M.C. Fox, born in Edinburgh and raised in the scenic Scottish Borders, has had a diverse and inspiring journey. She built a successful career as a general manager for a prominent retail company and contributed as a writer for a well-known sporting magazine. After her marriage ended, she completed her degree with the Open University, before continuing higher education, earning a postgraduate degree with master's credits in Primary Education with the UHI.

M.C. Fox's achievements include being honoured as a Commonwealth Baton Bearer and serving as a poster representative for the Edinburgh Marathon. She currently resides in the Scottish Borders, where she finds joy in teaching at a local primary school. As a devoted single mother, she cherishes her time with her daughter.

Perfectly Woven Lies is her captivating debut novel, marking her first step into the world of fiction writing.

M C Fox

PERFECTLY WOVEN LIES

AUSTIN MACAULEY PUBLISHERS

LONDON * CAMBRIDGE * NEW YORK * SHARJAH

A CIP catalogue record for this title is available from the British Library.

ISBN 9781035884513 (Paperback)
ISBN 9781035884520 (ePub e-book)

www.austinmacauley.com

First Published 2025
Austin Macauley Publishers Ltd®
1 Canada Square
Canary Wharf
London
E14 5AA

From the moment I told my dad, Patrick Fox, about my first scribbled notes, his support has been unwavering, encouraging me, his unflagging optimism and positivity in life setting me a wonderful example. Thanks to my friends and colleagues, without whom I couldn't have written this book. My boundless gratitude goes to my Mary for her friendship and encouragement, to Holly for encouraging me to send my manuscript off, to Linda and Jacki for endless chats, to my bosses Kevin and Alan for believing in me, to Billy for being there for me. Finally, above all I'd like to thank my wonderful daughter, patient and wise beyond her years. She is the epitome of kindness, and my inspiration. Together we got through the tough times.

Do you ever get that feeling you are watching your life from the outside, that it is someone else directing and you've no control? That the lead actress looks like you, talks like you and walks like you, but no, it cannot be you because you would not act that way. Would you?

Prologue

On the surface, her life was picture-perfect: a grand house in the countryside, a thriving career, a devoted husband, and a cherished child. It was the life everyone envied—flawless, glamorous, and seemingly without a single crack.

But behind the closed doors of her perfect facade lay a chilling truth. Gradually, she came to the harrowing realisation that she had married a monster. Trapped and isolated, with no one to confide in and nowhere to escape, the question lingered—could she find the strength to survive?

Chapter 1

I am wide awake now, all thoughts of sleep gone. I lie staring at the moonlight, tears falling silently down my face, soaking into my pillow. Such a beautiful night, the moon, the stars, such a sharp contrast to the emotions I feel inside of me. I feel utterly powerless. Powerless to alter my fate. I begin to wonder more and more of late who am I and where have I gone? I have begun to not recognise the person within me, the person who speaks like me, acts like me, but surely isn't me? I wouldn't act that way, would I? As I shut my eyes tightly, trying to block out the day, my thoughts drift back to that fateful day where it had all started. The party of all parties.

Will it still be there? I wonder. *Or is this all a dream?* With much trepidation, I walk into my bedroom, bare toes sinking luxuriously into the depths of the soft cream carpet. As I pad nervously over to the walk-in wardrobe, my pace slows. Taking a deep steadying breath, I raise my arm slowly. Eyes squeezed tightly shut, I pull open the door, stealing a peek, one eye slightly open just enough to see into the dark depths.

Yes! It's still there. My dress. Waiting patiently, wrapped beautifully in its designer packaging, clear plastic protecting its delicate contents. It is stunning. Taking a short inhalation of breath, I let my fingers slide gently over the protective wrapping. I wonder how long it's been since I had a reason to wear a dress like this. I feel a small ripple of excitement tinged with nerves course through me. The reason, a 'Prince and Paupers' party I am hosting tonight along with my husband, James, has taken months of organising, and the day has finally arrived. I've been up preparing the final details since before 5.00 am this morning and with over 100 guests arriving in just over 90 minutes, I'm almost ready.

Having spent all day preparing food and setting out drinks, the canapés are chilling nicely in the large American-style fridge, the champagne drinks fountain is ready, a temporary bar is set up and the playlist is prepared. Sophie, our 6-year-old daughter, is at my parents' house for the evening; all that I have left to do now is get myself ready.

"It has to be perfect," I remind myself, trying to steady my nerves. "Alexa," I call to the music system, "play my songs."

I am desperately in need of some calm, for although I feel well prepared, I am still fretting. James had been telling me for weeks how important this evening is for his business connections. Everything has to be absolutely perfect for him tonight. As Alexa obligingly lets a gentle tide of soft music flood into the bedroom, I draw in a deep refreshing breath of air and feel the beginnings of calm start to ease over me like a warm sun after a cool night.

Picking up the dress and gently easing back the clear plastic wrap, I touch the silky soft red fabric. *If I didn't know how important tonight was before, I do now*, I think to myself as I hold the dress up against me. The dress is a floor-length strappy body-skimming number; a soft cowl neck at the front gives way at the back to a dramatic plunge that will fall to the small of my back. I'm glad the heating has been on all day in preparation for tonight; it is March, and March in Scotland can be distinctly chilly, but James has chosen this dress for me, and I want to make him proud.

Singing along softly to the music, I head to the shower; with no time to waste, I strip off and step into the steaming hot shower, letting the deliciously warm water cascade over my exhausted body. The combination of the hot water and the gentle music begin to work their magic, and, swaying softly to the music, I let my mind go blank for a few luxurious seconds, a skill I've learnt as my saviour. The powerful jets of water invigorate me, the music begins to ease my frantic mind, calm begins to envelope me in a soft comfort blanket. I am enjoying being lost in the moment and let my mind drift.

The boys are back in town, suddenly shrieks out at full decibel from Alexa, startling me, as James walks into the bathroom.

"What are you listening to that rubbish for? You need to get yourself into the party mode! This is more like it!" He hollers above the music as he raises a beer in salute at me and joins in a few lines of Thin Lizzy.

"Come on! Get yourself out of that shower; we haven't got all night; I don't want anything to go wrong tonight, Isla, get a move on, would you, and make sure you fix your hair right." He turns on his heel and leaves me with Thin Lizzy for company.

So much so for that shower, I think as Thin Lizzy sings out to me:

I still think them cats are crazy.

I lower the volume of Alexa as I come out of the shower. The lyrics of Thin Lizzy are making me jumpy. I shudder as an eerie feeling that I cannot quite comprehend begins to creep over me.

"Well, I have no time to be wasting in the shower anyway," I mutter quietly into the steamy air. Grabbing a towel, I quickly dry myself and pad back into the bedroom, the soft blue walls enveloping me as I sit myself down on the stool in front of the dressing table. I peer closely at myself in the mirror—a tired girl looking back at me.

"Work to do here girl," I say softly to myself with a sigh. Reaching into the drawer I start to apply creams before carefully applying my make-up. This is going to take every bit of skill I can muster; I'm not even sure I possess the skills, but I have no choice. Perfection is the only catchword of the night.

Forty-three minutes later, I am as ready as I can be. Hair up and make-up painstakingly applied, I slip into my dress before sliding on my shoes. *There. I can do no more,* I think, as I am about to have a quick look in the full-length mirror hung on the opposite wall.

"Hurry up, up there!" James shouts out from below.

I jump up. "Probably better not to overthink how I look anyway," I say quietly to myself. With no time to waste, I descend the oak staircase. I've always thought this a touch pretentious, the stair splits at the large landing halfway, leading off to each side of the house. James loves it. It never fails to impress people at first sight. The large hall, adorned with limited edition prints is perfect for entertaining, the many rooms leading off from the marble hallway into various oak double-doored rooms.

I walk carefully along the hall, the delicate clicking sound of my heels keeping me company as I head to the dining room to check everything is ready.

"I'm just going to check that the drinks are all out and we have enough glasses, you know we always need twice as many as we think! I'll put the food out in the dining room, the hostess server will keep the hot food till it's time to eat."

"Okay, we can't afford any mishaps tonight, I have a few calls to make before everyone arrives," I hear James's muffled reply as he disappears into the depths of his office.

It has to be perfect tonight, I remind myself. Yes, perfect…

My stomach is churning; my mind racing, as I go over everything I have done in preparation for this evening. I start to invent scenarios in my mind; untidy rooms, cold food, running out of glasses, guests who don't get on with each other, music cutting out, power cuts.

Stop being silly, you've walked around checking and double-checking everything for tonight. Well then, I answer myself*, a triple check will do no harm.* I'm going crazy. I sigh to myself; this party is sending me over the edge. I'm not only talking to myself, but I'm answering myself too.

I take yet another look around the house, the main rooms are all to be left open for people to mingle through. I try to look impartially as I walk across the marble floor of the hall. What would people see? I walk into the living room and sit down for a second on the sofa which faces the fireplace. The stove is burning bright and welcoming from the hearth. Over the beautifully carved cream marble fireplace hangs a gorgeous antique mirror. I see the reflection of multi crystal lights twinkling merrily from the ceiling above. The many lamps around the room adorning occasional tables. A beautiful rug sits proudly in the centre of the solid oak floor. I slip off my shoes for a brief second and curl my toes luxuriously deep within its midst.

Various paintings, limited edition wildlife prints, hang on the soft grey walls, intersected by two long windows. The far end of the room hosts a deep bay window with an intricately carved window seat hand crafted by a local joiner and upholstered in a delicate dove grey, adorned with a selection of soft cushions just begging to be sat upon. I drift momentarily back to when I selected them, it seems a lifetime ago now. I give myself a shake, no time to reminisce, there is very little time before the first guests are due to arrive. I jump up, putting my shoes back on before I head through the double doors into the kitchen.

I take a quick glance at my watch—twenty-nine minutes to go. Wishing fervently that the hostess server was a real person and not a food warmer, I set about moving food from the kitchen to the dining area. Into the hostess server go hot baby boiled potatoes, baked potatoes and a mixed rice. My stomach gives out a growl in anticipation. I cannot remember when I last ate, I've been in such a fluster getting everything ready for this evening, food has gone by unnoticed.

Carefully, and trying to remain unflustered to keep my hair and make-up intact, I work steadily, taking all the food from the kitchen, moving it over into the dining room. I look over the efforts of my labour; tables lay adorned with silver trays of eight different kinds of meat, including game and chicken, five vegetarian options. Seven different bowls of salads plus the hot food lay across the main table. *Vegan,* I panic, what about vegan? Frantically I search my mind for the ingredients of the vegetarian. Fortunately I omitted eggs and dairy in two of them, more luck than judgment. Relief floods through me. Nothing, absolutely nothing can go wrong tonight, and I have to be prepared for every eventuality.

The dining room is beautifully laid out, filling me with a sense of relief. Earlier in the day I ensured all the silverware was polished and glassware sparkled. The napkins I folded now lie at each end of the main table which hosts the food. Around the sides lie a tempting array of desserts, including mountains of strawberries with bowls at either end, and an extra bar table is laid to the far end of the room. I breathe a gentle sigh of relief. It looks perfect. Checking my watch, I realise with a start there are only minutes to spare. I have just enough time to light a few candles, dim the light and change the music. Thin Lizzy has moved onto *Bat out of Hell*, which is blaring from the depths of the house. Cutting Meatloaf off in his prime, I change him for a more appropriate gentle background music. I feel my heart clattering rapidly in my chest as I cast a final glance across the room. No time left. I can do no more, I realise, and, as if on cue, the doorbell chimes.

Showtime.

Walking across the marble hall, heels clicking softly, I pause by the huge gilt-edge mirror by the front door. Looking critically at the reflection staring back at me, I see a stranger; the floor-length scarlet dress revealing slim white limbs, hair and make-up immaculate. Taking a deep breath, I open the door to welcome the first guests of the night. What could possibly go wrong?

Chapter 2

"Abigail!" I declare, a big welcoming smile on my face. *Great*, I think to myself, it would be her. I do not let the smile drop as I welcome her and her husband in. There will be at least three Abigail's coming tonight. This is Abigail Lame.

"Pronounced Lamie, dahling! You do realise, dear!" She repeatedly reminded everyone. Obviously adding the 'i' to it was vital. Abigail had married old money and coming from a relatively normal background had suddenly developed a very affected tone and superiority complex. I will need all my perfect hostess skills to ensure she feels welcome. We were good friends once, but she fell in with a new popular crowd and our friendship faded. James was still friendly with both and had insisted I lend her my one, and only, designer dress, a stunning full-length black velvet with a cream satin halter neck, from the days of my old career when I went to black tie celebrations.

"You'll need a new dress for the party, what will people think if they see you in that!" James had informed me. Seeing it now on Abigail, who is a good two sizes larger than me, the dress straining at the seams, it makes me feel sad. *No time for that,* I think, giving myself a shake. I secure a smile on my face as I turn to my guests.

"Please come and get a drink. Champagne?" I query as I guide them towards the champagne fountain.

"But of course, why would one drink anything else, darling!" Abigail chirps in her faux affected voice.

"Ruari!" James came over to join us, calling a little too loudly, having, I suspect, spent most of his time 'making calls' sampling the drinks on offer for tonight's party instead. "What can I get you?"

"I'll have the champagne that Isla is serving up for now," Ruari booms. "What a gorgeous home you have here, James, you have done wonders with it."

"And what fun to have a party!" Abigail exclaims, determined to be not only seen, but heard.

"Well, thank you both so much for coming to our little get-together," James declares, handing them both a glass of champagne. The doorbell chimes cut across the conversation.

Grateful for an escape, I attempt to slip softly into the conversation, "I'll get that!" No one hears me, they are all too interested in what they are saying themselves and I leave unnoticed, James peppily competing decibels with the Lames.

The next hour is a whir; after the first thirty or so guests have arrived, I give in and leave the door open for guests to enter. Despite the chill air, it is warm and cosy inside for once. I circulate around from room to room ensuring everyone has a drink and knows where to get refills. Most of the guests seem to have descended into the hallway, keen to watch newcomers arrive, ensuring they have pick of the crop for conversation. I edge my way around the bustle, chatting politely but briefly as I pass, moving around from room to room introducing guests to one another, offering canapés and drinks and laughing at the guests' jokes.

Returning to the kitchen for what feels like the thousandth time, I stop a moment to take in the scene, the atmosphere is lively, music fills the air, laughter tinkles, and conversation is growing louder as rooms fill and drinks flow. Guests seem to be filling every corner of the house, some milling in the hallway, others lounging comfortably on the sofas in the living room. The hall still seems to be the hub; no potential VIP guests will be escaping from the inquisitive locals. The party, and more importantly, the guest list has been the talk of the village for months now, and no one will be allowed to escape if there is the chance of any networking to be done.

I slip gratefully into the kitchen, hoping for a tiny bit of peace from the throng. It is quite overwhelming.

"Isla! There you are!"

I jump, startled. I had not seen anyone in the kitchen. I turn around to see Cameron, a local, resting by the aga.

"I'm sorry! I didn't mean to make you jump; it is just I always find the kitchen the best place at a party. It's the real heart of a home, don't you think! So please, tell me, who does your catering?" he asks, a broad smile spreading over his handsome face.

"Oh, that would be me." I laugh, taken aback a little at finding anyone in the kitchen.

"Seriously? Wow! Good looks and you can cook too; if I were not already happily married, I'd be giving James a run for his money."

"Oh, you are an old flirt, you." I laugh at Cameron's teasing ways. It is no secret Cameron is absolutely head over heels in love with Serena, his gorgeous and internationally famous model wife.

"What's this, what's this, who's this flirting with my wife?"

I look around to see James has appeared at the doorway.

"That would be me, sir!" Cameron says jovially, not missing a beat. "I'm just saying to Isla what a lucky man you are!"

"Oh, I know that. Now, what can I get you, Cameron? Beer? You're not really a champagne man, are you." He looks pointedly at Cameron's casual, but smart jeans.

"Oh, nothing really, I was just toasting myself by the aga and wondering if I could help Isla here. She's been running around all night looking after everyone. I thought she might do with a little help, then she could enjoy the party."

"Oh, she's a hard worker all right, I don't know what I would do without her."

"Well, I'm sure you'll never have to find out," Cameron chuckles, oblivious to his previous remark.

I feel James's eyes bore into me as he approaches me. At six foot one inch tall and well built, he is hard to ignore. I can't look away; I know that look. Spreading his customary smile onto his face, he leans into me.

"I had better not find out," he whispers almost inaudibly in my ear. Nodding almost imperceptibly, I'm glad Cameron is at the far side of the kitchen. As I reach up into the cupboard to pull out a few more bottles, I feel James's arm around me as it slides to the base of my spine; his hands are rough and calloused against my bare skin, my skin prickles and I know I need Cameron out of here.

"Here," James says, louder this time, taking the bottles from me, "let Cameron and I take those for you, darling, I am sure you have plenty to do without this."

"Totally agree. Here, pass me some of those, James, and Isla, what a super party, you really have done wonders here. Please though, if I can give you any help at all with anything, you really should be able to enjoy your own party!"

"I'm absolutely fine, Cameron, but thank you, that's so kind of you, we are so glad you were both able to make it." I smile over at him, keen for him to get back into the party, away from here. James hands over some bottles to Cameron,

16

casting me a look I know all too well before ushering him quickly out of the door, disappearing into the throng of the party.

Left in peace, I turn around. *Now, what did I come in for?* Slightly shaken from the brief encounter, I have no time to steady myself when I hear someone approach from the hall.

"Well, look who we have here! If it's not my lucky day. I didn't think I would get to see you, and here you are all by yourself!"

Oh no, that is all I need. I shudder involuntarily. *The village letch.* With supreme effort, I managed to paint a smile onto my face.

"Hi there, Andrew, what can I do for you?"

"It's what I can do for you, Isla." Clearly tipsy, he comes straight over to me. I step back, trying to create a little personal space.

"Oh, I have everything under control, please, just enjoy the party!"

"Come on, what harm can a little help do," Andrew cajoles.

You'd be surprised, I think to myself, but say nothing. Andrew is clearly very drunk, and as such there will be no talking to him. I can see the easiest thing is to accept, so, picking up a tray of nibbles, I hand them over smiling as sweetly as I can. "Well, if you really don't mind, you could take these out for me."

"Delighted to help, Ma' lady, anything, anything at all for you, Ma' lady." Andrew replies and, with an exaggerated bow, he takes the proffered bowl and sweeps, a touch unsteadily, out of the kitchen.

Breathing a little sigh of relief that I have navigated this encounter without too much of a problem, I walk back out of the kitchen and take in the surroundings. The ambiance is warm, jovial, and welcoming. Gentle light bathes the chattering guests in a complimentary light, background music swirls in and out, filling in ever-decreasing gaps in conversation. Everyone looks happy and, judging by the increasing noise level, they appear to be getting along well with each other. I feel myself relax just a little.

Picking up a bottle of champagne from a drinks bucket on the hall table, I proceed to circulate, topping up drinks and providing wine, beer, or shorts for those who prefer. Just as I am topping up a glass, I feel a hand on my elbow. Turning to see who is seeking my attention, I find myself face to face with Mungo, the editor for a national sports magazine. I take in a breath, champagne mid-flow.

"Isla, have you a second?" He carries on without waiting for an answer, "I have it on good authority that you enjoy doing a bit of writing? I had a chat with

Euan, my co-editor, and we wanted to ask if you would be interested in doing some pieces for us? It would just be a sample to start with, to see your writing style, but I cannot see any problem with that."

"Oh, well I…" I start, taken aback at the suddenness of this.

"What's this, what's this? Are you accosting my wife!" James appears; his uncanny knack of being able to appear out of the midst of nowhere never fails to astound me. Complete with a glass of sloe gin, he puts his arm around Mungo's shoulders, narrowly avoiding spilling his drink over Mungo's sports jacket.

"I was just saying to Isla, we were wondering if she would be interested in doing some writing for us, just as and when she has the time of course. It doesn't pay much, but you would get free advertising out of it," he adds with an encouraging grin.

"Oh, she has loads of time, she would be delighted to," James answers for me before I can say anything.

"Well, that would be fantastic, if you are sure, that would be super. Just email me over something when you get a chance, Isla, here, hang on a tick." Mungo rummages in his pocket for a business card and offers it to me. James swiftly intercepts the card and raises his sloe gin once again at Mungo, clinking it glass to glass in cheers.

"Here's to new beginnings and the start of a mutually beneficial relationship!" Mungo toasts. He is clearly enjoying himself and, like the other guests, enjoying the refreshments. I am overwhelmed to be asked. I give Mungo a big smile, assure him I will get something to him before very long and excuse myself to circulate some more. I cannot help feeling lifted by this offer. It would give James access to free advertising UK wide and could lead to an increase in clients. He is sure to be delighted with that.

Mingling with the guests again, soaking up the atmosphere, I cast a critical eye around. Everything looks like it is going okay. Singing along quietly to the music and enjoying the house being full of people, I squeeze my way gently amongst different groups, smiling and acknowledging as I go until I feel a tap on my shoulder.

I turn to see Rose and her crew.

"Isla, you haven't stopped all night!" She pulls me in before I can say anything. "Come join us and tell us what you've been up to, we never see you at all these days!" She pulls a sad face, and I can't help but smile.

"Oh, I know, I am sorry, Rose, but you know what it's like, full of good intentions then work gets caught up and before you know it another week has gone by!" I joke. "But I am so glad you could make it; we must arrange something soon."

"I'd love that, what about…" Rose carries on, but James catches my eye, gesturing it's time to open the dining room for the buffet. Nodding in acknowledgment to him, I turn back to Rose, who is still chattering away, suggesting dates, oblivious to my lack of attention. I smile, agreeing to meet her, knowing full well I will not be able to excuse myself from conversation until I do. Satisfied with arranging something, and oblivious to the fact I would not be able to meet her, she lets me go and I head towards the dining room.

"Hey! There you are lovely; I have so missed you, darling!" Zara, my oldest friend, comes bounding up to me, blonde hair flying and looking the epitome of glamour. Zara is married to Mac who is completely eccentric.

"Zara! There you are!" I give her a delighted hug.

"You can't do everything by yourself, you won't enjoy the party! Let me help, I can escape the boring old farts, the clickers, and the cliques all in one swoop—plus I get first dibs on the desserts!"

I giggle at her descriptions of the guests.

"Oh, you are so naughty, but that would be fantastic! We just need to uncover everything and then let the hungry hoards in." I say a little breathlessly as we head to the dining room.

"Relax and take a breath, sweetie, everything is going swimmingly. I really don't know how you pulled this off with no help at all. You are incredible. Really. I would have just called the caterers," she laughs before continuing, "and sweetie?"

I pause for a moment and look at her quizzically.

"You are really rocking that dress! Red really is your colour." She spins me around. "And wow! That plunge, you go, girl!"

I smile back at her appreciating the confidence boost. "Thank you. I wasn't sure, it's a bit low, but James brought it back from one of his trips and insisted I wear it."

"It's perfect for you! I didn't realise he had such taste," Zara winks over at me. "I still don't know how you pulled all this off with no help, you really are wonder woman, my Tigger; tonight though, you are Tigger on Speed," Zara murmurs affectionately, giving me a big squishy hug, and reverting to my nickname of years only she called me.

"Thank you. I've been in a panic about it for ages, but you know, I love to be busy."

Zara gives me a curious look.

"Well, you know me," I add lamely by way of explanation.

"Yes, sweetie, I do, and…" she trails off.

I search her face for anything that might give me a hint about what she means but I have no time to question this as I hear James ushering the guests in our direction.

"Wow, what a feast!" The first guests declare, pouring into the dining room; just as I whisk the last of the wrap out of sight, the guests descend on the buffet like a swarm of locusts ready to devour the food and soak up the champagne in preparation for more drinks.

"Help yourself to a plate everyone," I call out cheerily, "you can line up both sides, meat and salads along here, vegetarian and vegan options over here," I gesture, "and baked potatoes, rice or pasta over here!"

"Ooooh!" Abigail Lame declares sidling up to me. "It all looks super yummy, but I doubt you will have made anything I can eat. I'm following a very particular diet you know!" she booms out even though she is only inches from me.

Zara says, "I'm off to check out the yummies, no diet for me," and with a cheeky wink, she heads off to the buffet table.

"How do I look?" Abigail asks me as she twirls in my gorgeous dress.

I can't help but feel she resembles Betty Boop, but I love Betty Boop.

"You look very healthy," I reply honestly.

She beams. "Thank you! I have lost 3lbs, but I really don't think you'll have anything I can eat," she groans theatrically and rolls her eyes. "No one ever does, it's very particular, you know."

"Oh, now Abigail, I am sure we can find you something, come with me." I gently hook her arm and take her along the buffet table.

"Now, what about this, it's very low in fat and high in protein," I suggest pointing out a delicious chicken salad topped off with light yoghurt dressing and pomegranate seeds, a favourite standby, and looks deliciously fresh and appetising.

"Oh no! I can't possibly have anything that has meat in it." She looks at me, shocked.

"Okay…Well, that's no problem at all, let's look at the vegetarian section." I lead her along the tables to the vegetarian options. "What about this?" I point out the couscous salad, topped with walnuts and fresh herbs.

"No, I can't eat anything with wheat in it," she sighs dramatically.

"Don't worry," I reply, beginning to feel a little desperate; the next options were ruled out also on account of containing butter or eggs.

"I can't have dairy; I can only have cold-pressed olive oil. I told you that you wouldn't have been able to make anything for me," she replies now a little testily. "It's a very specific diet, only the supermodels follow it, but I managed to get a copy and you really and truly must stick to it!"

Maybe if I had had advance warning of this supermodel diet, I might have been able to accommodate more choice, I think to myself a little uncharitably. I am panicking now in case James sees an unhappy guest. I look over, but he is chatting away to the local publican, Paige. I am safe for now.

"Don't worry," I try to sooth, "now, what about this?" I list off the ingredients.

Abigail beams up at me. "And you are sure that's everything?" she queries.

"Absolutely!" I say triumphantly. "And we can add a little green salad to accompany it, with some fresh strawberries to finish?" I suggest temptingly. She nods enthusiastically. "You are allowed strawberries?" I proffer.

"Oh yes! Thank you," she replies as I settle her off, very happy that the vegan dishes have come to the rescue. And with that, she grabs a plate, fills it up to the brim and disappears back into the throng to eat her supermodel diet meal.

I look around, the dishes are going down fast. I clear some of the empty plates as Mungo comes up to me.

"Isla, this is a delicious spread and so fantastic to see so much wild game on the table! Such a healthy choice and so sustainable. Do you think that maybe you would consider adding a recipe column to the pieces you write for us? I think they would go down a storm, and with a different twist from the boring old cut, stick and repeat stuff that's everywhere. A fresh young twist on it. What do you say?"

I am flattered beyond words; turning pink, I stutter out my reply, "That's so kind of you, I would love to. I shall certainly give it a go!"

"Fabulous," Mungo replies, oblivious to my deepening shade of pink, or perhaps too polite to comment. "I very much look forward to your first copy. Now, I must go and circulate, maybe past the dessert table first though!" he gives a cheery smile and disappears into the party. Everything seems so relaxed tonight. *Just like the old days*, I think wistfully. I feel a wave of sadness wash over me, that had been then though, before my life had become the life everyone wanted.

"Isla!" a cheery voice followed by a smart slightly older lady comes up to me. I recognise her from school but can't quite remember her name. "It's Alicia? Alicia from school," she adds. "My little girl is in Sophie's class," she confirms in greeting. "I have been desperate to try to catch up with you, but you are always so busy!"

Inordinately grateful that she has introduced herself so clearly, I reply, "How lovely you could make it tonight." I am genuinely delighted to see her. Alicia is immaculately dressed, petite and has a kindly face. I had a feeling I would get on with her when I saw her at the school gates, though I had not yet found an opportunity to speak to her.

"Now, have you had something to eat? I have been watching you looking after everyone and you've not had a morsel!" she laughs gently, motheringly.

"Oh no, I couldn't eat anything, I'm too nervous."

"Phftt, and poppycock! You will fade away, and besides, it's all going swimmingly. You should be so proud."

I glance over to James, he is studying us meticulously. Alicia glances at me and a fleeting knowing look passes over her face. "Look lovely, I can tell you are very busy, I just wanted to come and take the opportunity to say hi. It would be really lovely if we could catch up. I would love it if Sophie could come up and have a play. You can either stay with her or leave her if you are okay with that and take some time out for yourself. I am sure you don't get much of that," she speaks softly, not quite in an undertone, but with the practiced ease of someone who has spent years perfecting the art of ensuring her words never reach unintended ears; *An experienced party-goer,* I think, *or perhaps just very aware of the Border cliques.*

"That sounds really lovely," I reply genuinely. She seems such a lovely, caring person. Brisk and efficient, but my instinct is that she would be trustworthy if I had the opportunity to get to know her. She gives me a big smile; says she will be in touch and disappears into the crowds to rescue her husband from 'some intolerably boring sales rep'.

The next half an hour flies by. I circulate the room ensuring everyone has enough to eat and their drinks are filled, and the chatter grows steadily noisier and noisier.

"Tigger!" Zara bounds up to me, putting her arms around me. "This is such a fabulous party and I love you to bits!"

"Are you a little tipsy, my bestest friend!" I laugh as she squeezes me tightly.

"Maybe a little," she whispers in mock hushed tones. It comes out loudly, in the way that only the inebriated can manage when trying to be quiet. "But it's such fun! Oh, Tiggs, this trifle is divine!" she waves a large bowl of half-eaten trifle around.

"I simply don't know how you manage it. You eat like a horse and still stay gorgeously slim and radiant!"

"Hah! You only say that because you are my unutterably best friend in the entire world! Live for the moment, that's what I say!"

"And quite right; you are lovely, never change," I give her a big hug. How I miss her.

"I was just bursting watching you with Mrs Lame! How do you put up with her! *Oh nooooo! I couldn't possibly eat anything with animal products and positively no wheat! Darling, I am so very particular,*" she mimics. "But she seems to have forgotten that now!" She leans into me giggling and nudges me to look over, and there is Abigail standing with a huge plate of profiteroles.

"She can have a fat wad of chocolate and cream; does she not realise there's butter and wheat in the profiteroles and where on earth does she think cream comes from?" She giggles holding on to me. "She's so pretentious!"

"Zara!" I mock scold. "Well, at least she looks like she's enjoying them."

"Very true! Life is too short to give up on profiteroles! Talking of which, I must just see if any are left, just to tidy up you know!" and with that she is off. I smile happily to myself, it is so lovely to see Zara again, my best friend. I never see enough of her. She truly is the epitome of a mad scientist with a brilliant career and an even more brilliant brain. She deserves down time.

Left to my own devices, I flit around the room, catching the last of the stragglers hoovering up dessert, until finally the last guest disappears back out into the hall to soak up more drinks. I survey the room; the guests have certainly made short work of the meal, leaving behind empty plates, scraped clean of every morsel, lying haphazardly around.

I hear a rustle by my side. It is Zara who has slipped up next to me, armed with another plate of dessert.

"Do you think I made enough?" I whisper to her.

"Darling, you could have kept an army marching for weeks on this, you made more than enough. It is just so delicious. No one will need to feed again for a month!"

I smile over at her, satisfied. The desserts have been a resounding success and there is precious little left as I look up from the foody remnants. I am happy to close the double doors on the dining room and deal with the cleanup later.

"Ok sweetie, relax now please. I am going to see where my darling wayward husband has disappeared to. I'll catch you later though," and with another flurry of green velvet, Zara slips into the crowded hall.

Making my way into the throng of activity in the hall, out of the corner of my eye, I catch James looking over at me; he mentions something to the group he is talking with and nods before heading over to me.

"Well, there she is," he says theatrically, placing his hand on the back of my neck before letting it fall slowly to my waist, pulling me into his side. "What would I do without you?" The conversation quietens in our surrounding areas. "My little hostess with the Mo-stest." Referring to the pet name, Mo, he used to call me after the half-penny Mo-Jo chews. He laughs raucously at his own joke, sloe gin fumes spilling out over me as he nestles close to my neck. I slip a bright smile onto my face and look up at him.

"Look at the pair of you. He can't keep his eyes off you, even after all these years!" I hear one of the guests call out.

"You'd better believe it!" James calls back emphatically into the hallway, laughing and holding me a little tighter. I feel his fingers dig into my ribs under the thin fabric of my dress.

I give him another small smile before wriggling out from under him. "I have to circulate," I whisper.

"Ok, the love of my life," he booms ostentatiously above the music for all to hear. "You have worked so hard, enjoy and chat with your friends." Reaching over to pull me back in, he whispers softly in my ear, "Do what you must but don't be away for too long. I don't want you out of my sight."

I nod in silent agreement before being released into the bustling crowd.

I take a deep breath as I make my way around the room. I go through the list in my mind, mentally ticking items off one by one. Guests are happy. Tick.

Everyone has a drink, tick. Conversation flowing, tick. Music just right, tick. No one left out, tick. It is going well. I can't think of anything else that would improve things. I head on through the bustling throng of party-goers, passing Lara and her clique. I overhear her conversation, a mixture of champagne, wine and heady party excitement loosening her tongue and pumping up the volume of her usually discreet self.

"They have it all, don't they." Lara comments in an exaggerated whisper, and not a little spitefully.

"Look at James, he can't take his eyes off her!" Abigail number 2 giggles, nudging. "I wish my Callum would look at me like that!"

"What I wouldn't give to be her, and she does nothing all day except get to swan around this gorgeous house," Flora sighed wistfully. Lara's posse nods agreeably.

"Ladies!" I interrupt their chitchat. "Can I get you anything?"

"A piece of your life," Abigail number 2 whispers pseudo-quietly.

I laughed amiably before replying, "You wouldn't really want it."

The clique looks at me, then back at each other before laughing. "Right, who would really want a perfect life!"

"Tigger!" Zara appears as if from the very cavity of the walls. "Darling, you promised to introduce me to Oliver!" Linking her arm, she gathers me tightly into her. "Ladies, do you mind if I steal away the hostess for a moment? I'm sure you can find your way to the bar," and with that she pulls me away.

"Umm, who's Oliver?" I whisper, leaning in closer to her.

"I thought you might need rescuing!" she giggles whispering into my ear, "I don't think they have moved far from the champagne all night; I wouldn't want to be them in the morning—you know what they say, nectar going in, sewage coming out!"

"Your timing couldn't have been more perfect, there must only be about 4 people here that I would actually want to party with," I whisper back quietly.

"Why do you do it then?"

"Well, James has to entertain for his work. He works so hard you know."

Zara gives me that look again.

"What?"

"Nothing sweetie, it'll keep." Linking my arm, she pulls me through the bustling partiers before stopping suddenly. "Look over there!" Zara nods in the direction of the stairs. "Now that's a disaster waiting to happen!"

Paige, the local publican, is wrapping herself around one of James's clients, cleavage on full show.

"Eek, I think we should move on," I whisper, holding onto Zara's arm, I lean into her and try to hide my uncharitable giggle. "I'm not sure that's the kind of entertainment that was on offer."

We move comfortably around the house, chatting away and giggling like the old days. Oh, how I miss them, sharing silly anecdotes and giggling at nothing very much in particular.

"Isla! Over here," James calls over, raising his eyes, looking first at myself then to Zara before settling back on me. "I want you to meet Charles and Alicia."

"Oh dear," I say as I turn apologetically to Zara, "I'm sorry but I'd best go, lovely, but I'll catch you up later? Will you be okay?"

"Of course! I'm going to go for thirds of desserts. You know I just can't resist your profiteroles!" she calls, heading towards the dining room as I make my way to James.

"Charles, Alicia, meet my wonderful wife, Isla. I don't know what I'd do." I accept the kiss on the cheek and hugs proffered as Alicia informs that we have met briefly. I listen as attentively as I can for the next half an hour; the exhaustion of the day is catching up with me, I haven't yet had anything to eat and listening on about land deals and shares would test anyone's social skills. I try my best to add in some hopefully intelligent comments when, just as there is a pause, my stomach lets out a large and uncontrollable growl of hunger.

Alicia looks over at me and with a smile says, "Oh come now, Charles, I think we have heard enough; besides, I am just dying for more dessert, aren't you, Isla. I don't think I have seen you eat anything yet, you naughty girl, you have been so busy attending to everyone else! Come with me now, darling, and let us get something!"

I proffer a smile as Alicia kindly takes my arm; just as I am about to go with her, James puts a hand on my back, "Don't be long, I shall miss you!" he says dramatically before leaning down as if to kiss my cheek. "Dessert? Really?" in barely more than a whisper so only I could hear.

I say nothing but try to keep the smile on my face as, heading along with Alicia, arms linked, we head to the dining room, "Now what can I tempt you with?" I say brightly. "Profiteroles? Cheesecake? Tiramisu? Strawberries?"

"Isla, you need to have something, you are going to fade away to nothing!"

"Oh, honestly, I am not hungry. I ate before the party," I lie trying desperately to quash the persistent and traitorous growling of my stomach.

"Maybe a few strawberries?" Alicia tries to tempt, "just to keep me company. Dessert must have company. You can't eat alone, it's just not right!" she laughs.

"Well, maybe I could squeeze a few strawberries in." I look at the glistening fruit, encrusted with delicious sugar coating.

"That's my girl." Alicia picks plates for both of us up and proceeds to fill them both to overflowing before offering one to me; taking my plate from her, I pick up one of the juicy red berries and pop it in my mouth. Instantly, my mouth waters and my tummy let out another growl, this time in anticipation.

"Oh heaven," I groan.

"See, I knew you would manage some," Alicia cries gleefully and more than a little merrily. "And now for some champagne!" Filling a glass from the nearby drinks bar, Alicia hands me a glass. I let the icy cold liquid flow over my tongue and slip down my throat, the sparkles tickling, the bubbles releasing a warm sensation through me.

"Now that's more like it." Alicia says smiling over at me. She has a warm motherly way about her and I find myself relaxing in her company.

"Oh look! Here comes your beloved!" Alicia nods to the door. I freeze, strawberry halfway to my mouth.

"Ah, here you are," James calls loudly. He's on the wrong side of a bottle of port and getting louder with every glass. "I'm glad you managed to get her to eat something." He leans into Alicia. "I'm always telling her she needs to make time to eat," he confides to her conspiratorially. "Anyway, darling," he continues, "I'm sorry to break up your chat, but Martha and Richard are leaving now and we really must say goodbye."

Alicia turns to me, champagne glass wavering, and gives me a warm smile. "I have hogged your gorgeous wife long enough. I am sorry, but she's such lovely company! I really must go back and see what mischief Charles is up to now!" She gives me a little pat on the arm, turns and disappears into the crowded hall, leaving me alone with James. He puts his hand firmly on my back and guides me towards our guests.

"You were spending rather a lot of one-on-one time in the kitchen, weren't you?" he murmurs, leaning into me. I barely make him out when without so much as a breath, he continues loudly, "Martha, thank you so much for coming. Richard, a pleasure as always, I shall be in touch in the week to continue our conversation." James leans in to add something further in Richard's ear just as Martha turns to me.

"Isla, please don't be a stranger. I have been meaning to ask you for ages and now is the perfect opportunity, come join our book club, you would love it. Time to get away from our husbands," she adds with a conspiratorial giggle.

"That sounds so fun!" Merry from the glass of champagne, I look up at James for a response, but he is still deep in conversation with Richard.

"We have it once a month. We change houses to whoever is able to host at the time. You can bring Sophie with you too! There are a few other mums who have husbands who work long hours, it really is flexible. And the best of it is those of us with older children bribe them to look after the younger ones, they really enjoy it! We don't take it seriously, the books are just an extra," she declares, laughing triumphantly before continuing, "we really just sit around and have a few glasses of wine whilst putting the world to rights, but it's fun doing that and chatting about the books. We take it in turns to choose the book and we try to arrange a few girls days out as well; the Melrose book festival for one, it has some great events, some with champagne, authors come and chat—it is such fun!"

She gathers momentum, "And you'll love the other girls. They are not stuffy or in the least bit pretentious." She pauses before adding, "Unlike some," and offers another conspiratorial wink. "You'll know a few of them. Tabitha, Willow and Olivia, but there's a couple of others from a few villages along and I know you'd just love them!" She stops, to come up for air I presume. I have never had much of a chance to speak with Martha, her children are older and at high school, but I can't help but warm to her. There is nothing affected or showy about her and I can't help but feel excited at the prospect of joining their book club.

"That's settled then! Here, give me your number and I can message you the details." I give her my mobile number just as James and Richard stop chatting.

"What are you girls up to?" Richard asks, his big jolly face ruddy from years of working the land.

"I was just saying to Isla how much she would enjoy our little book club. Get her out a bit and mix with people," she leans forward in an exaggerated attempt to mask what she was saying, "who are not cliques!" she finishes triumphantly.

Richard roars heartily with laughter, nodding enthusiastically, his ruddy jowls joining in the fun, only serving to make him look more jovial and wholesome.

"I couldn't agree more! What do you say, James!"

"It sounds right up her street; I am sure she would love it."

"Right ho then! Well, it looks like we will be seeing you soon then! I heard rumblings about that Shades of Grey book," he chortles good-humouredly again.

"Come on, Richard, we best get you home. Thank you both so much for a wonderful night, and Isla, I'll be in touch." She gives me a warm enveloping hug and with that they are off. I want to stay forever in that hug, but I cannot. There are guests to see to, I cannot drop the baton now; taking a deep breath, I fix the smile back on my face and head into the revellers.

The next few hours fly by. I top up more drinks to a few hardy, well-seasoned party-goers before eventually people start to make rumblings to leave. I am starting to flag but am happy everyone seems to have had a lovely time. Finally, bit by bit and with many cheerios, ciaos, tattie byes, ta-tas and offers of returns lunches and dinners, the guests dwindle to just a handful. Zara and Mac come up to us.

"Isla, we really must get back before the babysitter phones the child line on us!" Mac laughs. He is very merry, not used to drinking much, and in extra good form.

"I'm glad you could make it," James shakes Mac's proffered hand before turning to Zara.

Zara gives James a quick hug, "James, you have a star here, she is absolutely amazing, and I just love her to bits. Look after my Tigger for us, will you? And Tiggs?" she adds, turning to me, "don't let it be too long before I see you again!" Zara gives me a big tight hug. I miss her already.

Kissing her on the cheek, I hug her back, replying as convincingly as I can that I will see her very soon as they bid their fond farewells.

An hour later as the grandfather clock in the hall strikes 1.45 am, the last of the diehard guests finally head off, the red taillights of their cars disappearing, little devil eyes into the distance, horns honking good-naturedly in extended farewells. I breathe a sigh of relief. There is no more I can do. I am absolutely wiped out both physically and emotionally. The thought of clearing up looms in front of me.

I look up at James. "Well, I think that went okay. What did you think? Did everyone arrive that you wanted to?"

"I made a few contacts and getting into that magazine was a real coo. How did you manage that?" James gives me a questioning look.

29

"Mungo just came up and asked me if I would like to try out a sample bit of writing." James has a strange look on his face. I let it pass, choosing not to question it too deeply. "It's just a trial," I add hesitantly as I start to clear up the mess.

"I have no doubt you are going to be fabulous at it, like everything else." There's an edge to his voice as he comes towards me. "Leave that for the morning. Come up to bed," he adds, softly this time.

The thought is appealing. I am bone-tired, but we have a new set of B&B guests coming in tomorrow and the place is in uproar.

"Are you sure?" I look up at James questioningly. "Tomorrow is going to be busy."

"Leave it," he insists. "You must be dead on your feet," he adds and steers me in the direction of the stairs.

I'm glad. There is nothing more that I want than to take off my dress, slide under the warm duvet and fall fast asleep. I can barely stand. I am so exhausted. Surprised at this uncharacteristic side of James, I allow myself to be guided up the stairs and into the bedroom. Sitting down at the dressing table I start to take off my earrings. I see James's reflection in the dressing table mirror looking over at me and for a while he says absolutely nothing. In the mirror's reflection, I see his lips move. I strain to hear what he is saying.

"I have no doubt in you. Just make sure you do not let me down, okay?"

Momentarily, I am confused. My fatigued brain stirs slowly, wading through a slushy pool of treacle. Through the fog of weariness, it clicks what he means. *The editorial piece for the magazine.*

I am about to reply when I notice his dark eyes grow cold.

"What were you talking about with Cameron? You know he has a thing for you, don't you?"

The earlier uncharacteristic kindness he had shown evaporates as quick as the devil in a night sky.

"N-Nothing," I could not help the stammer, the change in the room was tangible. "He was just offering to help take some food around."

"A likely story, more like offering to take you," James sneers before continuing, "I see you didn't deny he has a thing for you though!"

"No, no, he was just saying what a lovely house this is," I can see his face staring at me coldly, a trickle of fear runs over me as I continue, "and also what a great businessman you are." I pull white lies from the air as quickly as stars appear in the night sky, in the hope that this will appease him a little. It works; James puffs out his chest. It makes no difference what my comments about Cameron are. James has already made up his mind.

"Well, everyone was saying what a marvellous party it was and what a lovely house I have. I must have made a good lot of connections tonight. The guys were telling me what a beautiful wife I have. They could not keep their eyes off you. But you are mine, and I will make sure everyone knows it," James lurches towards me, a little unsteady on his feet after so much drink, even with his voluminous capacity.

"But you know what?" He repeats, "You are mine! Zara thinks you're her Tigger, but no, you're mine." Slurring his words now, he continues, "They can look all they like, but you are mine." Lurching forward he grabs me tightly and hauls me off the stool before pulling me up into him, kissing me hard on the mouth, the taste of stale port on my empty stomach making me feel nauseous; he gropes clumsily at my dress.

I try to move away, but he holds me tighter.

"James stop, please, you are hurting me," I attempt.

I try desperately to twist away but he is strong, far stronger than me, even drunk, I know instinctively, and I'm frightened.

"Please stop," I plead.

"Shut up," he hisses. Eyes darker than ever, he is on me, fumbling at my dress.

"You don't tell me what to do. I told you, you are mine," he repeats drunkenly as he pushes me hard against the bed, forcing his hand up my dress. I struggle uselessly. His arm leans heavily against my chest, the weight of him pressing down on me. He is dead weight and I am exhausted. I know it is hopeless to struggle now, to struggle will make it worse.

"Don't ever tell me what I can or can't do," he whispers hoarsely, his face just inches from mine. Strands of his curly, red hair dance on my face, droplets of saliva showering my cheeks, eyes black as night stare into me. I remain still. It will be over soon. It is easier not to fight. I've learnt that from experience. A few minutes later, he rolls off. I slip off the bed, heading for the bathroom.

"Mine, I tell you. Mine," I hear James mumble as if to himself, "and don't ever forget it."

How could I? I think to myself. He makes sure I can never forget. Switching on the shower, I strip off what is left of my beautiful dress and step into the shower. I tried to make everything perfect, tried to ensure I spoke to everyone but not for too long. But I must have failed.

Memories of lyrics from Thin Lizzy's song from earlier in the evening float past me in a haze.

The drink will flow, and blood will spill.

I let the water flow over me for the second time that evening, as the water streams over me, my tears merge with the rippling water before swirling down the drain. I wish I could disappear with them. Stepping out of the shower, I towel myself off before climbing into bed next to the now comatose James, fragments of conversation from the night floating around in my head:

"What I wouldn't give to be her."
"Oh yes, me too, who wouldn't want a perfect life!"

Yes, indeed, I think, a tear escaping down my cheek and onto the pillow, *who wouldn't want a perfect life.*

Chapter 3

I wake up early the next morning. Looking over, James still snoring beside me, I feel a mix of emotions pass through me as I remember how the evening had ended. Fear. Anxiety. The thought of cleaning up after the party leaves me exhausted before I've even begun; however, the sooner I clear away the remnants of the party, the sooner I can collect Sophie from my dad. I missed both Sophie and Dad. I don't get to see Dad as often as I'd like these days, there always seemed to be something to do and his visits are getting less and less frequent. I know Dad would be looking forward to catching up too.

Getting up this early also means I could avoid any further confrontations with James. Slipping as quietly as I can out of bed, so as not to wake him, I pull on a pair of old jeans, previously tight they hang loosely on my hips. I shrug on an old comforting sweater and with soft steps I pad along the hall and head downstairs.

It is far worse than I remember—drinks glasses everywhere, the plates still piled where I had stacked them last night looking like they have tripled in quantity and the floor is sticky with spillages. There's nothing else for it but to get stuck in. I don't mind being busy though. It keeps me from thinking too deeply about anything. To think would set me on a path too dangerous to contemplate for now.

As I set about cleaning, first filling the dishwasher then starting room by room, I let my mind drift to my conversation with Zara. Oh, how I miss her, I smile at the recollection of her little anecdotes, my friend of old. I wish I could see more of her but every time I tried, something came up to prevent it. I think back to being approached by the editor of a sports magazine. I had been quite taken aback. James had been particularly impressed with this, knowing he would get free advertising out of it, which surely would increase business and reduce some of James's stress.

I contemplate Martha and her invitation to the book club. It sounds such fun, the thought of having a few hours out of the house once a month to read and talk about books sounds absolute heaven and Sophie would love coming along to play with the other children, some of her friends would be there and it would be a great chance for her to meet new friends so there would be no reason James could complain. Also, it was on a Friday so Sophie could sleep a little longer on the Saturday. A thrill of excitement starts to trickle through me—could it truly work out?

My mind moves on to seeing Sophie and Dad today. I would try to get there around midday and then Sophie could come to the food shop with me, not very exciting as trips go for her but she enjoyed helping, being a 'big girl' and choosing the food for our guests. It means that I could also choose a little treat to go in. James has long since complained about the amount of money I spend on food, so I have to be uber careful; it feels the harder I try, the more I need to try. Sometimes I feel I am on a treadmill and just can't get off.

We are busier than ever, but James still says we are short of money. I try and try but it never seems good enough. Maybe if I could write a good article for the magazine, that would please him? I hear noises from upstairs, he must be awake. I look around, there's still a huge amount to do; I head to the kitchen and put the kettle on, James would certainly want coffee when he comes down. I flick on the switch and set about emptying the third lot of dishes that morning from the dishwasher before refilling it again.

"Morning!" James appears at the door. "Mmm, is that coffee I smell?" he chirps, pushing a stray red curl out of his face, he seems remarkably chipper.

"I made a fresh pot, just how you like it," I reply hastily, pouring a cup. "Would you like some toast?" He is in a good mood, and I want to keep it that way.

"I was thinking that I'd take you out for a coffee today," James replies, ignoring my question. "You must've been complaining you didn't get out to someone last night, were you? Someone, I forget who now, said you didn't have much time to go out so now I have to take some of my own precious time. I can't abide nosy busybodies; you know how hard I have to work."

I butter the golden toast slowly, his words a familiar white noise.

He worked hard. I did not. Fact.

I hand him the toast.

"That's burnt, what do you expect me to do with that? I'll get something decent when I go out," he takes a sip of coffee. "Urgh what is this? Tar?" he retorts, throwing down his coffee mug dramatically.

"What's wrong with you today, you can't even make a decent cuppa. Right, I'm going out to get a proper coffee. I'll be back at one o'clock to collect you. Make sure this place is cleaned up when I get back. I've important meetings today. Goodness knows how I am going to get everything done today now." Taking a deep breath, he continues his tirade, "And make sure you have time to get dressed properly for going out with me," he looks me up and down before emitting a little snort, "I don't want to be seen with you looking like that!" And with that, he turns on his heel and leaves.

I sigh, something I appear to do a lot of these days, *at least I've Dad and Sophie to look forward to later,* I think as I set about the rest of the cleaning up.

I work solidly until 12.27. I look around at my handiwork, pleased; you'd never know there had been a party here. I've just enough time to have a quick shower, wash my hair, and change before James comes to collect me. I dash upstairs and pull out a little skirt and top, pairing them with a pair of boots and thick tights as it is still cool outside. I could wear this with a little jacket. *Perfect,* I think to myself. I jump into the shower and vigorously scrub my body and wash my hair as quickly as I can.

Fifteen minutes later I am changed, and having carefully applied my make-up, I'm blowing out my hair. My mind turns to the afternoon. I'm looking forward to seeing Dad and Sophie, not to mention Lola, my faithful Dalmatian. I miss them all, they bring life to me and make things bearable. Glancing at my watch I see I have 8 minutes to go. I dare not be late; quickly I set the straighteners through my normally very curly hair, and as carefully as I can I take small sections and begin straightening my stubborn hair, bit by bit it transforms back into long glossy lengths, just the way James likes it. I stand back and look at my efforts.

"You'll do," I say aloud to my reflection, before quickly heading back downstairs to check everything is sorted. Glancing around each room trying to look at it from a stranger's perspective, I check everything is in order. The guests would be in later, I won't have much time when I come back, but it doesn't matter, getting up early means I have everything done ready for the guests' arrival and can spend some time with Dad. The rooms all look great. I'm relieved. The back door slams loudly open and a few seconds later James appears.

"You ready?" he looks me up and down before continuing, "What a morning I've had, I'm exhausted, well, I guess the place looks okay. I'm glad you've tidied yourself up at least, right let's go, I don't have all day." He turns and walks out the door leaving me to follow in his wake.

Grabbing my coat, I follow him out to the car, a once lovely Range Rover, but now beat-up and smelling of dog. James is too busy, he says, to change his boots to get into the car or put up the dog barrier so the Labradors can't spray their wet coats, fresh from the pond, all over the vehicle. I say nothing but slip into the passenger seat. I cannot think of a thing to say, every topic I know will be wrong. I can tell from James's attitude that he's annoyed. He clearly does not want to be taking me out. I search my mind desperately for a neutral topic. I land upon the safe topic of coffee.

"Where are we going for coffee?" I ask lightly.

"Costa. It should be busy."

Yes, I think to myself, *and there will be plenty of witnesses making sure people see I am being taken out.* I chide myself for thinking such an uncharitable thought, it was nice to get out of the house for a change, and as James says, he is busy and he's taking time out to do something nice for me, I remind myself.

The journey feels long as I listen to James telling me how much work he does, how exhausted he is working 7 days a week, 24 hours a day and telling me I'm still spending far too much money on shopping.

"If you don't cut back, I won't put any money into the bank and then where will you be?"

I say nothing. There is no reply to this. I know he means it; it wouldn't be the first time I'd been to the shops and presented my card over only for it to be rejected. I have no card in my own name, he controls the money. It hadn't always been like this, of course. My mind drifts back to when I was a career girl. I had earned good money. When we got married, James had persuaded me that it was pointless having different bank accounts, so, giddy with new love, I had readily agreed to joint accounts. I hadn't realised at the time however, that what this meant was it would be his account with myself added as a subsidiary name. The credit card was also changed to be the same. The result—I am solely reliant on James now financially.

"What are you dreaming about?" James snaps, pulling me out of my musings.

"Nothing, just things you know," I reply, looking out the window. We have pulled in at the car park along from the coffee shop.

"No, I don't know. I don't know what goes around in that tiny mind of yours." He passes over a glare at me. "Right, here we are, let's get this over with."

I try to ignore the look he throws me and focus on being out for coffee. I open the car door and jump out. It's fairly busy and the weekenders are out in full force. There's a pleasant mix of families and couples wandering about, further over on the other side of the road I see a small group of youths waiting, from what I can make out, they look as though they've been playing football, and, judging by their happy faces and their muddy attire, I assume they must have won, or certainly had a good game. James joins me on the pavement and is about to say something to me when I hear someone call out my name.

"Isla! Isla," the caller repeats. "Over here!"

I look around to see Alicia and Charles, Alicia waving frantically and approaching from the car park opposite.

James mutters under his breath; his face dark as he looks at me, before quick as flicking a switch, he turns on his public face to them.

"Charles! Alicia! What a lovely surprise!" he calls jovially.

As they approach, I feel a knot of fear; this is not in James's plan, he'd be furious.

"How lovely to see you both!" I say as they arrive beside us. Charles shakes James's hand and proffers me a kiss on the cheek. I try to overt my eyes from James as he casts me an all too familiar look before returning the gestures to both.

"We haven't seen you guys for ages then we see you twice in two days! The party was so wonderful, Isla. What a night that was, it was fabulous, we both had such fun!" Alicia gushes warmly.

"We were so glad you were both able to come." James effuses. "We absolutely don't see enough of you."

"I was just saying that to Charles, that Isla and I really must get out for coffee and have a really good catch-up, you are always so busy, Isla," Alicia says turning to me, "and I hardly got any time at your fabulous party to catch up properly with you. Can I steal her away from you for a few hours?" This time she turns to James with an innocent smile on her serene face.

"Oh, she's been so busy getting our new house perfect she simply can't bear to be away. I'm always telling her she must go out, but if you can persuade her then it's fine by me, in fact, that's where I am taking her now, it took me a lot of persuading I can tell you," as if butter wouldn't melt, the lies slither smoothly off his tongue.

I put my game face on knowing full well James won't let me go. Well-rehearsed excuses spill from my lips as though I am playing the part of someone else.

"That sounds simply marvellous, absolutely! I would love that, Alicia, just let me know when suits you."

"What about next week, Wednesday? How does that fit in with you? If we arrange now, then you can't slip out of it!" Alicia chuckles good-naturedly.

I turn to James. "What do you think? Do we have anything on that day?" Taken aback at the immediate offer, I don't know what to do.

"Of course! Why on earth do you need to ask me?" James replies with a big smile and puts his arm tightly around my shoulder, squeezing it hard. I try not to wince as his strong fingers dig into my flesh. "I know you ladies love to escape from us men don't you." I see him give Charles a conspiratorial wink. Charles readily agrees.

"Oh absolutely! And can I say, Isla…"

I hold my breath, praying silently he's not going to say what I think he is going too. My heart sinks as he continues.

"You are looking more beautiful every time I see you!"

"Oh! You charmer." Alicia laughs and pats Charles' arm warmly. "But I have to agree, you are looking wonderful, please let me into your secret!"

"Umm, happiness?" I laugh uncomfortably not sure how to reply but trying to ensure it would please James. I know how pathetically lame a reply this is, and I cringe inwardly.

"Well, it is certainly working for you, can I have a bit, you look like you have plenty to go around," Alicia replies cheerfully, unaware of my discomfort.

"You look marvellous in it; James, you are a very lucky man."

I can feel James looking at me but daren't catch his eye. The squeeze gets harder, digging into my collarbone. I try not to show my discomfort.

"Oh, by the way, James, I saw you this morning! Up by the A7, you were in a layby. I think you were having a sneaky sleep! I would have rapped on the window, but you were out for the count, it seemed such a shame to waken you, you sly old dog you, was the party too much for you!"

This time I turn to look at James, his face is a picture, the usually composed expression he reserves for the public slipping. Hastily, I interrupt, trying to pacify the situation.

"He's been working flat out of late, 24/7, he works so hard all the time, he has to travel so much with work, it's exhausting for him working such long hours." I have a set list of responses; James would make it very clear later if he's not been happy with my response.

"Hah, yes 24 minutes working and 7 days in the pub!" Charles laughs at his own joke, oblivious to the darkening atmosphere. James is deathly silent. This was getting decidedly dangerous.

Alicia thoughtfully cuts in, "So, that's settled then! I'm really looking forward to catching up, does 12pm suit? I know you'll have changeovers in your wonderful bed and breakfast, will that give you enough time before collecting Sophie from school?"

"That's perfect," I beam out a big smile, "I'm looking forward to it too."

"Well, we better get on," James cuts in, public face back, friendly as ever again. "I must get this one off for her coffee, I never see enough of her, so I insisted she come spend some time with me."

"Oh, how romantic!" Alicia leans forward to give me a kiss goodbye on the cheek, Charles, about to do the same, is caught midway by James who leans forward to him and says something I cannot hear. Both look at me, a smile on James's face, but gone from Charles. I do not hear what Alicia is saying to me now, there is a rush of noise in my ears akin to waves crashing upon a beach. Charles looks at me then looks away; his skin a few shades paler than when we arrived.

"Well, it's been lovely seeing you both again," James grips my shoulder tightly. "I'm sure you two ladies will have a good catch-up on your coffee date, Alicia."

I repeat my goodbyes as Charles ushers Alicia quickly up the street muttering goodbyes and half-waves. I hope the smile and the cheery wave with promises I would meet up soon are convincing…

I am trembling inside as we head off, I know there will be a retaliation but what it would be, only time would tell.

As we head into the coffee shop, James turns to me, "Did you ever see such a look on your face," he mocks. "Anyone would think you'd been invited to the Oscars, not for coffee," he laughs to himself as he pushes past a family and in through the door. The coffee shop is crowded. I say nothing as James sends me to get one of the few remaining tables.

Sitting down I look over at James as he jumps in front of a couple oohing and aahing over which cake to have.

Bringing back 2 coffees and one cake, he sits at the seat opposite me. "I assumed you wouldn't want one since you had dessert last night?" He looks at me pointedly. I look at the delicious-looking traybake, the gooey caramel sliding down the chocolate-covered shortbread but say nothing. I sip my coffee, the steaming black liquid scalding all the way down. I try to make conversation; it's stilted and I get one-word answers. James's phone rings and he answers it immediately. He chats away, laughing with the person on the end of the phone. I wish I know what to say to interest him, for him to talk and laugh along with me again. I used to be able to hold a conversation. Where had that gone?

Left to my own thoughts entirely now, I look around. The aroma of fresh coffee hangs in the air, warm and welcoming, mingling with the mix of chatter and laughter from all different classes and cultures combining in a united goal; to take time out from a hectic week and enjoy company.

The steam from the cappuccino machine draws my attention, a girl in a jaunty hat waits in line for her drink, the barista expertly foams the milk, tossing a tea cloth over his shoulder he pours the light frothy mix over the dark liquid, topping it off with a flourish of chocolate powder and a cheery smile, he says something I cannot hear, the girl in the hat laughs and takes the tray.

A young couple walks in, the girl's ponytail swings merrily as she walks, the man walking beside her is tall and has a slight stubble, he is clearly nervous. A first date, I wonder. Stubble bustles anxiously around Ponytail and settles her into a seat with an anxious smile before going to the counter. She picks up a newspaper before quickly putting it down, unsure of what to do with herself till he returns. I see the barista chatting cheerfully to Stubble, I don't know if he knows him or is just friendly, he looks like he is putting him at ease.

Stubble returns to Ponytail with a loaded tray, kindness shining from his eyes, a nervous smile plays on her lips as they start to talk. A few seats over I see an overwrought young woman trying to settle her fretful baby, her partner comes back with a tray of drinks, lays it down and quickly scoops up the baby.

The relief on the woman's face is tangible as he murmurs something to her, she looks up at him, smiles and picks up her latte, I can see her body relax a little.

James hangs up his phone. I look up expectantly, maybe he will want to chat now? He looks over at me, then proceeds to text someone. It's clear he doesn't want to make conversation; I feel at odds with the warm bustling environment. I feel so lonely and out of place here, the chatter and friendliness surrounding me is a sharp contrast to my own world. I see an old couple in the corner, as he reads his newspaper, a lock of white hair falls forward, absentmindedly he pushes it back into place over his balding head, she is working on a puzzle book, curly white hair, and gold rimmed glasses, both are engrossed in silence. A moment later she reaches over and places a hand over his, he reaches back and covers her small hand with his large gnarly one, his mouth breaking into a smile, his eyes crinkling at the edges. This couple do not need words, the years have bonded them together. The smile still playing on his lips covers generations of love. I feel a flood of loneliness encompass me.

The noise of ice being crushed into a fruit cooler makes a welcome distraction from my lonely thoughts. I look back over to where the barista has now been joined by a chirpy young girl, fresh-faced and pretty, she chats merrily to her customers, she does not look like she has a care in the world. How I envy her.

"What? Sorry, I missed that." I am taken aback as James suddenly speaks to me.

"I said, do you like him? Coffee boy over there, I see you looking at him," he leans into me and hisses quietly, "do you think he would look twice at you?" He sneers, caramel is stuck in between his teeth and droplets of coffee-infused saliva spray my face. He is so close now.

"Are you trying to embarrass me? How do you think that makes me feel? I take you out for coffee and that is how you repay me." His eyes are flint like as he settles back into his chair, he stares at me for a full two minutes before returning to text on his phone. I feel utterly humiliated and stare down at my coffee. I wish I could sink right into my chair, to be enveloped in the imitation leather. I try not to let the tears that are fighting their way out to escape. I stare into my empty coffee cup, cradling it and pretend to take sips. I dare not look about me.

Silence prevails for what feels like an eternity before finally, he puts the last bit of caramel into his mouth and puts down his cup. The signal to go. I feel an unease, my stomach is lurching, I want to stay here forever. Whilst the warm aroma and buzzing conversation around me only serve to accentuate my own feeling of isolation, I cannot help but wish I could turn invisible, to stay and be a part of the warm aromas and chatter. Just a no one. But I must go.

A chill breeze is sweeping in from the east. Berwick is on the coast and prone to wind. It suits the mood. I walk around the Range Rover and slip into the passenger side. The smell of fresh coffee is instantly replaced by the pungent car smell. James puts the car into reverse and carelessly drives out of the parking space, narrowly missing a young couple pushing a pram, shopping bags perched precariously on top overflowing with nappies and groceries. Rolling down the window, James swears loudly and yells at them to watch where they are going. Mortified, I slip further into my seat; the young couple looks on, too shocked to reply. I can see their aghast faces in the rear-view mirror as we speed off.

Driving out of town I watch enviously at families out with children laugh together, an old couple sitting on a bench talking, a teenager on a scooter. Then the town is gone. The ride back home is in silence. I try to make small talk aiming for a few neutral comments, anything to break the deathly intensity of the silence but to no avail. I know this isn't good, there is nothing I can do but wait it out. I cling to the thought that I will be going to see Dad, Sophie, and Lola when I get home.

The atmosphere thickens in the car with every passing mile. There is nothing but James's outline against the green of the fields whizzing by, endless fields, endless journey, endless silence. I shut my eyes trying to block out his image, it doesn't work. His very presence is oppressive, filling the car with a thick gloom mixing with the smell of wet dog and dirt. We pass through Kelso, a lovely small country town before heading along the lone moor road. I hate this road, it is long and depressing, dry scrub, old heather, not a house to be seen. I can see James's outline, the wind from the part open window lifting his red curls revealing his receding hairline. His mouth is thin and drawn tight. With what feels like an eternity, we finally drive in through the gate. The tyres crunching loudly on the gravel announcing to no one our arrival.

I'm glad for once to see the house and as James turns off the ignition, I click off my seatbelt, release the lock on the door and slip out of the car. I need to see Dad and Sophie as badly as I need air. Pulling out my mobile, I begin typing in numbers.

"Who are you calling?" James asks over my shoulder.

I jump, not having heard him steal up behind me. "My dad? I'm just letting him know I'll be over shortly."

"You?" He spits, a smirk spreading across his dark face. "What on earth makes you think you are going there? I'll collect Sophie for you on my way back from my work this afternoon." He gives me a long hard glare; I stand frozen, mobile in hand, numbers only half entered, a cold wind tugging at my hair.

"For Christ's sake, what's that look for? It's about time you started cooking for me. Burnt toast and disgusting coffee this morning. I can't survive on that, I need proper food, soup, and can't you make a decent stew for once?" he disparages before continuing, "And we'll need some cakes made for the crowd coming in. Honestly, I don't know what goes through that pea-brained head of yours at times. What did you think? That I would take you out for coffee today then you could swan around at your dad's like Lady Muck!" he smirks as he watches my face fall, the realisation hitting me that I won't see Dad. Again. I miss him so much, he used to come over often, but the visits got shorter and less frequent until they dried up altogether.

"So, you'd better get started, the guys will be in at six and I'll expect something edible when I get back."

He leans into me, face inches from mine, I try not to shrink back. He stares straight into my eyes, his face unflinching. I nod my compliance.

"Good." One word of a reply before moving back from my face. "Good." I hear him mutter more to himself this time as he shuffles off, leaving behind him for company the dark cloud that always appears to follow him.

This time I let the tears flow unchecked. It is a lesson learnt. A rehearsal for the future, a future where my worst fears would land at my very being before long. I had been so looking forward to seeing Dad again. There was nothing I could do. James got his revenge for me daring to look at the barista today. The afternoon looms in front of me like an unwelcome visitor.

Chapter 4

Walking into the kitchen, I focus my thoughts on Sophie and Lola coming later, it can't come soon enough for me. I'll make a nice treat for her coming home, but what? I look in the cupboards to see what I have to work with. As always, there is plenty to make for James, he makes sure of that, but I want to make something special for Sophie. I know that my lovely dad will have spoiled her thankfully, but I desperately want to make something nice for her. Searching in the back of the cupboard I find pasta; luckily, Sophie loves macaroni and cheese.

James loves cheese so there is always plenty of that and pasta is cheap, so not complained about. I set about my afternoon of cooking, a chore I used to enjoy but is now filled with dread, there is always something wrong with what I cook. Too burnt, too lumpy or too cold. It feels like the three bears and the big bad wolf. I am too sad to have even a little laugh at this. I occupy myself with the thought of Sophie and Lola coming home.

The guests arrive promptly at 6, and I've just finished showing them their rooms when I hear James arrive back home. He is preceded by an excitable Sophie who runs up the stairs and hurtles herself at me with a huge, tight hug, she is followed by an even more excitable Lola dancing around my feet desperate to jump up. James has his usual public face firmly pasted on.

"I see Isla has you settled in. Beer chaps!" he calls out chipperly to the guys; a statement, rather than a question to which raucous calls ensue along with a clatter of heavy shod feet on the marble floor as they head for the kitchen to raid the fridge. Gratefully, I take the opportunity and leave with Sophie and Lola to the sanctity of the living room. James and the guys won't be seen for the rest of night, they would drink beer then head to the pub till the early hours. I take some comfort in that.

Sophie, now curled up with Lola and myself on the sofa, is excitedly telling me about her trip to Granda's, "And I helped him water all the seedlings in the greenhouse, Mummy!" she declares proudly. "Then I helped Granny make scones. I am really good at making those!"

"Wow, Granda and Granny will really miss you after all that!"

"Yes, Granda says his plants grow so much better when I water them!"

Bless Granda, I thought, *such a gentle and quiet man, he absolutely dotes on Sophie.*

"And have you had your tea yet?"

"I did, Mummy, but I could eat some more." She smiles up at me. "Granda says I have hollow legs."

"You must get those from me," I laugh. "Granda used to say the same thing about your mummy when I was little! Come on, let's go get something for you to eat, I've made macaroni and cheese, would you like some of that?"

"Absolutely," she says jumping up with a giggle.

"Are you copying your mummy?" I laugh good-naturedly, enjoying Sophie's merriment, following her through to the kitchen Lola close at my heels, her regular spot, black and white body bouncing up and down, tail wagging. "Oh, I think we can find a little something for you too, Lola, what do you think?"

"I think she would like one of these!" Sophie declares, triumphantly pulling out a handful of dog biscuits from her pocket. "Granda said I could bring some of Buddy's biscuits."

"Oh, how lovely. I am sure she will enjoy those; now shall we get your hands washed and I'll heat up some macaroni for you, shall we. Lola can have her treats when you have your tea, how does that sound?"

I could hear a commotion out in the hall, the guys must be heading to the pub. *So much so for the food I had had to prepare that afternoon,* I think but put it to the back of my mind just glad that I had my two girls, Sophie, and Lola, with me, an evening of peace beckons welcomingly in front. Sophie tucks into her macaroni and delightedly gives dog biscuits to an equally delighted Lola.

"…and Granda gave me a whole bag of them for her, Mummy, they are in my suitcase! He said not to give her them all at once though!" She looks up at me with an adorable smile, rosy cheeks, and blonde curls dancing in her excitement.

"Well, I think that sounds like very good advice, now there's some traybake, but I don't think you would really have any space for that now, would you!" I tease.

"Oh, I've always got space for that, Mummy," Sophie giggles.

"Well, if you're absolutely sure…shall we take some through and watch a movie before bed? What do you think we should watch tonight?"

"Lola told me she would really, really like to see 102 Dalmatians!"

"Oh, she did, did she? Well, in that case, we had better not let her down," I giggle; what a difference when he is not in the house, it is so much more relaxed.

"Right McGinty, it's getting very late now," I say after we've finished watching *102 Dalmatians*. "I think it's time for teeth brushing and bed! And I think that cheeky little face of yours could do with a good wash too!"

"Lola needs hers brushed too! Can she sleep with me tonight? Granda lets her up with me, he says she might be scared by herself, she might be scared here too."

"I'm sure she would love that," I agree. "Right, let's go! Quick march, left, right, left right." We giggle our way up the stairs and before long Sophie is safely tucked up in bed, arms wrapped tightly around a very happy Lola. I kiss her goodnight, switch on her night light, and quietly close the door. I hear her chattering away quietly to Lola telling her a good night story, she's exhausted but happy.

Heading down the stairs, I quickly check the guest living room; as I suspect it's littered with beer bottles, crisp and nut packets, and a few spillages, how can people make so much mess in such a short time, I wonder to myself. Gathering up the debris and going to fetch a cloth and a mop, I know the answer; it's James. He leads and guests follow. It's become the new norm. I work as quickly as I can, keen to finish so I can study. I don't have long before this assessment is due, so even a few hours are precious. Once I have the room back to its original condition, gathering up my study things and pouring myself a coffee I set about my assignment.

I'm enjoying this course, it gives me a little escapism from reality, and so far, James has not stopped me from studying. I have to be careful not to rock the boat, making sure I study only when he's out of the house, or in the evening when Sophie is in bed and I've completed my chores, usually finishing around 11.00, then I can have a few hours' study time.

Tonight, I'm in luck, it's only 10.00 pm. I'm tired from this morning's early start and the previous nights' late party, but time is against me. This is my final assignment for this course and worth 40% of my total marks. Opening my ancient laptop, I have a quick look at my notes before reading over my assignment. I'm pleased with my work so far, and don't have much more to do. It's going to be tough going tonight though I think as I set about reading and rereading, writing, and correcting myself, checking, rechecking until I can do no more that's worth anything.

Closing my laptop, I head up the staircase to bed. Quickly checking on Sophie, I see she's sleeping, still with her arms wound tightly around Lola. Lola opens one eye, cocks a lazy ear, and, seeing it is only me, snuggles back down with a contented groan, closing her eye again. I envy her simple life. Heading to my bedroom, it is about as much as I can do to wash and brush my teeth before falling exhausted into bed.

What feels like seconds later I'm being shaken awake.

"Well?" he demands.

I struggle to comprehend what's happening. James is swaying in front of me.

"Well," he continues, "when did you see him?"

"I…I…I don't understand," I reply hesitantly, confused and sleep-deprived. I try to shake myself awake in order to work out this latest interrogation.

"See who?" I try again, my voice comes out muffled with fatigue.

"See him!" he spits out, "*Charles*, and I quote: *you get more lovely every time I see you* so you must be seeing him regularly."

"N-N-No! No I haven't." I struggle to waken myself, to understand and make sense of this latest accusation, of what James means. I look at the clock. It blinks out a traitorous 3.57 am.

"I don't believe you! Were you planning to see him when you went shopping? Is that it? Is that why you wanted to go yourself?"

I get no time to reply before he continues, his tone now mocking. *"I know! I'll sneak out and see my boyfriend whilst James is out working, he'll never know."* His accusations are getting louder and louder.

"Shhh," I try quieting him, "you'll waken Sophie."

Ignoring me, and intent on his accusatory mission, there's no stopping him, his voice is getting higher and higher in pitch. I know there is to be no reasoning with him. I just pray Sophie does not waken, or worse, hear him when he is like this.

He thumps onto the bed which bounces under his ever-growing weight, pulling off his jeans and throwing them carelessly onto the floor, seconds later his sludge-green t-shirt joins them, the moonlight shines through the open curtains reflecting off his white belly, the rolls of fat now undeniable.

"Thought you were too clever for me, did you?" Throwing his socks onto the floor to join the growing mess, he interjects with a sudden, "I'll get the food shopping from now on, you spend far too much money, and when I don't have the time, then you can go online and do a shop from now on, there is no need for you to be gallivanting out to the shops spending all that money on fuel is a waste." He follows through with a triumphant, "it'll give you time to write those articles for the shooting magazine, make yourself useful for a change," he leans back heavily against his pillow and seconds later he is snoring loudly.

And there it is I realise. The retaliation. The retribution for today's actions, for the audacity of someone giving me a compliment, not only did I not see Dad, but I have now lost the few precious hours I get away from this house.

I am wide awake now, all thoughts of sleep gone. I lie staring at the moonlight, tears falling silently down my face, soaking into my pillow. Such a beautiful night, the moon, the stars, such a sharp contrast to the emotions I feel inside of me. I feel utterly powerless. Powerless to alter my fate. I begin to wonder more and more of late who am I and where have I gone? I have begun to not recognise the person within me, the person who speaks like me, acts like me, but surely isn't me? I wouldn't act that way, would I?

I don't know how much longer I can take this. Bit by bit, day by day, things are getting worse. For every action, there is a retaliation. I sense that things could get a whole lot worse. I can feel it. A plan has started to formulate loosely in my mind of late. I know I have to get away with Sophie, but how?

Chapter 5

The next day, walking Sophie to school along the small country road, I feel her pace slow. I know today is going to be another battle getting her into school. Mr Toledo, Sophie's teacher, said once she is in school, she is fine, enjoying her lessons, it was just such a battle getting her through the door though. Sophie, her usual quiet self, holds my hand tightly, tugging me closer to her as we walk, her pace slowing. I try to distract her with chat, the exciting things she would be doing in school, the upcoming school trip, and her friends. It's not working today at all.

"Mu-umm…I want to stay with you, I feel really tired today and my tummy hurts." Looking up at me with those big blue eyes, I want to scoop her right up and take her straight home, but I know not only does she have to go, but she will be safer in school.

"Let's get you in and see how your morning goes," I suggest as brightly as I can. Looking up at me with a mixture of doubt and hesitance, Sophie lets me walk her into school. Step one. I breathe inwardly. Step two, off with her coat and if only she can see her friend, I could be forgotten in an instant—such is the ability children have.

Alas, no, luck was not in my favour though, Daisy, Sophie's friend, is not in sight. As I continue scanning the throng of children buzzing about, chattering excitedly with their friends, I experience a pang of sadness. Just once would I love a whole week of setting Sophie into school, seeing her bound off excitedly to find her friends. Today is not to be that day though.

"Ok sweetheart," I try again, "Mummy needs to go now, so why don't you look around for Daisy? I'm sure she will be here somewhere." Even to myself I hear the desperation in my voice. Looking up at me, Sophie, ever willing, agrees hesitantly, and, with a final tight hug I watch her walk slowly away, blonde head lowered, in search of Daisy.

Taking my opportunity, I head out through the school doors, the bell ringing loudly signalling the start of the school day.

"M-U-M-M-Y!" I hear a wail behind me, my heart thuds, stopping in my tracks I've no sooner turned around than a tiny figure hurtles into me enveloping me in a bear hug. "Mummy, please don't go, I want to come home," Sophie wails.

I can sense rather than see Mr Toledo rushing up to us.

"Now Sophie, come on," he comments briskly. "School is starting, and everyone is waiting on you."

Sophie clings tighter to me. "Nooooo," she whispers almost inaudibly. "I want to go home with Mummy."

I try to peel Sophie off, fighting back the tears which will make the situation worse. I try to encourage her back to school, all to no avail, in desperation I look up at Mr Toledo.

"Right Sophie, come along," Mr Toledo interjects all brusque business. "Let's have no more of this nonsense, you don't want to get your mummy into trouble now, do you?"

Sophie looks alarmed. I can see the confusion in her eyes, torn between wanting to come home with me and not wanting to get me into trouble. She hesitates briefly before solemnly shaking her head. Reluctantly, she lets me go. Taking Mr Toledo's hand, she meekly follows him. It is heartbreaking to hear her crying, her tiny body wracked with sobs.

Holding back the tears of my own, I am emotionally drained, seeing the pain in her eyes as she unwillingly heads into school. I push my now trademark sunglasses further up trying to stifle the tears. People see what they want to see.

"Sunglasses on such a dull day, who does she think she is," I would hear them whisper behind my back.

I don't care though, the sunglasses shelter me from more than just the sun, they sheltered me from the world, from people—well-meaning people perhaps—asking questions I could not answer, curious stares at tears from 'informants' asking my husband what was wrong, what had happened—oh I know exactly what that would lead to if I presented our lives as anything less than perfect. So, my sunglasses are as much to me as my mask, both donned daily serving their duty to protect me.

"Isla!" I hear someone call out. "ISLA!"

50

I walk on, picking up my pace in the hope they would give up, thinking I had not heard them. I'm exhausted, the encounter with James last night just adding to the emotional baggage that I carry around with me daily, getting heavier and heavier, the repetitiveness of his comments is wearing me down no matter how hard I try to turn them into white noise, I just can't.

"I-LAAAAAA," the voice shouts, louder this time. My heart sinks as I hear quickened footsteps behind me, gaining on me over the tarmac.

Please go away, please go away. I think silently, walking faster and staring straight ahead.

"My goodness, you set quite a pace!" Rose laughs as she catches up and falls into step alongside me. "I didn't think I was going to catch you up!"

"Sorry," I apologise. "I'm just in a bit of a hurry as usual, the guys are on their way back for breakfast already," I lie, feeling ashamed. I'm not in the mood to talk. I'm afraid she will hear the wobble in my voice, evidencing my teary state. I can't risk that.

"It's okay. I'll walk and talk. It won't take long," she replies breezily. "I didn't quite get a chance to talk to you about this at your wonderful party, Isla, but we're in desperate need of new blood for the school board, and with all your previous management experience, we thought you'd be perfect!" she looks on at me encouragingly, showing no sign of letting up her pace with me.

My silence must have spoken volumes because she continues, "With you at home all day, you'll be perfect! Well, it's not like you can call what you do there actually work, is it?" She tries to laugh this off as a joke, but I can feel the undercurrent there just as clearly as if she has said: *Come on, do your bit, you only have one child and since you don't actually go out to work then it's not really work at all*. I know from experience all too well people use jocular tones to get out what they really feel or want to say.

"Umm," I stutter, "I'm not sure what James will say, the meetings are in evenings, aren't they, and he sometimes doesn't get back till late."

"Oh, that's okay," Rose replies brightly, "Hamish already spoke to him in the pub last night and he was up for it. You see you can bring Sophie along to the meetings and we'll make sure she's kept occupied, a lot of our mums bring their wee ones along, it's no problem!" she replies cheerily oblivious.

"Great," I think, James would love that, cornered in front of everyone he would have had to agree.

"Super," I reply as brightly as I can muster, tears welling up behind my eyes are desperate to escape, to break the dam wall, on the brink of flowing forth disloyally into the world and ready to break the cover I'm trying so hard to create.

I take a deep breath, cornered and with no escape, I reply as brightly as I can muster, "I really must dash now, just let me know when I need to be there."

Rose, happy to have got her own way, lets me escape, but not before calling out a cheery, and possibly a touch smugly, "Oh, didn't James say? It is tonight! See you at 7.30!"

As I walk the short distance back along the road, I read the small sign staked proudly beside a large display of cheerful blooming flowers in the neatly manicured verge:

Wisteria village
Winner Britain in Bloom
Best Wee Village 2010

Our wee village's proudest achievement. I glance up at the hanging baskets that agree adorning the lampposts. Deep red and snow-white trailing petunias nestle alongside blue trailing lobelia dangling cheerfully, dancing as if to their own little melody in the light wind. Letting my gaze trail into the distance, past the grey slated rooftops and across the neat green fields where cattle grazed serenely on the grass. Black and white sheep dot the fields to where the Eildon hills rise majestically; framed against the horizon.

I feel uneasy and at odds with this tranquil setting. I should have felt happy here. I cast my mind back to when we had just arrived here, fresh, happy, and over the moon with having finally given birth to our baby after years of trying. The village had welcomed us with open arms. It would do that to you. The beautiful winding roads all set for romantic walks, the village school where Sophie would eventually go, the pub where I had envisaged many lazy chatty Sunday lunches and the ancient church where Sophie was to be christened. I imagined it to be like my favourite time of the year. Christmas.

When as a child you walk into a room to see a beautifully decorated Christmas tree with bundles of multicoloured gifts wrapped in ribbon bows cascading around its base, music playing and the delicious smells of cooking wafting through the air from the kitchen. Then, as you excitedly step towards the gifts ready to unwrap them, heart drumming loudly in your ears with anticipation, you start tearing open the ribbons and pretty paper, only to discover the presents are in fact empty boxes, put on only for display. The tree is carried away in front of your eyes the day before Christmas and the Sale banner goes up. Then you wake up and discover it was all a bad dream.

But this is no dream. This is my life. Taking a deep breath and exhaling gently, I turn slowly into my driveway and make my way towards the house, footsteps crunching noisily on the gravel driveway, neat lawns lining either side, flower beds letting their residents nod a cheerful welcome. Sometimes, I wish for a reason not to come home, any reason, it doesn't have to be a big reason, just a reason to have a few hours away.

I look up at the house. Large, cream-coloured and double-fronted with a large slate roof protecting its inhabitants. Window boxes adorn the front and hanging baskets dangle brightly at the door swinging gently in the light breeze. It was as though the house was cosseted, safely enveloping, and offering protection to all who entered.

Protection or suffocation.

Pushing the door open and wandering across the marble hallway, I make my way past the utility room and into the kitchen. Putting the encounter behind me for now, I set about my usual routine. Collecting my cleaning basket, I make a start on the bedrooms, hoovering the carpets and preparing the dining table. I appreciate the monotony of it all. It stops me having time to think. The call declaring the imminent arrival of James and the guests had come 5 minutes ago, they would be home in half an hour.

Chapter 6

I can't shake the jittery feeling I have as I walk back along the marble hallway and into the kitchen. The kitchen, once my favourite place, now fills me with angst. Trying to dismiss the feelings of foreboding that are washing over me simply as tiredness and concern over Sophie, I pull the bacon, sausages, eggs, mushrooms, tomatoes, haggis, and black pudding out of the fridge before heading to the cupboard to reach up for the tinned beans and potato scones. Leaning down, I pull out two heavy cast-iron frying pans and gently arrange the sausage and bacon in them, setting them to one side on the countertop ready to move over to the aga. I appreciate the order. The routine. Routine where chaos is the norm, this simple daily duty is a reminder that there could be norm, a sort of norm even if it was monotonous.

I work quickly and efficiently, needing to have everything cooked ready to the point of serving for when the guests sit down or risk yet another dressing-down. James wants the breakfasts ready for the guests as soon as they arrive, the guests are happy to wait, James not so, as he reminds me often enough.

Hearing the crunch of tyres on gravel, I look around to see 3 four-wheel drives coming up the driveway.

Taking a deep inhalation of breath, I realise he's done it again, that he's set me up to fail. Quickly, I set the frying pans on the aga top. He knows there's no way I can cook 8 full cooked breakfasts in that time; resignedly, I carry on, mushrooms, tomatoes, beans, all in their pans, sliced haggis, black pudding and potato bread all joining alongside the bacon and sausage now sizzling merrily on the aga.

The door crashes open, making me jump as it ricochets noisily off the wall. James appears at the door, his six foot one bulk filling the frame, his customary outfit of green moleskin trousers hanging off his rear end, paired with a sludge-green polo shirt and size 15 wellington boots. I look over at this giant, red curls thrown back from the morning wind revealing a receding hairline, thick beetling eyebrows almost joining above small, dark, flinty eyes. I shrink back as he strides into the kitchen, mud from his boots dripping off in his wake, dispersing mud over my freshly washed floor. I know better than to comment on this, not after the last time.

"Good morning," I attempt as cheerily as I can, trying to gain a sense of his mood. I needn't have bothered; one glance and I can tell today isn't a good day.

"I hope breakfast is ready. I'm in a hurry today," he barks out abruptly.

"They won't be long, almost ready, by the time they get their toast and cereal, I'll have them ready," I try to appease him.

"Almost? For goodness' sake, what do you do all day? One simple task, one! That is all you have to do, and you can't even do that right."

Nothing, I think to myself, *absolutely nothing. I just get our daughter ready for school, clean up after your mess and then go and clean the guest rooms, often which resemble a nuclear disaster, before trying to prepare breakfasts in time for your arrival, the time can be anything from 3 minutes to 2 hours, not to mention that they are expected to look like something out of Jamie Oliver's cook book regardless but apart from that absolutely nothing. I sit on my bahookie all day reading gossip columns and painting my nails.*

However, I say nothing. It's a rhetorical question. One in which he has all the answers, and my answers are insignificant. Unnecessary.

Glancing back at James, I see his face is as dark as thunder, with no guests close by and free to show his true emotions, he turns on me.

"You set that up, didn't you?" he accuses.

Confused at the sudden change of tract, I stutter, "Wh-Wh-what?" There is no hint, no clue. No preamble. Nothing to give me a hint of what he means.

"You set that up," he repeats, eyes cold as steel now. "You want to go out, meet new people, you want a boyfriend. A new husband perhaps?"

"N-N-No…" I stutter again, the penny dropping, he was talking about the school board. Not daring to look up, I concentrate on the sausages turning a lovely golden brown, sputtering cheerily in the pan, so innocent and comforting—contrasting sharply with the now black atmosphere in the kitchen.

"I'd no idea they were going to ask you, honestly no one said anything to me before about it," I continue. I can hear the wobble in my voice, pathetic and pleading.

James takes a step towards me, his face murderous.

"You're lying," he hisses, looking quickly behind him, checking to see if the guests are coming in yet. "Things like that don't just happen, you must have asked him to ask me. What did you think? Ask him whilst he's in a good mood, did you plot it together? Maybe you're already seeing Hamish, is that it? You want more time together. I can see it now, the two of you laughing behind my back. Was it when you were in bed together?"

He's getting worked up. I can see where this is going, the customary line everything takes if I so much as look at someone. It means I must be having an affair. It it's exhausting, debilitating, and humiliating.

Footsteps from the hall are getting louder, the door to the kitchen opens. I am saved. For now.

"Isla! Oh my, that does smell good!" Jack, one of our guests, declares as he pops his head around the door. "Apologies for interrupting you both," he continues, looking over at me again, he smiles kindly. "I can imagine you don't get a lot of time together."

I offer Jack a grateful smile. James's face changed from dark to jolly, flick-knife fast as soon as the door opened.

Winking cheerily at me, Jack turns back to James and continues, "I wondered if you would have a quick look at my gun before we head out again, I thought it was slightly off this morning."

"No trouble at all," James replies, face now one of pure virtue. "I'll have a look just now. Isla is behind with breakfasts this morning, again, so it'll fill in the time until she serves up," he retorts, the slight, obvious, floats in the air reflected with a joking manner for Jack's benefit.

"Oh, Isla can take all the time she needs, I don't know how she manages but it's absolutely worth waiting on!" Jack looks over at me again and gives me a cheerful wink before continuing, "This is the best bit about coming here, getting our delicious Border Belly Buster for breakfast."

"Okay," James mutters. "I'll be along in just a minute. I just have to help Isla with this, or we'll be here all day."

"Super, no problem, and certainly no rush, I'll just go get what I need and catch you along there, James." With that, he retreats out of the kitchen but not before giving me a kind smile.

Turning to me, James hisses, "I'll speak to you later," almost inaudibly, his public smile still spread on his face, hiding the true meanings of his words to all but me. As he moves towards the door after Jack, I look on. He turns and gives me a look. The look. I know that look, and he knows it. Shuddering, letting out the breath I have unconsciously been holding.

I was grateful to Jack's diversion; it gives me a bit of time to think to myself as I turn back to the aga and carry on cooking. I work quickly, preparing toast to keep the guests occupied. They would have cereal first, and hopefully by the time they've washed themselves and settled themselves down at the breakfast table, I'd have their cooked breakfast ready. Popping through to the dining room I set two big pots of coffee down, following this with 2 pots of tea before returning to the kitchen.

James is there, picking up the toast to take through. He doesn't like me to be in with the guests, so I'm relieved of the task of taking through the toast and enormous plates of cooked breakfast. The air in the kitchen is deafening in its silence, ominous and menacing. I shudder but say nothing. It's safer. I wait to see if he's going to say anything, but nothing is forthcoming. Giving me the look again, he leaves the kitchen in silence. I wonder if he'll return but I can hear him laughing raucously with the guests at the far side of the house. I am safe. For now.

The waiting to see what he's going to say or do is often worse than the outcome. The wondering what direction it'll take. What the retaliation will be, for retaliation there would most certainly be. Retaliation for the audacity of my being asked to be on the school board. An asking that would mean time out from the house.

I set about my routine of cleaning and tidying the kitchen. Some of the guests are nice, oblivious to the recurring nightmare I find myself living in as they chat away. I'm careful to be polite but not too welcoming. I know the effect that would have on James if I'm too friendly. Others are not so nice, and it's like having multiple James's in the house. The dirt, the noise, even soiled beds but I dare not complain.

"*We need the money,*" is the constant war cry. "*You spend too much*" and when he is in that mood, I get the brunt. It's easier to carry on and say nothing, to keep the place as clean and as well organised as I can. I know from experience it's much easier to not poke the bear.

Chapter 7

Lifting the cleaning basket from the shelf, my sleeve slips down; staring at the bruise on my arm, I wonder how I got this one. I can't understand how I seem to be getting so many. I don't remember knocking myself on anything. The bruises have started appearing over the last few months on my arms and legs. It doesn't make sense. *I must just be clumsy and getting more forgetful,* I think, giving myself a shake.

James is still not back from having breakfast with the guests. Checking my watch, I see it's 1.34pm. Hearing a commotion in the hallway, I'm relieved to hear James getting ready to head out. I hear the guests collecting their apparel. They'd been scheduled to head out at 2pm, so a few extra minutes of peace whilst they sort their guns was bliss. I know this means waiting to see what James has to say when he had said he would 'see me later', but I've just over an hour before I go to collect Sophie from school. I hate to admit it, but I have to acknowledge I'm safer when she is with me. He does not dare to shout, or worse, in front of her.

Sophie is the most precious thing in the world to me and I have to protect her. I try to keep her in a routine, regular bedtimes, make her bedroom cosy and happy. I know though that as soon as I put her to bed, the access to assault on me is a ticking time bomb. I never know where, why, or when, always on tenterhooks, trying to judge his moods, pacify the unpacifiable and predict the unpredictable, always trying to think ahead, thinking how I can prevent problems. Had I said anything out of place? Had I spoken for too long to someone? Was anything out of place in the house? Trying to predict what he would like to eat. My mind is in constant turmoil, and it's wearing me down.

Taking advantage of the peace, I set about my tasks, clearing the breakfast dishes, Lola following me up and down the hallway, tail wagging, big brown eyes looking up at me in anticipation of some leftover sausage from the breakfast table.

"I'm afraid you're out of luck this morning, there's not much left, beautiful," I murmur to her as she prances playfully around my feet. "Not so much as a bite of sausage!" I bend down to fondle her silky black spotted ears before lifting the remaining dishes, cleaning the table, and resetting it again. The next hour speeds by, as I hoover and clean the house, I let my mind wander to the dangers and pitfalls that lay ahead tonight at the meeting. Nothing would be simple, for that I know.

"What should I wear?" I wonder aloud to Lola. Cocking her ears, she gives me a wag of her tail. I haven't been to one of the meetings before, would jeans be too casual? Who would all be there? What time would it finish? Would I be expected to stay and socialise after, or could I leave quickly? So many questions. One guarantee is that James would know the exact second of when it was due to finish, any deviance from that time plus the walk home with Sophie would be unacceptable.

"I shall say I need to get Sophie to bed, after all it's a school night; no one can say anything about that, that's one problem sorted," I glance over at Lola, who rewards me with an adoring look from her big brown eyes.

I wonder who'll be there. Will it be busy? What would be expected of me? I would find out soon enough. "And I shall wear my smartest jeans and a simple top, James can't complain about that, can he Lola?" Lola wags her spotty tail at me as though in complete agreement and I bend down to give her a big cuddle. I don't know what I would do without her, she had come into my life as a six-month-old, one of my braver actions many years ago. I remember one of the following days as though it was yesterday. James had been away for his usual 4-day 'business' trip at Christmas and, just before his return, I had got Lola. He'd not spoken or said a word about her.

Three days later he'd come into the house, I was with her in the living room adjusting the lights on the Christmas tree, the double doors into the kitchen were wide open. I hadn't heard him come in, but she clearly had, the next thing I knew she flew from my side towards him growling and snarling. I had never seen her do that before or since then. She had not bitten him but rather tried to scare him off. Thinking back on it I couldn't help but marvel at her uncanny senses.

"Well, girl, I am so glad I have you, you are just the gentlest and kindest dog in the world aren't you, but we'd best get going, are you coming to get Sophie with me, she loves to lead you back from school!" Another wag of her tail, her black and white spotty body jumping around me in excited anticipation of the

59

forthcoming outing. I couldn't help but envy the simple life she led, being fed, cuddled and adored.

Collecting her lead, we head off to the school. It's only a few minutes' walk, and I hear the bell ring as we walk up the road. Perfect timing. I'll arrive just as the pupils are all pouring out and I'll escape from having to awkwardly try to make conversation with the clique who equally obviously don't want to make conversation with me. I silently thank my lucky stars as I see Sophie running out of school, having got herself ready quickly. She's one of the first to stream out of the building, school bag trailing along beside her, blonde curls flying; she looks so tiny in her red and blue school uniform.

"Mummy, you brought Lola! Can I take her! Mummy, you are coming to the meeting at school tonight? Can I come? Can I come please! Daisy's going to be there!" The words come tumbling out and as I hand the lead to her, a warm glow engulfs me as I answer her questions one by one, listening to her delighted chatter as we head back along the road. Sophie is in full flow as we get inside, and after washing her hands, I hand her a frozen yoghurt stick as a snack whilst she gets her homework bag out, sitting herself up at the kitchen table.

"Mummy, I am so excited that you are coming to school tonight. Inside the school with me. Actually inside it!" Sophie repeats. The holy grail of places to visit. I laugh alongside her; her enthusiasm and good-natured banter is contagious and for a few minutes I forget about any potential side effects the evening outing may bring.

"Ok sweetheart, yes, it'll be fun, quite an adventure, won't it! But first we need to get your homework done and then you can have a play before tea. How does that sound?"

"Perfect Mummy, I have my spelling and Mr Toledo gave me a new reading book too. I'm on the next level of Biff and Chip!" she announces proudly pulling out her new book entitled *Lost in the Jungle* with a flourish. "Doesn't it look exciting, Mummy!" I look on at her, just seeing her innocence and excitement fills me with such pleasure, helping me forget about my own day.

"It does, sweetheart," I agree. "It does."

I look at the clock. 7.08. I've just enough time to go up and change into a clean pair of jeans and change my top before we need to head along to the meeting, which is due to start at 7.30, finishing at 9.00. I'd settled Sophie in front of the TV, she's happily watching *Fifi and the Flower Tots* on DVD for the umpteenth time. James isn't home yet, and I'm hoping I'll be out with Sophie before he gets home. Everything is clean and tidy, and I've laid out coffee cups and some biscuits in case anyone wants something when they get home. It's unlikely, there'd be more chance of them having a quick wash and change before heading straight back out to the pub.

Pulling out my jeans, I slip them on along with a little top, before popping a little jacket over the top. I take a look in the full-length mirror. *I think that's okay.* I hear a creak as the door opens and I spin around quickly. James is there, standing in the doorway, leaning on the jamb, his large frame fills the space, he says nothing but looks me up and down slowly. Eyes travelling down my length before stopping on my jeans.

"Jeans? That's a strange choice."

"I thought they'd be casual and smart. Don't-don't you think they'll be okay?" I add hesitantly.

"Yes, if you are going to be going there to clean the school," he scoffs, "you're going to a school meeting and going as my wife; as I am letting you go there, the least you can do is look presentable." He stares me up and down slowly before turning on his heel, leaving me standing there staring at the empty doorway.

My heart sinks, I've only a few minutes before I need to leave, or I'd be late. Looking desperately in my wardrobe, I wonder what can I wear. I've lost all sense of what is right and what is not, I used to know exactly what to wear for different occasions. But what now? A pair of smart black trousers catch my eye. Perfect. I grab them victoriously along with a smart little blouse. Quickly changing into them, along with a pair of low heels. I survey myself once again in the mirror. I'm running out of time.

I feel, rather than see, James appear again. I turn slowly, he is leaning against the door frame, this time holding a bottle of Becks in his hand, he looks at me before taking a long swig of the bottle almost draining it in one.

"You look like you're going to a funeral!" he smirks, draining the bottle fully this time he turns, I assume, to go for a refill.

I feel tears prick at my eyes, now what? Time is running out. 7.29. I can hear Sophie coming up the stairs.

"Mummy, Fifi has finished, is it time to go yet?" she asks bounding into the bedroom.

"I'm just changing, sweetheart; I couldn't decide what to wear."

"You look lovely in that, Mummy," Sophie says loyally.

"Oh, I noticed a mark on it," I lie. "I'll just change quickly." I look for the third time into my wardrobe and fumble about in desperation trying to think what would cause the least comments. Sophie picks up a little skirt.

"What about this one, Mummy, it is very pretty!" I look at it, I know James likes it, it was the skirt I had worn when we had gone out for coffee, besides I'm running out of options and time, so, changing for the third time and running desperately late now, I pull it on along with a simple rollneck, failsafe thick tights, and boots.

"Ok sweetheart, we're good to go! Let's have a little game now, shall we, and see how quickly we can get from here to the school! Do you think we can break our previous record?"

"Absolutely!" Sophie replies looking up at me, excitement showing in her eyes for the night ahead. "Absolutely!" she repeats.

I laugh, knowing she's trying to make me giggle by repeating my usual word of choice for agreement. Grabbing my hand, she pulls me along enthusiastically.

As we head downstairs, I hear James along in the guest living room laughing raucously at something and I know I'm safe for now from further comment.

"Let's go!"

The evening's meeting passes in a blur. I'd rushed in, apologising profusely, everyone had been so lovely and said they understood trying to get children out in the evening was hard. I'd agreed, oh how I wish that's all it was; however, I was glad Sophie had been excited about going into school with me at night and seeing some of her friends that would be there too. There had been a mix of teachers including the head teacher, a few parents who were far too busy working to take up any official position, and I had spent most of the night battling for Vice Chair rather than the Chair the committee seemed overly keen to foist upon me. There would be far too many meetings away from the school, each one had a potential meeting with someone James would disapprove of. That I can't do. That'll spell instant disaster for me. James would be furious.

Eventually, the committee agreed to Vice Chair with the proviso that I consider Chair at the next election. I shall cross that bridge when I come to it. Various topics had been discussed and re-discussed. Lack of school funds seemed to be a recurrent theme. *Home from home,* I think to myself. I'm glad when the meeting is at last declared over. I've survived. I make my apologies that I must go straight away and swiftly scoop up Sophie and flee, ushering hasty goodbyes.

Sophie is indeed tired, she's enjoyed the late night out at school playing with Daisy, whose Mum had also been at the meeting, she offers no resistance when I get her ready for bed and, tucking her in, with only a few pages of her book read she's out like a light, thumb stuck firmly in her mouth, snoring softly. It's almost ten o'clock and my own eyes are closing. I could've easily headed to bed myself, but I need to study.

Heading down to make a coffee, before reluctantly padding through to haul out my study materials. Sitting down, it would have been so easy to close my eyes; giving myself a shake, I open the laptop, I'll be glad to finish my end-of-module assessment.

Tired as I am, I'm so grateful to my dad who encouraged me to get 'a proper qualification' a few years ago. James had been reluctant, however, my dad had, with keen foresight of the old, mentioned it in front of James, the result being I am studying from home with an online course through the Open University. If I ever manage to finish, which just now feels infinitely debatable, it will lead to an honours degree in STEM. As long as I manage to get all my daily duties done, James has ceased to complain. It's exhausting trying to keep up with the coursework whilst not letting any other of the balls I felt I was continuously juggling, drop. I can only study when Sophie is asleep, and ideally when James isn't in the house, having learnt from previous experience not to remind him I am studying.

A few hours and several coffees later, I give up, I can do no more that is beneficial and decide to call it a night. I'll give it another look-over tomorrow. The deadline is looming, and I'm finding it difficult to study. Satisfied, I click save and turn the laptop off for the night. James is still out with the lads at the pub; the lads still have another night before heading home to England, having made the most of partying every night, no doubt it will be a late one again for them.

Brushing my teeth, I gratefully sink onto the bed, pulling the duvet around me. No sooner had I drifted off to sleep I awaken with a start; loud noises are coming from downstairs. Looking over at the clock, it glows 4.07am. How do they do it? I wonder with a groan, they'll all be up again in less than an hour to go out shooting, the noises grow louder as 7 very drunken men stumble through the door's downstairs, in their efforts to be quiet they are making more noise.

"Ssh," one whispers audibly and theatrically.

"You'll wake the baby," another slurs.

"She's no baby, she's all woman," another giggles.

I cringe inwardly at their comments, hoping they'll quickly go into their rooms.

"Flip don't talk about his wife that way," another pseudo whispers back in mock horror. "You'll be for the rubbish end of the shooting tomorrow if he hears you."

"It is tomorrow," another chortles.

The words fade to muffled expressions as I hear doors slam, water running, toilets flushing, and floorboards creaking as drunken bodies finally drop heavily onto beds into deep and instant sleep. I listen carefully for any noise from next door indicating Sophie has woken but there is silence. *Thank goodness Sophie is a deep sleeper*, I think. Just at that moment I hear the stairs creak again. James this time. I can hear his unmistakable thud, thud, thud on the stairs getting louder as he gets closer. I catch my breath trying to regulate my breathing, a pretence at being asleep. Luck is on my side as he stumbles into the room, not bothering to brush his teeth. I hear him struggle to get out of his clothes, he flops heavily onto the bed to remove his boots, the bed bouncing like waves on a stormy sea all the while I try to stay quiet as a mouse.

I can hear him swear as he battles with his clothing before throwing his boots across the room. They hit the far wall with a thud as he finally flops heavily back, hauling the duvet over him. I'm completely exposed but I dare not react for fear of what may happen. I lie stock-still, but I need not have worried tonight for only a few seconds later, deep, drunken snores emanate from James's side of the bed. Letting out a small sigh of relief, I immediately feel guilty. I wait a full five minutes to be sure that he's sound asleep before cautiously stretching down to the bottom of the bed and, as gently as I can, pull the throw towards me and slip it over my naked body. It's at times like this I desperately miss wearing pyjamas, but James has made it clear there will be no pyjamas, declaring them old lady clothes, another argument I failed to win.

I must have eventually dropped off to sleep again because, what feels like seconds later the alarm pierces the silence announcing 5.00am. James is up and out of bed thumping noisily around the room, switching the main light on. When he's awake, the whole house must wake.

"Can I get you anything?" I ask in the hope that he will quickly be ready before Sophie could waken in the next room. James mumbles something unintelligible. Unsure of what to do, I get up and hesitantly offer him a clean shirt. I know better than to offer him clean moleskins. I once made the mistake of washing them and he had gone ballistic, declaring that the scent of the washing powder would scare away the wildlife and that I had ruined them. I recoil at the stench of them, but wisely say nothing, that combined with the baby powder he's so fond of using makes me want to vomit. James says nothing but proffers me a glare before grabbing his shirt and socks from last night off the floor, throwing them on before disappearing downstairs.

I slip back into bed and draw the duvet tightly up around me; stealing a few precious moments to myself. The day is beginning. I just need to wait for the group to go out. The door slamming would signal the start of my day. I hear coffee cups banging noisily, the smell of burning toast drifts up through the air, the acrid scent assaulting my nostrils. I hear the hilarity from below, the laughs and excitement at the day ahead evident from the tone of the lads. They're on holiday and I'm pleased they are enjoying themselves.

On the whole, the guys are generally a good bunch, oblivious to the real James, to them, lewd jokes and drinking was part of being away from home, but for James, he lived it all day every day, he partied with the boys and became more and more lewd and arrogant every day. I can hear him shouting at the guys to hurry up, a door slams, vehicle engines start up, moments later the back door swings heavily and noisily open again, and I hear a few of the boys stomping back up and down the stairs with their thick heavy outdoor boots on. I can picture the mud and try to put it out of my mind.

"Have you got them?" I hear James's voice roar upstairs.

"Aye," a voice calls down and clatters back down the stairs.

"Good, because I was going to leave without you if you were any longer."

I can't hear the reply over the noise of the door clattering shut again.

"Mummy…" I hear Sophie call out anxiously from next door. "Mummy?"

"I'm here, sweetheart, I'm just coming." I throw on a robe and head into her room.

"I'm scared." A tear slides down her cheek and she holds out her arms.

I wrap her in my arms and reassure her that it was just the lads going out for the morning. "They are just being a bit noisier than usual sweetheart."

Sophie, not looking convinced, clings onto me a little tighter.

"It's still early yet, hunny, what if I read you a little story and you can have another little sleep before it's time to get up?"

"I can't sleep now," she whispers falteringly, "can I stay with you?"

I think for a moment, it's Friday, a half day at school, Sophie's obviously distressed, she'd be better getting up now, maybe I can distract her enough to cheer her up.

"Okay sweetheart, you know what, it's Friday and I bet you Lola would love it if you were up early this once and you could give her an early breakfast!"

A smile spreads over her angelic face, and I know I've made the right decision. "Right then, McGinty," I say referring to the name my own granny had affectionately called me. "Let's get this day started, shall we!"

Chapter 8

One hour blends into the next for me. I'd managed to get Sophie off to school, she'd be dropping with tiredness later, but I couldn't have got her back to sleep, I knew her well enough, sensitive and sweet, the best thing was just to reassure her and distract her. She was clingy going into school again but with the reminder it was a short day, I finally managed to get her safely in.

James has been in such a bad mood of late, complaining about money, or the lack of it. I am frustrated as it seems we are busier than ever, the house never seems to be without guests, but it is a constant war cry with him. I wrack my brain to see what else I can do to improve his mood. The house is spotless, I've made all his favourite foods, my mind goes back to the party. Of course! I realise with a jolt. The article I was asked to write! I guess if I admitted it to myself, I've subconsciously been putting it off. Fear of not being good enough adds to my anxiety. However, I have a little time this morning. Maybe I could have a wee go, see what happened. *Just pull out your old trusty laptop and try a few words. Just a few words*, I encourage myself.

I'm glad this morning's cleaning has gone without a hitch, it'll give me the time I need, after all I can't put it off forever. I pour myself a large black coffee and pull out my old laptop and make a start. Just a few words I tell myself again as I look at the blank page blinking tantalisingly in front of me. My fingers hover hesitantly over the keys as I allow myself to drift back to happier days, days when everything had been different.

As my fingers caress the keyboard, words magically appear on the screen. I start to lose myself in the words, drifting back to a happy place. It all starts coming back as I write, when I write I'm in another world, enjoying the escapism the words allow, words flow onto the screen and time ticks easily by, before I know it, I have written 1500 words of an article. I read it over, then again. Happy with my work, I do a quick search for the email address as James had kept the business card, however, it's not hard to find with google. I don't want to tell

James; I'll send it off and wait to see if I get a positive answer. I'm nervous. I haven't included a recipe with the article, I'll see what Mungo thinks of this first, he might hate it. However, it's worth trying, and it might just cheer James up, put him in a better mood.

Just as I load it, my finger hovering above the send button, I get a sudden increased pang of nerves. What am I doing? What do I know about writing articles? What if it's really terrible? Worse though, I think with sudden realisation. What if he rings James and says what a ridiculous article to send in. James would be furious at me embarrassing him. But then again, Mungo had approached me, had asked me to send one into him. If I didn't send one in, then he would contact James and ask if I were ever going to send anything in, and then James would be mad. I'm stuck between a rock and a hard place.

Impulsively, I click send before I can change my mind. There! That's it. I can't do anything about it now. I let out a sigh of relief, it's done. The cards are tossed in the air, I have to leave it to fate to see where they might land.

Chapter 9

Another day has flown past. I can't believe it is evening already, my mind is constantly occupied with the thought of the article I'd sent in. I'm petrified it will be rejected. James would be furious at me for embarrassing him, I know that, but what can I do? *I'm in a no-win situation,* I think, as I finish cleaning in the kitchen.

"Are you listening to me?" James roars, walking towards me, and slapping my rear. "I think it would be a good idea. You're getting fat."

I jump, turning around to see what he is talking about. James has just returned from the pub, and I know it'll be easier to just agree with his latest scheme.

"Sorry, what was that? I was miles away, sorry," I murmur.

"What's new?" mutters James in retort as he grabs a sloe gin bottle from the cupboard.

"Here, let me get that for you," I offer as he tries to fill his glass, spilling it over the worktop and floor that I had just spent the last hour cleaning. "After all you have had such a long day," I add hoping to appease him.

Slumping into the nearest chair, he replies, "Hmmm, well, it's about time you realise how much I do for you. Drefen and I were just saying, there's a race on and we think you should do it."

"A race? I don't understand."

"No, well, you wouldn't, you are as thick as mince and pay no attention to anything do you? Honestly, I thought you were supposed to be bright! I said there is a race, a…half-marathon…you…should…run…it," he repeats, emphasising each word loudly and slowly.

The words hit my face like a slap. I turn away to hide my face, knowing I'm on the verge of tears.

Fat. Thick.

Words could hurt deeper than any fist or any boot. Insults. I try to treat them as white noise, but the constant torrent, like the ocean on a stormy day, is relentless. Unlike a bruise, they don't fade. I try hard to gather myself as I turn back around.

"Run? A half-marathon? But I can't run," I utter falteringly.

"What is there to running," he scoffs, tipping back his drink in one go and carelessly refilling it again. "You put one foot in front of another, surely even you could do that or are you that pathetic," he laughs darkly and downs the glass in one again, refilling it for the third time.

I pause for a moment, unsure of a reply to this.

"How did you get on at the pub tonight? Were there many in?" I try to change the subject.

"You make it sound as if I go for fun. I have to go, it's part of my job to entertain the clients, they wouldn't come if it wasn't for the social life I give them," James scorns.

"Oh, I know, I know, would you like a coffee before bed?" I try to quieten him for fear of waking Sophie.

"Are you telling me I have had enough to drink, Isla?" he roars.

"No, no, not at all, it's just I know you have to be up early with the guests, that's all."

"I'm just having a nightcap, so, what did you do when I was out? Did you have anyone around?"

"No, of course not."

"What about Cameron? He was not in the pub tonight. Was he here?"

I want to scream at him for being so ridiculous but instead I reply quietly and patiently, "I have everything ready for the morning, the 6 go out tomorrow, don't they, and I'll get the rooms changed over for, is it 7 coming in? I'll make sure Sophie has her things with her for her school trip, she's so excited."

"Bloody school trips, they are wanting money for that, I guess. Work, work, work. That's all I do. You'll need to cut back on what you are buying; you are still spending too much. I am not putting money into the bed and breakfast account just for you to spend it, what do you spend it all on anyway?"

I breathe a sigh of relief, I can cope with this constant rant about money, it's just white noise now and it takes him off his accusatory track, that is dangerous. The constant accusations have left their mark, I'm now afraid to talk to anyone for longer than a cursory reply, the early years of having fun and chatting with both guys and girls for a laugh are a dim and distant memory.

"Where have you hidden the other bottle, Isla?" James roars at me from his position by the larder, breaking into my thoughts. "What's a man gotta do to get a drink in his own house?"

I rush to get another bottle, keen to quieten him, and put a stop to him hauling about the meagre supply of produce that I had laid neatly on the shelves. How much could he put away? *That amount would kill a normal person,* I think, grabbing a bottle from the larder and quickly pouring him another glass.

"What's that? I've seen more in a dirty glass; you saving it for your boyfriend? Is that why you were asking how I got on at the pub, were you wanting to know if Cameron was in? Is that it?" he glugs back his drink and refills it taking another long gulp.

My heart sinks, he is on a roll. Honestly, I think with a sigh, he must think I either have more energy than Duracell or more time than there are drops of water in the ocean, the number of men he accuses me of having an affair with.

"Or is it William? Is that who you have your eye on, well, you are mine, you know, no one else's."

Oh, I know, you'll never let me forget it.

"Would you like some supper?" I ask, hoping maybe food will help.

"You know I can't eat anything. It's because of you I gained weight, before I met you, I'd lost weight. It's your fault." He glares at me.

"I have made soup and pureed it, just the way you like it," I offer, trying to appease him, a bubble of fear rising in me, I know I have to get him off this subject, the subject where the blame fell firmly at my feet. James had had treatment a few years previously, to lose weight, and, he said, stop his depression at his size. At great expense, we had found the best specialist in the business, sadly though neither had considered the mental effects and overeating and drinking too much had been replaced solely by the latter. The weight was piling back on now and this did nothing to help his moods.

"Aye, yes, give me some of that," he mutters, grabbing the bottle from me and tipping the contents into his glass.

I hurry over to the fridge, take out the pan of soup and hastily put it on the aga to heat. A few minutes later, I pour it into a bowl and lay in front of James.

71

"Here you go, you must be ready for that, it's been a long day," I try placating him.

"You wouldn't know what a hard day's work is like. Get me another spoon. What do you think I am? A baby?"

Hastily, I go to the cutlery drawer and replace the soup spoon, this time for a dessert spoon, there's no talking to James whilst he's in this mood. Laying it down beside him, I turn and head for the door. I still have to check the dining room is tidy for morning, I had set it prior but it's not uncommon for James to take the guests in and use the items for an impromptu drinking session before going to the pub. "I'm just going to check on things to make sure they're okay for the morning," I say as lightly as I can.

"Haven't you already done that? Are you going up to sneak up to see one of the guests? Who is it? Malcolm? Is that why he was talking to you before? Tell me! Tell me! I'll soon sort him." Picking up his glass, he takes a long swig before throwing the glass down on the floor, it smashes into a thousand pieces. I look on in fear, in this mood he will have the whole house up. What can I do? I open my mouth trying desperately to say something as he stands up. I look on, fear striking me silent. He looks titanic in size, drink fuelling his emotions, he sways violently as he tries to take a step forward. "Tell ME!" he roars, taking another step he raises his fist at me. I can see the anger in his eyes. I take an unconscious step back. I can see the hatred in his eyes, pure hatred, and for the first time I am truly scared.

His face closes in on mine until I can see my reflection in the black souls of his eyes. The rage as he raises his fist then spins around, punching the wall.

I turn and make to head out. I need space. Away from the ominous presence of him. I have nowhere to go. I need fresh air.

James steps in front of me blocking my path.

"You'll never get away from me, Isla," he screams. "Never, you hear me NEVER, you'll never get away from me. I will find you wherever you go, I will find you." He slams his fist down on the island unit. "Now clean up this mess!"

Shaking, I hesitantly creep forward and began to sweep up the shards of broken glass. "Would you still like your soup?" I ask hesitantly, unsure of what to do.

"No," he roars, "it's cold now, get it cleaned up and get out of my sight before you force me to do something I don't want to do."

Look at her, James smirks to himself. *All trembling, cleaning up the glass, oh how I want to slam my fist into your face.* However, the wall had to do, although it had driven him mad. *I can feel it now, my strong hands slamming into your pale face, those big brown eyes closing and turning purple, closing over the red trickle of blood against the white skin.* The urge was so great, but he couldn't. He watched her flee out of the room. No, it was better she was out, he couldn't risk his gun licence, he could not risk someone finding out, no he had to be far cleverer than that. He was a man and shooting is his identity. It made him a powerful man. A memory crept up from the back of his mind. A conversation he had had with Tavish in the pub a few months back, a slow smile spread over his face. That was all that was needed. Why he hadn't thought of it years before was a pity, all that time wasted. Never mind it was sorted now. Satisfied and inordinately pleased with himself, he went to the larder and poured himself another drink, taking a long swig he laughed out loud. Oh yes, yes, yes, he had the power now he knew exactly how to use it…

As quickly as I can, I sweep up the broken shards before tipping out the now cold soup before flying out of the room. Padding softly up the stairs and along the hall, I check on Sophie. She's asleep. Thankfully, she hasn't heard any of the goings-on. I look at my watch. 2.07 am. I need to be up early in the morning. My mind won't settle. I can still see the hatred in his eyes. I know he'd wanted to hit me. To hurt me. Where would it stop. What was next? The thought terrifies me.

As I slide under the duvet, fragments of a conversation float around in my head.

"…there's a race on and we think you should do it…a race, a half-marathon, it's an obstacle race you should do…"

I sense somehow this is an opportunity for me to get some space. But run? I can't run to the gate let alone a half-marathon. How far even is that? I google it. 13.1 miles I must be mad. I laugh. 13.1 miles? But as I think of the peace I might get whilst I train, a plan starts to formulate in my head. As it rumbles around loosely in my mind, I begin to want to run most desperately, in the way people crave for things they consider elusive. It is, in my peace-starved mind, a real possibility, a real chance, a chance because somewhere in the deep recesses of my mind the cogs are turning. This is a chance for something. How or what, I have yet to mastermind. It's a challenge because I'm a fake. The moment I attempt to run I'll be exposed. But it's a chance, nonetheless.

Of course, James will stop me training once he realises that I'll be away from him, I'm sure. I need to think of something else. The feeling this is my only hope of a little sanity stings at me like a persistent wasp. Fragments of a conversation from the school meeting float into my conscious. What if I combine this with the fundraising the school so desperately needs? There is a tiny chance this might work.

However, James needs to be the one taking the credit for this, I realise. I'm merely a support for his image, for James' image and his status in the village are key to him, how he is viewed by others is more important than anything else to him. If I were to raise funds for the school by doing this race, then he couldn't stop me. Could he? He'd already complained at the expense of school trips. Maybe this is the solution I need; however, I will need to be quick. If I get to the school first, offer this fundraiser, tell them it's James's idea, they'd be delighted. Surely, he would not be able to renege on this. I feel a niggle of self-doubt wash through me. Being so underhand could surely not bring about anything good, could it?

However, 13.1 miles? Can I do that? Actually run a full 13.1 miles, not only run that distance but complete the course with the obstacles, tough obstacles? The thought terrifies me. Am I crazy? Perhaps, however, the thought of the peace, the tranquillity, the calm serenity of the open roads that wait for me, the time away from the house I so desperately crave spurs me on. That's it! The decision is made. Tomorrow I'll speak to the school. The cards are thrown in the air now and where they may land who knows. I just have to wait and see the consequences, for there are always consequences. A little tremor of fear trickles through me sprinkled with a sliver of hope. *What am I doing* is the last thought that swims around my mind as I drift fitfully off to sleep.

Chapter 10

The next morning, as soon as I hear the door slam behind James and the guests leaving for the morning, I jump up out of bed and head to the bathroom. Today is the day. The day I may just start to get control over my own life. I glance over at the alarm clock. 5.34 am. Splashing my face with cold water and giving my teeth a quick brush, I pull on my clothes before heading quickly for the kitchen. With James gone, I am only faced with the remnants of him, the coffee cup he favours, the cups and plates the guests had their tea and toast from, a top-up before their Belly Buster cooked breakfast which they would return to after their outing this morning.

Thankfully, it isn't too bad. I quickly clear up the debris and make sure the guest bedrooms have fresh towels. The guests are leaving today, which means the changeover will be later. Back in the kitchen I work like a demon, setting up the breakfast trays, I slice mushrooms, cut tomatoes, and prepare the sausage and bacon into the big heavy cast-iron frying pans ready to go on top of the aga the moment I get the call saying the guys are returning. I reach into the fridge, bringing out haggis and black pudding, a quick dig around in the cupboard I locate the potato scones before placing big jugs of orange and milk through in the breakfast room, carefully covering everything I stand back, pleased at my work.

I glance at the time. 7.27 am. Time to wake Sophie up. Today is the start of a plan with a capital P. Will it work? I'm placing a lot of hope on James's vanity, his eagerness to always be the main man, but time would tell. I head up to get Sophie and a mere 45 minutes later I have her ready for school.

"Come on sweetheart, today is a big day! Do you remember where your trip is?"

"Dynamic Earth, Mummy!" Sophie looked up at me with her beautiful innocent blue eyes.

"That's right, darling, have you got your packed lunch?"

"Yes!" she proudly shows me her lunch box, "I can't wait to show Daisy my new lunch box! She loves Fifi and the Flower Tots too!" I put her coat on and tied a scarf round her, it was chilly this morning, taking her hand she chatters merrily all the way along to school.

"…and I am going to share my snack with her too," Sophie excitedly adds.

"Oh, that sounds lovely! I hope you have a fabulous time. Now, have lots of fun, and it is going to be such a lovely trip for you, I can't wait to hear all about it!"

"Sophie! Sophie! There you are! I have been looking absolutely everywhere for you!" An excited voice calls over. Looking up, I see Daisy hurtling towards us. Sophie looks hesitantly at me as Daisy arrives at her side.

"I'll be here for you when you get back from your trip, sweetheart," I say encouragingly, "now go have fun, I need to chat with your teacher before I go."

"Sophie, I brought us some yummy snacks, and we can we sit next to each other on the bus!" The words come tumbling out of Daisy, and I am grateful to this young girl knowing that she will be with Sophie today.

"It's okay, sweetheart, the sooner you go the sooner you have fun!" It breaks my heart to see her so reluctant to go, surely, she doesn't know what is going on, does she? I put the thought to the back of my mind, I can't cope with that just now.

"Isla! Is everything okay?" Mr Toledo comes over to me, breaking into my thoughts.

How I wanted to tell him *No, everything is not okay*, but instead I reply the stock answer, "Yes, I'm fine, thank you. However, I wondered do you have a minute? I know today is a busy day though; I can come back later." I wouldn't usually disturb Sophie's teacher on such a busy day, but it's imperative I speak with him before James can change his mind.

"Yes of course. Is everything okay?" He repeats.

"Absolutely," I lie but add, "I have something I'd like to run by you."

Five minutes later, I walk home with a spring in my step. Well, the first stage is easy. Mr Toledo is delighted with the fundraising suggestion. I've absolutely no idea how I'll manage to run it or complete the mad-sounding obstacles, but I'll cross that bridge when I come to it.

Now, just to pick my time to tell James. I set to work on tidying the B&B rooms and preparing breakfast, it keeps my mind occupied. I feel sick at the thought of what I am doing. Would James even remember? Would he go with it? Would there be any repercussions? Of course there will be, I remind myself. However, the thought of the escape is overriding my fear of possible repercussions for now.

Two hours later, the guests have returned; happily, the shoot had gone well and James is in a good mood. I look up from the plates I'm stacking in the cupboard as he walks in.

"There you are! I wondered where you'd got too! I missed you." He was in a remarkably good mood.

Uneasy at this unusual expression of affection, I turn around and notice that James is not alone, Lachlan, one of the guests, has joined him.

That makes sense, I think to myself.

"How was your morning?" I ask Lachlan politely.

"Oh, it was great, lots of wildlife going over, and to come back to that wonderful breakfast, now that was the cherry on the cake!"

"You're too kind," I say, flushing at the unusual compliment. James looks over at me.

"Oh, she just loves keeping everyone happy, does our Isla."

The undertone of his comment is not lost on me; however, I seize the moment.

"James," I interrupt, "I mentioned your idea to Sophie's teacher today and he was thrilled." I feel uncomfortable taking this line, but I have no choice.

"Idea?" James looks at me questioningly.

"Yes, you had the brilliant idea to fundraise for school trips with the running and Mr Toledo thinks it is such a super idea, he said to thank you," I add trailing off, hating my deviousness.

"Oh, yes, yes, that…" James mutters clearly confused, but more than happy to take the credit in front of clients. "Well, it is important to support our schools."

"What's this?" Lachlan asks, as Murray, another guest, walks into the kitchen.

"Oh, James had this brilliant idea for me to run a half-marathon to raise money for school funds," I reply. I have to ensure everyone knows it's James's idea.

"So, which one are you running?" Lachlan asks.

James looks over at me as I reply, "Tough Cookie."

"I didn't know you ran!" Lachlan answers.

"I don't, yet!" I laugh.

"Oh well, good on you, put me down for £20.00."

"And same for me too, Isla, good on you!" Murray adds.

"Super breakfast, Isla, and thank you again for looking after us so well, it can't be easy having all of us mucky lot in your lovely home!"

I smile over and assure them it's a pleasure, which is the truth, they are a really lovely bunch.

Lachlan turns to James, "Right, we must get sorted out how much have you skinned us for this time!"

James grins over at the two, his favourite day, payday. *He'll be in a good mood today,* I think to myself as James, Lachlan and Murray sweep out of the kitchen.

I let out the breath I'd unconsciously been holding. *Well, that is it. I'm running an obstacle race and it is 13.1 miles long.* I try not to think too much about it, the thought scares me silly.

The rest of the day I spend in a whirl. My mind is in chaos. I have no idea where to start with running, or even when I'll get time to train, but the fact James thinks it is his idea helps enormously, he's spent most of the day telling people about his brilliant idea. Every time I pass him, he seems to be telling someone about it. As I load the last of the dishes into the dishwasher, James comes into the room, he's on his phone.

"Yes, she is! Can you believe it…hah…yes…she did…no…probably. I would say so…Ha-ha, yes it should tone her up, her backside has got so fat! Yes! It has…Oh, how would you know." I hear the one-sided conversation as he walks back out of the room, clearly ensuring I'd heard him.

"Don't let it worry you," I say to myself. "Clear your head. Think happy thoughts." I repeat my mantra, switching the dishwasher on to a fast wash.

Just then James walks back into the room.

"Well! Fuck me!"

I look up startled to see him grinning.

"Well, fuck me," he repeats, "if you did not only rise to the bait. Do you know what the Tough Cookie is? It's 13 miles of sheer hell, smoke, water, electric shocks, and the toughest obstacles this country has seen. Everyone is on about it in the pub. You'll never do it. It's only for strong people and you look like a dishrag. It's over from America, the raffle tickets were only for fundraising for some stupid local running group they had one spare ticket, no one else was up for it, they tried to get me to do it when my ticket came out the hat, but I'm not stupid enough to do it, imagine if I broke a leg! You're a bigger idiot than I thought," he sneers. Glancing around, he adds, "Why is there no coffee on? I'm in a hurry. You know I'll need coffee and be quick."

I say nothing but quickly go to the cupboard, I'm about to open the door to get a cup out for his coffee when I feel a thwack landing hard on my mouth. I stand, reeling in shock as pain courses through me. I can feel my lip throbbing. Gasping, I'm confused as to what's happened. I turn to look at James standing next to me.

"What are you doing, you stupid cow, didn't you see me?" He stares down at me, no expression on his face. His elbow had caught me full on the mouth as he had opened a cupboard next to me. I put my hand up to my mouth in shock.

"I was getting a mug out to make you coffee," I stutter.

"I said I'd make coffee. I'm in a hurry, didn't you see me, or hear me for that matter?"

Looking down at me, all six foot one of him, a faint smile plays on his lips. No, I neither saw nor heard you, I say silently to myself. James's legendary stalking skills have made him silent as a ghost, appearing out of nowhere when you least expect it. For a big man, he moves without a sound. Had I misheard him? I put my hand to my mouth, my tooth was throbbing and felt loose, I feel a trickle from the side of my mouth as I taste metal. Blood.

I watch on as he leaves the room. I hear him back on his phone again minutes later laughing. I hear my name being said. I turn on the little kitchen TV to drown out the noise. Humiliated again, I set about my work. Mouth still throbbing, I reach for a tissue and keep my mind firmly on my plan. Trying to keep my mind from going to dangerous places, dangerous thoughts, I clean the kitchen till it shines. A few short hours later, I feel accomplished. I'd stripped and remade all the beds, cleaned all the rooms, the bathrooms sparkled, and I'd reset the dining room.

Now, finally I could turn my mind fully to my plan. My mind flips back to conversations about the Tough Cookie. My stomach lurches. What have I let myself in for? I flick on my old laptop and do a search, minutes later I wish I hadn't. The obstacles that loom on the screen look pure torture. I am filled with dread, more for the cut-off time. The word cut-off strikes me with fear as I recall James's parting words as he left as soon as the guests were driving out the gateway.

"You'd better get training today. I don't want you embarrassing me over this! I'm off. I never get any peace, working 7 days a week. I need to go check out the hunting grounds. The guys will be in later tonight, make sure there's something I can actually eat in this house when I get back."

His words float over me like stormy clouds in a gale. After all these years of hearing the same words, the high pitch of his tone if I so much as start to say anything. I know nothing I say will make a difference. I've long since realised it's easier and safer not to poke the bear. I turn my attention to today's run. My first training run.

"Where could I go? How do I start?" I begin to panic.

"Now keep calm," I say quietly in reply to myself, trying to settle myself. "Thousands of people run daily, even more thousands must surely do these obstacle runs."

Just how I'm to do it, I'm not so sure. I try to quash this niggle.

I pull the pan of stew I am making for James off the stove. Beef stew, my stomach growls as the delicious aroma floats upwards. There is only enough for him. He would not eat the game, declaring it too strong on his stomach, choosing to leave the mountains of goose and other game for Sophie and I. The constant outbursts from James about spending too much money, the fear every time I go to the checkout that my card will not be accepted if he hasn't put money from the B&B into the account, mean I only spend the bare minimum. I detest game now, the singular food choice for years, along with bacon and eggs from the bed and breakfast is now my solitary diet, but it means I can slip a few nice things into the basket for Sophie to enjoy. I'd skipped breakfast again; the thought of eating bacon or eggs again turning my stomach.

Absentmindedly I reach into the drawer for the wooden spoon and begin to stir the stew. I needed advice. Putting down the spoon, I pick up my phone and google *how to start running*. Thousands of hits come up, 20 minutes later I've enough of an idea as to where to start. I finish mashing the potatoes, followed by the carrots, and ensure there is plenty of gravy.

"Right, it is now or never!" I tell myself with a shiver of anticipation, the thought of getting some space drives me forward and I head up to change. Rummaging around in the bottom of the wardrobe, I try to find something I can run in. Finding an old pair of leggings and a vest top, I realise this will have to do. Delving further into the depth of my wardrobe, I excitedly pull out a pair of very old but hardly worn trainers bought many years before. Perfect! I throw off my jeans and shirt and pull on my adapted running wear. Four minutes later I'm ready. Pulling my hair into a ponytail, I check my watch. 1.57 pm. I have 1 hour and 3 minutes precisely before I need to be at school to collect Sophie.

Putting on my headphones, I call Lola and we head out the door for my very first run. I think of my own wee plan; walk, run, walk, run. *Simple.* I think. I can do this. I take a deep breath and head out of the gate, turning right and proceeding along the road. My plan is to just walk until I get to the 30 signs, out of sight I will then try to run. I can't see anyone but that means nothing in this village…*Brown-Eyed Girl* blasts in my ears, the 30 signs beckon, encouraging me, I sense freedom and walk fast, my mouth still throbbing from earlier I carry on and, in just a few minutes, I'm passing the 30 sign.

Looking around and confident no one could see me, I break into a run, slow, almost at the same speed I was walking but I feel liberated, the road disappears beneath me, the road in front beckons me forward in its winding embrace, the trees wave in the distance, large hands waving, encouraging me forward.

I let out a laugh, how ridiculous is this! I can't help it though. I feel free! I run faster. I can feel my lungs beginning to burn as I stride forward, every step is a step further from the village, from the pain in my mouth, from the ties of home, the only joy I have is Sophie and Lola. I hope desperately that she's having a fun day with her friends at Dynamic Earth. I wish I could've been one of the volunteer mums that went with the school, to be with her, to be away from here. But that is a wish too far.

I begin to run out of breath, my chest tightens, I slow to a walk before reaching into my pocket for my inhaler and take two deep puffs. The road stretches out in front of me, no people, no cars, no houses, just silence. I'm exhilarated. I can't believe I'm out. Out without James. I am free. The road curves ahead, and I know just around the corner there is an entrance that leads into the woods. Here there is a track which leads down to the lake.

I gather my breath and power forward walking from one telegraph post and running to the next to gain my breath back, allowing my inhaler to open my lungs enough again. I round the corner and there, like a giant welcome sign is the entrance. I head towards it and break into a slow run, turning down into the tree-lined track I find it's slightly downhill. I let the weight of my body take me down the hill and find it easier to run, the trees sweep by me, a blur of fuzzy green new friends. Run, walk, run, walk I carry on until I've cleared the lake and head for home. If I take the shortcut up the top road, there is a nice long downhill stretch. I'd be back in enough time to collect Sophie from her trip.

The narrow road winds in front of me. *God's own country,* I think. My pace relaxes into a gentle stride, feet drumming rhythmically on the tarmac road. Walk, run, walk, run…I settle into a pattern. Tussock-lined hills, the heather long since purple, rolls out either side of me, the fields spread out like a patchwork blanket, dry-stone dykes the stitching holding the small fields together. I let the rhythmic sound of my feet hitting the tarmac work its magic on me.

My mind drifts to what I still need to do today, the third load of washing would need to go in, the ironing, my studies. I try not to focus on this, this is my time, think positive thoughts, I remind myself as I watch Lola lolloping happily ahead. I had been paying little attention to my surroundings as I dreamily enjoy my escape, the sun warming my body. Suddenly my eye alights on a familiar sight, I'm surprised to see the village school looming. I'm almost finished!

I walk quickly and soon pass the 30 signs, heading round by the school, checking my watch I realise I don't have enough time to change, so, sweaty-faced and windswept I have no choice but to head into the playground and wait with the mums for Sophie. Thankfully, the school bus returning with the pupils from their trip is already there and empty. Brilliant, I realise, there will not be any holdups.

"Isla!" Lara calls out and I look over to see a clique of 'cool' mums, the clickers I call them due to the sound their heels make on the school tarmac.

"My goodness! What on earth have you been doing?" she laughs as she looks me up and down. "You look like you've been dragged through a hedge backwards!" she giggles. Despite having been at the party, neither she, nor the rest of the clickers give me the time of day unless there is a point to be scored. For the most, I try to ignore it, the points they scored I knew were childish, but still hurt. My heart plummets, *Great,* I think, *just great,* but thankfully at that minute the bell goes, and Sophie heads the stream of children running free from the school. I can escape having to get into conversation.

"Sorry Lara, gotta go, you know how it is!" I turn from the clickers towards Sophie.

"Mummy!" Sophie calls out gleefully and runs towards me throwing herself at me in a huge hug, oblivious to my sweaty body or scruffy attire. To Sophie, nothing else matters other than I am her mum; she grabs hold of my hand. I hold it tightly and together we walk back along the road towards home. I listen to her excited tales of the day, pleased she had had such a lovely day.

"…and they have this giant ice block, and you can touch it!" she adds to the stream of excited chatter. I'm so happy she's had a lovely day away.

"Wow, that all sounds amazing, sweetheart, right let's get you changed, and you can have a little play in your room before teatime; how does that sound?"

"Can I play with my sea animals? I want to be a scientist when I grow up!"

"That sounds lovely, and of course you can, I'll get the box down for you. So, you don't want to be the tooth fairy anymore then?" I gently tease smiling at Sophie's excited face.

"No! I think Jacob wants to be a tooth fairy now. I am going to be a famous scientist, Mummy!"

"Well, I think that sounds just lovely," I reply as I bring down the box of sea animals for her.

Half an hour later with Sophie safely upstairs, I give the kitchen one final wipe-over and flick the kettle on. James will be back any minute and he'll want coffee. I think back to my run today, a smile playing on my face. I've walked a lot of the route, interspersing it with a slow jog but I did it! I managed to do it. My first run. I'm exhilarated!

"What are you grinning at?" James hisses from directly behind me. I jump having not heard him come in again.

"N-N-Nothing," I stutter. "I'm just making your coffee." Hastily I grab a cup and start spooning coffee into it.

"Yes, well I hear you got out for your run; I hope you lose some of that fat when you're out."

I don't rise to it, but, instead realise with a sinking heart there is nowhere, absolutely, and unequivocally nowhere I'm safe or alone. James has eyes and ears everywhere.

"I don't want coffee, I want a man's drink, get me a sloe gin, and make it a decent one this time."

I abandon the coffee and head to the larder to get the bottle of sloe gin out.

"Did you see anyone when you were out?" James queries. "Cameron perhaps? Is that why you're grinning?"

"Not a soul, it was quiet, would you like dinner, I made it just the way you like it." I try and fail yet again to make these accusatory comments into white noise, but they hurt too deeply. Death by a thousand paper cuts.

"Well, I'm glad you did something with your day, honestly I don't know how you cope with doing nothing all day," James mocks before adding, "of course, I want some dinner. Are you stupid? I'm starving."

I set him out a drink and proceed to heat his dinner, making sure it looks nicely set out. I lay the plate on a tray, my legs protest after the efforts of the day, but I say nothing, not wishing for more ridicule. I walk around the island unit towards James and before I know what's happening, I lurch forward, the marble floor speeds towards me and I hit the floor with a crash, the tray scatters across the floor. Momentarily winded, I'm disorientated.

"Did you not see my legs!" James sneers, "Idiot, honestly you are such a clumsy bitch these days, you better get that cleared up before clients arrive. And hurry up, they'll be here soon!"

I look up at him from my position on the floor as he grins down at me, and I see for the first time how yellow his teeth are getting. I am at a loss. He gets up from his chair, still laughing and leaves me lying there on the floor, a jumble of stew and broken plates scattered around me. I feel tears pricking at my eyes, but I can't allow myself the luxury of tears; with guests due in at any minute, I need to make sure everything is just perfect. I slowly get up, rubbing my arm. I can see a large bruise already starting to form. I set about cleaning up. I'm not sure how much more of this I can take. The elbow to the face, and now this. The 'accidents' are getting more frequent.

Later that evening after I've given Sophie her tea and bathed her, she excitedly tells me more of her day. "They let us dress up as *as-to-nuts!*"

I smile at her mispronunciation. "Really, that sounds such fun! I let it slip, enjoying her excitement."

"Yes, and we went to the moon, we got to touch real space rocks, Mummy, real space rocks!"

"Well, it sounds like you have had a very adventurous day sweetheart, now I think it's time for a story before you go to sleep, school tomorrow!" and with that I pick up the book we've been reading.

"But I'm too excited to sleep, Mummy," she looks up at me beseechingly.

"Is that right! Well then, let's read our book and see what happens tonight, shall we?"

She nods sincerely, and I start to read aloud. I'm exhausted and sore, but I love this quiet time together. I finish the first page and I look down at Sophie, tucked up in bed, her blonde hair curling around rosy cheeks, thumb firmly in her mouth and eyes struggling to stay awake, she looks happy. I carry on reading and before long she is sleeping soundly, the excitement of the day catching up. I lean forward and kiss her gently on the forehead, "Sweet dreams, my beautiful girl," and turn to gently pad out of the room.

I head to the kitchen and make myself a coffee, carrying it through to the living room. I set it beside the ironing table, I would get this finished and then I would have a little time to study before going to bed.

I finish up the ironing and pull out my study books. I've been working on my final assignment for what feels like ages, it is due within the week. It's been difficult finding time to study, catching only snatches of time where I can, however with it being due later this week I've no choice. Deadlines don't care about family life or dramas; they are just there—deadlines. So, I sit down and try hard to focus. I work away steadily with only Lola's gentle snoring beside me for company. As I find myself reading and rereading the last paragraph which has begun to swim in front of me, I decide it's time to call it a night. Switching off my ancient laptop I head to bed.

James is at the pub; I'm thankful for small mercies. I feel guilty for this little bit of peace. Once back in my bedroom, I pull the curtains back and open the window. The feeling of cool air rushing in is soothing. I take a deep, calming breath and stand perfectly still for a few moments just gazing up at the night sky enjoying the contrast of the stars, bright and twinkling cheerily next to the deep dark depths of night-time. Picking up a glass of water from my nightstand and taking a sip I try to process the day's activities, what it meant, the small piece of freedom in running won, but my mind refuses to consider anything except sleep. I slip under the duvet pulling it up around me and watch the gentle rise of the moon. As I drift off to sleep, legs aching, a large bruise turning red-blue on my arm, I think about the trees and the fresh air and I feel a slight sense of, not quite joy but something akin to it, wash over me.

Chapter 11

I wake up groggy the next day, my mouth feels thick, I slip out of bed and into the bathroom for a drink of water, splashing my face I try to waken myself. I crave my run desperately like a drowning man holding onto a lone piece of driftwood in the open sea. I had heard James leave with the guys for the mornings shooting and as was my usual routine now, I set about my work with renewed gusto, I got my work done, made sure Sophie was safely in school, the routine was banal, but it was routine. The guys go out to shoot, I clean up after them, they come back, have breakfast, go out to shoot. I clean up after them. Routine. Routine. Routine.

The only difference now is the open roads are calling me. The trees beckon like crowds at the finish line. It is my salvation. I needed these runs more than I needed air. I couldn't wait for the part of the day where all my work was done and the guys were back out on their midday shoot, I would have just enough time for a short run. Today was no different. As soon as I hear the crunch of gravel on the drive signalling the guys are away, I put the last of the dishes carefully away and bound up the stairs two at a time to put on my running wear. Without a second to lose, I throw them on. It is a stiflingly hot summer day, double-checking my watch, I see I have an hour. "Perfect!" I announce to the ever-waiting, ever loyal Lola. I pull on an old pair of shorts and a vest. "We can do the circuit if we are quick!" I say to her as she looks up at me, adoring big brown eyes, tongue lolling as if in a smile, ears cocked forward listening.

"Come on, girl, let's go!" I call as I pad across the soft carpet in anticipation of the run. I catch a glimpse of myself in the long mirror. I notice even more bruises on my legs, running from my thighs round to the back of my calves. Hmmm, not from where I fell. How on earth have I got these ones now? I don't remember banging into anything. The bruises are getting more frequent and quite alarming in colour.

"Well, Lola, one thing is for sure, sweetheart. I cannot, simply cannot go out looking like I have just run ten rounds with Mike Tyson in the boxing ring." Reluctantly, I pull off my shorts and don a pair of long, old leggings. *There that's better, no one could ask questions now.* I quickly pull my hair back into its customary ponytail and grab a pink baseball cap, *there*, I think to myself, *that should help a little with the sun.* It would still be unbearable not wearing shorts in this heat, but I'm left with little choice.

As we head outside, a wall of heat hit us, "It'll be a slow one today, but we have water with us!" Lola wags her tail in agreement with me. The heat was immense, but I'm just grateful to be out. I'm getting used to my little routine now and getting a little fitter. As we turn left out of the village, I feel lighter as my feet hit the tarmac, run, run, run, my feet call out with every step I take. Run, escape, run, escape they drum to the beat. Leaving the village in our wake we head towards the tree-lined entrance to the lake, the trees offering up their branches in sanctuary.

Turning down the slope, we head along the tree-lined route. As my feet pound the mud track, rock solid from weeks without any rain, I couldn't help but wonder what kind of man I had married. Was he always like that? Had I been so ridiculously in love, the love only the young can appear to achieve that I was so blind? Oh, so true that saying, act in haste, repent at leisure. My head spins. I need my runs so much these days, they are my sanctuary. I run on a little further before stopping to rest against a tree, taking a drink out of the bottle of water I pour some into the little portable dish I carry for Lola, she laps it noisily, water droplets spraying in all directions messily from her.

"There, that's better, sweetheart, isn't it, are you ready to make it back, we should make it just in time to spare to collect Sophie from school!" Having stopped, the beads of sweat were now trickling down my neck and back, it was a relief to get going again; to feel the soft breeze against me, it calms me as I try to clear my head. One thing's for sure I know I can't carry on like this, not for my sake, and certainly not for Sophie's. I need to work out a plan, but what?

Nearer and nearer the village we get, I'm looking forward to seeing Sophie, her happy little face appearing at the door of the school was the light of my day. I see the school in the distance, quickly I check my watch, bang on 3. I'm cutting it tight today. I speed up a little, grateful for the downward slope helping my pace. Just as I round the corner, I hear the bell ring. Dash it. I'm going to be late after all, I pace on a few minutes before reaching the final stretch and turn into the school yard, mercifully it's deserted. I'm spared the angst of the clickers ever ready to mock.

Mr Toledo appears at the door with Sophie.

"Mummy! You're here! I thought you'd forgotten!"

"I think Mummy deserves a few minutes grace, Sophie," Mr Toledo interjects kindly before continuing, "she's in training for a half-marathon, that's a long way and it's to raise money for our school library!"

"My mummy is very clever." Sophie beams up proudly and innocently before hurtling into me to give me a big sweaty hug. "I love you, Mummy."

"And I love you too, my darling, now let's get home and get your mummy tidied up!"

Mr Toledo waves us off with a few supporting and congratulatory comments which I appreciate, I need all the support I can get, the mocking at home not helping I try to, unsuccessfully, drown out the comments of 'you will never make it, do you actually realise what you are doing?'

I look up from my plate, realising that Sophie had been talking to me.

I slip a smile onto my face. "I'm sorry, sweetheart, I was miles away, what did you say?"

"I said, are you feeling sad, Mummy?"

I shake my head. "No. No," I affirm, "I was just thinking what fun we could have with the summer holidays fast approaching!" I realise with a start I'd need to be more careful. Sophie was very sensitive, and I had to be on my guard.

Forking up some beans from her plate, she gives me a cheeky smile. "Maybe you were in Canada with Auntie Sandy."

I laugh genuinely this time. "Yes now, wouldn't that be lovely? We would have such fun building snowmen and going sledding wouldn't we! They get such terrific winters there!" As I think back to the wonderful time we had visiting my sister in Abbotsford, my two nieces and two nephews out there, thinking fondly of Ben, my oldest nephew, and his gorgeous girlfriend Paige, I wondered when I would get to meet them again.

My mind drifts to the whale-watching on trips to Vancouver Island, the giant redwood trees in Vancouver, the hours we spent browsing through the books in Indigo, the trip to Capilano suspension bridge, all before we had headed south to

Seattle. I give myself a shake, no sense in letting my mind drift there, happy times I remember with a sigh. I can't imagine ever getting back there. I glance over at Sophie, relieved she seems content with the distraction, and it gives me a much-needed break from the turmoil in my head. I need to work out a plan, I can't let things go on like this. What the plan was though, as yet I have absolutely no idea.

The next morning brings the same routine, I am glad, the boring repetitiveness stops my mind from going to dangerous places. I'm looking forward to today's run. Sophie is in school. I've worked non-stop and as fast as I could this morning to make sure I have a little time to go for a run later. It would be tight, but I should be able to make it. The guys have returned quicker than usual this morning, I'm flat out preparing the breakfast things as my phone bursts into life startling me. Looking down, I'm delighted to see it is Zara. My face breaks into a smile.

"Zara!" I say picking up. "How lovely to hear from you."

"Tigger! We never see each other, and you can't call the party seeing you, you were so busy being Misses Hostess, I barely got speaking to you, so when am I getting to see you again!"

"Oh, I'm sorry! You know what it is like, busy, busy, busy!"

"Well, all work and no play, Tig, is no good at all! You must come out."

"I have double changeovers all this week, and then next week I—"

"Tig," Zara cuts me off, "I knew you would say that!" she laughs, "You must stop for coffee! I'm off today, so I'm coming around, I'll see you soon. I'm just around the corner—no excuses!" And with that she hangs up. I have no choice; I'm excited to see Zara, but I know James will hate it. I try to put it out of my mind and distract myself with work. It helps a little, but my mind is a whirr. I'm so looking forward to seeing her again, but I know James doesn't like it when she comes round.

I set about making yet more pots of tea and am just about to load the toaster with more cheap white bread when I sense rather than hear James come into the room. Like cold, dark, drizzly mist enveloping you on the Scottish moors, James has the uncanny knack of dampening the spirits just by his very presence.

"We need more toast, hurry up the guys are waiting," he states. No pleasantries, no 'How was your morning', or 'How was Sophie this morning', just continuous, ever continuous demands.

"Won't be a tick," I return as I flick on another round of bread into the toaster and return to plating up the last of the breakfasts ready for him to take through, when I see Zara's car roll up in the drive.

"Who's that?" James demands as he heads to the window and takes a squint out. "Oh. It's her. What does she want. Always looking for trouble that one. Flighty she is you would be far better off…" he tails off as Zara bursts cheerily through the door.

"Tig! At last, I see you!"

My heart lifts as I see her. I could cry. I just want her to give me a big hug and for her to say everything is going to be okay. But before I can say anything, James cuts in, "Zara, how lovely to see you again, I feel we don't see enough of you," he's all smiles now, charm personified.

"Oh, have you not got a pinny, James," Zara laughs, "well, don't keep the hungry hordes waiting on you now," and with that she bustles him away with a flick of her hands.

He's not going to like that, I think to myself but instead give Zara a big hug. "You'll have to chat whilst I carry on, lovely."

"Oh, don't worry. I shall just sit here out of the way." She plonks herself down on one of the stools at the island unit. "Now Tig, what have you been up to? I'm worried about you; you never seem to come out anymore."

"I'm sorry, lovely, I do miss you, it's just we are so busy at the minute I just never seem to get a chance. Tea or coffee?" I reach up to get her a mug from the cupboard.

"A water will be perfect. Oh my gosh, what have you done?" she gasps as she catches the red-purple bruise on my arm; hastily I pull my sleeve back down, it had slipped up as I reached into the cupboard.

Just then James walks in, "Oh, she's always catching herself, clumsy, always bumping into things, aren't you?" he looks over at me before sitting down next to Zara.

"Oh, that's baby brain!" Zara laughs, "I don't think it ever goes away does it, the mind is always somewhere else and before you know it there's a big pile of something just appearing!"

I look over, she catches my eye and gives me a smile and a wink. This is surreal, James sitting next to Zara and not talking with the guys. It's obvious I'm not going to get any alone time with her. I search for neutral topics, but I needn't have worried. James is holding the conversation. I listen to him talking to her, he turns and faces me.

"Isla, can you just take some more toast to the guys? They'll be finished now," he asks, his tone sweet as honey, it makes me want to scream out to Zara. *Can you not see what he's doing? Keeping us apart?* But instead, I dutifully slip another 4 slices of bread into the toaster.

I feel alienated from the conversation now anyway, James has cut me right out. I listen to the pair of them as I wait on the toaster. I can smell the delicious aroma of the bread as it turns a gentle golden colour, my stomach lets out a growl. I can't eat it even if I wanted to it makes me very breathless, and I can't let anything interfere with my running. My sanctuary. The toaster pops up with a little ping, I start filling the toast wrack and take it through to the waiting guys, my feet padding softly and slowly through to the dining room.

"Isla, what a lovely surprise! I didn't think James let you out of the kitchen! Come join us, you'll improve the conversation a hundred-fold from this motley crew!"

"Aww, that's very sweet of you, and I shall come back," I stall, "but my friend has just popped over to say hi."

"Well, bring her through too!"

"Ok," I laugh, "I'll see what she says." There's no way I can sit through there with the guys, even with Zara, but they don't know that; besides, I assure myself as I walk along the hallway towards the relative safety of the kitchen, they'll probably have forgotten as soon as I left the room.

Walking into the kitchen, it's empty. I look out the window to see James and Zara talking, I can't hear what they are saying but Zara's face is still, she nods her head several times before replying something back, her face solemn. I want to go out to see her, I don't understand why she's leaving, especially without saying cheerio to me. I hesitate…should I go out? Before I can make up my mind, Zara looks over and catches sight of me at the window, she says something to James, gives me a wave, blows a kiss, and jumps into her car. She's leaving. I'm taken aback. James is heading back into the kitchen.

"She had to leave," he states, with no further explanation. He looks over at me and for a while says absolutely nothing, his dark eyes growing cold. "What were you talking with Zara about? You know she is just a menace. Always interfering."

"N-N-Nothing, we were just talking about the party and things, I haven't seen her in ages, she said you worked really hard and that I must be really proud of you." *I am pathetic,* I tell myself, *why can't you just say what is on your mind?* I know the answer to this though. I know that actions always have consequences, and the consequences are getting worse. I look at James, his green moleskins are filthy, hanging off his behind, his customary sludge-green polo shirt stretched tightly across his hemispheric stomach, beetling black eyes twitching as a slow smile spreads across his rotund, purple face. I look at him still saying nothing, he looks as though he is going to say something else to me but instead, he turns and leaves.

I feel a tremor shudder through me. *Things can't get any worse though,* I think to myself. I have lost any remnants of who I used to be and am fast losing any sense of who I am now.

I was wrong though, very wrong. Things can always get worse, much worse.

James was inordinately pleased with himself. That was so easy, he thought, women—he could play them right out of his hand. The right word here and there, nodding sympathetically in agreement with him, all he had needed was the right moment and he had pounced. He hadn't liked what Zara had said to him at the party, that Isla didn't get out much and she was going to insist that she went for coffee with her, he had to make sure Isla didn't call her back replying to her coffee invites. That part was easy, Isla was so weak, all that was needed there was a comment letting her know how much he disapproved of Zara, she was too scared of him to go against him. What he hadn't reckoned on was the strength of their friendship, he had thought he had headed her off at the pass, that she wouldn't come around anymore, however it turned out to be better than even he could have hoped.

It was a bonus that she had seen the bruise, he had panicked at first, but she'd bought it, even agreed with him, and came up with the reason for the bruising! It was genius! No one would believe Isla now even if she got up the nerve to tell anyone, who would believe her now, they think she is such a clumsy bitch. Besides, who would she tell? What would she tell! He was sure he had gotten rid of that interfering Zara. Told her that Isla was too busy, but too polite to tell her she was holding her back.

Zara had looked a little astounded by this but nevertheless took it, then he'd managed to take Isla's phone whilst she was clearing up, all he had needed to do was change a couple digits on Zara's contact details and put a block on her incoming from her, and whilst he was at it he altered a few more, he wished he could block everyone but this would do, for now…Isla would never know why Zara or the others had stopped messaging her, so that sorted that little problem, then it just took a word in a few peoples ear in the village he had made sure people were starting to think that she was unfaithful; people believed what they wanted to believe, and it just took one person to spread the word.

He had poured his heart out in the pub to Paige, she was the biggest gossip around. All he had needed to do was call her and say he was worried about Isla, and could she come around. She jumped at the chance, he knew she would, she just loved the attention, craved it. She had listened dutifully to him as he spilled out his concerns about Isla, how he thought she was having an affair, how she didn't want to meet any of her friends anymore, she was too interested in meeting up with her bit on the side.

Getting away with it, now that was genius. All he needed to say was she spent money, all the time. The extortionate phone bill was genius, a word here, showing it to the right person, people see what they wanted to, a little hint that she must be phoning her lover to stack up that bill. Of course, he'd cleverly stopped paying her phone, then when the bill came in, it was for two months, but they didn't need to know that.

The designer sunglasses she had bought were just the ticket he needed. People were gullible, he just needed to make the arrows, people were more than happy to fire them for him. It had not mattered she had bought them when she was working. All that mattered was a seed of doubt. He let out a haunting guffaw, delighted with himself, he took another long swig. Oh, this was coming along brilliantly, just brilliantly he thought. It was only a matter of time before word got out, and she would stop getting invitations to go out altogether.

The thought of the power bolstered him enormously. He was getting ridiculed by the guys about his weight, telling him Isla would be finding herself a fit man now if he got any fatter; well, whose fault was that he'd put on weight, it was hers, of course he needed to eat things like nuts or chocolate to give him energy, he worked hard and needed it. Well, she need not think Zara and her were going to go out together. Zara was a flighty one; she would be finding Isla someone, he was sure. No, he reminded himself, he had done well today. He picked up his pace and went, bolstered, back to the guys.

It's been a very long day, monotonous and exhausting. Lovely as it was having Zara around, I'm confused that she left without saying goodbye, frustrated that I had not been able to have a good chat with her, but James had gone in a strange mood after, and I knew something was brewing. However, with Sophie and Lola safely tucked up in bed and sleeping soundly, I know I must read over my final assessment and sort any last-minute corrections. It'll be a relief to finally get it emailed off, I've just enough time before the midnight deadline. Pulling out my laptop, I take a deep breath. It's been a long haul getting it to this stage.

Chapter 12

James walked home from the pub early, leaving the guys sitting with their drinks. Stupid men. They'd been teasing him all night about Isla. Saying she did so much. That she could do better than him. That if she took people out shooting, she could do the whole thing herself. He'd gotten mad, but he knew he had cleverly hidden it. Said he needed to go back home to finish off something and he would catch them later. It had not helped that Zara had come around earlier. Who did she think she was telling him how lucky he was to have her Tigger? What did she mean HER Tigger, she was his and his alone was she not? He needed a boost; the attention of the landlady was not doing it for him tonight. He needed a bigger rush. He didn't know what yet, but he knew it wasn't with these guys. Then it hit him with a clarity, he would find it at home.

This house, he loved it. The biggest in the village, he had had it built. He laughed to himself as he remembered how he had got Isla to organise it. Well, it's not as if she'd anything else to do, he recalled, she was on maternity leave and still had 6 weeks to go, he recalled her waddling around trying to pack up the last of their previous house, he had cleverly managed to stay out of the way, she's just so gullible. Then watching her negotiate prices with the builders that would keep the stupid idiot from having too much time on her hands. Then when the baby came along, he'd managed to make sure she was there to coordinate the build, watching her pack up the baby to take along with her, he'd made sure she was plenty busy! He went away just far enough for her not to see where he went, but he could still see where she was. Oh, it was too easy! Silly cow, it was almost too easy.

This house had been witness to many victories for him, the first was the house itself, then the huge housewarming, the hog roast with over 500 guests. That showed everyone who the man in the family was.

And more. The scene of his personal rise. When he had met Isla, he had been a painter and decorator, oh how he'd hated that job, seeing everyone with their beautiful homes and having to skivvy for them, no, he'd hated that. The work had dried up though, it wasn't his fault. Then Isla, of course Isla had to step in, he'd been so angry when she'd suggested turning his hobby into a business. Pre-booking clients in. Just because she was a big shot manager of a gallery, she need not think she could manage him!

As he wandered through the house a little unsteady on his feet it was like taking a walk through a film of his life. He was the star! Emerging from the shadows of his previous life, the life where he had been adopted, given up, abandoned at the door of a charity shop. He laughed wildly. He was the star now! He'd show everyone what he had become.

Oh yes. He thought as he walked into the dining room. He loved it here because it was the scene of so many great screws. Right there on the table he had had two young girls from the local riding stables, a couple of nearby lonely housewives, and from here he could see the hot tub on the patio. He grinned as he remembered that auld years' night when he had brought back some willing ladies who were visiting some locals. Not much to look at but impressed with the big house enough to get naked with him in there. Stupid cows were too noisy, and he had almost got caught when Isla had woken up with the noise.

He took a deep breath, here he had power, here he could lay on the charm, show people how brilliant he was.

The grip of alcohol swept over him, allowing melancholia to enter. What did it all mean? He thought about his wife. He had fallen in love with her humour, her looks and most of all her business sense, everyone had loved her, but he had gotten her. Yes! HIM!

An unwelcome thought arose, what if he lost her? What if she went off with someone? What would he do then? He let out a loud wretched sob, he could not let that happen. She was his. His alone and he would make damn sure no one else was having her. He thought back to the conversation he had had with Charles earlier when they were going for coffee; he'd soon put him right! Told him in no uncertain terms what he would do to him if he so much as caught him looking at his wife again.

James was feeling piteously sorry for himself. He did not deserve any of this. People everywhere were trying to take her away from him. What was she studying for? She was trying to leave him. She meant to leave him as soon as she could. She would get a job as soon as she got her degree for that, he was sure.

The maudlin wash of regret peaked on another alcohol dip. He reached for the bottle, pouring himself yet another glass, it flooded over the top as he filled it to the brim. Slugging it back in one the dip turned into anger. He would show her. Throwing down the glass, he went in search of Isla.

It's now 11.43pm and I'm pleased with my work. Reading it over critically, I make a few corrections checking my references, looking to see where I can pull in a few extra marks. Losing myself in my piece, I relax for once, able to enjoy my reading, the hard work has been done. Pleased with my efforts, I give it one final check and spot a word error. I begin to change it when the door slams against the wall. I jump as James comes storming into the room.

"Where is it!" he demands. "Where have you hidden it? Tell me. TELL ME!" He lunges at the bookshelf and sweeps the contents onto the floor. I shrink back at the clatter.

"W-W what is it?" I stutter in confusion and fear. "Where is what?"

"Tell me!" he roars again, his full height standing menacingly dark in the small room, red curly hair dancing. "What are you doing that for? Tell me!" He demands again, lunging at my laptop.

"Nooooo!" I scream uselessly as he grabs it and proceeds to press buttons in a frenzied manner.

"Please," I beg, "it needs to be in by midnight."

"Oh, it does, does it," he scoffs darkly, his face right up against mine, "well, you had better get on with it then." Holding my laptop high in the air, he punches a few more buttons before slamming it shut with a clatter, tossing it back at me. I clutch at it before it hits the desk. Looking over at me, his lips parting into a sneer, showing his yellow teeth, the evil smile reserved only for me, before folding his lips over them, covering them up. James looks me up and down before turning and leaving.

I am aghast, in shock I pull my laptop open, holding my breath. Searching frantically for my work, I begin to panic, I see nothing. I look in all the files, but to no avail, they had been permanently deleted. I click on file after file. Nothing. I look at my watch 11.54 pm, I realise with a sinking heart I will need to send in an earlier draft, there are no substitutions this late. I could cry. I frantically hunt for any previous copies; he has deleted them all. I keep hunting for anything, any

97

copy at all, finally I locate a previous draft which is no more than a rough copy, the only copy left. Logging onto my Open University account, I attach this and send. I can do no more. I'm still none the wiser what he was after; bursting into tears, I set about putting books back on shelves.

I know I've gone from desperate to pathetic. I've become someone I don't like, the kind of woman I didn't believe existed. What frightens me isn't the hurt he has already bestowed on me, what frightens me is how much more he wanted to hurt me, I can see it in his face, what frightens me is I have finally realised I fear my own husband. I can't take much more of this.

James slipped back along the hall into his office, grabbing another bottle of sloe gin along the way, he slumps into his office chair and opens his laptop. He needed some relief he thought as he clicked on his favourite site. Slopping out the sloe gin, he thought about her. He had so wanted to hurt her, to ram his hand into her bony little ribs, to hear the crack. To show her who was boss. The only thing stopping him was the thought of losing his gun licence. No, he had to control himself at all costs.

Chapter 13

Several weeks had passed since that incident. My University marks had been returned; a bare pass with some very scathing comments from my tutor about the unprofessional nature of the work I had handed in, and at this stage of my studies I should know better what was expected. I try to dismiss the thoughts; it does no good to brood over or to contemplate too hard. *You passed* I remind myself, *what is done cannot be undone. Move on and focus on the present and the future. Easy words to say,* I think to myself.

However, today is special. It is a day I've been looking forward to. The day I am meeting Alicia for coffee has finally dawned, and I am so looking forward to meeting her. We have finally, thanks to her persistence, managed to get a date we can both make. Just the thought of a few hours' peace away from the house was like winning the lottery. If I'm honest, I'd thought that it wouldn't really happen. I had wracked my brains thinking about all possible scenarios that might stop this happening; however, I had not reckoned on the force of Alicia's determination or forethought. Alicia, determined not to let anything stop her, had got James's number from Charles and rang him to confirm that she would pick me up at 12pm as previously arranged. Unable to say anything, he had had to agree.

The morning has gone surprisingly well and not only have I managed to do all the breakfasts and subsequent room changeovers after the guests had left, but I have also managed to make some jams. One of my guests had brought me some trays of fruit from their fruit farm, slightly past their prime but perfect for jams and chutneys. The timing of this arrival was perfect, I've squeezed in some time to make them, and I know these will be a welcome addition to the sparse cupboards. Standing in the kitchen, I slip off my apron, settling my gaze upon the array of jars laying neatly in rows like cheerful little soldiers. In one row nestles strawberry jam, made from delicious fat strawberries, another row contains apple chutney using apples fresh from the orchard and the final row displays rhubarb jam. Lifting them carefully, I begin to stack them neatly in the pantry. I'm ridiculously overjoyed to see these cheerful additions to the bare shelves. Not only do they add much-needed colour and variety, they'll also see us well into the winter. I let a small, rare smile play on my lips as I imagine Sophie's joy when she samples these. I lift the last jar onto the shelf just as James walks in.

I hate what I'm about to do but have no choice. Gathering a deep breath, I ask hesitantly, "Could I have some money please?"

"Whatever for," he retorts.

"I'm going out with Alicia today. Remember?"

"Oh yes, so you are," he looks at me slowly appraising me up and down. I flush slightly at my obviously dishevelled appearance, waiting for a comment, however nothing comes out, instead he turns about to head in the opposite direction, retorting offhandedly.

"How much do you need. What is it for?"

"Well, we are going out for coffee," I reply hesitantly.

He lets out a dramatic sigh before digging around in his pocket he pulls out a handful of change, opening his fist he slowly counts out £1.90 in small change into my hand. I say nothing, I can't. I am mortified I cannot even buy Alicia a coffee. I hope we don't go anywhere fancy, or the price of coffee has gone up.

Just then, my phone buzzes into life from the island unit signalling an email.

"Who's that?" James demands. I say nothing but head over to my phone, picking it up I see it is a message from Mungo, the editor from the magazine.

Isla, fantastic piece, send in a few photos to accompany and I'll get that in the next issue, I have his nibs contact details so look out for an influx of guests! It will be three pages so that's £150.00; don't spend it all at once! Oh, and if you maybe have the time, I really think a little bit on your recipes would make a great column! Just a thought, I know how busy you are!

A surge of excitement flows through me, he wants to publish it! "It's Mungo," I reply excitedly to James, "from the magazine! He says he's going to publish my article in the next issue, he just needs some photographs, isn't that great!" I tumble the words out in my excitement as I look over at James. Looking at me, his face is expressionless.

I'm not sure what I was expecting, but I had hoped he would get a kick out of this, being in such a prestigious magazine and getting not only free publicity, but there would be money for the article as well.

James looks across at me, a strange look passes over his face. "Yes, well, we shall see."

I feel deflated. "Oh, okay, umm well, do you have some photographs?" I ask hesitantly.

"Aye, I'll get them sent off soon as I get a chance."

I hear tyres on the gravel outside and turning I see Alicia coming up the drive.

"Right, you'd better go," James says dismissively before turning and heading out the kitchen door. "I'll have a look for some photos," he adds as an afterthought.

I've no time to think as Alicia opens the door with a cheery, "Come on lovely, coffee beckons, and I am desperate for a good girly catch-up!"

Gratefully, I accept the diversion and allow myself to be swept along in her cheery company.

"Right, I know this gorgeous little coffee shop, I just need to collect something in Melrose first, perfect for a quiet little catch-up! Let's take a little detour along Scott's View, it's simply heavenly," she chatters away companionably about her morning as we drive along. It's a delight to be in her car, so beautiful and clean and I settle back as we drive along, the car making easy work of the steep climb up to Scott's View.

"I never fail to tire of this view," I say almost inaudibly as we pause to take in the glorious sight.

"Me either, we are lucky to live in such a beautiful area; right, those scones are calling," she laughs as she puts the car into first and we make our way steadily down the winding road before joining theA68 and cutting across the famous Leader Valley Viaduct. It's not long before we arrive at Melrose. While Alicia collects her parcel, I admire the ancient ruins of the beautiful medieval Abbey, believed to hold the heart of Robert the Bruce. It never fails to fill me with awe, I realise as I sink further into the comforting leather seats.

"Right, it's not far, it's such a darling little place!"

We drive a little further before reaching the coffee shop. As the car pulls up, I can't help but think about the last time I'd seen her when I'd also been going out for coffee. What a difference today is. I am enjoying the constant stream of chatter about nothing really in particular. Alicia is good company; warm and friendly.

"...and you should have seen his face!" she continues; I hadn't heard what she'd been saying but I could tell I was meant to laugh. I did so obligingly.

"Right then, darling, what are we going to have? They make the most divine scones in here fresh from the aga, raspberry and white chocolate! That's what I had the last time, I wonder if they'll have it on again?" She muses as I line up beside her, homemade scones are piled high on plates, I read the signs, rhubarb and ginger, goats' cheese and red pepper and the infamous raspberry and white chocolate. The delicious warm scent of the homemade goodies combined with freshly ground coffee makes my stomach growl.

"Oh, they look amazing, but I think I shall just have the coffee."

"What? Oh, Isla, you really must try one! They are simply heavenly!"

I think about the £1.90 nestling in my pocket. "I'm in training for the race, less weight to lug around for my race," I joke.

"Oh, don't be so silly, darling, you are so slender you could have ten and not gain an ounce!"

I laugh this off, not feeling the slightest bit humorous, "I have to pop to the loo; powder my nose," I fib yet again to Alicia, what choice do I have, I realise as I hand over my £1.90 to her. "Do you mind awfully paying? I'll be straight back, sorry but I am desperate."

"Oh no this is on me," Alicia tries.

"No, I insist." I slip the money quickly into her pocket before disappearing quickly into the nearby loo. I feel awful not being able to offer to pay for both of us as it is. I've seen the price up on the blackboard; £1.90 on the dot. I don't want to get into further conversation about scones no matter how delicious they look so I head for the sanctuary of the bathroom, the coward that I am. I wash my hands and use some of the hand cream attached to a dispenser on the wall. Walking back out, I notice Alicia sitting in the corner on a sofa beckoning over to me a huge smile on her face.

"Isla, I insist you must try one! I am positively not eating by myself!"

I look down and there, sitting proudly on the table are two giant scones alongside two steaming mugs of coffee.

"My treat, and you cannot possibly offend me by not joining me."

I smile up at her, she smiles back as gratefully I accept and descend on the scone; raspberry and white chocolate, Alicia is right, these are simply gorgeous.

"Oh my gosh, this is the most divine thing I have ever tasted!" It's absolutely heavenly, my mouth waters as I savour each bite, enjoying every morsel as we chat companionably about life in general, work, children, and hobbies.

I am deep in thought, I love being out and being able to chat, it doesn't matter what we are talking about I'm just enjoying being in her company, however, I realise with more than a little sadness, it just emphases how isolated I am becoming.

"Is everything okay, Isla?"

No, it is not, everything is wrong. I cannot do anything right. James is getting more and more angry with me, the harder I work and the busier we are the more he complains about having no money. I am not allowed out by myself unless by some freak chance he has no choice and when I finally do get out there is always some retaliation to look forward to, I live in fear, I am black and blue, and I just want to run away from it all.

"Isla?" Alicia looks at me questioningly. "You've gone awfully quiet."

I want to confide in her; to open up, I do, I really do, but I cannot. I've tried before, and it always seems to have a way of getting back to James. I had tried to confide in Abigail when we had been closer, her reply had been derisive. "What? You're just being silly, why would you go start making trouble for yourself, look at you, look at what you have! This is one of the oldest families in the area, they wouldn't hurt a fly surely, besides," she pointed up to the house, "would you seriously give all that up?" She had looked me straight in the eye. "It's not as if he beats you every day, is it!"

So that was it, the marker that I should adhere to, it was at that moment I knew, and she knew I knew; it was woman's intuition, but she was defying me to say anything, to rock the boat; the Borders are a tight-knit community, old names mean as much, if not more, than old money. She had cut across me unable or perhaps unwilling to comprehend the unhappiness and the increasing fear I felt daily, all she could see was the house and the name. It had gotten back to James. Everything gets back to him eventually. No. I cannot risk it. The words stay firmly locked inside me.

"Isla?"

"Yes, yes, sorry of course, sorry. I was just thinking about something I must do."

"Well, you really need to try and relax once in a while, you are out now so enjoy, the B&B won't fall apart if you are not there for a few hours! She gestures our now empty coffee cups. I think I should take you for a nice leisurely walk around Abbotsford House, the grounds are simply delightful at this time of year. Now, no arguments. I shall have you back in plenty of time to collect Sophie from school!"

And with that she quickly orders two more coffees to takeaway, insisting it is her treat.

"I have to have an ally in my caffeine addiction!" she laughs gently, as we head back to the car and head to Abbotsford House, Sir Walter Scott's ancestral home. A beautiful, imposing building set in luscious grounds with a stunning walkway from the main house, down to the River Tweed, and then back up through the woods.

"Now, tell me what you have been up to," she continues, as I make a concerted effort not to think about home. It was so good to have a conversation; I know I feel isolated, but I'd no idea just how much until now. I look over at her as she chats away telling me about her life and the goings-on within the village, the social politics, and I tell her excitedly about the book club. The only thing I really have to say that's not child or work-oriented.

I love this distraction from my life, the relative normality of it all and I feel ridiculously grateful, indebted really. Without this I have nothing.

"Well, Isla," Alicia sighs dramatically as we come out of the path next to the main house, "I guess I need to be taking you back, I can't believe how fast time goes."

"I have loved being out today and thank you again for that scone, you are right they are absolutely delicious; I cannot remember the last time I tasted something so lovely." I'm not lying this time, after a diet of bacon, eggs and game, it tasted like a little piece of heaven.

"Oh, Isla, please stop thanking me, honestly you were doing me the favour, I hate to eat alone! Besides, I think you should have more of them, you could do with a little bit of fattening up!"

I wish James would agree with you, I think, reminded again of the relentless jibes about being fat. The thing is, even if people tell me I am not fat, I don't believe them. I know that I'm not fat, but I feel fat. I've hovered around a size ten for years but the constant snide remarks and put downs have worn away at me over the years and now, every time I look in the mirror all I see is a big elephantine girl standing staring back at me, every flaw magnified a thousand-fold.

As we head back to the car and inevitably back to the village, I try not to think about home just yet, relishing being in the moment, it's so easy being with Alicia, talking about anything and everything it reminds me of days gone by, but before I know it we are pulling into the driveway. I thank her again and wonder if I will get the chance to go out again, as she insists that I have made her day and we must do this again very soon.

I walk slowly and reluctantly across the driveway, crunching my way as quietly as I can and into the back porch. James greets me at the door.

"What time do you call this?" he asks before I can say anything.

"Sorry, Alicia was driving, and I guess, I guess we just lost track of time."

"It's okay for some, isn't it," he sneers at me. I feel the happiness of my outing drain away, a black cloud descending in its place.

"Well, how did it go?"

"It was lovely. I—"

"Where was it you went?" he interrupts before I can continue.

"We went to the Old Melrose Tearooms, where is Lola?" I ask looking around as she is usually the first to greet me at the door.

"Lola?" He asks innocently, "How would I know? I thought she must be with you."

What? I think looking at his face, it is expressionless except for a tiny movement of his lips.

"I haven't seen her for," he pauses, "well, since just after you left. She must have got out, I guess," he looks over at me I see him trying to read my expression which is one of horror, the smile that had been playing on his lips stretched a little wider. "I've been in and out all day I guess the door must have been left open, I don't have time to be looking after your dog whilst you are out gallivanting with your friend..."

"But I left her safely in the other room as she's in season..." I say falteringly.

James shrugs, making no effort to now contain the smirk on his face. Panicking, I dash out. I have to go and collect Sophie from school, but I need to find Lola and fast. I run as quickly as I can calling out for her on my way but to no avail, she is in season but also what if she is hit by a car. I arrive at the school door and am relieved that Sophie is already waiting, coat on, school bag in hand waiting in line in the hall ready. Mr Toledo sees me and lets Sophie out.

I welcome her childish hug and hug her tightly back whilst explaining and trying to make light of it that Lola decided to take herself for a walk, but my heart is hammering so loudly as we both hunt, calling out for Lola, we head back into the village green.

"Lola," Sophie calls as we hunt around, asking other mums on the route back from the school but no one has seen her I see Linda the local gossip looming in the distance, *anyone but her,* I think, *but I have no choice.*

"Ummm, Linda, you haven't seen Lola anywhere, have you? She managed to escape."

"Oh yes actually! She is over there, I think she's having a bit of fun with an old sheepdog." She laughs openly and I just know this is going to feed her gossip for the coming weeks ahead, I thank her not wanting to engage in more conversation, rounding the next house, I see Lola, just breaking off her join with the sheepdog; *that's all I need, Lola,* I think to myself.

"Lola! There you are, you are such a naughty dog!" Sophie calls running over to Lola. I've been so careful to only take her on the lead to make sure this didn't happen. I slip the lead onto her. Sophie is delighted to have found Lola after her adventures and chatters away to her whilst my mind starts to drift on the way back to the house.

James would not have let her out on purpose, would he? That was just cruel, I think back to the time though when I had my 2 cockapoos and he'd constantly let them out when I was away at work, one resulting in a litter of cross puppies which he'd drowned at birth. I had cried for days after, and then when I had given birth to Sophie, he had ramped up the escaping of the two dogs so much so the neighbours had complained about them doing their business in their garden. I'd no choice but to rehome my two dogs. I'd passed this off at the time as just him being careless leaving doors open, but this seemed to be too much of a repeating pattern, but surely, surely, he would not do this, not deliberately would he? A shiver runs through me, I have an awful feeling in the pit of my stomach.

Back in the house, I send Sophie up to start running the bath. "She smells like an old wet sock," I try in an attempt not to let her sense my mood. Sophie giggles at this.

"She does, maybe even two wet socks, I'll put lots of bubbles in the bath for her, Mummy, then she will smell all nice again."

"Okay sweetheart, I'll be up in two shakes of a lamb's tail. I just need to ask Daddy something." As she heads off, I have no choice but to say to James what has happened and ask what to do.

"Well, if you think I'm wasting money by taking her to the vet, then you have another think coming. You should look after her better, and if you cannot then I'll get rid of her for you, if you have a dog then you need to be here to look after it, not gallivanting around the countryside. If you'd been here today, then it never would have happened. Would it?" he looks directly at me, challenging me to disagree.

And there it is, I realise with a resounding thump as I head up to the waiting Sophie and Lola. He did it on purpose, the audacity of me going out for coffee today was retaliation. It was as clear as day, he could not have been clearer if he had said, *Well, Isla, if you dare to go out without me, you will pay the price.*

This on top of my essay last night, I feel another little piece of me dissolve. I'm at breaking point, drained both physically and emotionally. I text one of the farmer-type mums and explain what has happened, the brief version, and she replies back reassuringly that the old sheepdog has been doing that for years, it's firing blanks and has indeed got to some of hers in the past but not to worry, she won't have a litter of pups. I am still shaking inside from the realisation that not even Lola is safe now.

Chapter 14

It has been a rough week, I tried to put the incident with my beautiful Lola behind me. I had something really lovely to look forward to, something I had been looking forward to since the party and the day had finally come when I was going to the book club meeting. I had a text message saying they were starting up again, now lambing and calving were over, and they would love it if I came.

I am beside myself with excitement. I feel a little nervous about meeting some of the new girls, however I do know a couple of names, they aren't from round here and their children don't go to Sophie's school but from what I've heard they are friendly there and it would be lovely to get out. Most were mums and a couple of the mums were bringing older children who were going to play games with the little ones in another room. I can hardly believe that I am actually going!

Martha has been so warm and welcoming, she has texted me a couple of times since the party reminding me to come and her bubbly warmth is contagious, she seems relaxed and free-spirited. I feel a genuine warmth and connection to her. The most recent text I'd got was last night suggesting that she pick up Sophie from school.

Hello Poppet! Soooo looking forward to you coming to our little soiree tonight! Richard met James earlier today and he mentioned something about him having VIP's in, how exciting! However, I know that will probably bring about you heaps of extra work darling so why don't I just pick up Sophie from school, the girls will absolutely adore her and w…

I looked quizzically at the message, trying to formulate what the next part of her message could have been when my phone tings again.

Sorry my text ran out. Oh, what a silly thing texts are, darling, but soooo useful in today's age! Anyway, where was I? Oh yes that's right, the girls will absolutely spoil her rotten and don't worry we shall give her tea. That gives you a bit more time to get sorted. CU soon! TTFN!

I think back to the night of the party again and can almost hear Martha speaking in her wonderfully enthusiastic tone. Delightedly, I accept and ring the school to let them know. Martha and Richard are a wonderful couple. Martha is so warm and vivacious she brightens any room she walks into whilst Richard is so jolly and open you can't help but see why they are perfect together. I wonder what book we would be discussing tonight; it really doesn't matter to me. I am just so excited to be out. I can't believe James has agreed so readily to this either, but I am not going to question it. Just then, a message pings up on my phone. It's from James. My heart sinks. Was this it? The VIPs Martha mentioned? The sudden change of plan which means I can't go tonight? Slowly, and with trepidation, I open the message.

Red or white wine for taking tonight?

I can't believe it. It's still on! Stunned, I pause a moment before gathering up my phone. I eagerly type back.

White please!

Breathlessly I wait. Is this a cruel joke?

Ten minutes later a text comes back, I can hardly bring myself to open it, to open it will either raise or dash my hopes for tonight. Car crash style, I open it and wait for the message to pop up.

Sauvignon Blanc, New Zealand. Hope that's okay.

I could have passed out in shock had I not been so happy. No, that's the wrong word. I'm ecstatic! Maybe after everything James really does want me to go out. Maybe, just maybe James is back to his old self! Maybe the articles in the magazine are taking some of the stress from him? I am so thrilled I could cry. Quickly I text back:

Perfect! That's my favourite, how on earth did you remember!

And with that I do a merry little jig and then laugh at myself. Stop being silly, I mock scold myself. You have lots of work still to be done. Nevertheless, I can't wipe the big smile off my face. Everything is changing. Changing for the better! I pick up my cleaning box and set about the house with fresh gusto. So, James has important clients coming tonight, he must have forgotten to tell me, that's all. I want everything to be extra special. I'll make a cake too! A big chocolate one. I always reserved ingredients to make birthday cakes for any of the groups that are up celebrating a birthday. James will like that; I know he would for sure.

Several hours later, I have finished the cleaning. Looking around me, everything is in its place. Polished and sparkling to within an inch of its life. I've plumped the cushions, cleaned the windows, polished the woodwork, hoovered every carpet, and washed all the floors. I love the clean smell. It takes me back to my childhood. To another time. Now for the cake! With renewed hope and excitement, I dance into the kitchen and pull open the baking cupboard door. *Now what have we here,* I think to myself. Pulling out bags of self-raising flour, cocoa powder, sugar, baking powder and the rest of the ingredients. Hopping between cupboards and fridge, I call Alexa to play *My Happy Playlist*. I feel a wave of jubilation wash over me. *Things are changing,* I think, as I pull out mixing bowls, all the while singing tunelessly along to *Brown-Eyed Girl.*

I spend the next whilst in a blissful trance, whisking, mixing, and beating my chocolate cake into a delicious dark, gooey, sticky perfect treat. My mouth waters in anticipation. I don't even mind that there will be no part of this cake for me; life is good again! That's all that matters. As I pour the mix into the lined baking tin and pop it in the oven, I take a quick taste of the rich, silken, chocolatey mix still lining the bowl. The best part of baking my mum always said was being able to lick the bowl! *How right she was,* I think, as I take another taste. *Mm hmm, now that is delectable!*

But enough, I check myself. James doesn't like your being fat. A moment on the lips, forever on the hips. Hesitantly, I head towards the sink to put the bowl in to wash. I waver before quickly turning on the tap full blast before I can change my mind. Quickly washing all traces of the mix, I watch it swirl round and round the sink before disappearing eternally into the abyss that is the drains. Who cares for chocolate cake when I can go out tonight, I happily remind myself, setting about making the icing for the cake.

Two hours later and I am still dancing happily around the house. The house is filled with the warm aroma of chocolate cake, music, and the smell of fresh polish. Sophie will be at Martha's now and having a ball no doubt! I cannot wait to join her. Checking my watch; it shows at 6.07pm. I glance over to my cake; the only thing left to do is ice it then I'm free to get myself ready. Yes. Cool enough to ice now. I love this part. It's rare I have the time to make such an extravagant cake I think as I place it atop of my one and only crystal cake stand, a wedding present from my mum who had shown me a love of baking. I pick up the icing bag, piping and swirling the delicious chocolate icing on to the cake, reaching for my palette knife. I smooth it around the sides before finishing it off with a triumphant flourish. There I think as I look on happily. Even if I say so myself, that is one fine-looking cake! Just one thing left now is for me to get ready, and with a delighted skip I turn and head up the stairs two at a time.

Stripping off my clothes, I jump into the shower. I'm a hot sticky mess, and the water is so refreshing as it trickles over my bare skin. Reaching for the shampoo I use extra in an attempt to lather it up into a thick mound, giggling to myself as I try and fail to make a unicorn spike. The soap is too weak to lather and the spike flops. *I must be losing my mind;* I think to myself laughing. I've not felt this free in an age and it feels wonderful. Rinsing it off I apply conditioner, cheap but better than nothing and at least I can slip it in with the B&B shopping unnoticed. I let this soak in whilst I wash my body and brush my teeth. A habit I've got into to save precious minutes off my day.

Jumping quickly out of the shower, I grab a towel, quickly and vigorously rubbing myself dry. What to wear? I open the wardrobe. Pulling aside item after item nothing seems just right. I come upon a little blue and white floral summer dress. It's been in the wardrobe since not long after we got married. *Perfect*, I realise in jubilation, with James changing and being more like himself, he will like me in this. It couldn't be better! Changing quickly into it, I slip on a pair of summer wedges, ancient but thankfully they look almost as new since they get precious little wear. I dry my hair and style it simply with a loose ponytail. Applying my make-up, I look at my efforts. Staring back at me is a youthful girl, a faint recognition of the past I could see in her, she looks almost happy. I apply a quick slick of nude lip gloss when I hear a rustle behind me. James is standing in the doorway.

"What do you think?" I ask giving him a playful twirl.

Looking at me, he says nothing.

I wait. Still nothing. An anxious knot is starting to twist its way up into my stomach. Maybe my choice of outfit is wrong?

His face is still. Vacant, as if in deep thought.

"Wine is downstairs, is everything ready for tonight?"

"Oh, um thank you and yes," I say momentarily taken aback. "Yes, yes, and I have made my special family-recipe-millions-have-tried-to-get-the-recipe-for chocolate cake!" I add hoping to get a smile or something, anything, in fact from him. His face stays expressionless except for a tiny straightening of his mouth.

"Right. Okay. Well, I need to pop out, my meeting is not here until 9 so long as everything is in order, I shall be fine to entertain them myself," he stops again, giving me a long hard look before continuing, "enjoy your evening." A slow smile spreads over his face as he turns and disappears back into the depths of the hallway.

I feel a bit odd; I can't put my finger on it, there's nothing he's actually said, nothing he's done, but I can't help the strange sensation that passes through me. *Now come on,* I say to myself, *you've only a few minutes before Tilly comes to pick you up.* I try to focus on the positive. How lovely it was that Martha had sent a lift. Remembering fondly our last phone conversation I smile.

"Oh, darling, you can't possibly come and not have a delicious glass of chilly Sauvignon Blanc, that's positively the whole purpose of our get-togethers!" she had let out such a tinkling little laugh before continuing, "…and Tilly is so sweet I just know you and she will get on like a house on fire!" I have a feeling that Martha has sent Tilly in order that I don't have to walk in alone and I am eternally grateful. I try to quash the feelings of unease, after all, I have everything looking just perfect in the house and the big chocolate cake is sitting pride of place in the kitchen, I've laid out the special cups and James has said to me to 'Enjoy your evening' not to mention the fact he has bought me a special bottle of wine to take. Yes, I'm just being silly. I reason with myself, most likely because I've not been out by myself in such a long time.

"So, come on," I say aloud to myself. "Get moving and don't be looking a gift horse in the mouth." I check my watch and with a shock realise I have little over a minute to go before Tilly will be here. "Right Lola darling, are you going to sit here and have a jolly good sleep whilst I'm away?" Lola wags her tail and cocks her ears in answer before joining me: her customary place, 2 inches from me. I give her a hug and with a renewed bounce to my step the smile arrives back on my face without me having to try, I lightly head downstairs and clack across the marble hallway, heading towards the kitchen.

Chapter 15

Turning the corner into the back hall, I stop mid-stride and let out an involuntary gasp. Mud has been trailed in from the back door, scuffing along the oak doors and through into the kitchen, the half open door leads my eye further into the devastation, the mud trail leading an inescapable thick gluey brown path, beckoning the way, pushing the kitchen door open a little wider I freeze to the spot. It looks like a cyclone had just passed by. Trying to get a breath, I survey the scene in front of me.

The mud is only the start. Almost every cupboard door is open, the contents of the larder are spilling out onto the floor, self-raising flour bags burst open, dredging their innocent white contents over the floor, fine white particles still in the air coating the surrounding area in a fine white blanket, dented tins join smashed jars of pickled beetroot and onions, the pungent aroma of the vinegar assault my senses. The precious jars of jam merging strawberry into rhubarb. The rubbish bin is on its side, spilling its once secret contents into the open, the recycle bin suffering the same fate, vegetable peelings now join the dried lentils and pasta, strewn across the floor.

On the countertops, a jar of coffee spills its dark brown crumbly innards over the surface, a half-drunk cup of coffee on its side, the contents trickling out to join the coffee granules, creating a stream of sticky brown goo which steals across the countertop before descending down the cupboard door to join the chaos at foot. Looking around to the island unit where my chocolate cake had stood proudly in the centre, I realise it's gone. The chocolate cake I was so proud of lay on its side in the dog bowl, moist chocolate sponge lay defeated, half in half out, gooey chocolate icing sliding innocently down the side, escaping onto the marble floor. My precious crystal cake stand lies shattered amid the chaos.

A knock at the door tears me back to reality, amid this chaos I had not heard the tyres crunching on the gravel outside.

Tilly! I realise in panic. What am I to do? Tilly cannot see this, and it's now achingly apparent that I cannot go out tonight. James's guests for his meeting will be here very shortly and he has made it very clear about his expectations. Fighting back tears, I have no choice; the smile now gone, I haul the now customary mask of composure across my face and proceed to the back door pulling the kitchen door behind me. Opening the door, I am met by a bright and cheerful Tilly. All wild hair and sparkling eyes.

"Isla, I'm so glad you are coming tonight, Tilly burst out before I could say anything, I have been absolutely dying to meet you Martha said you and I would get along so fabulously, I am new to the area and hardly know a soul, well I have seen a few of the locals but they are a bit stuck up for me, ooops sorry I shouldn't have said that should I, oh what am I saying you hardly know me and here I am babbling away!" Words fly from her like a river in full flow as she laughs merrily. "I get like this when I'm excited!" she adds by way of explanation.

I could have cried. Tilly is so lovely, Martha's right, this would be exactly my type of friend. I knew we would have got on like a house on fire but how can I explain to this perfect and kind stranger what I'd just left, and worse, what the consequences would be if James walked into that with his guests. She wouldn't understand, how could she? So, I do what I do best. What I always do now. I don't poke the bear. I lie. I feel awful.

"Oh, Tilly, I'm so sorry, but I've just developed this most awful migraine, I don't think I can make it tonight, I'm so sorry I didn't ring, it just came on so suddenly."

A fleeting look of disappointment crosses Tilly's face before quickly being replaced by a gentle and compassionate smile. "Oh, that's such a shame, darned awful things they are, I don't get them much but when they hit they are just the worst aren't they? Can I get you anything or do anything for you that would help?"

I want to tell her everything, I want nothing more than that at this exact moment, but I can't. I know what the consequence would be for me, and I can't risk that, instead I heard myself say, "Thank you, but I'll be okay." My automatic response and I dredged up a smile as best as I could.

"You should go lie down and get some rest, you've probably just been overdoing it, don't worry about Sophie, sweetie, I'll bring her back, and we can arrange something for next time, or maybe, we could catch up for a coffee at some point, you can fill me in on the ghastly locals too!" Standing on my doorstep, about my height, a big mop of curly brown hair and a sprinkling of freckles on her pretty face, she gives off such a warm welcoming vibe I could have cried. I needed a friend. I needed a friend I could trust more than anything in the world, but I knew this could not be, with an aching heart I bid her farewell, thank her for her kind words and slowly close the back door behind her before promptly bursting into tears. I can hear her car door close and the tires crunching their way out of the drive, taking with it my hopes and dreams.

Turning back into the kitchen, I see Lola head towards her dog bowl. "No Lola! Sorry hunny but that'll make you sick, mind your paws, come, sit in your basket." Settling her out of harm's way in her dog basket in the corner, I give her a big hug. Letting the tears flow unchecked as I set about clearing up the debris, sweeping up the broken fragments, the dried food, I wash the floor trying to remove the pungent smell of the vinegar, the acrid stench amid the chaos contrasting sharply with the homely aroma of chocolate cake, the kitchen that less than an hour ago was immaculate.

As I wash and clean the debris as quickly as I can, aware he could arrive home at any minute, the realisation dawns on me, I feel sick. How could he have worked so quickly? And so quietly? My mind flashes back to the last thing he said to me…

"Enjoy your evening" and the slow smile that had spread over his face as he turned. That was it. He'd not ever really had any intentions of letting me go. I feel such a fool for thinking he had changed.

Idiot, Idiot, Idiot. I chastise myself as the tears slip down my cheeks, I clean. This is the last one. The last hope. It had gone. Puff. Just like that, it had gone as quick as a wisp of smoke on a windy day, the crashing of dreams melting like the chocolate off the cake. This time however, it feels like the biggest betrayal. The pain I feel is almost physical, the impact of that final realisation. I look up and down the kitchen shocked and saddened. The last hope spills from me, mingling with the mess on the kitchen floor.

I work solidly for over an hour and am just slopping the chocolate cake into the bin when James arrives home. I hear him say to the guys just to head along to the other room and he'd join them shortly.

I look up as he comes through, his massive bulk filling the doorway of the kitchen.

"You're home early?" he states.

"I didn't go," I mumble.

116

"Whyever not?"

"I came down and it looked as though a bomb had gone off in here, I know you need it to be just right for your meeting."

"Oh, those blasted dogs, I meant to say but I was in such a hurry, they got out just as I was heading out, it must have been them, did it take long to clear up?" He had his back to me so I couldn't see his face.

My mind is racing. *Very clever dogs we have, that are able to open jars of coffee and lift entire cakes complete with a stand and place it in a dog bowl but not actually eat any of it.*

"Didn't you get my text?" He adds, "The meeting was cancelled so I invited a few of the guys around for a drink instead."

I look up at him, too stunned to speak.

Convenient, a sudden mention of VIP guests only today, the day I am going out and then they don't turn up?

He turns around to face me staring, unblinking, directly at me; a hint of amusement playing on his face.

"No. I didn't get any text…"

"Mustn't've gone through, you know what the reception can be like," he replies dismissively. "Here, let me pour you a glass of wine, it's too late to go now and no point wasting the night. Go sit down, the guys are here now though so I'll have to join them."

I stand, staring, like a rabbit caught in the headlights, *go sit down*, I repeat to myself, *go sit down*? Obediently, though, I go and sit through in the living room. Something feels strange. Oblivious of the usually calming tones in here I sit down on the sofa, sinking in deeply, I throw off my shoes and sink deeper into the sofa, I wish I could keep on sinking. Sinking into oblivion. Lola joins me, I cuddle into her. There are no more tears left. I switch on the TV; the distraction of a monotonous soap burbles on in the background. I feel so bereft, bereft for what could have been tonight, possibilities of what could have been fill me with such despair that I can do no more than just function on autopilot. I wonder what book they are discussing, who is there, what Tilly must have thought.

The excited high I had been on today contrasts deeply with the low I now feel, the opportunity that has been ripped from me only serves to heighten my desolation. A vague thought begins to niggle its way into my thoughts. James had offered me a wine hadn't he. That was an act out of the ordinary for him. What brought him to offer this act of kindness? Maybe he was sorry. Genuinely sorry? Maybe I had got this all wrong? I begin to feel guilty. Maybe I've misjudged him.

The living room door opens, and James comes through, handing me a glass of wine. "So, who did you invite around tonight?" I ask, accepting the proffered glass. I can hear in the background the roars and laughs from further along the house.

"Oh, just the usual crew from in the pub, there was meant to be a football match we were going to watch, but the SKY TV wasn't working, they suggested darts and dominoes, but I said we could come here instead."

"You were at the pub?" I question before I can stop myself.

"What do you mean, are you trying to cross-examine me? Are you trying to provoke a fight? I told you I was out sorting some things. I said I met them coming out of the pub." He fixes me with a glacial stare, daring me to say any more. I say nothing. There is nothing to say. He turns and leaves to join the boys.

I try to process the events of the evening. I am confused. Thoughts are spinning around in my head. I take another sip of the chilled white wine. Was the mess intentional? Had he been sorry? Was I picking a fight? I'm so confused; I don't know which way is up anymore. Tears roll unchecked down my cheeks, spilling onto Lola's black and white warm spotty body. I'm oblivious to these as I try to make sense of things. Nothing seems to make sense.

The thoughts spinning around in my mind are at war with each other. Every thought I bring up has a counter argument. One thing's for sure, I know I cannot ask him outright. I hear roars of very drunken men laughing raucously followed by a crashing of glass splintering across a floor. I take another sip of wine and flick channels, trying to drown out the noise and find something, anything that will distract me.

Chapter 16

The next morning, as I waken, I feel groggy and confused, a sick feeling lurches in my stomach. Oh, that's not just a sick feeling, I think as I rush out of bed and into the bathroom just in time before being violently sick. After heaving the contents of my stomach into the toilet bowl I sit, gripping the side of the pan weakly, beads of perspiration lining my forehead. I can hear Sophie calling me from the next room.

"I'm okay, hunny, just wait there. I'll be through in a minute." Sitting there without a stitch on, I don't want Sophie seeing me like this. Grabbing the edge of the bath I haul myself up, running the tap I splash my face with cold water and brush my teeth. Stumbling back to the bedroom, I pull on the first clothes that come to hand. James is nowhere to be seen. I try, unsuccessfully, to focus. What day was it? Saturday. No school today. That's something. I make my way through to Sophie and pick her up. "Mummy, are you okay?"

"Yes sweetheart, I'm fine, Mummy's just a little tired. Come, let's get you and Lola some breakfast, we'll need to sort out things for the lads coming back; they will be hungry, won't they!"

It's all I can do to keep it together going downstairs. I feel awful, how much had I had to drink? I can't remember even going to bed let alone changing out of my clothes. I must have had a lot more than I thought, not being used to having a drink. It must have gone straight to my head. That must be it, I reason as I hold onto the banister, steadying myself as we descend the stairs.

"Sophie?" a thought suddenly struck me. I couldn't remember Sophie coming home. Oh god that's awful, what an awful mum I am. I was drinking and had so much I couldn't remember my girl coming home.

"Yes Mummy." Sophie looks at me, a puzzled look on her little face, curious why I had not finished my query.

How can I put this; I wonder frantically.

"Tell me all about your night, I want to know all the fun things you did and who brought you home, did you fly!" I tease, trying to keep the mood light and the concern out of my voice. I am finding it difficult to stand let alone function. Sophie proceeds to regale me with tales of the nights, it sounds like she had had a ball. Tilly had brought her home, lovely Tilly.

"And Mummy," Sophie continues, "Tilly says you and her are going to go out for coffee and I can come if I want, and we are going to get a big piece of cake or maybe even ice-cream!"

"Well, that sounds just lovely," I reply as enthusiastically as I can, the thoughts of ice cream and cake make my stomach churn making me want to be sick again.

"And when I got home, you were all tucked up in bed, I came in and gave you a big kiss and a cuddle and you were sleeping and didn't wake up, so I put myself to bed. I am a big girl now, Mummy," she declares proudly. "And I made sure Lola was safe too, Mummy, I tucked her in with me just like you do."

The realisation that I had not only been oblivious to Sophie coming home but not even been there to see her safely into bed hit me full on like a truck, shame mixed with horror overcomes me and I feel another tide of nausea wash over me, this one was not to be quelled.

"I'll be back in a sec, hunny," I call as I tear out of the kitchen to the downstairs bathroom making it just in time to empty my now empty stomach; my stomach heaves and lurches in protest at not being able to bring anything up. *This is the worst hangover I have ever had,* I concede, pulling myself up yet again from the toilet, splashing cold water over my face again in an attempt to gain a bit of perspective. I head back to the kitchen. Thankfully, Sophie is sitting at the big pine table telling Lola about her adventures last night. I see she had placed cereal into a bowl and given Lola her breakfast.

The two are sitting contentedly eating, Sophie chattering away in between mouthfuls. Everything looks normal.

I set about getting breakfast ready for the guys return, they had arrived early this morning and headed straight out for an early-morning shoot so I didn't need to tidy the rooms just yet thankfully, by the time they came hopefully I would have more energy, the thought of cooking 7 full Scottish breakfasts was not appealing.

I open the fridge door to get the milk and orange juice out. Staring at me from the door was the bottle of Sauvignon Blanc. I pick the bottle up and look at the contents, it is three quarters full. It doesn't make sense. How could I have such a horrendous hangover when I had only had one glass? A hangover so bad I could not remember even going to bed let alone going upstairs. It makes no sense at all. *I must be such a lightweight,* I think to myself as I try to let the mundane tasks of the morning distract me.

The day drags on, I could manage to keep coffee down now and at least that gave me some focus. I head back to the kitchen for what seemed like the thousandth time that day for coffee, the only thing that could give me the energy to get through the day. Without the food my body so desperately needed, the caffeine hit was the only thing in abundance. The rich strong liquid slipped back to my throat, its warming glow gentle on my throat. I felt calm, for a while now there had been the flitting's of a plan, a plan of how I could escape starting to formulate in my mind. *I can do this,* I think, *I can, I will, one day I will get my chance, but for now I need to keep Sophie safe.*

As the nausea begins to wear off, I am aware of something else. Something more alarming. I am in considerable pain in an intimate area. It hits me then with a jolt. The realisation. I am mortified. But I can remember nothing about it. Not one thing.

I try to focus on the events of last night. To piece together the events. Think! I tell myself. Think! I remember cleaning up the mess in the kitchen. I remember the ruined chocolate cake. But that was it. Nothing. What is wrong with me? What normal person does that? I feel sick. I need to feel clean. I am embarrassed. Disgusted. I dash upstairs and switch the shower on full, stripping off. I wince as the shower water hits my sensitive areas. Looking down, I notice yet again there are large bruises appearing on my legs. This doesn't make sense. I would have to ask him. I had to know. I reach for the soap and clean myself over and over. I still feel dirty. Humiliated.

He'd have to be more careful, he thought to himself. *She was onto him. He had not thought she would say anything, and he was taken aback when she'd come right up and asked him straight, straight out like that, imagine the cheek of her. At first, he had tried to deny it but then she had said she knew they had. He had simply replied, "Prove it" and walked away. He had been trying out the drug on her for a while to see how much he would need, she'd woken up before when he hadn't given her enough, but now he had it sorted, how good it had made him feel.*

He couldn't slap her about during the day, oh no, he was much too clever for that, he said to himself proudly, she needed pulling into line a bit. Oh she was getting a bit cocky now, all that running, people saying how committed she was, well, men for as long as time itself had given their wives a slap to keep them in check, and since she had started getting her writing in the magazines, well, it was only a few pages for Christ sake, anyone would think she had cured cancer the way the guys reacted when they realised it was her that was in the magazine.

Well, she needed more than a slap, and as for sex, well, imagine trying to tell him he couldn't have that kind of sex. She was his, she belonged to him, husbands and wives had sex. That was fact, and he was going to make dam sure he got what was rightfully his. He took another long drink. No, he was doing what was right. He was married to her. He was justified.

He took another long swig, draining the contents of the glass. A wave of anxiety swept over him. What if she told someone? That Zara maybe? What would happen then? She would get her to leave him, leave him like everyone leaves him, his dad had abandoned him with his mum shortly after his birth, then his mum had abandoned at just 9 months old on the door of a charity shop. Yes, she would leave him too. Just like everyone did. He would have to make sure she didn't. But how? Think, think, THINK!

Picking up the bottle, he didn't bother to pour, this time choosing to drink straight from the bottle whilst he paced the room. After people started noticing the bruises, she couldn't keep saying she was so accident-prone, he had to be more careful. More discreet. He had to maintain control, but above all he had to maintain his image. She was provoking him. When he had seen her all playful and twirling like that in front of him, she was not dressed like that to go out to a book club, there must be men there. No one would get dressed up and go and sit talking about books all night, no there was more to it than that. Did she think he was stupid? Well, she was his, she couldn't leave him. He wouldn't allow it.

Taking another slug, he let the liquid trickle down his throat, he could feel it slide down, the warm glow he felt as it oozed into his very core. He needed a release. Snapping open his phone he looked at the pictures, pictures he kept of her, pictures he kept for when he needed a boost. Flicking through, he was momentarily satisfied, he took another long glug draining the bottle, he looked at it, the clear glass of the bottle taunting him. He threw it down in disgust, the shards scattering in all directions over the hard floor. He looked about him as a wave of maudlin swept through him. She's going to leave me, he muttered into the darkness, then who will I have? No one, that's who. Everyone leaves me, he thought morosely. I can't let that happen. No, he needed to find her. To stop this. She was his, his and his alone, she couldn't leave him, no he couldn't allow that. He knew what he needed to do now.

I felt myself waken from a dream, or was it a nightmare? It would have been easier to finish the nightmare, but I have no control over that. I have no control over anything. I listen again, trying to work out what had awoken me. Was it Sophie? I tip my head to the side and listen, no noise from her room. I pause, still groggy from sleep, my head feels thick, I can hear noises from downstairs, a crash, I start, about to get up when I hear footsteps on the stairs. Heavy footsteps getting closer and closer, I pull the duvet up around me as James came stumbling into the bedroom.

"Isla," he slurs, "I love you; I'm sorry, I love you more than the world itself, you're going to leave me aren't you, that's what the study is for, you're going to get a high-falutin job and leave me. I just know it. You are out with someone aren't you," he let out in a rush, staring at me from the bedroom door.

Taken aback at this onslaught and barely awake, I'm about to say something when he continues, "I can't live without you, whatever I have done I didn't mean to, I can't live without you."

"I-I-I'm not leaving you," confused, I stutter, trying to get the words out as James, his voice getting higher and louder continues.

"I know you're going to leave me, why wouldn't you? I can't live without you. I'll kill myself if you try to leave me, you just see if I don't." He slurs, tears starting to roll down his face. "I'll shoot myself right out there, right on the lawn, right there," he points dramatically to the window. "I'll get the gun now, then see how you go about trying to sell this place and setting up with your new boyfriend, my blood will be on your hands. It will be all your fault."

I am worried about Sophie waking up, he's getting louder and louder, losing all sense of reality and I'm scared, this is a new tack, I don't know what to do.

"I am not going to leave you, James," I try pacifying him, speaking in soothing tones I don't feel. I am at a loss. This is beyond me.

"I will kill myself!" he repeats, the sobs getting louder. "Everyone lets me down, it's not my fault. I will kill myself, right out there," he points to the window again, "just there, right on the gravel, that'll serve everyone right." He lets out a sob. "I can't lose you; you're everything to me."

"James, I can't go on like this though, I…"

"I won't hurt you again, Isla, I love you."

"This isn't a life. This, this life, I can't go on like this, and neither can Sophie."

He drops onto the bed and cries like a baby, his whole body shuddering. I can do nothing but comfort him. I have no choice; I accept his apology fearful of his suicide threat.

A few months have passed, and James was feeling inordinately happy with himself, he had had a good few weeks at the shooting, the house had been full, and the money was flowing in faster than he knew where to hide it. He would need to organise a trip somewhere, he realised, his mate had suggested Singapore, now, if he could arrange to go out there that might be just the place, there were only so many places to hide money without people getting overly suspicious. That's the trouble nowadays; no one minds their own business.

He knew he had to control the money. To make sure Isla couldn't leave him. If she had money, then she would be able to leave him. He couldn't allow her to do that. Telling her he would commit suicide had worked better than he thought it ever could. That was a stroke of genius, he applauded himself, she'd been walking on eggshells ever since, doing whatever he wanted, whenever he wanted, he loved that. It made him feel powerful, it gave him a high. It was like a drug.

And what was all that crying about? The bitch had started to cry, actually cry, fuck, he liked to do it a certain way; it was the way he could stay hard. It wasn't his fault, after all a man had a right to that didn't he. Some girls just loved that. He saw that every time he went to the lap dance club. The girls there were all over him. Up there at the lap dance club the girls loved him. Money was power, these girls didn't make you feel bad. No, they made you feel on top of the world. Well, he needed to make more money, as much money as he could. She didn't need money, she had a house, and she had food. Besides, if she had money of her own, she would leave him, wouldn't she. No, he couldn't take that hurt. There's some hurt you just don't get over.

Jealousy. Jealousy makes you do crazy things. He couldn't help it. Seeing her talking to Cameron in the kitchen at the party, it was obvious he fancied her. No, he needed to ensure she thought there was no money. She couldn't leave him then, could she?

Power and control. That's what he had, and it made him feel so good.

Chapter 17

The weeks passed in a whir of mundane activities, one day milling into the next, before I knew it, months had passed. I'd hoped foolishly that James would have changed after his suicide threat. But no, the words I had said that night had come back to haunt me.

This isn't a life. This, this life, I can't go on like this, and neither can Sophie. James would remind me how traitorous I was. How everyone wanted my life. How lucky I was. How I wouldn't, and couldn't, survive without him. I've been at a loss that night; he'd threatened suicide. I couldn't live with that. Who could?

Since that night, I feel like I have turned into a robot. I focus on work and Sophie; I don't allow myself any time to think. To think is dangerous. Staying safe means not to poke the bear. I need to keep Sophie and I safe. My only joy in the day is being with her or escaping during the day for my run. I look forward to this so much, realising that with the right motivation, you can achieve anything. Escape is certainly a powerful motivator.

I'm feeling more isolated and fearful each day. I need to go for a run today more than ever. Today has been particularly stressful, the guys arrived back for breakfast with no warning at all and James is in a foul mood. Putting the coffee and tea on as soon as I can, I settle the guests with toast, tea, and coffee before making a start on cooking their breakfasts. James hovers around me, a black thunderous cloud enveloping me as he paces around the kitchen tutting whilst I cook under his watchful stare.

I try to focus my mind on the job at hand and not his stares. The room feels ominous, a dark oppressive cloud contrasts sharply with the bright surroundings. I work as quickly as I can, relieved as the sausages turn a delicious golden brown signalling their readiness. Hastily, I serve up the breakfasts for James to take through. Glancing at his hands as I pass over the plates I shudder. Dirt and blood spatters cover them from this morning. He hasn't bothered to wash his hands. I say nothing though, I could hear in my mind the reply, the high-pitched tone he defaulted to. No, safer not to poke the bear. Eyes averted; I continue in silence until he has taken the last of the plates through. Then, and only then, I know I can relax for a fraction whilst they eat their breakfasts.

The group has left, it will be later on today before the new arrivals come. Enjoying the peace, I load the last of the dishes into the dishwasher, letting my mind drift to my planned run later. I desperately need to run today. I'm still not fast, but I'm finding my legs are getting stronger, I can run for a little longer each time before I need a walk break. My asthma is sporadic, and I'm getting more reliant on my inhalers, the pollen is at an all-time high, but it's a small price to pay for being out. The mysterious bruises I'm getting are increasing in frequency. Long-sleeved t-shirts and running tights stop questions on the rare occasion I meet anyone.

I am going to let nothing stop me and I cannot wait until I head out today. My plan for today is to try for a slightly longer run. Thinking about the amount of work looming in front of me, I wonder how I can get through it all and still have time to run. Letting my mind drift to the long peaceful run, the open roads, the trees waving friendly branches, encouraging me along settles me a little, for weeks I have had a growing anxiety gnawing away at me.

Working as hard as I can to get the place ready for today's new arrivals, I fold the last of the towels neatly and place them on the bed. Standing back to appraise my work I am satisfied. I nod to myself, yes. Perfect. I check my watch. Time for a quick run. James won't be back till later and the guests aren't due till this evening. I can run and be back for when Sophie is back from playing with her new friend, Imogen, who is Alicia's daughter.

I make my way up to the bedroom and change as quickly as I can into my makeshift running gear. As I slip it on, I can feel myself changing; just like a police officer changes from being a regular human being as they put on a uniform, I change into someone else when I put on my running clothes. Who? Of that I am not sure, but someone far removed from me. For now, that is good enough for me.

127

Just as I am scooping my hair into a ponytail, my phone pings into life.

James, I need a list of food for the B&Bs.

I know it will be a bargain basement whatever he buys, but I proceed to reply with the items I need. I wonder how long it will be before he realises that his getting the shopping actually gives me time to run…

I look down at Lola, her tongue lolling out, lips parted as though in a smile and my heart melts, oh how lucky I am to have her.

"Come on, girl, we haven't got long," I rub her ear affectionately as she looks up at me, tail wagging in anticipation.

Finally, I get out the door. I feel drained, it won't be the long run I have hoped, but a small run is better than nothing, and a run will invigorate me. Running is my saving grace. It keeps me sane. It helps me cope. The trouble with that though is the problems are still there, waiting for me like an unwelcome relative as soon as I get back home. I longed for the fresh air, the trees waving as though new friends in greeting. I give myself a shake. This wouldn't do. It wasn't like me, however with each passing day I feel as though I am losing more and more of myself.

I have just enough time for the 10k around the block. Turning left out of the village, the road looms in front of me. The world displays how I feel, branches are grey, nothing but ragged limbs and a despondent sky mimicking exactly how I feel. I know I won't feel easier until I head down the forest path, all sights of the village gone. I run faster, the road starting to clear my head. I feel freer as the trees sweep by me, tall, majestic, welcoming me, listening to my thoughts, keeping my secrets safe high amongst their branches, the leaves at the top of the tree privy to my innermost thoughts.

You're so strong, people always say to me, that makes me feel worse, it brings home to me how weak I really feel. I am not this strong person; I am a person trying to survive. I am a coward. If I was strong, I would up and leave, if I was brainy, I would have worked out how to get Sophie and I out, to keep us safe. But I was still here, still in danger. How can I leave? I have no money of my own. I have to come up with a plan. A plan to stop this ever-decreasing circle I find us caught up in. Think girl, think. I repeat to myself as my feet pound the long winding narrow road, Lola's paws clattering delicately as she lollops alongside me, tongue lolling happily. Trying to formulate thoughts in my mind as second by second the hedges and trees lining the roadside wave me past. Lonesome friends.

As I get further out of the confines of the village, the sky above is darkening, it matches my innermost thoughts. As I gaze up, stride after stride, desperation swims through me, I want to be sucked up into the abyss, to keep running. To never stop, but I have to return home. My beautiful girl will be home from her friends very soon. I run on and on, oblivious of the usually welcoming trees. I run faster and faster, my mind in turmoil, I need a plan, I want, no, need to escape with Sophie, but how? How?

I need to work out the details. Nothing could be left to chance. Frustrated with going around in the same futile circle, I feel anxious. Every time I replay the possibilities of escape, I start right back at the beginning.

Truth is, with no money I am stuck. I have no friend that I can confide in. I am stuck with no means of escape. I am getting increasingly worried about our safety. I can see the anger, the hatred in James's eyes. I wonder what his plans are. What he is thinking. I dare not let my mind go there. I run on, the skies are darkening, the wind is rising, rain isn't far away. I pound along the dirt track alongside the lake. I need to run today, oblivious of the time pressures I decide to take in another lap of the lake adding another 1.2 miles. Lola lollops alongside, oblivious to the turmoil that is my mind.

I try to let the endorphins from running seep into me, it's not working today. Looking out across the lake, I watch as ducks and swans swim close to the edge. I run on, second lap done I turn off at the dirt crossroads and head up through the field to the gate. Puffing, I run up the hill the air thick, warning of a storm coming. Slipping through the gate and along the track I turn right through the arches. The patchwork of fields, stitched together with dry-stone dykes that usually lifted my mood have no effect today. The closer to the village I get, the more a sense of disparity fills me, stealing away any sense of joy from my run, every step closer to home.

No! Not home, I correct myself, every step is a step closer to that mausoleum of a house. *Nothing feels less like a home than that building,* I think, as I turn the corner, just one last run downhill and then back there. It's just a house. I long for a place I can call home. Hearing the rhythmic thump-thump of my feet hitting tarmac, I start to slow. I force myself to keep running. Running to that house in that village, the place that should have been so warm, so welcoming, the house and life that so many wished was theirs. I laugh. I can feel it bubble up inside me, hysterical and uncontrollable I laugh until I have to stop running. Tears are rolling down my cheeks and I grip my side which has a stitch now from laughing so hard.

"Oh my lord, Lola, I am going insane!"

Lola dances around my feet clearly thinking this is a fun game. I gather myself up. "Right, this is no good, lass, come on, there is nothing else for it; we have to go back at some point."

As I proceed to carry on back to the house, this time at a walk, my head is whirring. Money. Safety. Escape. Weak. Danger. Safety. Plan. The words whir uselessly around in my head. What can I do? There must be something.

The lights from the street are on now, as I run closer the shadows from the light dance playfully on the damp ground, light-hearted dancing, contrasting sharply to how I feel.

There must be some way to get out. The thought keeps going over and over in my head. Entering the driveway, I see the guests have already arrived.

The door beckons.

"Crap," I murmur quietly to Lola, "he's going to be hopping mad now, with any luck they might all be along in the guest living room and we can slip in, eh girl." Quietly I ease the back door open and slip in. Lola, eager to see if there is any food in her dish, bounds straight past and crashes through the kitchen door noisily. I can hear raucous laughter now emanating from there as I take off my running shoes and lay them neatly aside the door.

"Isla!" I hear James call. "Come through here, I have something for you!"

Baffled by this turn of events and James's cheery tone, I walk in.

Seven guys and James are all standing in the kitchen, surrounded by port, sloe gin and whiskey bottles in varying states of fullness.

"Well! What do you think?" James demands of me, with a strange look I know so well on his face.

And there, right in the middle of the kitchen, is my prison sentence.

An old beat-up treadmill.

"Well, with all your writing now, you will not be having time to go out running the roads, you can train whilst Sophie is in the house. I knew you'd love it; it was in Abigail's garage. I was down there today, and she was saying that she'd heard from everyone in the village that you were seen out running on the roads. She said it was just gathering dust in the garage. And when she told me how much she loved the dress you'd let her borrow, I said we could swap the dress for the treadmill."

I stare at the machine, sitting traitorously in the middle of the kitchen.

James turns to me; a triumphant smile covers his face. "Well, it's not as if you'll wear that dress again, and this will save you having to go out running on the roads now, won't it!"

He gives me a look, a look meant only for me. It's said with such apparent helpfulness, but I know exactly what he is saying:

See! You think you are so clever, but do you think I am going to let you go running outside where everyone can see you, you can't win against me!

I'm dumbfounded. I don't know what to say. My heart sinks, my one escape is gone…my beautiful dress is gone. Swapped for this. I feel like a prisoner, giving up her finery for bars. I can almost hear the clunk of the key in the jail door.

The guys are all looking at me expectantly, I know the response they want to hear.

"She's so happy she doesn't know what to say!"

"Well, that'll make a change."

"I should get my wife one if it keeps her that quiet!"

Jovial banter but it is all just a buzz in my ears, I couldn't believe it. However, I take a deep breath, fix a smile on my face, and I reply with the answer everyone wants to hear.

"Thank you, this is wonderful, very thoughtful." I look at the expectant faces, and as soon as the words fall from my lips, I see the smiles on their faces.

At least, someone is happy, I think.

The inane chatter continues for a bit, I ask how everyone is and obligingly let them take my new 'gift' through to its 'pride of place' in the living room which pleases them enormously. They are a kind bunch, but they have no idea I am breaking inside.

"Right boys, let's go through and chill for a bit, there's new sporting DVDs through there in the other side and a few crates of beer, let's get the party started! Isla has her new toy so let's give her peace," he ushers the guys out along to the guest room but comes back almost immediately.

"We're going out to Edinburgh tonight, taxi is coming at 6 for us, bring us a few snacks through, we won't be at the Chinese till 8 o'clock. The guys want to go to this lap dancing club they have heard of…" he breaks off watching my face intently. "It's not as if I suggested it, for flips sake, Isla, take that look off your face, you know this is my job."

I say nothing. What can I say? A lap dancing club? One rule for him and one rule for me. Meekly and pathetically, I say nothing. As usual. I hate myself.

"The shopping is over there, I got everything on your list, it took me ages to get it, it is really eating into my day."

"I can go shopping next time if you like, I really don't mind," I suggest hopefully. I am afraid now to venture out by myself, I know going out by myself brings the risk of being accused of having affairs, but I crave the sanctuary of busy shops. Busy shops where I feel safe, safe in the numbing anonymity of the shops surrounded by strangers, strangers who knew nothing of me.

"Remember to bring the snacks." James ignores my comment as he heads out the kitchen door with a fresh supply of beer.

Taking a deep breath, I let out a long sigh. *Snacks, right, get the guy's snacks, after all they have a hard evening of going out for dinner and partying ahead of them.* Opening the bags of shopping, I expect only the bare minimum; I'm not disappointed with my findings. He's not let me down. I take out the groceries, putting the sad little shop onto the counter. Getting only items off the list I had sent on his request, the only criteria apparently was price, the lowest value of everything, budget sausages which I know at least half the guys would make comments about, cheap bacon which would leak white all over the pan, discount mushrooms on their date which would cook black, battery eggs that would be pale, own brand beans that would be more sauce than beans, cheap white bread, all lie in front of me.

He had apparently found money in the tight budget for his snacks, prawn crackers, nuts, 4 large boxes of beer and some energy drinks for himself. I can no longer abide the sickly-sweet smell. Picking up his prawn crackers, I'm tempted to crush them in a brief moment of rebellion, but think better of it, there are no treats here for Sophie.

I have long grown tired of James's continued chant, I could repeat the last conversation word for word:

"At least I can eat those on the go, you are so lucky you can eat whatever you want," before continuing, *"I can only eat things that are easily digested, it's*

your fault that I had to get this treatment, I was doing okay on my diet until I met you, I'd kept on it for almost a month and then bang, your 21st and you put those pork pies out. You knew I like those and that put me right off my diet. Now look at me, I can't get the weight off."

This was another argument I could not win. The fact was he could eat whatever he wanted, it just took more time to prepare, but he chose not to, easier to eat the crumbly comfort food he desired. His voice would get higher and higher-pitched in reply until he had the last word, "I make sure you have plenty of meat though."

I dare not argue with him on this, the meat he referred to being the game he shot. I could see it far enough, any variety in my diet now came from eating bacon and eggs from the B&B, and that was wearing thin. The sight of this cheap bacon does not fill me with relish. Slowly, I stack away the meagre shopping before taking through the snacks for the guys. It's not their fault. They don't know the living hell I've found myself in. They are just here on holiday, and they deserve the best I can do.

Chapter 18

A few hours later, the guys are away on their jaunt up to Edinburgh in high spirits. I stand beside my treadmill gazing through immaculate windows, the rain which had been threatening, now lashes down, flattening the peony roses in the flower bed. Sophie, having been dropped off by Alicia earlier, joins me, slipping her small hand into mine as she leans against me. I can feel the warmth from her. I can't remember the last time we did anything as a family. I don't know how or when it had stopped, it had just petered out, like a leaky pot, drip, dripping away until nothing is left. I look across at the treadmill standing treacherously staring back at me, and I know that another bolt has just been put on the prison door.

It is imperative now to think of a plan. A way out. As I get more and more isolated, more afraid of James, the more the chance of escape reduces. I need a way out for us. Looking down at Sophie, I ruffle her hair.

"Come on, sweetheart, let's see if we can rustle up some hot chocolate before bed. I'm so glad you had such a lovely time with your new friends. It sounds so fun!"

"Yes, and they have a trampoline, and we had a steak on a BBQ for our dinner! A whole steak; you would have liked that, Mummy, Alicia says you can come next time."

"That sounds lovely!" I'm happy for Sophie, she needs security and routine in these early years, and I fear more is getting to her than she lets on. We set about making the hot chocolate. I know that after her bath, Sophie will sleep like a log tonight, thankfully.

It has been three full weeks now since the arrival of my 'gift'. I feel like I am losing myself more and more, where has the once bouncy, happy chatty and confident girl gone? I feel but a shell of myself, unable to make my own choices about anything, I feel so isolated, my friends have stopped messaging, I have given up on messaging them. I get no response back, the blank screen on my phone, the unanswered messages only serving to remind me how alone I now am. The only hope, the only thing that keeps me going is waiting on Tilly's longed-for message, she said she'd get in touch as soon as she'd finished unpacking.

Wandering over to the bay window next to my treadmill, I gaze out over the gravel drive and beyond to the winding road that had once offered me the sanctuary of running. The view from here filled me with joy once upon a time, how things change, now it saddens me. Saddens me to realise how much of a prisoner I have become. There is something more than a little unnerving about the amount of people willing to report back to James my every move. The control he has over people is frightening.

Looking out the window, I see the whole sky is dressed in a thick woolly jumper of drab grey. Drab, but somehow comforting. I open the window and lean out as far as I can, I take deep breath after deep breath, practically inhaling the sky. I feel myself drifting away, away to another place, another place that was safe. I feel jittery again. I can't settle. I need to go for a run, my head is spinning with thoughts I cannot as yet process properly. Little fragments of ideas are coming together but lack the glue that will hold them together. Sophie is asleep upstairs with Lola, and James in the pub with the guys. I can run now without being mocked.

Quietly, I slip upstairs and slip on my running wear before heading back to the 'gift'. Jumping on, I switch my running tracks sounds on, and as I slowly warm up, the steady thump-thump of my feet hitting the tread combines with the beat of the music. I pick up my stride as the music changes to a faster song and pace myself to run in time to the music. I feel my stress attacking me like a jujitsu professional. I increase the speed and pound away, mile after mile I see the monotonous grey counter click by. Numbers don't mean anything to me. I long for the open road, the green friendly trees, the patchwork fields, even when the clouds are dark, grey, dramatical, I had felt in sync, they had captured my mood. When I was outdoors, I felt at one with them. I pound harder and my mind is racing. I need a plan. What can I do? Safety. Sophie. Danger. Escape. Money. Spies. Fear.

The words are whirring around my mind, syncing with the whir of the treadmill belt racing under my feet. I run and run and as my mind races, my legs move faster. Finally, I slow down. My legs are weary, my brain wearier. I complete my cool down, click off, and head for the shower. It is now gone midnight. Quickly, I check my watch. 12.37pm. The boys could be back at any moment.

Quietly, I slip upstairs and enter the bedroom as silently as I can. I heave a small sigh of relief that he is not there. Heading into the bathroom for my shower, I'm grateful and feeling more than a little guilty to feel so relieved that he's still out. I turn the shower on full blast and undress as speedily as I can before sliding under the powerful jets. I feel a little more refreshed and more at one with myself after my run. I shower as quickly as I can, eager to slip into bed before he gets home. I have begun to dread his advances, guiltily lying stock-still in bed pretending to be asleep when he returns nightly from the pub. I often ask myself, *What kind of wife am I that cannot stand his advances?* Trying to avoid the inevitable pain that will ensue if he finds me awake.

Turning off the shower, I hear noises from the bedroom, the hairs stand up on my arms, he's back. I am not in luck tonight I realise; he must have come back whilst I was in the shower, having entered stealthily as a cat, I hadn't heard him. Towelling myself dry and prevaricating for as long as I can, in the hope he will fall asleep, I have no choice but to leave the sanctity of the bathroom. The warm steamy mist which had enveloped me, abandons me as quickly as snow melting from a dry-stone wall in spring sunshine.

I enter the bedroom, having wrapped a towel around me. He stands watching me, beady eyes not saying a word as self-consciously I slip off the towel before trying to get into bed.

"Wait a minute, have you seen yourself? You look like a boy; all that running, you are straight up and down." he mocks.

I blush bright red in humiliation. I cannot win. Either too fat or too thin.

"Who would want you now?" he taunts not ready to stop until I am in tears. "Here, come here, let me have a feel of that body, it's quite a sight that you are. Jeez Belize, have you seen your ribs, all poky bones." A lecherous grin spreads over his face as he lurches forward, heavily and drunkenly, towards me.

I try unsuccessfully to wrap the duvet around me. He hauls it off and rubs his sweaty calloused hands over my body; still hot from the shower, I shudder involuntarily, "humph," he lets out a grunt as he pushes his hand down between my legs. I can smell the drink on his breath. He is sweating profusely.

"Christ, it's hot in here," he says hauling the duvet off leaving me exposed, "a rickle of bones that's what I have for a wife, why can't you be more like Felicity. Now that's a body a man could do something with." Hauling me round to him, he heaves himself onto me.

I cannot move, he is dead weight on top of me. I know what is coming, willing it to be over I can't help the tears that spring to my eyes—no longer able to pretend, to make the noises he likes, the noises that would give me momentary peace. I feel floored.

"What are you crying for?" he roars in disgust.

"Shh, please," I plead. "You'll wake Sophie."

Hauling a pillow from behind me, he covers my face. I am panic-stricken. Is he going to kill me? I lie as still as I can, saying no more. He pushes harder and harder. I want to scream out, but fear stops me, the pillow a reminder.

"So, you can be quiet then?" he mocks as he rolls off, finished with me. "I'll have to remember that."

I say nothing. What have I done to deserve this? It must be something I have done, or something I have said for him to treat me like this. I try to understand what is happening but fail miserably. I lie staring at the moonlight, tears falling silently down my face soak into my pillow. Beside me James is snoring loudly, seemingly without a care in the world. I try again to piece together a plan. I cannot take much more of this. Escape. Help. Danger are my last thoughts as fitfully I drift off into a turmoil-filled sleep.

Chapter 19

I have turned into complete autopilot now. One day runs into the next and race day looming. I am missing my freedom to go out running on the roads. The work is getting unbearable now. I feel the harder I work, the more James piles onto me. I dare not complain. I dare not poke the bear. It is easier to keep the peace. I miss Zara dreadfully, but since that strange encounter in the kitchen, she hasn't returned any of my calls. Tilly sadly had had to cancel her meet-up with me and every time we try to reschedule, there is always something to stop us, until finally, she also stopped replying to my messages.

The very last text message I had received from her played over and over in my head as if on an old-fashioned cinema reel:

So sorry darling I would have loved so much to meet up, but James said you are intolerably busy! Anyway, I have almost finished organising everything after the move and am terribly excited for our get-together. I will be in touch next week when things settle a bit for you! And then we shall have such fun, us girls together! TTFN Tilly xxx

And that was it. No more text messages. I tried a couple of times but with no reply. I have to accept that she simply must not want to meet up. I can't understand it. I really had thought she genuinely wanted to meet up. I had been excited, not being from the village I had hoped there was a tiny shred of hope that she might not fall under the village spell. But no, it appears I am wrong.

I try to put the thought out of my mind and continue with my daily routines. Anything to keep my mind occupied. Days have become a dull routine of cooking, cleaning and working out on the treadmill, and most of all, keeping my head just under the parapet.

Three weeks later and the day has finally arrived. It is Sunday morning, the date etched in my mind has finally arrived. Today is race day. The day I have been training for. I try to quell the nerves that are gnawing at me, I try to tell myself I can get through today.

"It's only a race, an obstacle race, some people even do it for fun," I repeat to myself as a mantra but to no avail. I am beyond nervous, but I have to go through with it. James's repeated taunts that I could not do this float persistently in my head, stinging away like that persistent wasp.

The smoke from the challenges will stop you breathing properly, and if that doesn't, then the toughness of the obstacles will, he had derided.

I was continually the butt of his jokes. He enjoyed it and took every opportunity to poke fun at me.

Weak mind, weak body, that's you. No amount of running is going to help you in this race, you are just going to humiliate yourself and me too.

I fear he is right. I am going to humiliate myself today. And for what? Why did I need to go out? It had not been easy to get away today. James had arranged for us all to go together with Ivor, one of the guys from a local running club that had been in the pub and won the other ticket. Ivor apparently had been happy to drive us all, having stated that he was more likely to go ahead and do the event if he had others egging him on. I had been so looking forward to having the support of Sophie, wondering what she would make of her mum getting all wet and muddy, but at 1.43 am after getting home from the pub, James announced that he had a meeting in the morning and had to leave at 6am.

Waking early from a fitful sleep that morning, I realise I have two choices, cancel and give back all the sponsorship money I have managed to raise for the school, or find someone to look after Sophie whilst I run and then get back as quickly as I can. Frantically, I ring up Daisy's mum, Fran, on the off chance she might be able to look after Sophie, and as a parent on the parent council committee, I feel this is a good place to start. However, I feel more than a little guilty asking her, especially first thing in the morning. As the phone rings out, I begin to panic, maybe I should hang up. Maybe this is a sign, a sign I shouldn't do it. Before I can hang up, the phone is answered, a bright and breezy Fran answers. I explain the situation, apologising profusely for the early hour.

"Heh girl, stop worrying, I am always up early so don't worry about that and whilst I might think you are crazy doing that to raise money, we will be delighted to have Sophie to stay with us today, in fact send an overnight bag along with her so they can have a sleepover together! That will give you the night off. I'm sure after today, you'll want to celebrate with James!"

I babble back my gratitude and apologise yet again for the early phone call as she reiterates, "Oh, stop worrying, please! I always get up early to feed the animals, you should see the medley of animals we have here, it is like a zoo! I'll pop along now and collect her, James's away you say? I shall be 15 minutes, is that okay?"

I agree gratefully. It would have been an ideal excuse for me so say I couldn't do the race, that I'd to look after Sophie as James was unavailable to bring her with us. After all, I could easily stay at home and be humiliated here. However, I have sponsors and the school relying on me. I can't let them down; besides I had experienced an element of freedom on the back of this, the times I had been able to go out running on the road. It had been increasingly more difficult to find time to train even on the treadmill, dull and monotonous as it was, it still gave me a sense of something. I was not quite sure what that something was, but I knew I needed to strengthen myself in preparation for this day.

The workload seemed to increase daily, the constant stream of bed and breakfast guests, the writing articles, the studying, all meant trying to do the normal daily routine of B&B duties whilst ensuring Sophie was kept in a happy routine.

As soon as James left for shooting, I am up, it gives me a little more time to make a start on the cleaning and preparing for the day's activities now Sophie was on her summer holidays, studying or training fitted into whatever time I have left after clearing up after the guests when James leaves for the pub with the guys at night. Of late it seems that as soon as I have tidied up and left a room, by the time I come back the mess has magically reappeared, it is relentless. I yearn for some cleanliness that lasts for more than a few minutes of me leaving it.

However, today is the day. The day I had an opportunity to prove that I could accomplish something. Maybe, just maybe, James will be proud of me after all. As long as I didn't embarrass him.

Now here I stand. Fran had collected a sleepy Sophie and here I was by the gate in my running tights and an old t-shirt waiting for a lift. I had time not only to think, but for the nerves to really kick in. Sophie had been a little confused but eager to go to Daisy's, I knew she would have a lovely time there.

Hearing a car come up the small road beside our house, I watch as Ivor pulls into the drive. *Well, there's no going back now*, I think to myself as I pop as cheerful a smile as I can, raising my hand in a small wave of greeting.

"Well, you ready, lass?" He calls out cheerfully from his open window. "No James or Sophie? Well, if they are anything like my wife and kids, they'll be doing something far more Sunday-like than what we are doing! I am pretty sure my kids will be in the paddling pool; my wife will be having a nice cool G&T!" He laughs good-naturedly.

"Here, hop in," he says as he opens the door for me. I slip into the front passenger seat of his ancient Volvo, a comforting clean smell, polish and something that reminds me of my dad, Old Spice perhaps, washes over me as he chatters away, putting me at ease and admitting he was 'shitting bricks' as he put it when I asked him how he was feeling about today. "But we will give it a go, it's a day out, isn't it," he seems remarkably laidback.

Less than an hour later, we arrive at the venue. It all feels remarkably surreal, there is a hive of activity, music blaring, hundreds of people are milling around, excited chattering and laughing. I try to quell the anxiety gnawing at me as I look around.

"Well, Isla, this is it now! We shall be champions in our little world after this!" Ivor is the most chilled out person I have met in a long time and is easy company.

After signing some alarming looking accident waivers and having our race numbers pinned onto our t-shirts, we head to the start line for our allocated time slot. We are as ready as we were ever going to be. Arriving at the starting line I look about; I can see there is an incredible mix of people. Some look incredibly strong and fit, others out for a jolly. I can see one group clearly there for the fun, a hen party with the bride in full white wedding dress, complete with sash declaring to anyone who may have missed the wedding dress that she was, in fact, *The Bride*. The rest of the party with feather boas and pink ruffle skirts over the top of the shorts, t-shirts adorned with *Annie's wedding party* in pink writing. Another group appears to be from some sort of military bootcamp, dressed in fatigues with huge rucksacks. With the heat that was already building up, I could not help but admire their confidence.

Excitement starts to push its way in alongside the nerves. When we had arrived, I was so anxious I could do no more than follow along nervously, but now, having a little time to actually stop and take in my surroundings I felt connected. The atmosphere is electric. The air is buzzing with hundreds of people milling around. Energetic music plays out on loudspeakers around the grounds, which are adorned with flags and bunting. Hot dog vans, burger sellers and ice-cream vans all vie for business amongst the happy crowd. Nearer the start line though the atmosphere is a little different. I can hear fragments of conversation and judging from that, most people seem a little apprehensive.

"We made it this far so let's give it a go."

"This is going to be awesome fun."

"What's the worst that can happen."

"Holy cannoli, did you see obstacle 17?" alongside more competitive comments and good-natured bantering of each other, bets as to who would finish first, or indeed finish at all.

The fact that everyone else seemed to be a bag of mixed emotions helps me somewhat and I begin to relax a little. Ivor chatters away in the background, telling me his kids will tease him mercilessly if he jibs out on any of the obstacles. I begin to lose myself blissfully into the atmosphere.

The music is loud, and the warmup crew are enthusiastically getting us psyched up for the challenge.

"Are you ready!" The loudspeaker booms through the noisy crowd of spectators and participants, competing to be heard above the increasing noise of cheering crowds and music.

"Three…two…one…and you are off!" a loud siren wails, and we all surge forward.

"Come on, Isla, we have this!" Ivor calls out encouragingly as we head towards the first obstacle—the stinging nettles—thankfully, we get off lightly as the early groups have flattened most of them. I am oblivious to the few stings I get but hear a few mutterings of 'ouch, you bugger' coming from beside me. We pass this one relatively unscathed and head towards the next one. Panting slightly as we head up the hill, I wonder what we will encounter next. In the near distance, I can see people on all fours crawling along; as we near it, I can see it is a barbed wire framework, quite simple, I can see that you just have to get down and scuttle along keeping your back low so as to avoid the barbs. Not too bad I think as Ivor and I pace along. Ducking down low we crawl on all fours along the muddy grass under the wire. I hear Ivor, who is a much bigger rugby build getting caught on some of the barbs and so I call over to ask if he's okay.

"Aye lass, nothing worse than a bee sting!" We successfully manoeuvre this obstacle and appear triumphant at the other side.

"We have this girl!" he shouts over as we trot up the field in front. It is unlike the running on the road or the treadmill that I had been practising but my breathing is steadier than it has been in a while, and I am enjoying the freedom. I can understand now why people do this for fun, a little tremor of excitement and euphoria slips through me. As we head towards the next obstacle, I grow nervous. I can see exactly what it is. It is the one obstacle I fear most, it was not the smoke, it was the water trough, filled with iced water you have to swim under to get to the other side.

We join the group in front, waiting to be given the go-ahead. Waiting in the queue I am ready to bail. The euphoria I felt moments before is only a fleeting memory now. I look at Ivor who understands and replies comfortingly, "Don't worry, lass, you'll be fine. It's nowt more than some chilly water and I shall go first if you like, make sure there are no wee sprats to tangle you up!"

I nod hesitantly at him and appreciate his support. I look anxiously on at the water, listening to the excited squeals as people emerge victorious from the other side.

Ivor, at the head of the line now, lifts himself up onto the top of the trough and without delay nods me a quick wink and submerges himself, the icy water cascades over the side as his rugby build fills the tank, I hold my breath subconsciously, tick, tick, tick I hear in my mind as I watch for any sign of movement on the other side of the tough. Suddenly, he bursts triumphantly out the other side in a shower of icy water, shaking himself like a giant horse. "Nowt to it, Isla, and nae wee sprats either!" he gives me a wink.

I laugh despite myself. I have to do this. There was no going back. I take a deep breath and remind myself dead participants are not a good advert, if I get stuck, they'd surely know and pull me back out, so, with one last deep breath and an encouraging pat on the back I climb up onto the trough. I can see large chunks of ice floating in the dark water, however, without giving myself a chance to back out I slide into the trough. I gasp as the icy water hits me. Stealing all my resolve I dive under the icy water, battling the large chunks of ice.

Jesus H Roosevelt Christ! That wakes me out of my musings. I gasp as the freezing cold water hits me, a shock after the heat of the sun a few moments ago. I struggle and flap about, pushing my way down through the ice blockages, I swim my way down, pushing further until I can feel the bar I have to swim under, pushing as many ice blocks from me the sounds from above are eerie and muffled as I struggle to crawl under the bar.

Fear and panic grip me as I haul with both arms and feel myself slide through, blocks of ice swimming past me as I emerge onto the other side of the bar, my arms flail on the other side I feel for something, anything, to haul myself up, grabbling for the side, I am trying not to let the panic take hold, I turn myself around and get myself the right way up in order that I can get my feet onto the ground before giving as hard a push with my feet on the bottom as I can, I push off back up to the surface, as my head breaks into the air above I let out a gasp. I can hear a loud shriek of joy—I wasn't aware that it had come from me, but I hear cheers of support from around me. I break into a grin and accept the help of proffered arms to get me out.

I did it, I did it! I was ecstatic.

"See lass, nowt to it, you are a natural!" Ivor laughs before continuing, "Right, let's get to the next one, I wonder what hell they will have in store for us there!"

I follow suit and we head to the next obstacle; the wedding party left behind us in a pool of icy water. A long underground tunnel half-filled with water and stinking of rotten flesh waits for us. Yuck. Why am I doing this? I hesitate in my pace as I look on anxiously at the long dark tunnel, the thought of the pillow incident stabbing at my thoughts, I couldn't bear the thought of enclosed spaces anymore.

"Right Isla, nae worries here either," Ivor senses my hesitation. "If you like, just follow me, I'll make sure there are nae wee creepy-crawlies waiting in there for you!"

How could I not, with such support, there were people filling up behind us excited at the next challenge, so, watching Ivor disappear into the depths of the dark tunnel and not wanting to be too far behind I take a deep breath, close my eyes, and pretend it is not a tunnel. I crawl on all fours, the sloppy mud dragging at my limbs tiring them out. Inch by inch I crawl through. I can hear excited squeals coming from the tunnel behind me, I plough on until I could sense, rather than see, daylight. I open my eyes and see Ivor waiting at the end, hand held out ready to haul me up.

"Well done, lass, that's another yin done!"

A smile breaks out onto my face, I am doing this! I am actually here and doing this! My only regret is that Sophie and James are not here to share this with me. To be cheering on from the sides, waiting for us to finish.

We head down the hill only to be faced with electric fence wires dangling to shock us as we yelp our way through, inexplicably these help strengthen my resolve as we tackle this one.

"Just a few wee bee stings!" Ivor laughs as we are showered crazily by hose pipes as we make it through.

A signpost is in front; it states *Mile Six.*

"Mile SIX!" I say incredulously. No way. We have been running for hours and I am beat.

"Ah but what fun we are havin', lass, all the more time for you to enjoy yourself!"

I look at him like he's half-crazy, but I can see the humour in his face and laugh. "Well, that's one way of looking at it I guess!"

We run around the corner and come face to face with another sign.

Mile 7

"Mile 7? That wis a quick yin!" Ivor laughs. We head towards another obstacle, over and under logs, out the other side another sign welcomes us:

You have made it to Mile 8!

Well done! Keep going.

Obstacle after obstacle we make it, jumping off 30-foot-high bridges into water, using ropes to climb up oily slides, leaping over the Berlin Wall. I feel alive.

Heading down the last stretch, the signs are just a few hundred yards apart.

Mile 9.

Mile 10.

Mile 11.

Running towards the last obstacle, a particularly testing metal slide with only a rope to haul our exhausted bodies up, we pass the sign Mile 12 then another with a grinning face.

You made it, Tough Cookies!

Mile 13!

They are really playing with our minds, I realise as I look up at the gargantuan obstacle. Every part of my body screams *No! You've done enough*, but having come so far, I couldn't jib at the last, could I?

"Right lass, give it a good run, grab a hold of the rope and cling on for dear life, the lads at the top will haul you up, and dinnae worry, they winnae let go!" he enthuses as, after two attempts I begin to despair I will ever make this last obstacle.

"I'll go on ahead, and see if I can pull you up too, just do your best, lass, there's nae shame if you need to go aroond the side of it, lass," and with that, Ivor, much stronger than I, takes a leap and with what appears like effortless control, glides up the slide, hand over fist on the rope and appears at the top; swinging his leg over, he sits grinning astride the top, alongside a host of other rowdy successful challengers.

"Right Isla, your turn. You've got this, lass. Look how far you've come!"

I look up at the mammoth obstacle looming in front of me, with one last attempt I gather every bit of energy I can muster and throw myself up the slope, grabbing hold of the rope I cling on for grim death, it feels so high up here, I can hear the guys calling from the top.

"Come on, you can do it, just a little more and then we will have you!" anonymous voices call from the top. I feel my limbs burn under the strain, I am spent, nothing more to give, then I think of Sophie's face, the support she would have given me had she been here, of the people that had faith enough to sponsor me and finally of James. His taunting words. The repercussions if I embarrass him. I give one last push, haul myself up a little further until I feel many strong hands pull me the last little bit until I too am sat proudly astride the top of the very last obstacle.

"You did it, Isla! I told you that you could!" Ivor, still sitting astride the obstacle, gives me a matey punch on the arm. "Look at you now! Officially a Tough Cookie!"

We hear shouts and cheers from below reminding us that the finish is in sight, all that's left is to slide down to victory and run across the finish line. Sliding our legs around, we slip down the oily slide and land with a sloppy bump into a giant pool of mud, scrabbling about I come yet again to the surface, Ivor, stronger than I, is already up.

"Ready, Isla? The victory line awaits us!" To the tune of almighty cheer, we run to the finish line.

Ecstatic to have finished, I can't believe it. Elated does not begin to cover it. The toughest obstacle race known, and I actually finished it! A wave of emotion floods over me. I felt so alive, so different, I can't explain it. There is no medal to show, but pictures are taken and we are presented with an orange towelling headband to show our efforts.

The comradery of the entire participants of the race is amazing, I have never felt so alive, so connected before as I do when I'm running with everyone, mud spattered and grinning, such a mix of people with one goal in common, to finish. All sorts of people, all walks of life. Some highly competitive, others in fancy dress. I had seen Scooby Doo, Desperate Dan, Where's Wally, not to mention the bridal party, further on we had seen what must have been the entire wedding party complete with groom and best man. It's been tough, there's no doubt about that, and the signs definitely played with our minds.

"Well, lass, there might not have been a medal, but I don't think I'll ever take this headband off," Ivor laughs, "right, best get our muddy asses back home or the wife will eat me alive. I left her with both the wee ones today," he laughs good-naturedly. I listen to his chat all the way home, but my mind is drifting. I am so happy I completed today, as Ivor said there may not be a medal, but I had gained something better than that, and it wasn't the £357.63 I had raised for school funds, this had shown me that maybe I am capable of something. I had managed to do this. I and many others thought it was impossible. I am getting through my degree, and I have had a few of my articles published, with Mungo requesting again that I send in the recipe column, I had finally gathered up the courage to send that into the magazine. Maybe now James would be proud of me, see that I was capable, that I could help. Maybe if I earned a little more money for us then he would not have to work so hard.

Yes, that was it! If he were not working so hard then he would not be so tired all the time. I couldn't believe it. I have a solution. I can't wait to tell James. Oh, he is going to be so happy, I think jubilantly. My body aches from using muscles I didn't know existed. But it is worth it. Yes, I answer my previous question to myself. This is why I am doing this. Ivor breaks into my thoughts, and I turn my focus back to what he is saying.

"Here you are, back home! I wonder what James has got planned to celebrate your achievement, he was only saying the other day he'd have to think of something to mark the occasion. Anyway lass, it was a pleasure having your company today, maybe see you at our wee run club, it's really friendly and lots of lasses go too. Tuesday night 7.00pm, no need to book, just turn up, we meet at the village hall, bring your own water bottle!"

I thank him as I get out of the car stiffly; nice as it is for him to suggest running club, I can't see it happening. But maybe if James can see how hard I am trying to make extra money for us and he wasn't so tired, then maybe it would be okay? Maybe I would be able to go? Actually, when you come to think of it, he'd let me go today in the car with Ivor, hadn't he? Was this his way of saying he's changed? That he didn't mind me going out running? Maybe, just maybe, he's proud of me after all! I'm sure he would have come today if he could have, after all who wants to go to a boring meeting on a Sunday. He would have come if he could have. Yes, that was it! As I open the house door, I'm jubilant. I finished the race, I didn't let him down. I can't wait to tell James all about it.

Chapter 20

"James!" I call excitedly bursting through the back door and into the kitchen. Clattering through the kitchen door I look around. James, sitting by the window, has his back was to me, looking down the driveway watching Ivor drive off.

"Hi," before adding needlessly, "I'm home."

The excited expression on my face slips faster than butter drips off a hot scone as James rises from the seat he is sitting on; he turns to look at me. His face is thunderously dark.

"James, are you okay?" I ask hesitantly.

He says nothing. The deafening silence speaks louder than any words can.

The excitement I'd felt on the way home falls.

I look at him. I can't look away. I am a rabbit caught in a headlight. Transfixed. I want to move, to be anywhere but here.

Time stands still. Nothing but the tick, tock of the clock in the background marking the sound of time passing. All the words that have been bubbling up inside me, all the excitement I'd been ready to share, all the newfound thoughts I had that James would be happy and excited to share my news that I had completed today melt away, evaporating into a fine puff of smoke and disappear.

"You're home," he says eventually, the low tone of his voice doing nothing to betray his fury.

I open my mouth to say something, anything just to break through the thunderous atmosphere that is now surrounding the kitchen, but before I can say anything he turned his back to me and heads towards the door.

"I'm off to see some folks, make sure everything is ready for the new guys coming in tomorrow," and with that he's out the door.

I feel flat, deflated. I turn around and look about me, taking in my surroundings for the first time. The previously tidy kitchen is its usual customary mess. I don't even have the energy to cry.

Chapter 21

James slams the door of the pub behind him, all he had wanted was a few drinks. He couldn't take the 'good-humoured banter' any longer from them, as the drinks flowed in the pub, everyone had been talking about Isla's race. That's the thing with villages, he thought angrily, everyone knew everyone's business. He had enough of hearing from them how amazing Isla was having done that course, how they couldn't have done it, how *a little slip of a girl was* doing that course when he, a big man, wouldn't even attempt it, and she was out running it with another guy, well now how did he feel about that, her running with some fit guy. Then the comments about his size, okay so he had put on some weight, but that wasn't his fault, was it. Normally, he would have given as good as he got, but as the drinks flowed, his mood had got darker. He wanted to be home, home where he could drink in peace.

As he staggered along the few hundred yards of single-track road he could see his house loom, its huge presence outlining against the skyline. A sense of satisfaction overcame him. He was the man. The guys in the pubs were just talking crap. He hadn't seen them putting themselves up for the event, had he? No! Well, he was just the same, the same but better! He was smart. He was sensible. He couldn't risk breaking a leg on that course. That was only for idiots. He let out a snigger, yes, he was the man.

Stumbling across the gravel driveway, he opened the door, letting it ricochet noisily off the wall, and headed along the hallway to his office. He needed a drink, pulling open the cabinet he hauled out a large bottle of sloe gin and threw the cap off. Slopping some into a waiting glass, he took a long slug; as he felt the warm soothing liquid flow down his throat and seep into his body, he felt more relaxed. He poured another and took a long drink, letting the warm feeling ooze into him. That's better, he picked up the sloe gin bottle and emptied the remnants into his glass before tossing it into the bin, taking another long gulp as he consumed the contents. Reaching over to the cupboard, he pulled open the door to see if there was a spare. It was empty.

"Damned be, never anything where you want it," he muttered to himself and hauled himself out of the captain's chair. In search of another bottle, he headed out the office door and shuffled along the corridor, passing himself in the long mirror hanging in the hallway he stopped short. Looking at himself in the mirror, was that really him? He leant closer into the mirror before pulling back, looking himself up and down before settling at his waistline, the rolls of fat bulging that he tried to hide from himself were clearly visible for all to see. He stared for a moment, a wave of pity sweeping over him, he leant in unsteadily before lifting his top. He looked in disgust at the image staring back at him. Taunting him from the confines of the mirror.

"Look at you," he cried angrily into the dark. It's her fault. It's her fault you're so fat. She should have been helping you get fit; she does it for herself, doesn't she, and all the time you are getting fatter. It's her fault, she should be helping him, helping him with his meals but no, she's running all the time, making him feel bad about himself. *Out running all the time, she doesn't want me, she wants someone else.* Angrily, he pulled his top back over his bulging, flabby stomach. Punching the wall hard, as the mirror falls crashed to the floor, he went in search of the sloe gin.

Locating a bottle in the pantry, he pulled it out along with a box of pistachio nuts and headed back along the hallway to his office. Staggered in and sank heavily into a chair; *the treatment was meant to work—she was meant to make sure it did—after all, wasn't she the one with all the qualifications?* Unsteadily, he leant forward and poured himself another drink, throwing it back in one go before refilling it. No, she couldn't be allowed to go on like this. It was her fault. Hers and hers alone that he was like this. He rose from the chair which creaked and groaned as though sighing in relief as he staggered along the hall. And that's why I have to do what I'm about to do. He had to. He had no choice.

Chapter 22

I stand back to survey my work. I heard James come back earlier but decide to stay clear of him; when he is in this mood, there is no telling what could happen. Don't poke the bear, I remind myself time and time again as I carry on with the clearing up. My body protests with each and every move, every muscle aches from this afternoon's exertions. I plod away, knowing that the sooner I have this done, then the sooner I can stop for a rest. I hadn't bothered to stop earlier for a shower, choosing to get the jobs done first. When James is in this mood, I know from experience that it is safer to just carry on and get the work done. However, I can see progress. The dishes are done, the counters are clear, the floor is swept and washed yet again.

Finally, the place is starting to look tidy again. I step back to check my work. It all looks fine. I am beyond exhausted but feel a faint satisfaction seeing the neat and tidy order the kitchen is now back in.

I think back to the events of the day. A faint buzz of something is whirring around in my mind. Reminding me that, despite everything, I did it. *I completed the Tough Cookie.* No one can take that away from me. Reality hit though and somehow it doesn't feel like something I can be proud of anymore. I turn around and head to the kettle. My body feels heavy. My mind feels sad. A coffee is just what I need, then I'll head upstairs for a long hot shower. I flick the kettle and reach for the coffee jar just as I hear a noise at the kitchen door. Turning around I see James. His huge bulk filling the frame. His dark red brows furrowed, face puce as he stares at me.

"Who was that?" he demands, his voice menacingly low.

I start at his tone, my body and mind so weary I am having difficulty processing. "What do you mean?"

"I said who was that you were in the car with!" he roars this time, any attempt at keeping a low tone gone.

"In the car, you mean dropping me off? It was Ivor, you kn-kn…" I begin falteringly.

"Ivor? Who the hell is Ivor?" He spits.

"You know," I try again, "you had arranged it. We were all going to the race together…" I trail off.

"No. I didn't. You were going by yourself. Now I see what you have been planning all along. It makes perfect sense to me now. It's him isn't it. All along I thought it was that prat from the village that you were seeing. Do you think I am stupid? This sudden interest in running? I work all the hours I can and for what reason? So you can go sneaking off on a Sunday with another man?"

Confused at this sudden turn and fearful of the thunderous expression on James's face, I try again, valiantly, thinking this is all going so wrong. I have nothing to lose by replying back, do I?

"No, you came back with the raffle ticket, you won, you suggested I do the race, remember?"

"Are you trying to tell me what to think? To make me angry? He steps towards me. "Are you deliberately trying to provoke a fight? Look at me! Look at me!" His face inches from me the madness no one else sees; the side of him reserved only for me, his jowls wobble; his face puce with anger. Saliva splatters my face, close up I could see his teeth are actually going green, I shrink back."

"Well, answer me," he roars but before I can answer, he lunges forward and punches me full on in the stomach. Catching me off-guard, I gasp in pain, momentarily winded and shocked. I reach for the island unit for support, but before I have time to recover another strike hits, harder this time, sending me careering across the room. I land heavily on the hard floor, my aching muscles stiff with today's exertion are no use to me now. Winded and in shock, I try to get up, but a heavy kick, this time to my leg, causes me to scream out in pain, another blow, and another, they rain down on me, a heavy boot to my side.

I gasp as I try to protect my face, putting my arms up, shouting for him to stop so that I can explain, blow after blow come raining down, arms, legs, side, any part he can reach, his huge heavy work boots digging into my flesh, exhausted after today I could put up little fight. I can't not hear what he's saying. The pain that's shooting through me is unbearable. I can't remember pain like this, not ever, it's terrifying. I have only one thought in my head.

Survival. Sophie needs me. I have to survive.

The kicks have stopped, I realise. Please god, let him be gone I pray as I try to get a breath, a shallow, stuttering breath. Please. I looked up to see if he is gone. I can make out his bulk towering above me.

"Well, get up," he roars at me.

My head is swimming, I use drawers on the island unit as leverage to get up, I struggle to get a grip on the edge of the unit as I heave myself upright. I am in so much pain I do not know which part of my body hurts the most.

"Now you listen to me," James leans into me; he is inches from my face. "I make the money. I make the rules. Is that so difficult for your baby brain to understand? When I married you, you became mine and I am not going to let some shitbag lowlife, rugby bloke crawl all over you. Is it such a big thing to ask for me when I give you such a lovely life? A beautiful home? Is it? Why, everyone wants your life."

I could say nothing. The spray from his face lands on mine. His jowls are wobbling right in front of my face. His eyes, blacker than I have ever seen, are staring right into my soul. I am frozen in terror. His face is more purple than ever.

"Don't you ever, EVER, embarrass me like that again, you hear?" He leans forward into me, I grip the island unit for support, the black granite offering cold comfort. I feel his hot rancid breath on my face, but I am unable to move away. It is the last thing I feel before everything goes black.

Chapter 23

As I come to, I'm not sure how much later; the place is in darkness. Silence surrounds me. He must have gone out again. I feel my head is sore. Sticky blood where he has hit me, my head throbs. What to do now? I don't know how much longer I can go on. Pretending everything is okay…living life in fear.

I must have been on a high from the endorphins, I realise miserably, why would I think anything would change? Stiffly, I get up from the floor, glad Sophie is safe with her friends. I crawl upstairs and switch the shower on, stripping off my clothes, thick and crunchy now from dried mud and blood. I step into the shower. I wince as the water jets hit me, the water stinging every bit of my body, but I don't care. I wash myself trying unsuccessfully to lather as many bubbles from the cheap soap as I can, trying to hide my body. The bubbles traitorously let the black, red and blue skin shine through like a beacon. I lather and lather, but it does not work. I ache so much I don't know what to do, where to turn.

Giving up on the lather, I rinse off, dab myself dry with the rough towel and slip into the sheets, their cool surface a temporary respite for my bruised body. I lay there for a while trying to make sense of things, hard as I try, I cannot, I am beyond even tears. I lay as still as I can, trying to quiet my anxious mind. It was a beautiful clear night, the stars twinkling in the rich dark sky, a beautiful blanket covering the world. Such beauty, but how could such a beautiful night be witness to such violence? I pray James does not return home anytime soon. I do not even feel guilty at that thought tonight.

He couldn't help it, he thought morosely, the red mist had just come down. Drunk on gin and jealousy, he had watched her, lying there on the floor, not knowing what to do. The pent-up rage inside of him had been building, it wasn't his fault. No, he knew it was her fault. He turned, grabbed his car keys, and headed out the door. He needed a drive, to drive away from everything. From the taunts of the guys in the pub. From his friends. From her. From himself.

Slipping into the driver's seat of the Range Rover oblivious to the stench, he put the key in the ignition before turning the key and jammed his foot against the accelerator, with a screech of tyres and gravel spewing, he spun the vehicle around and headed down the road.

Chapter 24

Waking the next morning, I can barely move. I open my eyes and look out the open curtains. It is daylight. I look to my side, and I'm glad James is already away, or perhaps he didn't come home? I'm unsure. The only thing I do know is the pain I am feeling. I ache more than I have ever ached before. The new guys will be here early today. I think it is 11 o'clock. Did that sound right? I can't think, my head hurts so much, I try to put on a pair of jeans, but my legs hurt so much I can't even get them on.

I hunt around for some loose clothes, slipping them on. I think these are better, however as I walk, the constant brushing of the fabric screams at me, everything hurts, I go back and change again, this time I choose a thick pair of tights and a flippy skirt. My arm is swollen and bruised; it aches so much as I struggle to put the tights on. Finally, and beyond caring what I look like, I make my way down the stairs and set about trying to organise last-minute things for the new guests arriving. I skip breakfast and make coffee after coffee for myself in an attempt to keep myself going. I am on my fifth coffee of the morning. I am exhausted physically and emotionally after yesterday; the pain is making me very nauseous.

I check my watch. 10.38. I am about to make another coffee when I hear a knock at the door. The guests, I realise in alarm. Have I done everything? Too late I comprehend as the door opens before I get there and in rush two liver and white spaniels, tails wagging, tongues lolling they hurtle past me, followed by a posse of green camouflaged guests.

"Isla," I hear them whoop.

I'm so relieved to see Ralph and his group coming in through the door, instead of a brand-new lot of guys, they are one of the nicest groups and so easy-going.

"How are you! So sorry about Moss and Rusty, they must be keen to see you too! *Down boys,*" Ralph mock-scolds his two dogs as they bound about

157

excitedly. He adores his dogs and treats them better than royalty. "We have been waiting for this trip since last year. I thought it would never come, but here we are! Can you believe it's been a year already!"

"It's great to be back, oh I can't wait for your Belly Buster breakfast, it's the thought of that that's been keeping me going!"

"Have you made any of those scones again, they are the only reason I come up here!"

The guys babble on excitedly. The sounds of excited chatter mingle together to become one long clamour, as one by one they rush forward to give me big hugs in welcome. I try unsuccessfully not to recoil in pain.

"Here let me have a look at you," Jake relinquishes me from the tight bear hug and looks at me. I see his face turn from jovial to one of aghast.

"Isla! What on earth have you done to yourself?"

I try desperately to think of something, unprepared this time, my brain is sludgy and stubbornly refuses to think. I feel my mouth open and close like a fish, when through the fog of my brain words appear from the distance.

"She was at a Tough Cookie competition yesterday, it's an obstacle race."

I have not noticed James coming up the rear of the group.

"Did you hurt yourself yesterday?" James asks me innocently, and without waiting for an answer he continues, "Right guys, you know where the rooms are, go and get yourself sorted and we'll head out for the first of today's lot as soon as we have had coffee and a bite to eat."

Never let yourself panic, he reminded himself. *Stay calm. Don't give anything away*. He had trained himself over the years. *Keep the image*.

The guys disappear, I can hear them clatter about the hallway, one by one going upstairs to claim stakes on the rooms that would be home to them for the next few days. James stays with me as I struggle to make coffee. The only sound is the kettle boiling, and cups clinking until a few moments later I hear footsteps come along the hall towards us.

"Don't say a word," James hisses.

I pull out the tin of scones and put them on a tray as one by one the guys filter into the kitchen.

"We just thought you might need a hand taking the cups through, James, poor Isla shouldn't be lifting anything with that arm, you don't need to wait upon us, we are quite capable you know, lass, why not take a wee seat, put your feet up for once."

"I was just saying that just now. She needs to take it easy." The words slide out of James's mouth as smooth as butter, an instant look of caring crosses his face. How does he do that? I wonder briefly as I busy myself with the cups.

"Here, let me help you with that," Jake offers as he sees me struggle with the coffee.

"You really should go and get that arm checked out, maybe pop along to A&E. It looks very badly bruised and swollen? Isla?" He looks at me gently. Questioningly.

"Oh, she doesn't like a fuss, isn't that right?" James interrupts. He looks over at me. I hear the tone in his voice, it's a statement, not a question. I say nothing.

"Right guys, on you go, we'll have this through in the other room, give Isla some peace," James commands.

"Well, if you don't want to go to A&E, if you like I can look at your arm?" Jake asks me, ignoring the coffee for now, a kindness in his voice I have not heard in a very long time. "I've dealt with a few injuries like that over the years in my line of work. How did you manage it?"

"She fell, didn't you," James replies before I could think of an excuse. "Off one of the obstacles."

"Ah. Okay. And you finished the race too? Even with your arm like that? You must be a tough wee thing." Jake smiles kindly as he heads towards me.

James steps in front of him, "Actually, I was just saying before you guys came in that I thought it might be best if she goes to the hospital to see about it. If you could take the milk through?" The look on his face is insistent.

Jake pauses, looking up at James before returning a look at me. "Probably best to get it checked out though, Mo, A&E can be busy these days. Hope you get on okay," he adds, giving me a further look up and down. I see him pause as he looks at my legs before looking back up at my face, a curious look on his face. I try to pull my skirt down a little further, I hadn't thought of the bruises showing through. I say nothing.

"And Isla, don't be fussing about us guys, remember, we are more capable than we look, you know!" And with that he turns back to the other guests, organising them with military precision, he ushers them out, one by one handing them trays of coffee, tea, milk, sugar and the scones, they filter out along the hallway giving me 'peace and quiet'. James comes up to my side, I stand stock-still knowing how much he will have hated that encounter.

"Well," he hisses, his tone so quiet I can barely hear him. "Did you wear that on purpose? I suppose you had better go to the hospital now since you're finished with the coffee or I'll never hear the end of it, but I warn you, one word out of line and you know what will happen, you make sure that you say that happened at the race, okay?" His face is inches from mine. I nod, unable to say anything, my mouth has gone dry, my tongue stuck to the roof of my mouth.

Three hours later and I'm sitting in front of a kind nurse, my stomach gives out a protesting growl. I had simply not been able to face anything. The choice of bacon and eggs, no matter how merrily they sizzled in the pan, turn my stomach. How many ways and times could I eat that? The delicious tasting scones make me wheeze. It's easier to skip breakfast, I just can't face bacon or eggs anymore. I'm beginning to resent the fact this is what I'm allowed to eat, day after day, to eat bed and breakfast food but James would get the best, all made for him he insisted, because he decided he couldn't eat these, for whatever reason I'm unaware, no mention is ever made of the array of takeaway meals or dinners out he has with the guests There appears to be an unwritten rule that can never be mentioned. I choose yet again not to poke the bear.

I'm dragged back to reality with the nurse repeating herself to me.

"Those are some quite nasty bruises there; how did you say you got them again?" Gently, the nurse examines me, I am on my guard, she has asked me the same questions in different ways four times now.

I repeat my story.

"Ok love," she says, as she looks down at my legs, I can tell she has noticed the bruising on the rest of me, big ugly bruises, old bruises on top of new ones vying for top place shining through my tights.

"Right love, I just need to check something with the doctor, I won't be a moment, just sit here quietly." She gives me a gentle motherly pat on the shoulder as she disappears into the corridor.

I sit there quietly as directed. It's peaceful here, so calming against the turmoil of my head. Outside I hear the chaos that is the accident and emergency department—sirens outside, buzzers calling overworked doctors, shouts from patients, anxious and in pain. The door opens and a kindly but harassed-looking doctor comes in.

"Well now, what have we got here?"

I repeat my stock answer. I know what they are thinking but I have rehearsed my speech well. There is nothing they can do if I say nothing.

Secrets keep you safe. Secrets keep you alive.

He looks at me then discreetly back at the nurse. Neither of them say anything, they do not need to, I know what they are thinking.

The doctor lets out a small sigh before quietly saying to me, "Well, there's severe bruising, I suspect there may be a small fracture but it's unlikely that will show up on X-ray yet, and you did all this at an obstacle race? That was quite some event." He looks at me questioningly.

I try to put a cheery smile on my face, at odds with how I feel. "Oh well, what we do for fun…" I falter off as the doctor looks at me kindly, his face open, his eyes gently questioning.

I say nothing and the doctor gives an almost imperceptible nod to me before continuing, "So, I'll leave you with the nurse to finish off, it is difficult to tell with the swelling, but with that much we can't do much more than support it and treat the pain until the swelling goes down, now, if you feel it gets worse then you'll need to come back before we send you an appointment."

He gives me a kindly smile, but I can feel his frustration. He knows he is helpless to stop anything, he leaves the room and the nurse chats away to me. I know she wants me to open up to her, but I cannot. The repercussions would just be too great. She straps up my arm.

"There, that'll help with the swelling whilst giving you a bit of support," she says adding, "now, as the doctor says if you have any problems, anything at all…then just come back, we are here, remember we don't close…"

She is so kind, I want to tell her everything, I want to open up, but I cannot. James has already warned me, so I say nothing. I know I shall not be back.

"Well? What did they say?" James barks at me as soon as I walk into the house.

I am exhausted and not ready to face him. I am so tired, freezing cold, and frightened all in equal measures. Hesitantly, I repeat what the doctor told me.

"You'd better make sure that no one finds out what you have driven me to. How do you think that makes me feel? You'd better post something on that Facebook page of yours, and I want to see exactly what you are writing."

I look at him, my foggy brain trying to process what he wants me to say.

"Go!" He roars. "Go do it now!"

I flee and get my laptop. Unsure of what is coming, I bring it to him and log on to Facebook.

"Right, you had better make this good because by goddam if anyone, and I mean anyone, gets wind of this, you know what will happen; if anyone finds out you will lose everything. I will lose my gun licence and then you will have no job, no income, we will lose the house. Sophie will have nowhere to live," he growls at me as I type out what he wants me to say. I feel nauseated, not just with the pain, but with the lies he is making me say, so jovial sounding and at such odds with the way I am feeling inside.

OMG! I had such fun today at the Tough Cookie but look what happened when I fell off the Berlin Wall obstacle and managed to injure my arm! But I still managed to complete the race! I am bruised from head to foot, but it was worth it to finish! All that for a headband!

"Right, now can you add a photo to that?" James checks, I nod, everything feels surreal. "Ok," he continues, "take one showing your arm and add that to the post."

I do as he says and show him.

"Ok," he confirms, "post that, don't you tell a soul, you hear me? Not your dad, not your friend and definitely not the police, understood? And if I hear anything, anything at all..." he warns, but he need not say any more. I understand. I understand all too well. I sigh and start to clear away the debris that had been left in the kitchen for me.

I hear a gentle tap at the kitchen door, and I jump as a soft kindly voice drifts into the kitchen.

"Isla?"

I turn around to see Jake at the door, a look of concern on his face.

"Hope you don't mind, or think I am interfering, but..." he trails off hesitantly. "Well, I just wanted to check on you and see if you're okay? You look like you took quite a bashing from the…" he pauses before adding firmly, "the race," and looks at me directly this time.

He knows, I realise. *He knows.*

Oh, how I want to shout out, to cry for help, but what if he can't help? What if James had got to him, what if it was a trap? It's not worth the risk. I couldn't escape, not just yet anyway…

I bluster my way through a response, touched that he cares, but unsure if he has been sent by him. I can't trust anyone, I realise sadly as I watch Jake retreat out of the kitchen.

I work away tidying up the kitchen until I hear the back door slam, signalling the start of a night of drinking for the boys. I am beyond exhausted and in so much pain. I call it a night and curl up on the sofa with Sophie and Lola. Having heard my 'adventures' repeatedly, they are content to cuddle up on the sofa. Sophie, once assured that my arm is fine, protects it from Lola, thumb contentedly in her mouth sitting next to me, as Lola, wrapped in a tight ball, sits next to her, both oblivious to the reality of what is going on.

It is with relief later that evening I finally head to bed. I try to make sense of the events. It is clear James doesn't love me. How could love turn to hate, because surely there must have been love at one point? I pad softly over the thick cream carpet in the bedroom to the French windows of the balcony overlooking the garden. I'm glad he's still out with the guys; it is their last night so I know they'll be out a long time.

The promise of tomorrow hangs thickly in the air. The fear of what it may bring. Still disbelieving of his attitude, I'm at a loss. It must be a mistake—surely, I hadn't married this monster—was it his depression making a big resurgence? Was that it? Or maybe, he simply wants me away? Why not just divorce me? Would that not be easier? But I realise with a sinking feeling he won't ask me for a divorce, I know he won't, that's too clean for him, he wants everything, he won't share, he wants all the control, to share is not enough for him, in his mind I am nothing more than an object, a device, a mechanism, just a gadget to be used for his end purpose. Success, power, and money; a little ant in his workshop.

I could run away, but I have nothing, nothing to support Sophie with, nothing to take care of her, no money, no friends to rely on, nowhere to go. The threats of his suicide taunt me, a constant tirade in my ear. I wish my dad was here, but he's headed off to New Zealand to tour both the North and South Islands for the winter and is currently without any communication and would be like that for several months in what is fondly referred to as the Wop Wops. I am glad for him, he deserves it, and the weather is so good for his arthritis, but I miss him so much.

And as for telling friends, they are further and further from me. I can't understand why no one is replying back to me, but would they even believe me if I could actually confide in someone? Believe in me when even I don't know if I can believe the truth? Can I really think James would want me dead? Am I being paranoid? Crazy? It's just that I would feel better with a plan. My head is fuzzy, I wander over to the bedside cabinet and take a drink of water from the glass, yuck it tastes weird I think as I put it down, I would go get a fresh one, but my body feels heavy. Then nothing.

Chapter 25

He was getting addicted to the high but the thrill he was getting from that was diminishing, the accidents when he was able to hurt her had not been enough, he craved the first high he had gotten when he had cleverly managed to drop the mell hammer on her foot, to see her hobble around powerless filled him with amusement. The 'accidents' had become more inventive, he got off on that but now he needed more, he needed to be more elaborate, he needed to feed his habit, but how? He needed to get more creative. The planning was giving him a high, knowing what was coming, knowing she was unaware was exciting to him, it was easy for him to get away with, under the cover of marriage, in his own house, no one suspected. He was safe. He could do what he wanted.

Exciting to him, he could portray two lives, two existences. Play two roles.

It felt good to dominate and humiliate her, he had begun to resent the achievements she was getting, she was gaining notoriety in the magazines, the guys were all impressed with her, she had completed that Tough Cookie and he hated her for that. That was a man's race. She had humiliated him with that. He looked at her, feeling himself rising at her boyish form he pushed the reason to the back of his mind. He had to leave no evidence. Nothing that could be linked back to him. The sexual release he felt after, when he was on his own was sustaining him between occurrences. It gave him great power, he felt in control, it gave him a thrill, it filled him with excitement to plan what he could do next, how far he could go. He felt intimate with her when she was unconscious. Having her prone body at his disposal. When she was prone, she was only a pretty body.

As he looked on at her motionless body, he reached down and pulled out his phone, clicking it onto camera he took a photo, standing back he grinned, oh this was perfect, moving her arm just enough so he could see her naked body perfectly he clicked again, walking around the bed, he clicked and the flash went off. Shit, he thought, waiting with bated breath for her to rouse, nothing, not even a blink of her eye to show she had been disturbed, he took another shot, nothing, on a high and gaining confidence he arranged her for a perfect close-up as she lay motionless and oblivious.

Now for the good stuff, he couldn't believe how easy this was, flipping her back over onto her front; her arm caught the bedside table with a thwack, he paused holding his breath to see if she would awaken this time, he could hear his own heart beating, nothing, he gave her a prod, nothing, he tried again, harder this time, nothing; she was out cold, he felt a surge of amusement flow through him, rearranging her again he was exhilarated, oh this was more like it, too prudish she is, well, take this Miss high and mighty, as he pulled at her, taking photo after photo, just knowing he had these pictures gave him a feeling of power. She was completely oblivious of this, he could look at them whenever he wanted now, do whatever he wanted with them. She was his, and who was she to say what he could and could not do.

Anger rose inside him, it had been waiting to erupt for a long time, he always had to be so damn careful around her, oh he was able to have the odd 'accident' but not really show her who was boss. Self-pity mixed with loathing for her welled up within him and he took a kick at her leg, no movement from her, he grinned to himself, oh this was good, he took another kick this time on her shins, he couldn't believe it, lying there motionless she could not look up at him with those big brown doe eyes, he gave one last snap, checked the photos had been saved then with a smirk to himself he slipped the phone back into his pocket.

Yes, he thought to himself. *He was the man. He was in control. He had the power. Looking at her like this, he could easily forget about her achievements. She was weak. Seeing her quiet, unmoving body, he felt another surge of power, another thrill run through him. He liked her like this. He took his phone back out from his pocket and took another photograph, arranging her just as he liked it; she was just an object now, he could use her as he wished, he took another close-up of her, giving out a lecherous grin, his lips spread across his yellow teeth, pleased with himself. Moments later, after satisfying himself, with a quick check the photographs were there, he left the room leaving her exposed without any blankets.*

Chapter 26

I can't take much more of this. Every day is worse than the previous. I spend my days thinking how I could improve things. What would make life better here? What could I do to make things stop? I am losing options. I have one last hope. I think back as momentarily, a kind face flits across my mind. A kind face that gives me hope. A chance. But dare I? Should I take him up on his offer?

The door slams open, jarring the kind face from my mind as James storms straight into the kitchen, wet mud dripping its sticky foulness onto the clean floor. I try to ignore the dark atmosphere that has descended. I feel uneasy and unsure what to say when I turn around. James, gun in hand, is staring straight at me unspeaking.

I look at the gun, wet and mucky in his hand. "Would you like me to get the gun cleaning kit for you?" I ask hesitantly.

"What for," he sneers. "It'll be fine. You think hardworking people like me have had time over the centuries to clean guns—just a little bit of wet and muck."

"I just thought…" I add falteringly.

"What! What did you think?" he scoffs. "You've suddenly become an expert in guns now! Your new man been telling you how to do things, has he."

"James, there is no one else for me."

"Aye, so you'd like me to believe," he retorted as his lips folded across his green-tinged teeth.

No one. I think to myself, *absolutely no one, why would I want to put myself through this again?* I think to myself. I do not know how much more of this I am able to take. A friendly face emerges in my mind's eye as a wave of despondency flows through me. I push the thought of the friendly face out of my mind, how could I see him? I just couldn't though, could I?

"Get me a beer," he interrupts me as he turns to take the shotgun through to the gun cupboard, mud trailing in his wake. It has been raining all day, but James wanted the pub and nothing, but nothing, would get in the way of that. I was glad though. James going out to the pub would at least give me a little peace and quiet. Doors slamming behind him and knowing he would be in a bad mood with the weather interrupting the day's shooting, I ran through wondering how I could keep the peace. I enter the kitchen just as he was popping the lid off a bottle of Stella, seeing me enter, he growls at me, a dark flash crossing his eyes.

"I work 24 hours a day, 7 days a week and what do I get?" he slugs back half the bottle in one go before continuing, "a wife that won't clean the dam house!"

My heart sinks as I enter the kitchen. I keep my eyes focussed straight on James, the repetition of these words ringing in my ears was all too familiar, now a common mantra for him. I knew he would not settle till he went to the pub. I recognise the all too familiar signs…

What more could I do? I'd cleaned the house, the washing is done, the guestrooms are all clean and tidy, the table set ready for the morning and Sophie is playing quietly in her room and his tea is prepared ready just the way he likes it. I can feel my heart thumping…scanning the room, my heart sinks; the room I'd spent hours cleaning is in uproar, muddy, wet footprints he'd trailed into the house, wet coats and equally wet dogs lying on the floor, flasks and lunchboxes strewn on the counter—James glances over to the island unit next to where I am now standing, his dinner laid ready, an hour ago it was beautiful but now I would have to reheat.

My heart beats rapidly as he crosses the floor in three giant steps, towering above me, his eyes, once warm and affectionate during our engagement now glacier cold and dark as the devils waistcoat—the eyes reserved only for me he pushes his face close to mine, and, in tones so hushed I can barely make out he spits, "And what the hell is that muck I'm meant to eat?"

I tremble fearing the hushed tones, hushed tones were worse than any volume he could create.

Hesitantly, I reply, "Venison casserole, it's beautifully tender…" I trail off hesitantly, "I thought it would warm you up after being out all day."

"Did you now!" he sneers. "You expected me to eat that?" One sweep of his arm sends the dish I had spent hours preparing hurtling across the island unit and into the wall leaving a miniature sea of brown in its wake, venison and gravy slip down the wall, shards of broken crockery splintering across the floor. There is deathly silence. Seconds pass that feels like minutes, I can hear the giant clock on the wall tick. James says nothing. I feel his eyes on me. I can't look at him.

I am frozen to the spot. I know I must get a cloth and start to clean the mess before anyone comes. Rabbit caught in a headlight, I am still unable to move. James raises his arm again, this time he catches me, a clean blow to the jaw, caught unawares. I reel in pain, try to steady myself but slip on the congealing mess and land on the floor amongst the shards of crockery and venison.

"Get this mess cleaned up before I get back," he hisses again, "the guys are already in the pub, thank god that they don't have to see this mess."

With another kick for good measure, he turns on his heel and heads off to the pub.

Winded, I take a breath, the kick had landed heavily on my leg. With difficulty, I raise myself up, hearing the front door slam. I breathe a sigh, at least he would be out till the early hours. *Thankfully, I haven't landed on the broken fragments of crockery, the kick has caught my leg, the bruises are getting harder and harder to hide, these would be hidden, a small mercy,* I think to myself as I set about cleaning up the mess before checking everything is ready for the morning.

Rinsing the cloth again, I pause for a moment as the poisonous truth bleeds clarity into my mind. I have married a monster. An idea had been formulating in my head for a while now and tomorrow would be the day I plan to make a start on the idea. I have been having serious doubts though about going through with it. I now know I want, no, I need to, and everything has to go smoothly. I am pinning my hopes on tomorrow. I take a deep breath and set about my tasks with renewed vigour. Yes, I know this is what I have to do. And tomorrow is the day.

Chapter 27

"Mummy! I woke up early. I'm a big girl now!"

I turn to see Sophie's cheery face at her bedroom door.

"Well, good morning, sweetheart, you certainly are! I think we need a super-duper breakfast for such a grown-up girl this morning. What do you think?"

Lola dashes past us tail wagging and tongue lolling.

"Oooh, Lola, you woke up too, she was under my covers, Mummy, all night! Yes, please, I think boiled eggs and soldiers today."

Relieved that she could be so happy with eggs and toast, I reply, "I think that sounds lovely," as Sophie slips her hand into mine and we descend the stairs towards the kitchen.

"Ooh Mummy, the men have been really messy this morning!" Sophie gasps as I look on, too stunned to say anything. Inwardly, I sigh looking about me, just one day it would be nice to come down to how I had left it the night before, however, today is not that day. This morning the kitchen is strewn with dirty dishes, floor filthy, my favourite cup smashed in the sink.

"Oh dear, I think a mini whirlwind must have come through here!" I try to joke although I feel anything but laughing. "Right McGinty, do you think you could put on the toast ready for your soldiers and I shall get those eggs on to boil!" I suggest, distracting her in order to clear the broken cup discreetly before she can see. I'll have to work quickly after dropping Sophie off at school to get this all cleared up. I dread to think what would happen if it wasn't right when he got back with the guests, and I still have to get Sophie ready for school. Thankfully, the distraction works and she happily gets the bread, sliding it into the toaster all the while talking away to Lola explaining how to make soldiers for eggs.

It doesn't seem like two minutes later when I am walking back from dropping Sophie at school. I feel my legs slowing. The summer holidays have long gone, and we are heading into October, the days getting shorter, the nights longer. The thought of going back to the house fills me with dread. I need a run, but I've a busy day in front of me. I desperately crave the welcome open roads, the branches of the trees waving as if in welcome the fresh air. The peace. It is not to be. I dare not risk going out anymore, not now that I have my 'gift'. I know the consequences of going out. He never fails to remind me. However, today is the day of my plan. First things first, I need to clean the kitchen. I push open the once welcoming door and head into the kitchen to collect a bucket, filling it with warm water. I put in a squeeze of cheap cleaning liquid and pick up the cloth, wincing in pain as I kneel down to scrub the floor.

I wonder if I'll have time to write today, the next article is due. I used to love writing; I remember when I used to write my diary. All my thoughts, feelings, hopes and dreams. A record of my life not to be forgotten…so honest and true…I had written a diary since I was a child, but when I realised he was reading my diary the pleasure evaporated, he didn't like honesty, I found that out, he made sure I did, reminding me that "I had a roof over my head and food on my table, a million woman would kill to have your life, ungrateful that's what you are, ungrateful." I could still feel the slap, the pain that had stabbed at me.

I had to lie then; the diary stopped. I couldn't do that anymore. Now when I write I would write whatever he wanted to read, in my diary, in the sporting magazine—I feel a fraud. Writing lie after lie a happy idyllic life was portrayed. I have no choice. Every day I remind myself, *Don't poke the bear*.

As I get up stiffly from cleaning the floor, fresh bruises rich red mixed with purple on top of older bruises now turning yellow green. The thought of a kindly face flashes briefly across my mind. Conversations I had had with him, times he has been to the house, someone of no threat to James. Someone I could speak to when he came shooting. And now, I have finally plucked up the courage to see him later that day. I am wracked with nerves; can I really go through with this? My phone pings into life, quickly I answer it. I glance about me, all is quiet.

"Hi, thank you for calling me back, I wasn't sure if you would."

I could picture the kindly eyes on the other end of the phone. I felt inextricably embarrassed, unsure whether I could go through with this.

Outside in the hall, James leans in closer so he could hear better.

"No, I can't make it until after that…" There is a pause as she listens to the person on the other end of the phone.

Chapter 28

A red mist boiled up within James as he listened, his mind in turmoil.

"I need to go back for Sophie at school. Yes, 1 o'clock works for me."

There was a silence, he craned his neck.

"Brilliant, I'll see you then."

He heard her put down the phone as he quietly slipped back along the hall. *She mustn't know I've heard her. I have to know who she's seeing.* James's mind was in turmoil.

I have to know. I knew she was seeing someone. I must find out who, but how? He couldn't follow her; she would recognise the car. He paced up and down his office for a bit. Yes, he grinned to himself in realisation. *Yes. That's what I can do.* His lips parted in a smirk before returning to fold across his green-tinged teeth as a plan formed. He picked up his phone and punched in a number.

As it nears 1 pm, my stomach is in turmoil, rising and falling. My breathing is rapid and shallow. I couldn't help my thoughts of hope turning to fear. Could I really go through with this? Be so disloyal? What would be the retaliation, for retaliation there would be for sure if James found out? I need to be extra cautious I thought as I busy myself with my work, guiltily rushing through my jobs.

"You seem in a hurry today!"

I start as James appears behind me. I haven't heard him come up behind me. For a big man, he moves stealthily.

"Are you going somewhere?" He queries, more of a statement than a question.

"Umm," I stutter, caught unawares and off-guard. "I need to collect a book from the library," I improvise feebly.

"Oh, that's okay, I can collect that for you. I am going that way anyway," James volunteers, "save you rushing." There is a slight smirk playing across his lips as he looks intently at me, his eyes scrutinising my face.

Fear forms a knot in my stomach.

"Umm thank you but I err…" I stutter, faltering off, "I need to collect my prescription too and they need to see me in person."

James looks me up and down before grunting something unintelligible and turning on his heel.

I have a sick feel running through me, but the thought of the kind face flashes in front of me tightening my resolve.

Yes, this is it. This is what you need to do. I tell myself, more reassuringly than I feel. *I need to see him again. He will know what to do. He has always taken care of me.*

James watched from his office as she scuttled out the door. Who does she think she's kidding? Library and prescription, his ass! He would know soon enough where she was going. One phone call was all it took, and he'd have all the answers.

Chapter 29

It hasn't been easy to get away today, but I have just enough time, my resolve is faltering. What if he finds out? I can't take much more of this. I know I have reached the end of my tether. I am emotionally and physically scarred, and I know it's passing through to Sophie, however much I try to hide it. How much she knows though I don't know. Pulling up my car, I take a deep breath, turn the car engine off and pull up the handbrake. I release my seatbelt. It's now or never. I open the car door and a few short minutes later, I'm opening the door to him.

"Isla It's been far too long! I'm so glad you came. I wasn't sure if you actually would," he says. I feel a fleeting moment of guilt as the door closes behind us; however, as I look up into his kindly face, I know I have done the right thing. I had thought for a moment James knew but I'd got away with it, for now. *Yes,* I think, *this feels right and as I sit down in the chair, the closeness of him in the chair is comforting as his familiarity fills me with confidence.* He smiles over at me and as he starts to talk, his voice gentle and soothing, I know I am doing the right thing.

Chapter 30

James stormed about; the red mist that had descended before had arrived back with vengeance. Where was she? He had to find her. What time was it anyway, he slugged back another sloe gin, the heat flaming his anger on its way down. His mind went back to the conversation he had had earlier. It hadn't taken much with Leith. One phone call. He'd gotten him to follow her from the village and tell him where she had gone. Who she was seeing. His answers later that day had infuriated him.

"What! I knew I couldn't trust the bitch. She's where? Right, thanks mate, yeah see you down the pub tonight. I owe you one," and with that he snapped off his phone.

"Well, that was easy! Free pint out of James? That's unheard of! Just tell him what he wants to hear, and I get some peace. Peace and a free pint!" He chuckled to himself. "I'm not going to waste my time following Isla; she's a dog's life but I'm not getting involved in their mess, he's one crazy geezer and I for one am not getting on the wrong side of him!" And with that, Leith settled back into his chair where he hadn't moved all morning.

James paced about, mad as a bear in a trap. He knew it. Knew it all along. She'd been seeing someone else on him, he had to have it out with her, he would show her, he got up and refilling his glass carelessly, he threw it back in one before lurching unsteadily to the door. He had to have it out with her once and for all.

As I finish my last job of the night, I think wearily of my bed, how I long to pull the blankets over me and sink into oblivion. I lean over to pick up the last load of washing.

"WHERE WERE YOU TODAY?" James bellows, startling me from my thoughts.

"Wh-Wh-what do you mean?" I stutter.

"Today! Today! Where were you!" he demands, his voice rising a pitch in his hysteria, grabbing my arm and pinching it painfully, he presses his face up against mine. I can see the whites of his eyes threaded through with red veins, his stained teeth against mine, foul-smelling water droplets spraying me as he demands to know.

"You're hiding something!"

Yes, I'm hiding something. I'm hiding how afraid I am of you, afraid of my own husband. When I talk to you, you roar and shout. Your voice goes higher and higher and there's always payback for me and I can't deal with it. I can't cope. I wish I could say the words out loud, but I can't.

I wish I could disappear into a big hole. I can't tell him the truth, not about where I had been today. I can't admit it, I just can't. The shame is just too great, I hang my head and try to wriggle free from James's grasp as shame washes over me tinged with fear.

James's face is inches from mine as he spits.

"You were seen! Hah yes! You didn't expect that, did you! You thought you'd get away with it, didn't you trotting off to see your man whilst I work hard to provide you with your every need."

"I-I-I don't understand," I whimper pathetically trying to pull away. He grips harder.

"I said *You. Were. Seen*!" he thunders, repeating each word slowly.

Say anything, say anything but the truth, I tell myself, come on, think…

Fearing he would waken Sophie, I try to appease him but before I could say anything he interjects, "Who were you seeing? You were seen at Berwick train station. Who were you seeing?"

Caught off-guard, I hesitate, confused, I hadn't been anywhere near Berwick, let alone a train station.

James raged on as I shrink back. "You'll pay for this. Who do you think you are? You little trollop, after everything I do for you. You'll pay for this."

The alcohol merging with his fury he couldn't contain himself. "Oh yes you will pay for this," he mutters as the spray lands on my face. As James pulls away, the pupils of his eyes are midnight dark, the furrows on his brows deep as he swings his fist back and lands me a full blow in the stomach.

Winded and caught unawares, I fall to the floor. I try to gather my breath.

"This isn't the end of it," James mutters to me, his eyes flash cold and hard as he turns on his heel. "I'll see you later."

Looking around me, I'm grateful to be alone. I can't take much more of this I realise, trying to stop tears from flowing. I pull myself up, feeling nauseous. I ache all over. Guilt floods through me as memories of the afternoon flood back. I thought I could trust him. I thought after everything he had said before that I would be safe, that it would be okay to see him. How did he find out? With my heart fit to break, I pull myself up from the floor.

Chapter 31

"That showed her," James murmured out loud as he paced the guest living room with alcohol in hand. He had done the right thing having her followed. Thought she was cleverer than him, did she? If he hadn't had her followed, then he would never have known she had been to Berwick. She said Duns so she must be seeing someone, after all why would she lie if not for another man. Oh yes, he was definitely the clever one. Who does she think she is? She thinks she's so smart. He let out a long low chuckle. Oh, he would get her and get her good, so he would.

Reaching for the sloe gin, he slopped more into his glass, letting the sticky sweet liquid run freely and slowly down watching intently, spellbound he watched the red liquid pool at the base of the glass. The trickle reminds him of something. But what? James let his mind wander. Through the alcohol fog it came to him. Blood. Yes. Blood. He took a long drink finishing the contents in one and let a slow smile spread across his lips before letting it slowly spread across his face. That's it, he thought, that's it, that's how he can make sure she never leaves him, she can't leave him if she is dead, better dead than leaving him.

At last, I have finished the last of my jobs for the night. It's been a long and exhausting day, and I'm at the end of my tether. *One mercy though,* I think to myself, at least I'd heard James go out. I feel guilty at not feeling guilty. *I'm going mad,* I think to myself, but I'm just grateful to have the house to myself with Sophie. I head upstairs, my sore and tired legs protesting at every step. Pausing at Sophie's room, I pop my head around to see if she's sleeping. Against the small nightlight I see her cuddled tightly with her teddy bear; thumb firmly in mouth with Lola curled up in a neat ball at the end of the bed. I let out a small

178

sigh of relief and enjoy the warm glow that always spreads over me when I see she's content.

I head to my room, slipping into bed too exhausted physically and emotionally from the day to even shower. The events of the day begin to replay in my mind like a bad rerun of a movie.

I'd pinned all my hopes on today. His kind face flashes before my eyes. I can remember word for word everything he had said. I take a deep steadying breath, trying to calm myself. I feel foolish. Foolish and hurt. Mostly I feel hurt.

"Isla, come in, how lovely to see you." Smiling over at me, he gestures for me to sit down. "What can I do for you today?"

I look over at my doctor, he's the only person left who can help me. He knows James. He would know what to do, so slowly I open up to him.

"Isla, hold on a minute," he pauses as he looks up at me peering over the rim of his glasses. A slight hesitation before my doctor is back to his usual jovial self as he booms, "Well, I can't write anything down for obvious reasons." A big hearty chuckle follows.

It was then with a resounding thump I'd realised he's won. I hadn't realised until that very moment It was time to be honest with myself. To face the cold hard truth.

The shock hit me like a physical blow.

How weak I have become. It was a drip, drip effect.

One by one, my friends had become alienated from me. I have no one. No one to turn to.

His control had quietly and stealthily won, like a panther waiting on its prey; all the patience of the world waiting to pounce at exactly the right moment.

I have no money, no friends, he has fabricated my 'perfect' life to others, the illusion he has created, the power he's built. I can't even go to the police. He's drinking buddies with them. Now, even my doctor is with him. The people who are meant to keep me safe are turning against me. He has connections everywhere. I am entirely in his hands, and he knows it. I sigh deep within, trying not to let the tears welling up in me flow out.

I slip out of bed, defeated.

Who was I and where have I gone?

The once-strong happy-go-lucky girl. It all makes sense now. The drip-drip effect had mushroomed. There is no escape, no secret stash of cash, no friend I can confide in. I am all alone. I am exhausted and drained from continually defending myself, the emotional attacks worse than the physical attacks—when it's physical there is an end to it, with emotional they are a constant presence, always with me, they control every word I say, every look I give, they control the actions in my day, my running, the clothes I wear, there is no escape—ever, I have no career, no money of my own, no friends, no family, no trust and no confidence. I am trapped. There is no escape. Ever.

The barriers he's built to prevent escape are not physical. Fear is my prison, locals my guards. I can stand no more of this but what can I do? He has won, I realise. I can't control my own thoughts or actions anymore. I've reached the lowest of the low, I am pathetic. I take a deep gulp trying to stop the tears that are ever present now from flowing. I failed. I'm so afraid, afraid for myself. Afraid for Sophie. I feel like I've been kicked in the stomach. I realise there is no one I can confide in.

Who would believe me?

Yes. The penny has well and truly dropped—he has won—he has succeeded in getting everyone to believe the persona he put on. The carefully constructed image that is his public face. But I cannot give in. I have to fight, after all it was I who had chosen him, agreed to marry him and live happily ever after, but Sophie hadn't, she had not chosen to live in this world of abuse. She had no choice. An innocent amongst danger. No, I must fight to save both our lives.

I have to come up with a plan.

As the darkness envelops me, I try to clear my mind. To think. The soft dark air stroking me gently, featherlight wisps tickle at my skin. I let it wash over me, taking deep steadying breaths. I wish I could evaporate into the darkness, merge with this soft dark peaceful night.

Where am I, I wonder, and where have I gone? I think to myself again as I have begun to wonder this more and more of late. I let out a shaky, stuttering gasp of air. I know I am still here. Still here in the deep sanctity of my being. I am still here. Just as day follows night, I have too, I must believe there is some part of me left. Some part of my former being. With every minute that passes, life is getting harder. Days keep passing, nothing changes, the world keeps spinning, time moves forward relentlessly, weeks, months, years are passing whilst I try to make sense of things. No, not to make sense, just to survive I realise. To survive and keep Sophie safe.

I try to look ahead to a better future, a safe future, but the truth I realise is the road ahead has grown darker, impossible to envisage. I feel so alone, so lost, I am desperate for something, anything that will show me a way, show me a way to keep us safe, to provide Sophie with a future, to get our lives back. I feel despair, despair that there is no glimmer of light to show me the path, to provide a beacon. I know I have to keep trying, keep trying to find that glimmer of light, the path to follow, I need to keep dreaming, keep hoping, without hope I have nothing so that's what I must do every second, every minute of every day, for Sophie, I have not given up and I won't, I cannot. I gaze out of the window into the darkness, the deep pitch black that only the countryside could provide, no stars are out tonight. In the darkness I could disappear. A thought begins to roll around, nudging an idea, it grows force, tap, tapping away at me before thrusting forward.

Darkness. Disappear. Of course! We could be gone, and he would never notice if we went when he was off to the pub. We couldn't go during the day, there were always people in the village watching, spying, reporting, then there were the guests to see to. But in the dark envelopes of the night, he would never realise we were gone. He would come home drunk from the pub, fall into bed and with any luck he may not notice until the morning.

But in the dark with Sophie, we could be going on an adventure. I feel fear. Fear deep-seated in the very core of me, on the other hand, I can also feel the bubble of excitement that comes with the ecstasy of an idea, not daring yet to imagine its complications. Just for the moment, the idea is enough. Executing it would be another matter. For now, it gives me hope. Much-needed hope in desperate times.

Chapter 32

"Isla!" I hear a shout and I recognise the voice. It is Cameron, he pulls up in the car alongside me as I am about to head into the school playground for Sophie. It is the last day of term before the October break, and I need to get back quickly to get scones made for the group returning. I daren't speak for longer than a brief moment because everywhere there are eyes.

"Isla, how are you doing, it's been ages since we saw you guys! You must come over for drinks during the holidays."

I nod a brief acknowledgement and murmur that would be lovely, but I am in a tearing hurry.

"Oh, not to worry, I just don't see much of you and only the other day I was saying we must get you guys up!"

I could feel James's eyes on me. Wherever I went, I could feel them on me, imagining what he would say or do if a gaze lingered a fraction too long at me or I uttered a single word to anyone, it didn't matter where I was. It could be anywhere from the school gates to the checkout at the local supermarket. There was no place to relax, I was always on high alert…Fear was my prison guard. I needed no walls, no doors and no padlocks. It hadn't always been like that of course it hadn't. After all, who would willingly marry a monster?

I think back to the days when we'd met. I had felt so young. So carefree. I loved my job, my life, we had travelled, USA, NZ, he'd proposed in Barbados. Looking back, I realised it had all been on my pound. I hadn't thought much about it. If I had, I wouldn't have cared. Young, innocent and in love, what was mine was his. I was in a good job, with great prospects and had no cares in the world. Oh, the innocence of youth. Oh, how things change.

I shake myself back to reality. I can't be seen talking to Cameron, the outcome doesn't bear thinking about; trying to think of an excuse, I am rescued by Sophie as she bounds out of the school gate and across the tiny, tarmacked area to where I'm standing.

"Mummy, we had such fun! We watched a movie and had popcorn. I sat next to Daisy, and we got to draw pictures too!" I turn from Cameron and bend down to scoop her up in a big hug before setting her down again.

"Well, that sounds like such a lovely day, sweetheart, and you got to eat popcorn when you watched your film, well, now that sounds like a perfect afternoon at school to me." I smile as I look down at Sophie, her small hand slipped into mine, school bag hanging loosely on her small shoulders, curly blonde hair bobbing along in the breeze. With Lola by our side, we look like any normal happy family heading home after the last day of school. I turn back to face Cameron and give him a small smile and a shrug hoping he would see I couldn't stay.

"Okay, Isla, I understand, always busy-busy with a youngster, you'll be off having some fun in the holidays, young Missy, won't you," he turns around addressing Sophie kindly. "She's the spitting image of you, Isla!"

"What are we doing for our holidays, Mummy?" Sophie asks before I can reply to Cameron.

Taken off-guard, I think of the back-to-back and same day B&B changeovers that James has rammed into the October break, there would be no respite, every day would be full. I think desperately how I can give Sophie some fun.

I put it off for now, I'll think of something that we could do, maybe make a tent in the garden if the weather is kind, if not maybe in her bedroom.

"We'll have a think and see what we could do, hunny, but for now I say we race home and bake some scones together!"

We say our goodbyes to Cameron, and he drives off.

"Oooh yes—I bet I can beat you!" Sophie calls, slipping her hand out of mine and racing along in front of me. Lola joins in the fun lolloped alongside Sophie as I pace along behind, enjoying the breeze on my face as I jog along the few hundred yards to the house. It brings back memories of running outside I realise with a pang. A sadness envelopes me with the realisation I'll be unlikely to run outside again. What a simple thing and yet I am too much of a coward to go against James.

Coward or survivalist.

"I beat you, Mummy!" Sophie squeals delightedly hopping around from one foot to the other inside the gravel driveway.

"Yes, you did, hunny, you did indeed! Right, I think that means you get to be the chief baker and I'll be your sous chef!"

Sophie giggles, "Come on, Mummy, Lola says she needs a hot scone!"

"Does she indeed! You know, I think you are right!" looking down at Lola, her big brown eyes, tongue lolling she always looked like she was smiling. Just as we push open the door, I hear gravel crunching on the driveway, a car followed by another, the guys are back early from their shoot.

"Mummy?" Sophie whispers in a small, worried tone as she slips in behind me, her arms about my waist, burrowing her head into my back.

"It's okay, hunny, it's just the guys home that's all. We'll have to be super quick getting those scones on, won't we!"

"Mummy, I think Lola wants to see my new maths homework. It was fun."

"Yes hunny, of course," I say distractedly, as I look over at James, now in the doorframe, red curls dancing wildly, black eyes thunderous, the look on his face is unmistakable and an icy waterfall of fear trickles through me. Sophie disappears to the safety of upstairs with Lola, any sign of the carefree child of a few moments ago vanished. I wash my hands as James slams into the house ahead of the guys.

"What have you been up to, why isn't the coffee ready and where are the goddamn scones, you're fucking hopeless you know that," he threw at me as he stomped inside, welly-clad feet hitting the floor.

Say anything, anything but the truth. You can't say you were speaking with Cameron and got delayed. So, I reply in the only way I can. The only way that won't poke the bear.

"I-I was just about to make them with Sophie," I stutter. "I didn't think you'd be back as quick."

"Don't give me your excuses," he hisses under his breath, "you must've been gassing with someone, the guys are coming in."

There is a strange feeling in the air that perplexes me.

"Is everything okay, how did the shoot go?" I ask hesitantly.

James ignores me and heads back out to the guys.

"Right James," I hear voices from the hall, "let's get squared up then."

I am confused, the guys are meant to be in until tomorrow morning. I wonder what has happened but choose to stay quiet. To stay quiet is safer. I keep myself busy making pots of tea and coffee, I pull out flour, salt, milk, baking powder and cheese ready to make a quick batch of scones, trying to distract myself from the growing noise from the hallway. I am glad Sophie is safely upstairs.

"Don't even bother with the scones now, you're too late." I start as James appears soundlessly into the kitchen. "You can't even get that right; hurry up and get that coffee on; the guys are annoyed now, is that too much to ask?"

I work as quickly as I can as James leaves the room again, black air the only trace he has been as I hastily pull together mugs, tea and coffee onto trays. The kettle boils and I make large pots of coffee and tea. I am about to lift the trays and take them through to the guest living room when I hear heated exchanges from the hallway.

"That's not what we agreed; it was all included," one of the guys says.

"There's a bank machine in the next town, I'll stay here with your guns till you come back," I hear James reply testily and coldly.

Louder voices float along the hall, I hear scraps of the conversation.

"You're a conman."

"Well, you were happy enough to pull the trigger, now you pay for what you have shot."

"You'll not hear the last of this."

I stay put in the kitchen. Doors slam. Moments later a screech of tyres and a crunching of gravel.

I hear nothing else.

Twenty minutes later and crunching of gravel and the front door opens. Footsteps on the hallway. More heated exchanges, noises from upstairs as the group gathers their things, footsteps on the stairs. The door opens to the kitchen, I jump.

"Bye lass, it was lovely to meet you, thanks for a lovely breakfast and looking after us so well."

"Shame your husband is a conman though," I hear from the back.

"Sorry about that, Isla, you take care of you and that darling little girl of yours, that's us away now; sorry we aren't staying another night; after all we have to get back."

"Oh, okay," I stammer, unaware of what to say, "lovely to have met you all, drive safely," I add, bewildered at this sudden change of events.

I hear the rest of the guys all troop out, muttering something under their breaths. I can hear James from further up the hallway, he is on the phone and shouting at someone.

I feel an icy trickle of fear return to run through me. This isn't good. I know it's not. Whatever has happened, I know I need to keep a low profile. I slip upstairs to check Sophie is okay. Opening the door a little, I see her lying on the floor, chatting contentedly to Lola.

"And this is what a ten-pence coin looks like." Sophie is drawing in her colouring book with Lola stretched out on the floor beside her. "Mummy!" she calls delightedly when she sees me standing at the door. "We've been working with money at school. Mr Toledo says if we can, can we practise in the holidays with real pennies at home?"

"I shall have a look and see what I can find, sweetheart, but in the meantime, I think you are doing a really lovely job of drawing pennies for Lola!" *Fat chance of finding any coins around here,* I think to myself, *the best I could hope for would be a few odd foreign coins left over from one of James's trips abroad.*

I can hear his voice getting higher and higher at the end of the phone downstairs, not a good sign, he was pacing dramatically up and down the hallway.

"I wonder if Lola would like to hear a story from one of your CDs?" I say louder than needed in an attempt to drown out the noise from downstairs.

"Oh yes, I think she would like to hear the one about the princess, Mummy, the one where the princess needs to find a new castle!" She jumps up to rummage in her bookcase. "Here it is!" She pulls the CD from an old pink CD case filled with audio storybooks. I settle down next to her, trying to quiet the noise from downstairs, a trickle of fear nibbling away at me. I can sense all is not well and experience has taught me that I would experience his wrath.

Chapter 33

James paces the room, scooping up the remains of the bottle of sloe gin he was consuming. Everything was falling apart, he took another slug from the bottle and continued pacing around the guest living room, recalling the phone conversation earlier; as soon as the guys had gone, he'd phoned his friend in the police force.

"Yeah, he's saying I was poaching his ground…no, no, that's not right, it was my ground…yeah, I'm sure, well, of course the deer ran, that's what they do, so yes it might have run onto someone else's ground and then the guys threw a hissy fit and said I was a crook…*Me*, yeah *me*…what do you mean…No, I'm not, well, yeah there was a bit of other stuff they weren't happy with…they shot a 6-pointer; they need to pay more for that…I know it's not the first time…Heh, you get your fair share for turning a blind eye, money is the same colour wherever it comes from…okay. Fine…You sure? Well, these guys reckon they are gonna sue me, said they are going to report me to trading standards or some such shit…you sure I won't lose my licence…okay, right, get back to me when you hear for sure, okay, cheers. I'll drop you one soon, okay?" And with that he hung up the phone.

Then came the call he had been dreading, inside information that he was indeed going to be investigated, it sounded a lot more shit than he could handle. He paced faster, he needed a release. He felt like he was losing control. It was slipping, slipping out of his grasp.

He reached for the sloe gin bottle and slopped some into a waiting glass. He took a deep drink, draining the glass in one, stopping to refill the glass, he took another long swig.

"I have the family name to live up to!" he spat out to the silent room, resentment building in him. *It's not easy trying to live up to a family name that's been in the Borders for hundreds of years. Everyone looked up to us. But then,* he let out a wailing sob, *when my parents abandoned me, everything went wrong.*

I can't risk her leaving me. No, No, I can't risk that. If she leaves me, it would be the end. How could he continue, no, he couldn't let her destroy everything, if she left him like his parents had left him, he'd have nothing.

People would laugh at him, just like they laugh at him for gaining weight again. Just like teasing him saying it was her that was the power behind the business, but he took the guys out, didn't he? He knew how to shoot. All she did was cook and clean and write. Refilling the glass for the third time, he watched as the thick, red, liquid slid down the outside of the glass. He paused for a moment. Reminded of his plan, he felt a comfort. Oh no, he would not let her leave him.

It was humiliating to him. Why didn't people see he'd have people coming without that? The guys wanted the pub and nights out at the strip club, lap dancing. Up there, he felt powerful. The girls wanted him, they came over and paid him attention. That's what he needed. He needed the attention of those girls. They knew him, they knew how to help him, he would sort her tomorrow but for now he knew what he needed.

Just one more night wouldn't make any difference; he consoled himself as he grabbed another bottle of sloe gin and headed along the corridor, he could hear her in the kitchen; ignoring her, he grabbed his keys and stumbled out to the car. Yes, one more night wouldn't make any difference; a night in Edinburgh at the finest lap dancing club would sort him out.

Chapter 34

I hear the back door slam, the screech of tyres on gravel, the roar of the engine as James drives at speed out the driveway. I feel myself release a shaky breath, he is out, and judging by the mood he was in, he wouldn't be back until late. I set about looking for something to make for our dinner. The air feels thick, dark, ominous, and I don't know what to do. I know the mood he's in. There will be repercussions for me. Just what, I don't know and don't dare to contemplate.

I pull some pasta out of the cupboard, before heading to the fridge and pull out some milk alongside some cheese. *Just for a change*, I think to myself. *Macaroni and cheese*, as I hear Sophie come through from the hallway.

"Mummy, Mr Toledo said I was really good with money, and the more I practise, the better I am going to get."

"Well, Mr Toledo is right, sweetie, and I saw you do a really good picture for Lola so I think she will be good too!"

"He said I'm really good at drawing pictures too."

I am glad she has a good teacher that has such an impact on her. Pulling out the pans, I listen to her sitting up at the table chattering away to Lola quite contentedly.

"Mummy, I found this. Is it okay if I use this to practise just like Mr Toledo said?"

"Of course, hunny," I reply as I whisk up the milk and flour, seasoning it a little before putting it on the stove to heat whilst I boil the pasta and grate the cheese. I'm glad that Sophie's found a few pennies somewhere to play with.

"Now hunny, would you like…" I trail off mid-sentence as I turn around to look at Sophie counting her 'pennies'. I walk over. "Sophie…" I say slowly and quietly as if there were a live line connected to a bomb on the table and any sudden move could set it off. "Where did you find those 'pennies'?"

On the table lay a pile of pounds in £50s and £20s.

"It was in Daddy's special box, you know the one under the stairs, Mummy, the one that looks like he puts guns in it, but he must have forgot to put guns in today and put this in instead. Silly Daddy!"

Yes, silly Daddy indeed. It looks like a bank robbery. But more importantly, a sudden flash of realisation hits me. This is freedom. This is an opportunity.

I know this is it. This is our opportunity to get out and get out now. There's no time to waste. I have our chance, but we need to go now. I look around me, afraid this is a prank. That he will come storming back in mocking me and ready to punish me for touching his things.

There is no time to waste.

"Let's go on an adventure!" I say to Sophie impulsively.

"What, now, Mummy!" Sophie's face breaks into a big toothy smile, blonde curls bobbing merrily in agreement. "With Lola, can Teddy come too!"

"Yes sweetheart, but we must be quick, that's the fun thing about adventures—you need to do them straight away!"

Without thinking, I scoop up the money, throwing it into a carrier bag we dash upstairs. Grabbing a few things, I throw them into another carrier bag; there is no time to waste, he could be back any minute. I stuff as many things for Sophie as I can into a bag. Sophie, giggling happily, is telling Lola we are going on an adventure just like the princess when she went to find a new castle. She picks up her favourite teddies and we run as fast as we can down the stairs. My heart is pounding. Can we really do this? What am I thinking? Could I just up sticks and leave with her? Make a new life for us?

The repercussions do not bear thinking about if he found us. As find us, surely, he will. He's a trained stalker. It's his livelihood. If he finds me, he will kill me for sure. But what if he doesn't kill me, what if he maims me so badly, I am dependent on him forever? That is a fate worse than dying. I can't overthink this, if I do, I will never do this. We will be destined to a life of imprisonment. We will have no life. No future, I tell myself. I walk into the kitchen where only a few minutes before I had been quietly making macaroni cheese.

"Come on, Mummy!" Sophie excitedly tugs at my hand.

I remember the look on his face earlier. The angry voices. The last time he hurt me. No, if I think too much about it, my resolve will fail me. We must go now, go for the sake of our lives.

"Yes, let's go!" And with that, I turn off the cooker and walk through the kitchen, the back door appearing frighteningly fast. I open the door, step out into the cool, dark night, and close the door behind us.

Heading out in the cold October night, reality hits me, *what am I doing, am I crazy?* We crunch over the gravel, Sophie and Lola in tow excitedly asking where we are going. My heart is racing, blood rushes noisily around in my head as we run to the car, our meagre supplies stuffed into two carrier bags. I pull open the garage door. Truth be told, I have no idea where we are going. I have thought no further than seeing an opportunity. Anytime I had even contemplated this, I hadn't got far because there were too many hurdles.

Inside the garage now, I unlock the car, glad for once it is tucked away here, at least there is a small chance he might not notice on his return that it is missing, giving us a chance to get further away. As Sophie slips into the front seat, Lola lolling along the backseat, I fasten Sophie's seatbelt before getting into the driver's seat. It's cold. I feel cold. It's dark. I'm scared.

I turn on the ignition. *Am I really doing this,* I wonder as I reverse the car hesitantly, edging it slowly out of the garage. As I reverse, I take a look at the house, it is in pitch darkness. No welcome light glows. I jump quickly out of the car and pull down the garage door. It might give us a few precious moments. Jumping back into the car, I take a deep, shuddery breath. No, I am not crazy, I am surviving. It is now or never.

"Come on, Mummy! This is exciting. Can we have music on?" She beams up at me, her little cherub face glowing with excitement in the faint light from the dashboard.

Music. Yes, music was a good idea; leaning forward, I hit the CD button and out pop some tunes.

"Yayyy," Sophie squeals in delight. "This is fun, Mummy, where are we going to go? The beach or camping?"

"I have no idea, hunny, but what I do know though is that's the fun part, let's just see where the road takes us, shall we?" And with that I put my foot down, crank up the heating and for the second time in an hour, tyres screech in the driveway as I edge my little Corsa out of the drive and speed up the little road. My phone glints in the glow from the village streetlights. I open the window and without a second thought toss my phone out of the window. No one ever calls me now anyway, feeling a sense of freedom as I catch a vision in the rear-view mirror of it bouncing along the verge. No chance of him tracking us on that now.

I allow myself the luxury of a deep intake of breath. *We are doing this; we are really doing this.* I settle myself deeper into the driving seat. Left or right? *Left,* I think. I don't know why, maybe because all my running was that way. Maybe it is the escape route. I have no idea why. I turn left at the end of the road and drive another few miles.

A sign on the side of the road glowed in the headlights from the car.

Edinburgh 32 miles.

Here we go, it's now or never. Turning right, I pull the car out onto the main road and head towards Edinburgh. Glancing to my side, I see Sophie sitting contentedly beside me chatting excitedly about princesses and new castles as the miles pass by. I feel more and more at ease, it is as if every passing mile is taking us to safety. I still have no idea where I am going or what I will do when we get there. I look at the fuel tank, it is just over half full. That'll see us a while. I think of the carrier bag stuffed with money, as of yet I have no idea how much is there.

What I do know is he will be absolutely furious when he realises what I have done; no, he won't be furious, he will be beyond that. I know we just have to keep driving. It is done now and the chance of escape is within our grasp. There's no going back. To go back would be incomprehensible. The retaliation unthinkable.

Sophie chatters away beside me. Lola lets out great noisy sighs of contentment in the back. It is a great adventure to Sophie; she hasn't once asked about her daddy or if he will join us. I think that's strange but decide not to question it. Time enough for that later. The adrenalin keeps me wide awake as the miles pass by. I can see the city lights of Edinburgh glowing in the dark, the place of my birth. Lights offering up a welcome blanket. Encouraging me to hide away in the autonomy of city streets. Two survivors hidden within hundreds of thousands of anonymous people. I think with a pang of sadness at all the beautiful places we could visit if we went there, of the happy times I used to go up with my friends, of climbing Scott's Monument, of visiting art galleries and the many beautiful book stores where we could while away many a happy hour encompassed in the comfy sofas, of the bustle of Princess Street, the anonymity of a city, but no, that was too close, he would find us there within 24 hours.

No, sadly, Edinburgh is too close to home. We need to be further away. I head on the city bypass where the sign reads:

North A9/M90

I have many fond memories of visiting the North as a child. The North? Somewhere that no one would ask questions. North seemed as good a place to go as any. I click the indicator and turn left off the city bypass for the M90.

As I drive along the motorway heading north, I keep looking in the rear-view mirror expecting his car behind us. As the miles and hours tick by, the car lights begin to fade into just an odd one every few miles until I am left mostly with trucks doing overnight deliveries. Sophie has long since fallen asleep, thumb in her mouth, she looks content. Alone with my own thoughts, I begin to panic. Every light in the rear-view mirror causes me to panic, thinking he has come home and seen we have gone; has he somehow managed to follow us? I long for the oblivion of sleep but adrenalin and the need to distance ourselves from him keep me wide awake.

I've stopped a few times, the last being just after Aviemore a while back to let Lola stretch her legs and for a coffee and a short nap. I couldn't sleep properly but it was enough to keep me going. I was too anxious to get as many miles as I could between us and the village that had become my prison. I drove through Boat of Garten and continue along the A9, passing through Inverness. I pause for a moment, exhausted. Inverness is beautiful, would it be far enough away? Anonymous enough? No, I have to keep driving. I forge ahead, a sign for Kessock Bridge. I continue along the A9, the darkness of the night mingling with my fear of what I have done hides the beauty beneath me as we head over the bridge continuing along the A9 we reach a roundabout; which way now? I wonder. Continue along the A9 or set off for adventure.

Well, we started this with no ideas where I was going so, I pull off the roundabout, the A9 gives way to a series of winding roads interspersed with a few houses and lonely farms. I glance at the lovely sounding names on signposts—Clootie Well, Munlochy, Fairy Glen Falls. I keep driving.

Chapter 35

I look down at the clock on the dashboard. 7.23 am. The dawn is beginning to break, the sun would be appearing signalling a fresh new day, oblivious to the major event that has just happened in my life. I can hear Lola waken in the back seat. Looking over at Sophie, I see her eyelids begin to flutter into a drowsy early-morning waking.

"Well, good morning, sleepyhead!" I try to keep my voice light and not betray any anxiety about what I have just done.

"Good morning, Mummy," she smiles up at me before turning around to look in the back for Lola. "Lola, are you having fun too!"

"I think Lola might be hungry, do you think we should stop at the next village or town and see if we can find some breakfast?" I ask.

"Ooh yes! I think she would like that too!"

Sophie chatters away happily about what the next village might look like, and if there might be a castle like the princess in her storybook, as I continue to drive, unsure now of where we are, let alone where we are going.

The roads are getting narrower, winding and tree-lined. I begin to despair of ever seeing humanity again when, rounding a steep bend in the road, a few houses appear, and beyond those opened up an expanse of water.

"Mummy! It's the sea! Oh, can we stop!"

I love the sea, evoking happy memories of family day trips to Portobello Beach, as a child with my parents when we lived in Edinburgh.

"I think we absolutely can!" I smile over. We trundle along a small road which begins to open up into what looks to be a small village, a tourist one too by the looks of the car park in front which is dotted with a few camper vans.

I pull over into the car park. An early-morning tourist bus is stopping, and the passengers are decanting like little well-organised soldiers from the bus into a waiting fuel station. I scan the area quickly, the seafront on one side, on the opposite side beyond the fuel station are a few little shops aligning the quiet road.

194

A few trees intersperse the pavement, and apart from the tourists from the bus, I cannot see anyone else. It looks safe for now.

I look out over the water, a light breeze playing with my hair. I can hear gulls squawking noisily in the surroundings, the noise floating lazily over the airwaves. A few boats bob lazily on the water. It looks so peaceful. I take in a deep breath, letting the salty air enter deep into my lungs, enjoying the fresh scent.

"Well, I think that it looks like we might get breakfast here, hunny. What do you think?"

"Yes, oh yes! That looks like a princess place!" Sophie jumps excitedly from one foot to the other as we get out of the car and stretch. I watch as the tourists get takeout coffees and hot rolls, using the facilities before heading back on the bus.

"Let's take Lola a walk down the road, shall we?" I ask Sophie who nods excitedly in agreement as we head in the direction of a few small stores. I want to take in the surroundings, see if this is actually a place we may be able to stop, even if only for a few hours. I hear the tourist bus engine rev up and leave on to its next destination, a tour of the highlands I assume.

"Look, a princess coffee shop, Mummy," Sophie squeals in delight as a pink striped awning with a large sign out front, also in pastel pink, proudly displays a large coffee cup.

"I do believe you are right! Shall we investigate?" I smile at Sophie who is already three paces in front now. As we near the coffee shop, I can see the door is wide open and the smells coming out are simply divine. My stomach gives a large growl of encouragement.

"Shall we?" I smile at her.

Sophie's reply is to nod eagerly before bounding in through the door.

"Well, good morning, cherubs," a wonderfully cheery, soft Scottish voice beckoned us. I look around to see where the voice is coming from but can't see anyone. "I'll be with you in just a minute, dear, just take a seat if you don't mind. I take it you aren't in a hurry. We don't usually get people so early; the tour buses usually stop at the fuel station. We are more of a mid-morning stop, but I like to get all my cakes out early." A twinkling laugh comes from behind a door set behind a glass counter which is already laden with a gorgeous display of baked goods.

I look around us, there is a wonderful eclectic mix of tables and chairs, a selection of pretty tablecloths adorns the tables, each set with a bud vase of wildflowers. In the far corner is a faded, well-worn, tan leather sofa with a low swung oak coffee table in front. The walls are lined with groceries, cakes, homemade preserves all along one wall and on the other, groceries of every kind you could imagine all neatly lined up. I head to the sofa and take a seat. Gratefully, I sink into the warm recess, the surface is covered in cracks, it has a fresh scent of polish, it feels well loved, and I can imagine many a conversation has taken place here. I take in my surroundings, a few paintings are on the wall, I peer closer at these, they appear to be the work of a local artist. A lamp is placed next to the sofa, perched on a tall narrow set of drawers, it offers a warm glow.

"Now then," a well-rounded lady appears from the opening behind the counter, a huge smile on her gentle crinkly face, wearing a white frilly apron with matching white lace cap, hair tied back neatly in a bun; she has a storybook granny appearance and oozes an aura of homeliness.

"My name's Dorothy, but everyone calls me Dotty." She lets out a gentle chuckle and her smile gets even wider if that is possible. "Now then, oh what a beautiful young lady you are," she smiles at Sophie, "just like my Milly, she's my granddaughter, a wee bit older than you now, lass, but the same lovely locks too, and what a lovely dog, what's her name? She's a beauty, you'll be hungry now, I would say you've had a long journey by the looks of you." She looks at me, a knowing look crosses her kind face before she continues, "Now, what can I get you?" The warm smile never leaves her face as she proceeds to list off the menu for us.

"Oh, the spelt flour buttermilk pancakes sound delicious but then everything does! What do you think, Sophie?" I looked down at her, her sweet face smiling broadly.

"Yes please! And this is Lola."

"Well, hello to Lola as well! And what about a nice hot chocolate for you, young lady, with extra sprinkles and marshmallows, and for Lola, I shall get a bowl of water and I have some leftover sausages? Do you think that she might like them for breakfast?"

"I'm sure she would love those, that's very kind." I'm taken aback by this lady's kindness and openness.

"Right then, I'll get you your drinks, just sit back and enjoy some peace," she smiles as she bustles away.

I glance over as Dotty pops behind the glass counter and expertly handles the coffee machine, the scent of fresh coffee fills the air as the machine bursts into life grinding beans noisily, it is a companiable noise, and I let the scent of coffee wash over me as, with a hiss of steam, Dotty makes the hot chocolate.

"Here you go, lass, you look like you need a large one." Gratefully, I take the coffee from Dotty, wrapping my hands around the large polka dot mug, as she places Sophie's enormous hot chocolate in front of her.

Sophie's eyes open like saucers. "Wow, look Mummy!" I smile over. I am inordinately tired after the long drive and coffee is a welcome boost. I can't help but warm to Dotty, her effervescence and constant stream of chat, she hardly takes a breath between sentences, and has such a calming air about her. The coffee smells delicious, and I warm my hands around my mug as Sophie delightedly hugs her hot chocolate with extra sprinkles and marshmallows. Lola is flopped at the table side as if she has been coming here every day of her life.

There is a lovely warm aroma here. I glance out of the window, still apprehensive of James having somehow managed to find us. However, all I can see is the open water, the early-morning sun rising in the sky, reflecting off the gentle ripples. I can see a notice board tucked at the back and get up to have a look, enjoying the gentle music that has started to play, the scent of our pancakes bubbling on the range cooker. I hug my coffee as I look at the noticeboard. There is an array of notices, all tourist-based, fishing expeditions, boating trips and the likes but what catches my eye is a slightly faded card that reads:

Log cabin available
Long or short term
Enquire through Dotty

I look up as I hear Dotty approach. "Now then, here's your pancakes and I have put extra raspberries on and cream. I grew the raspberries myself and the eggs are free range, they will put a spring in your step for sure."

"They look sumptuous."

Dotty beams with pride.

"Dotty?" I enquire. "The noticeboard up there says to ask you about the cabin."

"Oh, now would you be interested in that, yes, it's mine, been in the family for generations, I usually let it out over the summer but it's the end of the tourist season so it's sitting empty just now. If you like, I can take you for a look when you have finished your breakfast? My son will be in then and he can take over here for a bit."

"That would be fantastic, but only if it's not too much trouble," I add hesitantly.

"Ach no, not at all, lassie, it would be my pleasure, now just sit and enjoy your breakfast. By the looks of you, you could do with a wee rest," she says kindly before continuing, "I'll just be in the back, the bread is about to come out of the oven, I had best not scorch it!" And with that she bustles back into the kitchen leaving us to enjoy our sumptuous breakfast of pancakes and raspberries. My mouth waters as I pick up the cutlery and cut a sliver of pancake, carefully spooning a little fresh cream on before topping it off with a juicy raspberry. We eat in happy silence, the only sounds a few happy sighs.

"Oh, that was so yummy!" I let out a groan of satisfaction as Sophie and I finish up every last scrap of the deliciously light and fluffy buttermilk pancakes.

"I see Mum has her famous buttermilk pancakes on today!"

I jump, so engrossed in our pancakes I hadn't noticed when a man had walked in. Tall, with short light brown hair, he looks very relaxed in fawn chino shorts and a light pink polo shirt which sets off his long, lightly tanned strong limbs.

"Sorry, I didn't mean to startle you, good morning!" he says cheerily. "I see Mum has been making her specials, well, you can't go wrong with those!" He gives us both a wide smile before leaning down to give Lola a pat. "Now who do we have here? Aren't you a bonny wee thing."

"This is Lola," Sophie answers before I can say anything, "and this is Mummy, and I am…"

"Full of delicious buttermilk pancakes!" I interject quickly. I can't have anyone knowing our names. Not until I know we are safe, and by then I will have been able to explain more to Sophie of our new life, that we need to change our names.

Unperturbed at my interruption, Sophie continues, "Yes, Dotty gave her some sausages, she is really nice, and Lola wolfed them down. I think she thinks they are the best sausages she has ever had!"

"Well, I am very pleased to meet you both and young Miss Lola." If he is curious about my interjection, I can't tell, he simply smiles a friendly smile over at me and nods. I can see how blue his eyes are in his ruggedly handsome face.

I wonder if he might be a fisherman, he has the look of someone who spends a lot of time outdoors.

"Now then, are you harassing my customers, Noah!" Dotty comes in from the back and gives Noah a warm hug. "Now then, I was going to just show these girls the cabin, if you could take over for a while, and dinnae be eating all the cakes this time!"

"What do you mean this time!" Noah pretends to be affronted but with the warm smile on his face, it is obvious to all he is not in the slightest bit offended. *By the easy camaraderie between mother and son, it is easy to see where Noah gets his smile and easy manner from,* I think to myself.

"They are simply delicious, if you decide to stick around for a while, you'll get to try them for yourselves, I can highly recommend the lemon drizzle cake, made to make your mouth water."

"Awe, now son, you'll be embarrassing me and making my head swell!" Dotty pretends to shoo Noah away, but it's clear that she's delighted with her son's praise.

"Right then, if you girls are ready?" Dotty asks as I hand over some cash. *It feels so strange having actual money in my hand and a long way from my previous visits to the coffee shop,* I think to myself as I remember being embarrassed with the £1.90 in small change and how worried I had been that the coffee price might have increased.

As we all head out the shop, Dotty informs us it's 'only a wee stroll' along the waterside and we can come back for our car after. Sounds perfect, I think as Sophie slips her hand into mine and skips happily along beside me, Lola, a few yards in front stopping to sniff every few yards, her tail wagging ten to the dozen, had long since earned the name of Miss Wiggles-a-lot. As we head along the waterside, I feel a fresh wave of anxiety creep over me. Has James appeared back home yet. Has he noticed we are gone? Has he somehow found us? Every snap of dry twig, every rustle of the leaves makes me look around nervously.

Dotty carries on chatting, Sophie skips alongside, joining in the conversation oblivious. I try to appear as calm as I can. Dotty is lovely, but surely a nervous woman arriving with a young child and a dog looking spontaneously for somewhere to stay would arouse suspicion and possibly gossip. I can't risk that, I realise, as I try to think out a plausible reason for our arrival if asked.

We walk together for about 20 minutes, Dotty happy to carry the conversation, as I frantically come up with and dismiss many a scenario to explain our arrival. Fortunately, Dotty so far hasn't asked. I look to my right, the water sparkling beside us, a trail path making easy guidance, runs alongside the road, a few trees rustling gently in the soft breeze, the sun sending silvery fronds down amongst the trees. We turn up into a small copse and along a small track.

"It's just in here." Dotty tells me of the many antics she got up to as a child, how her grandfather had built this log cabin, and of the many happy memories she had. "Now, it's nothing posh you know, there's no internet signal up here or TVs, it's a wee bolthole, a lot of the city slicker types like to come out to find themselves." She laughs but it is a kind laugh, the laugh of one who understands the importance of knowing who you are.

Dotty picks up the key from under the mat, unlocking the door, she turns to me. "We don't get any trouble up here, it's perfectly safe," by way of explanation to the key under the mat. It reminds me of the old days my dad used to say the key was under the mat if I dropped by and no one was at home, those days of being able to do that are long gone. I shake myself back to the present as Dotty pushes the door wide open.

Peering inside, I let out a small gasp. Giant log beams form the walls and roof of the cabin, a delicate light from the window cast gentle shadows dancing from the soft breeze onto the floor, it's so homely I take in the warm smell of wood.

"As I say, it's nothing posh, but there's a generator for the electric and running water, a nice log fire with plenty of logs and if you run out then just ask and Noah will soon chop you some more, in fact, if there's anything you need, anything at all, then just ask."

Sophie races ahead with a delighted squeal, Lola not far behind in her wake.

I pause on the veranda, taking it all in. It is so peaceful. Trees on three sides, you can see the water from here. A little swing seat hangs on the veranda calling out for long peaceful days. *It's perfect*, I think to myself. No one could find us here and no internet or phone should make it easier to hide. Just until I can find my feet, get a job and we can start again.

"Well, what do you think, Missy?" I ask Sophie as she bounds out to me and envelopes my waist in a big hug.

"I love it, Mummy; can we stay?"

"I think we have our answer." I turn to Dotty, her kind face crinkling into a warm smile.

"Oh, how wonderful! It'll be so lovely to have the three of you here. Oh, and in the garage there," she points to a wooden shed alongside the cabin, "you'll find a few wee bikes, if you want to take them out for a wee cycle, get to know the area. I'll let you get settled, but just pop back to the coffee shop if you need anything, love." And with that, Dotty gives us both a hug, pats Lola and heads back down the path.

Left to our own devices, I look around the cabin. I love it. I knew from the moment I had read the little notice that I would want it. Seeing it in reality though, shakes me. It feels like I have stepped into a proper wee home. The walls are log-lined adding to the warmth and charm. It has two small bedrooms, a bathroom that has both a bath and a shower, and the kitchen is open to a cosy living room with the log fire Dotty mentioned. I wander back out onto the small veranda and take in the view; I could imagine in early summer, the woods would be alive with the chorus of birds. It is perfect.

Sophie comes out from exploring the little cabin. "Lola told me she really, really loves this adventure we are having, she thinks we should stay forever and ever!"

"Oh, she does, does she!" I laugh, it is so lovely to see her relaxing and enjoying herself. I push to the back of my mind what I have done.

"Right then, I think we should head back to Dotty's; we shall need to get a few things for our stay, won't we."

Sophie slips her hand into mine as we lock the door and head back into the village. I pay in cash for our stay at the cabin, buy some supplies from Dotty's which is a miracle of a coffee shop and grocery store, before thanking Dotty profusely and taking the car back to the log cabin, parking it out of sight in the garage.

Chapter 36

With the sun setting on our first day, night begins to drift over the log cabin, enveloping it in a warm blanket of stars. I lay in my new bed wearing a new set of pyjamas that both Sophie and I had been able to get at Dotty's. Sophie, tucked up with Lola in the bedroom next door, exhausted from our travels, has gone off into a contented sleep almost the minute her head hit the pillow. Staring at the ceiling, anxiety gnaws at me. I can't help but be apprehensive.

I'm still in shock about how quickly all this has happened. Just over 24 hours ago, I had been mundanely making macaroni cheese, anxious about what the retribution James's bad day would be this time. And here I am, Sophie safely tucked up in bed having had such a lovely day, sitting in this idyllic cabin in the woods. The contrast between our old life and new is vast, oceans apart, but I can't help but wonder if I'm living a fallacy. Will it all come tumbling down?

Thinking back to my mobile phone bouncing along the verge in our old village, I think with relief at least he can't track us here. To this tiny, but gorgeous piece of Scottish paradise where the people are so friendly. It's like stepping back in time. I think guiltily of the money I've taken, trying to justify it as half mine, for years I had no money of my own, surely it was half mine and only a tiny fraction of what I had brought in over the years?

Counting it, there was £2,320.00. Enough to keep us going until I can get myself a job. I could home-school Sophie, get a job that paid in cash. Get a burner phone to contact Dad, try to explain somehow. I wouldn't leave a trail. My mind races, fighting with my weary body as the exhaustion from driving all night and the relief of finding somewhere, somewhere that was away from that prison, catches up with me. I drop fitfully off to sleep to the sound of the waves lapping the waterfront.

I wake up with a start. Something has woken me, but what I am not sure. Nervously, I slip my feet over the side of the bed and pad through the hall, opening the door to Sophie's room a fraction. I can see she is sleeping peacefully,

Lola, laying on top of the bed, half opens one eye sleepily, realises it is just me and closes it again before letting out a sleepy contended groan of comfort. Closing the door quietly, I pad back along the small corridor into the kitchen. The window is wide open. I can see the cool white glow of the moon riding high in the sky, sending slivers of moonlight to play amongst the trees rustling in the light breeze.

Unfamiliar noises from outside, an unfamiliar cabin, an unfamiliar bed. The window is wide open, banging in the breeze. That was silly. *I must have forgotten to close it,* I think to myself as I pull it closed and draw the curtain. That was careless. I am sure I had checked everything. *I shall need to be more careful*, I think, as I head back along the corridor and slip into bed before falling back into an exhausted sleep.

Chapter 37

The next morning, I wake to the autumnal rays of the early-morning sun streaming through the light curtains. Momentarily confused as to where I am, everything comes flooding back to me. I can't believe what I have done. We have escaped. I never imagined it would ever happen, but here we were, miles away from the prison. No matter how tough things get from now, at least I have got us away from him. To safety. He can never hurt us again.

I look around me, the pale blue floral curtains at the window, I must have been too exhausted to close them last night, the simple wooden furniture, a wooden rocking chair with a cream rug adorned sat in the corner, a blue and white vase sat aboard a dressing table, a blue patchwork throw over my bed, all adding to the cosy homely feel. Slipping my legs over the bed, I let my toes burrow into the thick sheepskin rug.

As my mind begins to register what I have done, and what I still need to do, I feel a wave of anxiety wash over me. *I need coffee.* Quickly checking Sophie, I see she's fast asleep. I pad along quietly to the kitchen and put a kettle of water onto the stove to boil. The wooden scents in the kitchen are warm and encompassing. Hunting around, I try to remember which cupboard I put the coffee in. I must have been more exhausted than I thought. I laugh to myself as eventually I locate the coffee in the cupboard under the sink. *Why on earth would I have placed it there*?

Spooning out some into a mug, I put it back into the cupboard with the rest of our supplies. I jump as the kettle begins to whistle loudly, announcing it is ready. I pour the steaming liquid and slip quietly out to the veranda, sitting onto the swing chair. I hug my hot coffee, letting my feet dangle as I watch the crystal-clear water, a few wispy traces of mist floating lazily in the distance, promising a fine day. Geese begin their assent, taking off from the water, loud gaggling noises and the beat of their wings so close as they take off. The noise is spectacular. I have no idea what the time is, but it must still be fairly early as the sun is still relatively low. There are a few boats bobbing about on the water, out for an early-morning sail, I guess.

Draining the last remnants of my coffee, I hear a clatter of paws on the wood floors coming from inside as a black and white spotty bundle hurtles through the door closely followed by a blonde tousled-haired smiling Sophie.

"Mummy, this is a princess castle," Sophie declares.

"And did you sleep like a princess, sweetheart?" I ask, smiling at her fixation with the princess castle.

"Better than that, Lola and I both slept like princesses!"

"And would our princesses be hungry for breakfast yet?" I tease gently.

"I think my tummy is rumbly and so is Lola's!"

I smile as we head back into the kitchen. The simple pleasure of being able to choose what we wanted for breakfast is a delight. Half an hour later, we have made a selection of fresh fruit and granola with yoghurt and decide to have a picnic breakfast on the veranda. I make more coffee as I listen to Sophie chatting away. "Shall we try out the bicycles today and go explore the area?"

"Yes!" Sophie exclaims excitedly, spooning the last bit of yoghurt up; she smiles broadly at me and jumps up heading back into the cabin. I hear her clattering excitedly along the wooden corridor to her bedroom, chatting nineteen to the dozen with Lola.

I gather up the dishes, quickly washing them before putting them away neatly in the cupboard, I pop the coffee back alongside the granola in the grocery cupboard. It hits me then how simple this task is. How much simple pleasure I get from this small task. But the joy I feel comes with knowing that this will be as clean and tidy when I come back as I had left it. I feel ridiculously overwhelmed. Something so simple that makes such a difference.

"Come on," I chide myself; *it's only a few dishes,* but no, I disagree with myself, it is a statement of my new life, what it could be. The simplicity. The calm. The peace, more so, the freedom, the safety. I head through to my bedroom and pull out the bag of clothes I had hastily stuffed into the carrier bag and tip them out. One pair of jeans, two t-shirts, a sweatshirt, woolly jumper, varying underwear and OH! I exclaim in delight as I pull out an old pair of leggings and my tatty trainers. Delighted with my find, I hastily throw these on, pull my hair back into its customary ponytail and head back out into the kitchen. Sophie is already on the front porch, dressed and excited to try out the bikes.

"Race you!" I give her a small head start, before pacing a couple of steps behind her. I pretend to pant in exhaustion.

"My goodness, I think you could be in the next Olympics with a speed like that!"

Sophie lets out a delighted giggle. "We can practise lots up here, Mummy!"

"I think that sounds like a lovely idea. Okay, let's see what we have then." I smile as I pull open the garage doors.

"Look! There's a pink one!" Sophie squeals in delight as she runs to a small bike complete with bells and a little white basket, silver streamers adorning the handles.

Pulling out the bike, Sophie hops on and takes to it like a duck to water. "Come on, Mummy, which are you going to have?"

"Actually, you gave me an idea, I think I shall just jog along beside you. What do you think? I need to get some practice in order to keep up with you!"

Sophie giggles. "I could race you, Mummy, come on follow me!" and with that she heads off, a little wobbly, along the trail beside the water.

We head along the trail behind the cabin trees; either side the leaves are starting to turn brown and fall in crisp little piles on the track. I jog steadily along beside Sophie, feeling free, free like I haven't felt in a long while, as my feet hit the path in a lovely rhythmic beat it is as if they are cheering me on, cheering me into a new life, trees float past waving long branches, extended arms welcoming me back in friendly waves. I float on as though in a new world. I can't believe I am running outdoors again, something I never thought would happen. We round a bend, Sophie giggling in front calling out in support. This feels surreal, heavenly. Endorphins are flooding through me. The sun plays on my skin as it bounces in between trees. We stop for a break and a drink of water, as we overlook the water, stunning in its simple glory. Sophie looks so carefree and happy. I know then, irrespective of the way it happened, that irrevocably I have done the right thing.

Later that day and still on a high from our outing, we pull together a picnic and wrap up warmly, heading down to the waterside. I lay out the blanket and watch as Sophie dips her toes into the water, squealing in delight as the cold water tickles her feet. I hear her trying to encourage Lola in, but Lola flatly refuses. I remember how she wouldn't even step into puddles.

"Mummy, I am trying to tell her there's nothing to be afraid of. Dad tried to get Lola to swim once with the other dogs; he said if he threw her in, she would swim but she wouldn't swim, and I had to say to him he had to go in and get her because she was under the water."

Innocently said but it shakes me to the core. If Sophie hadn't been there, then who knows what would have happened to Lola. It was the first time Sophie had mentioned him. I wait to see if she is going to say anything else, taking the lead from her, but she is dancing around Lola playfully chatting, telling her she was okay, that no one would throw her in, she was safe here. I can't help but feel she is trying to tell me something, does she know more than she is letting on?

The sun starts to set over the water when we decide to go back up to the cabin, it has started to get chilly.

"Come on, I shall race you back!" I say as we gather up the picnic remnants. "I think we could light a fire and have some hot chocolate. How does that sound?" I say to Sophie as we reach the cabin.

"Yummy, yummy, yummy!"

"I shall take that as a resounding yes then, shall I? Okay McGinty, let's get ourselves washed and into our pyjamas and then we can have a story beside the fire before bedtime, do you remember how to work the shower?"

"Yes, Mummy, I am getting to be a big girl now!" she calls as she skips through to her room as I set about making a fire. There is plenty of paper, kindling and wood. I find the matches alongside the stove. I am so grateful to Dotty for leaving us so well stocked. The flames lick into life as the paper and then kindling catch hold. I put the fire guard over and make my way to have a quick shower before changing into my pyjamas, luxuriating in the simplicity of the task. I make my way back to the kitchen to warm up some milk for our hot chocolate.

I stop in my tracks, either I am losing my mind or…for on the counter are 2 cups and a jar of coffee. A teaspoon lying neatly beside it. No! No! I refuse to let my mind play tricks on me. Nothing else is different. Everything is neat and tidy, just the way I left it. An unease gnaws at me. I push it to the back of my mind as Sophie comes through.

"Can we read this one, Mummy?" Sophie bounces through with her favourite princess book. "It's just like us, we found our castle too!" She settles down on the rug beside the fire, Lola cuddled into her.

I push the thought of the cups to the back of my mind.

"Yes, we have, sweetheart." *We most definitely have,* I think to myself as I wash out the milk pan and take two mugs of hot chocolate over, settling myself down alongside them.

Chapter 38

The next morning, I check the fridge, we need some more fruit and some milk. I had woken in the middle of the night again fresh from a nightmare. He had found us. Sketchy fragments of detail which I could not piece together now float in and out of my head. One resounding memory from the nightmare was his leery grin, the grin with the green-tinged teeth up close. That I could not remove from my mind.

I need the outdoors. To numb my mind. I also need to keep some normality on this crazy expedition, for Sophie's sake. She seems utterly at home here and so far, hasn't even mentioned Daisy, let alone him. I feel this strange, however, day by day, hour by hour and minute by minute I grow more and more sure Sophie knew what had been happening at home.

I decide to risk heading out to the village again. I need to clear my mind, calling Sophie. I ask her if she would like to take the bikes along to the little village. If the coast is clear, we can have breakfast there. As we pull the bikes out of the shed, I can't help but smile. I love the bike I am using, it is duck egg blue, has two bells on the handles and a basket on the front. Heading along the small track, Sophie in front of me, I let the breeze wash over me. I feel like a tiny leaf in this giant forest, bumping along the little track, the wind tugging gently at my hair as we glide along. Two unknowns. I wonder how long it would stay that way.

It is setting up to be another beautiful day, the sun is beginning to rise high in the sky, a few white fluffy clouds drift along lazily as if unaware winter was just around the corner. As the bank of trees slither to an end, I look ahead, we are nearing the end of the track already. The trees have opened up revealing the water glistening to our left and the path stretches out in front leading to the car park and the little row of shops including the lovely Dotty's coffee shop.

Dotty's is far more than a coffee shop; it is a little Aladdin's cave selling almost everything you could possibly need or want. I think about the delicious array of baked goods, imagining them all neatly lined up ready to tempt the day's travellers. As of yet, it is very quiet. I scan the area. Nothing. Not a soul in sight. We should be safe to stop off for a bit before retreating back to our cabin.

"Right then, poppet." I look over at Sophie who is hastily scrambling off her bike, a huge smile on her face. "Are you ready for breakfast, or are you still all full up from yesterday?" I gently tease as we prop the bikes up alongside Dotty's coffee shop.

"I could eat a horse!" She announces as she rushes ahead into Dotty's, the door tinkling as she enters.

It does my heart good to see her happy, but I can't help feeling uneasy. This seems too easy. My mind flits uneasily back to Him. I wonder what he is doing right now. Would he have a search party out? One thing for sure I know he will be mad. If he found us...I give myself a virtual shake and try to block the image from my mind. *The nightmare has just unsettled you. How could he possibly have found you?*

I slip a smile on my face so Sophie can't see my concern as I enter the coffee shop.

"Well, hello there, I was wondering when we would see you. How are you settling in?" Dotty's cheerful voice welcomes us immediately. Her soft Scottish accent is as warm and welcoming as a fluffy fleece blanket on a wintry day.

"Oh, just wonderfully, it is a little piece of heaven!" I say as Sophie adds, "It is a princess palace! We rode the bikes along; I rode the pink one and Mummy rode the blue one. We came in for breakfast again, it was scrummy, I love the fluffy pancakes!" she continues before stopping to come up for air.

"Well, that's just wonderful!" Dotty laughs at Sophie's enthusiasm. "This is our specials board, and we have some lovely wild bramble berries this morning too, just take your time and let me know when you are ready." Dotty bustles around cheerfully, singing to herself as Sophie and I study the specials board. It all looks so tempting. We decide on the wild berries with homemade yoghurt and a stack of the fluffy buttermilk pancakes on the side, picking up a book for Sophie and I from the pile left for customers to read by the noticeboard.

"Mummy, can we sit outside, please Mummy, it is so pretty!"

I try as discreetly as I can to scan the exterior for anything of concern; I can't see anything. I look down at Sophie's face, wreathed in a beseeching smile. What harm could sitting outside do? It is quiet, and if we sit next to the tree, we would be quite hidden.

"Well, I think that sounds an excellent idea, we should make the most of the lovely weather," I say as she leads the way. "What about that table next to the pretty tree?" I offer as we head out towards the array of cheerful tables waiting patiently in front of the coffee shop.

"That's the perfect table," she announces as she jumps up onto the seat. Sitting behind the tall tree and facing out to the sea, I feel a little safer. I pick up my book, allowing myself the luxury of enjoying some time to simply read. I can't remember when I last had time. I look over at Sophie who is sitting smiling as she reads her book contentedly to her teddy bear.

Absorbed in our books, I am momentarily startled by a voice.

"It's grand to be making the most of the weather, it's due to change before too long, I would say." Noah appears from inside the coffee shop with two mugs of hot drinks, his long lean brown legs in what I assumed now were his customary chino shorts, this time teamed with a navy polo shirt and wearing a pair of sandals. He has the look of someone who spent a lot of time outdoors. I hadn't noticed he had been inside.

As if registering my surprise and by way of explanation as he settles our hot drinks down, Noah offers up, "I was just helping Mum out, she does amazing, but I worry that all the heavy lifting is a bit much although she never says anything."

"It is a wonderful coffee shop and has so many delicious things, I don't know how she manages to get so many different things onto those shelves!"

"Yes, she makes all the jams and preserves herself, she loves her garden and makes all sorts of pickles and chutneys," he stops and lets out a small laugh before continuing, "sorry, I'm going on."

"No, not at all, it's lovely to hear." I say honestly, urging him to continue. I enjoy the simple chat and listen as he tells me how his granny had started with a little market stall selling produce from her garden. Years later his mum had bought this store and turned it into a thriving bakery and grocers. Listening to Noah, it is clear how close they are, he is obviously proud of her.

"Now, now Noah, you'll be swelling my head going on like that!" Dotty arrives with a huge tray filled to bursting with food. "Here you go, dearies. Breakfast with a view, now you enjoy it, you look like you could do with putting some meat on those bones, dear."

I don't take offence at this comment, it's said in such a kind motherly way. "Wow," Sophie mouths; eyes as big as saucers as Dotty set the tray down.

I look at the plates overflowing with red and purple berries, a big stack of the delicious buttermilk pancakes we had indulged in the previous day, a blue striped jug of cream and another blue and white spotted one with what looks like raspberry syrup. I have to agree, and my stomach let out an agreeable rumble.

Dotty lets out a small chuckle and I join in. "Sounds like you are ready for this, my dear. I shall leave you to enjoy, Noah will bring out something for Lola, won't you, love."

Noah smiles at us before following Dotty back inside. Left alone with Sophie, I look about; the view is breathtaking. I take a sip of my hot coffee as Noah brings out some sausages and a big bowl of fresh water for Lola. I can't help but have a feeling someone is watching. I look around.

No, there is nothing and nobody there. I am just paranoid. He can't have found us. Stop being so silly, it's just years of being on high alert for something to happen. No, you are safe here. You threw away your phone, he has no way to track you. Just enjoy your breakfast.

I chide myself once again and set about my breakfast as Lola wolfs down her sausage breakfast treat. As we scoop up the delicious fluffy pancakes, the early-morning sun warms our faces, the light reflects off the waterfront. I try to let the serenity wash over me, but something is nagging at me. Time, I remind myself, it will take time to get used to being away. To us being safe. I pick up my book and flick over a page, trying to lose myself for a little.

A while later, as I try to settle our bill, Dotty insists that our breakfast is on the house and flatly refuses to take a penny as I try to press some cash into her hands.

"No, no not at all, dear, it is such a pleasure to have some new youngsters around the place, and please take those books, you can swap them when you are done with them."

I thank her gratefully as Sophie flies up to her and gives her a big hug, encompassing her waist.

"Thank you!" she beams up at Dotty. "I am really liking this book, I really like my princess one too, the princess found a new castle in the book just like we did, but this book is fun too."

"Well, you are more than welcome." Dotty looks over at me and gives me what I feel is a knowing look, a kind smile on her wise face she gives Sophie's curly locks a gentle ruffle as we head back to get our bikes and cycle along the trail back to the cabin.

"Are you ready for our adventures today then, McGinty? Another cycle, or maybe we should walk to the beach, what do you think?" I ask as we cycle back companionably.

"Can we take a picnic to the beach; we can cycle there, and I can race you again!"

"Well, now doesn't that sound like a lovely idea! I agree, but surely you won't be hungry again till much, much later after all those pancakes!" I tease gently.

"I have hollow legs, remember, I miss Granda, but I think he will be having a lovely time in New Zealand."

"Yes, I think you are right, and I miss him also."

I hold my breath waiting to see if she says anything about missing James, but she continues, "I think I will draw a picture for him in our new castle. Do you think he would like that, Mummy?"

"I think he would love that very much; shall we take some drawing things to the beach? I think I saw some paper and crayons in the kitchen."

A short while later, we are boarding the bicycles again. My legs still ache from the many bruises; I loved my first run here but there would be time enough to run.

The path is just wide enough for us to cycle side by side as we head around the waterfront along the path chatting amiably. The gentle breeze is refreshing but Noah is right, it wouldn't be long before the weather changes. I lift my head slightly to make the most of the breeze, it's very calming, brushing against my cheeks and playing with my hair as we bounced along the track, the picnic safely tucked in the front basket on my bike alongside a couple of blankets. I let out a laugh as hysteria threatens to overcome me. Three days ago, I was making macaroni cheese. It feels surreal.

I look ahead trying to block out images of discoloured teeth and giant boots as we bounce over the trail. I let the trees continue their friendly embrace, their long arms always encouraging, always waving as we head further around the waterside to the far side where Noah had told us lay a sheltered sandy copse, perfect for reading and making sandcastles; he had smiled at Sophie as he handed her an old bucket and spade. "Left behind from my nieces last time they were up, could you make use of them, young lady?"

Sophie had delightedly accepted and that had secured our plans for today.

Rounding the waterside, I gasp as out in front of us lay a beautiful copse. How right Noah was. This is perfect.

"Wow, Mummy look!"

"It's beautiful, isn't it, sweetheart? Right, let's get ourselves settled."

The breeze is increasing but down in the hollow of the sandy beach, it is perfect.

Sophie settles herself down and starts drawing whilst I lay on the blanket next to her with my book.

"What are you drawing, hunny?" I look over.

"It's us in our new castle for Granda, see." She turns the picture around, "That's you, Mummy, and this is me on my bike, and this is Lola, and this over here is the castle, and I'm going to draw the beach too."

"I think it's perfect, hunny, but I also think it's time to make a sandcastle!" Sophie lets out another squeal of delight and tucks her picture and crayons carefully back in the basket of my bicycle as I get up to join her in sandcastle-building.

Half an hour later, we look upon the efforts of our labour. "You've done a great job of this," I declare.

"No Mummy," she corrects. "We've done a lovely job of this, I think I'll draw this in the picture for Granda too, I think he will like this."

"I agree, hunny," I reply, sitting back and just enjoy the peace, no demands on my time, no accusations and no…No, I stopped myself short. No, I could not let my mind go there. This is a new start. I take a deep breath. I was starting to relax a tiny bit at a time. I know I had felt anxious this morning, but I was just being silly, paranoid. There was no way he could find us here. Even I barely knew where we were. We were safe, that was all that mattered.

The day had started to cool, the light starting to fade. "I think we should make our way back to the cabin, hunny."

"Can we read our storybook beside the fire?"

"I think that sounds just perfect, sweetheart."

We gather up our things, hop onto the bikes and make our way back along the path as we head to our cabin.

Chapter 39

I stretched satisfyingly out in the bed, letting out a considerable yawn, I can hear the geese gaggling on the waterfront. How simple life is. It is just what we need, both Sophie and I. We have been here 6 days now and already the colour is beginning to appear in Sophie's cheeks, in my own too. The bruises are starting to fade. I love the simple routine. It is lovely to know what we were doing in a day. I had parked the car in the garage, choosing to walk everywhere, cycle or take a gentle jog alongside Sophie as she cycled.

I couldn't believe how much our lives have changed in just a week. To know that our little cabin was neat and tidy, warm, and welcoming. To know that the day wouldn't end in pain and heartache. To know that Sophie could play free and easy, to laugh and giggle, to dance around like children should. The fear and anxiety had left her quickly and she had adapted to our new life with a speed that still surprised me. She hadn't mentioned James once which only added to the gnawing idea inside me that she had known more of what was going on at home, more than I had given her credit for.

As I stretch out in the bed, looking out the window, I can see the water glistening in the remnants of the moonlight. So beautiful and a sharp contrast from back home. No, not home. This is home. I remind myself with a grateful sigh. I need to make more solid plans for being here. I need to get a job, that has to be top priority. I not only need the money, but I need the routine. I am having nightmares, every footstep I hear I think is him, every rustle of the trees I wonder if it's him. I have started to run again, my legs slowly healing. I find running around the little tracks in the woods alongside the waterfront refreshing, blowing away fears and memories in equal measures. Last night's nightmare had been particularly bad and I felt tired this morning.

As I watch the morning break, I slip out of bed and head to the kitchen to make myself a coffee. I love the smell of the wood, the fresh scents of the forest and the gentle noise of the water lapping on the shore, the sound of the geese heading off for their day's travel before returning to roost at nightfall. Spooning coffee into my mug, I place the jar neatly back into the cupboard. I let out a small sigh as the water comes to a boil and I fill my mug, watching the black steaming liquid swirl in the mug. *It is the simple things that are giving me the most pleasure,* I think, as I lift my mug and head out to the front porch. Although it is getting a little chilly, this really is my favourite place I think as I look out over the water.

I try to put the nightmare of last night out of my mind; in my nightmare, he had found us, and the outcome was particularly graphic. I close my eyes trying to push it away, to focus on the gentle noises around me. The wind rustling, the chill air on my cheeks, the warmth of my hands wrapped around the hot coffee mug, the water lapping on the front, the sound of the car crunching along the leaf-strewn track.

My eyes shoot open. A car! There had been no one visiting us here. Has he found us? Has my nightmare become reality?

I jump up alarmed and am about to run inside to join Sophie when I see a red Mitsubishi 4-wheel drive come into view. A long, tanned arm waves at me through the window and a friendly voice calls out, "Good morning! I hope you don't mind me dropping by, but Mum has some excess that she thought you might be able to use."

It's Noah. I breathe a sigh of relief still shaking, it's only Noah.

I get up and walk over as he stops the truck and bounds out, reaching into the back he pulls out 3 large Tupperware boxes and looks around at me smiling. "Mum thought you might be able to use these, although I think there's enough to last you until Christmas."

"Oh," I say, taken aback. "That's incredibly kind."

I look on at Noah, still slightly shaken as he stacks each of the large Tupperware boxes on top of each other and lifts them in one sweeping movement of his long, strong arm. "Right, lead on, McDuff!" He gives me a cheery wink as he heads towards the porch. Setting down the boxes, Noah turns to me, about to say something when he stops abruptly, looking at me in concern.

"You're shaking, are you okay?" Noah asks. "Are you cold? It's certainly getting a bit chillier," he adds, "here, sit down, wrap this around you," he pulls out a rug from the blanket box on the porch.

I hadn't realised that I am still shaking, I had got such a shock hearing the car and it had come to me with a jolt just how much I had let down my guard, that it could quite easily have been James driving along the track, finding us. But how? I reason to myself. How would he find us here, here in the whole of the world? Why would he search here?

"Sorry, what was that you said?" I pull myself out of my panic-stricken thoughts as I realise that Noah has asked me something.

"It's okay, I was just saying you are as white as a sheet, are you sure you are okay, maybe we should get you checked out? I know a very good doctor locally," he adds with a smile. He is kneeling aside me, a gentle smile on his face; close up I can see the blonde hairs on his long, tanned legs, he smells so clean and so fresh, a sharp contrast to James. That brings me back to reality with a jolt. James.

"Sorry, no, I mean yes, I am okay, I…I…I just got a start, that's all," I stutter knowing I am making no sense at all.

"Well, I think I interrupted your coffee earlier," he replies with a twinkle, "maybe another coffee and a look in Mum's Tupperware might be just the thing then."

"I think you could be right." I laugh, I'm being silly, the nightmare has left me jumpy, that's all. I get up a little shakily.

"Steady there," Noah murmurs as a strong arm comes around to support me. "I think you should just sit down a moment, if it's one thing I can do, it's make coffee—Mum made sure of that!"

Tucking the blanket around me a little snugger, he gets another to place across my knee. "Now, you sit there and rest a bit, you've probably been overdoing it a bit, I'll make us some coffee." I watch as Noah disappears inside the cabin, taking the three large Tupperware boxes with him.

I sit quietly on the veranda, cocooned in my blankets, listening to the sound of pots clattering gently as Noah sets about making coffee.

Moments later, Noah appears carrying a tray laden with mugs and piled high with baked goods. He settles the tray down on the little table and hands me a steaming hot mug of hot chocolate.

"I thought hot chocolate was better," he winks at me, "and of course, some of Mum's lemon drizzle cake, a failsafe recipe to put you right back on your feet!" He cuts a fat slice and slips it onto a plate, handing it to me. "Now, if anything can put colour into your cheeks, that will!"

Gratefully, I accept the plate and take a bite, immediately my taste buds came to life, watering as the delicious lemony flavour hit my senses, it is delicate and moist with a light tangy sugar and lemon-crusted glaze. Noah is right. This is absolutely delicious.

"MMMM…" I groan, rolling my eyes heavenwards.

"See, I told you, it's Mum's secret recipe," Noah laughs delightedly as he lies back against the seat, one long leg crossed over the other; he looks over at me as he takes a leisurely sip of his hot chocolate whilst I nibble on my cake.

We sit in contented silence for a while, I watch, mesmerised, at the water in front of me when I feel his hand gently on mine.

"Look over there," Noah murmurs quietly in my ear.

I look over to where he motions and gasp. Turning to him, I see the smile spread across his handsome face.

And there, right in front is a pod of dolphins swimming and leaping in the air.

"Oh my!" I sigh in disbelief.

"They've come up to welcome you here." Noah smiles at me. I'm caught for a moment in his gaze, very aware of his large, warm hand on mine. We watch the dolphins playing for a while before they head off. Aware of the closeness of Noah, the comforting feel of his warm hand, the clean scent of him, I am reminded of the contrast to James. James Fear builds in me. I pretend to move the blankets so I can remove my hand surreptitiously.

"That was amazing. Dolphins are so regal," I say to Noah.

"Yes, no doubt we are lucky to live in such a beautiful part of the world," Noah replies, kindness on his face.

"Well, I can see the colour starting to come back to you now, that's much better, I declare a day of rest for you, lass."

I'm not used to someone caring for me, being so kind, thinking what I needed or what would make me feel better. I feel slightly out of my depth, not helped with the fact he is incredibly good looking, I admit to myself as I catch his profile again in the corner of my eye. I focus on my hot chocolate, taking small sips of the rich, warming liquid, nibbling my cake as Noah contentedly chats away, never asking invasive questions or prying. I begin to relax a little.

"Well, that was absolutely the best cake I've ever tasted, I must thank Dotty," I say as I pop the last delicious morsel into my mouth and suck the last bit of sugary lemon glaze from my fingers with a flourish.

Noah laughs, "Well, Mum will be pleased, she loves nothing better than baking," he turns to me, "now, I was thinking, if you like I could—"

Noah's sentence is interrupted as Sophie comes flying out, Lola in hot pursuit. "Noah!" she squeals in delight, wrapping her arms around his waist and hugs him tightly.

"Well, good morning, young Missy, I thought maybe this little princess was going to sleep till noon!"

Sophie giggles in delight. "Princesses have to get their beauty sleep, Mummy says."

"Well, I think Mummy is right," Noah looks over at me and holds my gaze. I can't look away and I feel a warm flush start at the tip of my toes that isn't from the hot chocolate.

"Are you staying to play, Noah, you can come out with us. We're going out for a walk today, we're going to take our books and a picnic too, we've almost finished them, mine is really, really good and Mummy is enjoying hers too, I read all the words myself!" She declares proudly, words tumbling over themselves in her haste to get them out.

"Well now, aren't you the clever one, I think Dotty has some new books in, and I think she might have found ones that you might like."

"Can we go to Dotty's later, Mummy, and look at the new books?" Sophie looks up at me beseechingly.

"Well, I'm sure Noah will be too busy to come out with us, but I think we can certainly manage to go along later today, sweetheart; the rate we are getting through our books, I think we will need a whole library soon!"

"Well, I am sure Dotty will be delighted to see you both too, and of course you too Lola!" Noah says as he gently fondles Lola's ears, Lola lets out a groan of contentment. "Well, ladies, I had better get back now, I am sure Dotty will have a long list of things for me to do, but maybe see you later?" He looks at me, holding my gaze and for a brief second, I am sure I see a fleeting look of hope on his face, quickly replaced seconds later by his broad smile. As he gets up from the seat, Sophie gives him a big hug again. I am surprised by this act from her. She is usually far more reserved, but I choose not to question this.

Waving Noah off, we head back into the kitchen as his red Mitsubishi trundles back along the lane. "Shall we have a look in the tubs that Dotty sent us then, although I don't think there would be anything you would be interested in!" I gently tease. Sophie climbs up onto a stool by the workbench and pulls open the lids.

"Wow Mummy! It is everything from the shop!"

"It certainly looks like it!" I have to agree, for inside the Tupperware there appear to be every kind of baked goods and grocery imaginable, all neatly labelled. I very much doubted that all this is near the sell-by date as Noah had proffered, looking at the vast array laid out in front of us—raspberry and white chocolate scones, fluffy buttermilk pancakes, soda bread, rolls, pots of jam, pickles, pita bread, hummus, a dozen eggs, thick sliced ham and even a jar of olives. Neatly packed in tin foil were two parcels both marked, 'For Lola'. Sophie opened these in glee. "Look Mummy, bones with lots of yummy meat on them for Lola! We can take one on our picnic!"

I am overwhelmed by the kindness and generosity of Dotty, I feel tears pricking the corners of my eyes, a lump appearing in my throat as I wonder how I could ever repay her.

We set about boiling some eggs and packing a picnic for our day's adventures. I know that Sophie would have loved to have Noah stay and join us for our picnic tea, but I can't, I am not ready. It is too soon, if I am being honest, I am scared to allow anyone close. I am not sure if I will ever be ready for that. I put the thought out of my mind and focus on making the picnic.

Twenty minutes later, we have our picnic made and cleared everything away neatly back into the cupboards. "Okay then, I think that's us ready, McGinty, have you got the books?"

Sophie produces them with a flourish. "Absolutely," she replies and lets out a cheeky grin, she always knows how to make me smile with her copying of my words.

"Race you to the shed, Mummy," she calls as she tears off in the direction of the shed.

Bouncing along the track on our bikes the trees shedding their leaves preparing to root down for winter, I lift my face to the breeze, it's getting a lot cooler, but I'm going to take every opportunity to come out that I can, the freedom of being able to do so without criticism or argument is still so new to me, I still cannot get used to it. My first thoughts in the morning are still of the B&B, the tasks I would have to do, then I would remember I am in a different life now. Sometimes when I wake in the middle of the night from a nightmare, I would think of the people I had left behind. No. I correct myself, no, they left *me* behind. They had left me behind when they stopped contacting me.

"Here we are, Mummy," Sophie calls excitedly, distracting me from my thoughts as she pulls aside and hops off her pink bike. We had chosen to come again to the little inlet Noah had told us about. It feels safe and protected.

Shaking myself from the unwanted thoughts, I hop off my bike and we lay them to the side, pulling out the rugs, books, and picnic basket.

"Gosh, next time we shall have to bring a trailer if we bring anything else," I laugh as together we bring the goods down to the sandy cove and set up.

The next few hours are bliss, I know I must take a reality check at some point, get a job, the money will not last long, I know that, but for a few days I need time to heal, time to give Sophie a bit of her childhood back.

Closing my book with a snap, I look up at Sophie happily playing in the sand running to the edge of the water squealing in delight as the cold water tickles her toes before running back up the beach. It does me a world of good to see her enjoying herself, how quickly she has adapted and apart from mentioning her Granda that last time she had never mentioned a word about anyone else. I know I would have to address this at some point, but I put it off, the time would come for that.

She comes running up, this time at full pelt, and throws herself down onto me in a big cuddle. "I love you, Mummy."

"I love you too, sweetheart. To the moon and back. Now, it's getting a little chilly. Do you think we should head back?"

"Can we go to Dotty's and change our books, Mummy, pleeeease?" She smiles her beseeching smile up at me.

"Well, how can I refuse that little face? I think we absolutely can." I wink at her as she giggles. "We can thank Dotty for the lovely treats as well."

"I drew her a picture of us all for her, Mummy," Sophie reaches over and pulls out a picture of the cove with us sitting with the world's largest picnic, Lola with her bone.

"I think she will love that, sweetheart."

"It's such fun here, Mummy."

"I love it here too, hunny, I love it too."

Chapter 40

Sophie runs inside Dotty's, eager to hand over her picture.

"Well now, isn't that just the loveliest picture I have ever seen! I shall put it up here for all my customers to see. They will think a new artist has moved in!" Sophie beams with pride. My heart melts at this lovely lady, the joy she spreads, kindness in her heart.

"Well now, Noah said you had taken a wee turn, dear. Are you feeling better now? My Noah will be here shortly."

"Oh, I'm feeling much better now, I just wanted to thank you for the incredibly delicious and generous box of goodies you sent around."

"You were doing me a favour, my dearie, they were going to be near sell-by soon enough. I just get carried away making things but with this being the end of the tourist season, I haven't adjusted yet." Dotty lets out a twinkling little laugh. "It keeps me out of mischief."

"And you certainly need that, Mum, don't you!" Noah laughs as he walks in through the door, his easy manner filling the room with a sense of calm. "Did I hear someone say my name?" he enquires teasingly of Dotty.

"Now, why would I mention you, son?" Dotty replies, smiling, batting him gently with the tea towel slung over her shoulder. "Why don't all of you sit down, I'm just making a fresh pot of coffee, and I have tried out a new recipe. I would love to try it out on you all, go take a seat outside, make the most of this beautiful weather."

Noah looks at me questioningly, brown eyes expressive as he asks softly, "Is that okay?"

Before I can say anything, Sophie pipes up, "Yes! Yes, come with us, Noah! We can tell you all about our day, it was such fun!"

I nod my reply with a small, shy smile to Noah. A ripple of anxiety runs through me, years of not being able to talk openly to a man, let alone sit and have coffee without repercussions are instilled into me. However, what harm can it do? It's just coffee. They are a lovely family and their kindness, openness, and generosity to us had made me feel that perhaps we could be safe here.

"Yes of course, and please, Dotty, it would be wonderful if you could have coffee with us, if you have the time?" I add.

"Well now, wouldn't that be lovely. Yes, I think I shall, it's been a long day and a wee cup of coffee in the fresh air sounds lovely."

"If you ladies would like to find a table outside, and I'll get the coffees, and don't say anything, Mum, you are always running around looking after things. I am perfectly capable of making a few coffees."

"I shall take you up on that, son, and be happy to do so." Dotty takes a hold of Sophie's proffered hand and guides us outside.

I let the fresh sea air wash over me as we wait patiently for Sophie to choose a table. I smile gently at her look of concentration.

"It has to be just perfect," she declares with the wisdom of one much older. "I want us to see the sea, and the trees, oh and the coffee shop, and…" she stops, "this is the one," she declares and sits down promptly, a huge smile on her pink cherub cheeks, the slight sea breeze lifting her curly locks she looked angelic.

"I do believe you are right, love," Dotty smiles affectionately at her. "I couldn't have picked better myself!"

Settling ourselves down, I let out a sigh of contentment. Dotty looks over at me and smiles a knowing smile, she leans over and pats my hand. "Coffee will be here in a moment, just rest yourself for now, my love."

I do as I am told, grateful for her quiet understanding. Although cooling down, the day is still beautiful, I feel myself relax a little.

"Now then, Missy," Dotty says looking over at Sophie. "I do believe I have some books if you would like to take a wee look inside and see if there were anything that would take your fancy."

"Yes please!" Sophie looks over at me.

I nod, smiling back at Dotty. "I think you have just made her day!"

"And what about you, lovely, what would make your day?"

I want to say: *James never finding us here, to stay safe and build a new life for Sophie and I here. To let my dad know that we are safe. That would make my day.* I couldn't however, so I think for a moment.

"Well, I shall need to find a job, I guess that must be at the top of my list of priorities. Trying to find one that fits around Sophie."

Noah appears back at the table with a tray laden with mugs of hot coffee and a plate piled high with scones and cakes.

"Hot chocolate for Sophie, and three cappuccinos, I thought I would try my hand out with your new machine, Mum. I assumed these were your new recipes, I couldn't decide which to bring so I brought a selection." He winks cheekily over to me with a broad grin on his face.

"Oh, you did now, did you." Dotty laughs. "You never were able to resist my baking. Now the scones are cranberry and fresh ginger, I added a few wee chunks of white chocolate, I thought maybe a wee hint of Christmas, what do you think?"

"Oh, Christmas is my most favourite time of the year," I pipe up.

"Mine too," Dotty agrees, a broad smile enveloping her wholesome face. "It's such a happy time of the year, especially when the snow falls and everything is clean and white."

"Well, aren't you two just out the same pod?" Noah smiles over. "Now, did I hear you saying something about a job?" He looks inquiringly over at me and then back to Dotty. "Mum? What do you think?"

"I know exactly what you are going to say, love, and I was about to say the same thing. I could do with a hand here, love, Noah helps out when he can, but he isn't here all the time with his work. I was thinking about advertising, but if you might be interested..." Dotty trails off.

"Oh wow," I'm overwhelmed, "yes! Yes please! That would be absolutely perfect and such a weight off my shoulders," I gush.

"Well, it's quite flexible and you could easily bring Sophie with you."

"Can we, Mummy, can we really?" Sophie asks excitedly hopping from one foot to another having just returned from her book hunt and was steadily scooping up marshmallows piled high on her hot chocolate. I nod over, smiling, which brings a whoop of joy from her.

Discussing details, I immediately feel lighter. To work here would be simply perfect. Dotty's company is so engaging and friendly. And the fact I could bring Sophie here with me is ideal. I love the atmosphere here at Dotty's. I am to start a week on Monday. Noah would be back at his job then and unable to help as much. Dotty would explain the comings and goings of the store for me. She'd been genuinely delighted to know that I had had previous retail experience before and loved to bake, although nowhere in the league of Dotty, who pooh-poohed this, replying baking simply comes from the heart.

I sit back and let out a small sigh, listening to the friendly banter, sampling the delicious baking, overlooking the waterfront. I cannot help but remember back to the coffee shop outing with James. The contrast between then and now is oceans apart. Sitting here with the easy, friendly chat, no one to stop me going out, to interrogate my every move, no one just waiting for an opportunity to give retribution for anything they deemed wrong. Simply being a part of conversation, it was worlds apart. There were never any intrusive questions, they hadn't asked where I was from, or thought that a woman on her own appearing with a young child and a dog, with no more than a few bags of belongings to show a life's achievement was strange. I wondered what they made of us, if they found any of this strange but I was glad they had simply accepted us. I was eternally grateful.

The coffee and baking are all gone now, I want it to last longer but know we must go, these lovely people have things to do.

"Right then, McGinty, I think it is time we head back to our cabin."

Sophie picks up the books and clutches them tightly to her, getting up she gives Dotty a huge hug. "Thank you, Dotty, I am going to read these tonight!"

"What! All of them, you will be up all night!"

"Well, maybe not all of them." Sophie giggles.

Dotty comes over to me and envelopes me in a big hug, I could have stayed in her embrace forever, so warm and comforting she is, the aroma of home baking surrounding her. Reluctantly, I pull away and we say our goodbyes, the skies are looking grey and it looks ominously like rain.

Refusing the offer of a lift back from Noah saying we enjoyed the rain and we wouldn't shrink, we set off. True to form, big wet splashes of rain come down as we head into the woods.

Nothing could dampen my spirits though. I feel a spring in my step as we walk along the track. I had secured a job! An actual job! I let out a whoop and dance around on the track, Sophie joins in, and Lola lets out a few barks, dancing around our feet, eager to be part of the excitement. The rain is pelting down heavily now, soaking us to the skin. Leaves are falling in swirls from the trees. Things are coming together. I start to feel alive. I feel the rain is washing away the remnants of my previous life. Maybe, just maybe a tiny little bit of me is making a comeback. Nudging its way back. It would be a long road, but every journey must start with a single step.

"Come on, Sophie sweetheart, let's see if we can both race Lola back home!"

Chapter 41

Once inside the cabin and shaking off our wet coats, Sophie runs to her room 'to show Teddy the new books', whilst I shake off my coat and head to the bathroom. It had been a long day, and I am ready for a long, hot bath, put my pyjamas on and just sit by the fire and read my book. There is no one to tell me I am lazy, that it was alright for me, I didn't work 24 hours a day, 7 days a week, the mantra that was ingrained into my head.

Turning the water on, I strip off my clothes. The bruises still evident are turning more green than angry purple and black. There will be no more when they are gone. My skin would return to its usual colour. I won't have to hide behind long sleeves and trousers any longer.

I pour bubble bath into the running water, creamy white bubbles jostled for top place with each other. A luxury to me, thinking back to the cheapest bath and shower gels I had been able to find. James grudging every penny, seeing them as an unnecessary luxury.

Slipping into the steamy bubbly liquid, I let the water caress my tired body, still achy and stiff from fists and boots.

My mind drifts to the lovely day we have had, the new job I would soon be starting, of Dotty, of Noah. Handsome, strong, kind, and calm Noah. His long, tanned arms, the broad shoulders. His clean, fresh scent, gleaming white teeth. Images of size-fourteen boots, fight for space in my head, stained teeth, strong hands, once caressing now only capable of inflicting pain flood into my thoughts, pushing Noah to one side. I sigh. No. I can't let myself go there. I can't allow myself ever to get that close to someone. To allow that to happen again.

I know that day by day, hour by hour, minute by minute I am entering a new life. There would be no fists. No size-fourteen boots. No stained teeth close up. No…

Stop! I chide myself. *Don't let your mind go there. Don't spoil your lovely day. You can be strong. You can be strong*, I murmur quietly to myself.

The water is cooling as I pull the plug, stepping out of the bath I towel myself off, wrapping the towel around me. I watch as the water swirls the last remaining bubbles down the drain, a flashback of watching water swirl down the drain after that awful night. I pull the towel tighter around me and quickly go to the bedroom, slipping my pyjamas on, I head to the log burner. It's not long before I have a fire going, the flames warm and cosy, letting out a friendly crackle.

I look out of the kitchen window, there is quite a storm brewing. Hot chocolate is what we need to finish such a lovely day, I think as I turn back into the kitchen to pull out the pan. I stop dead.

For there, on the work surface, are two mugs. Just sitting there on the counter. I swear I put those away. My mind flashes back to the first morning when the coffee had been misplaced. A roll of thunder breaks out in the sky above, making me jump. I try to think, think back to the morning. I know I put those away.

"Mummy!" Sophie appears in the kitchen. "I'm scared."

"It's okay, sweetheart, it's just a storm, we are safe inside." I have to ask, I don't want to frighten her, but I have to know. "Hunny, did you get these mugs out ready for us?"

"No, I was reading my book to Teddy."

Before I can say anything, the lightning cracks loudly outside, making us both jump.

"Mummy!" Sophie wails, holding me tightly. Spooked as I am, I need to keep her calm.

"Let's count how many seconds it is from the next roll of thunder until the lightning, then we will know how far away the storm is, shall we? Come on, let's get our hot chocolate first and cosy up by the fire, how does that sound?"

As I pull out the jar of cocoa and put milk in the pan to heat, my mind flashes back to the first morning where the coffee had been in the cupboard under the sink. The open window. Was it just a weird coincidence? Am I just being jumpy? Paranoid? A loud roll of thunderclaps outside.

"Okay Sophie, one…two…three…four…fi…"

Crack, a vivid streak of lightning splits the sky in two.

"Wow, that was a loud one! Okay, so a little more than four we got to, that makes the storm four miles away. Let's see when the next one is." The distraction appears to be working with Sophie as she now eagerly awaits the next roll of thunder to begin counting. The rain is lashing against the windows now, making it difficult to hear ourselves. The milk starts to simmer and I move it from the stove.

Another roll of thunder announces its arrival.

"One…two…three…f…" squeals Sophie in glee. "Mummy, it's coming closer, it's three miles away now!"

"I wonder if it will come closer?" Trying to keep her distracted, I spoon the cocoa into the waiting mugs and fill them with milk as another clap of thunder rolls in.

"One, two…thr—" I look out the window as a bolt of lightning lights up the darkness, showing a face at the window.

We both scream and I drop the mugs I have been holding; they shatter on the floor, spilling the sweet dark contents, the noise lost in the midst of the storm. "Sophie, go to your room and lock yourself in. I will be there in a moment." I am terrified, unsure what to do, how to keep us safe.

"Mummy, I'm scared, and so is Lola." Sophie's lip trembles.

"I know, sweetheart, everything is fine, it's just the trees making silly pictures against the window. Nothing more." I try to calm her, sounding more confident than I felt. Even I don't believe myself as she flees to her room with Lola in tow.

My heart is hammering. The mugs appearing has put me on edge, the coffee under the sink. Am I being paranoid? Has he found us? Is he playing with us? How have I just been able to forget what I'd done? Am I losing my mind? Imagining things. Imagining faces? His face at the window. Another roll of thunder quickly proceeds another flash of lightning. The rain is pelting down heavily now; the generator groans into silence, the lights flicker and go out. Nervously, I look towards the window, pushing my back against the wall as the thunder lets out an almighty rumble, hot on its tail comes the lightning. The face appears again, and I scream, every hair on my limbs standing at the proximity.

I can hear loud banging coming from somewhere. Fear tears through my very being. *He has found us. What am I to do. How can I protect Sophie now?*

The shouting is becoming louder, infiltrating into my fear-struck mind.

"Isla, Isla! It's Noah, I just came around to check you are okay," Noah shouts as loud as he can through the rain.

It takes a moment for his voice, his name, to sink into my terrified mind. I don't know whether to laugh or to cry, such is the relief and shock.

I run to the door and open it, "Noah!" I cry in relief letting him in.

"I just thought…" he trails off as he spots the broken crockery on the floor, the sticky contents of hot chocolate spilling from it. "I'm sorry to have given you such a fright, just Mum was worried about you getting caught in the rain and sometimes the generator packs in during a storm and she thought you might need help."

"That's really kind of you, I guess I am just jumpy, and yes the generator has given up." I look up at him, relief flooding through me. "You're soaking."

"Don't be worrying about me, I'll nip out and sort the generator, after all, I can't get any wetter!" Noah winks cheerily, his customary broad grin splitting his kind face, revealing gleaming white teeth.

Relieved, I gratefully accept Noah's offer and head back to Sophie. Knocking gently on her door, I call through explaining that everything is okay. That it's just Noah checking we are okay. As she unlocks the door from the inside, I see her small white face appear.

"Is it really just Noah? Lola thought…" she trails off. "Lola thought it was a ghost, Mummy." She pauses a moment as though deep in thought before adding, "Lola is happy it's Noah and so is Teddy!" A smile spreads over her face as she holds up Teddy. "Do you think Noah might like some hot chocolate?"

"I would think he might just, hunny, shall we go and see?"

Moments later, Noah comes back in with a stack of logs in his arms as I'm about to clean up the broken cups and spillages.

"I thought you might need these too; it could be a long night with the looks of that storm."

Laying them down gently by the stove, he turns around to look at me, a look of concern passed over his face. "Isla," he says tenderly, coming over to me, "you are as white as a sheet. I am so sorry, really, I am, here, sit down. I'll finish cleaning that up and make you a hot drink."

I try to insist that I am fine, that I was just jumpy from the first storm in a new place. Noah gives me a curious look as he insists that I sit down. Sophie chatters away alongside as he sets about making fresh cups of cocoa, making short work of the broken crockery and spilt cocoa; he brings over fresh mugs of steaming hot cocoa before turning to stack more logs onto the fire. This close, I can see the fine blonde hairs on his long, lean, shorts-clad, tanned legs, muscles flexing as he kneels to stack the logs. He has the kind of build that comes from being active rather than from the gym. Being so close to him, I feel the comforting aura that emanates him, his easy way that makes me feel more relaxed in his company.

Stacking another log on the fire, Noah turns around to me, he looks at me a moment before saying, "If it's okay with you both, I can stay a little while till the storm goes over, make sure the generator doesn't go off again?"

I pause a moment before nodding, realising that having his presence in the cabin would reassure both Sophie and myself. I hadn't realised quite how much on edge I had been since arriving here. "That would be kind, thank you."

"Noah, can I read you some of my books?" Sophie asked Noah. "I want to be a famous author one day!"

"Well, sure, young lady, I would be privileged to hear you read. I have every faith that you will indeed be a very famous author one day and I shall be able to say that you once read to me!"

I settle down, watching as Sophie reads aloud to us, the log fire crackling merrily in the grate I feel myself beginning to feel a little more relaxed. We drink our hot chocolate contentedly until Sophie finishes her story with a dramatic 'The End!'

"Okay now, Missy, I think it's time for your bed. Noah is going as well."

"Night, night, Noah, thank you for my hot chocolate." Sophie scoops up her teddy and climbs off the chair, Lola follows her, both tired out.

"Goodnight, princess, thank you for that lovely story," Noah calls after her as I walk her back along to her room. As I tuck her tightly into bed, I doubt it will be very long before she is fast asleep, Lola tucked in tightly beside her.

Heading back through to the living area, I see Noah standing by the door. "I shall leave you to it, Isla, as long as you are both okay?"

"Yes, yes of course, and thank you again so much for tonight."

"I'm just sorry I gave you both such a fright, it's just with no internet or phones that work out here, Mum was worried about you all."

"Well, I am very grateful you came, or we would have had no power! And you definitely made Sophie's night letting her read to you!"

"Any time, it is my pleasure, she's such a sweetie," he pauses again, his eyes linger on me, unwavering, until they draw mine to meet his gaze. "I really enjoyed myself too, Isla." He pauses before continuing, "I was wondering, I know how much you both love your books, in town there is an amazing bookstore, Leaky's Bookshop, I was thinking, if you like I could take you both there?"

I'm not sure what to say, I know Sophie and I would both love that but…I open my mouth and close it again without a word coming out.

Noah looks at me with a gentle smile, his expression knowing as he continues, "Anyway, I think the worst of the storm has passed now. Are you sure you're okay?"

"Yes absolutely!" I confirm, "It was just, just old haunts spooking me in the storm, I was just being silly."

"No, you weren't. You are safe here, Isla." He gives me a look I find difficult to discern.

I can't think of anything to say so I just nod.

Thankfully, Noah carries on, "Now, anything you need, anytime…" trailing off he adds, "remember, that's what friends are for, right then, I'll be off," and with that he leans down and gives me a gentle hug. I feel his long, strong arms about me and before I can think whether I should give him a brief hug back, he releases me.

"Get some rest, Isla, it's been quite a day for you, and I shall see the three of you at Dotty's!" His face is wreathed in kindness, a smile covers his handsome face as he gives me his customary cheery wink.

I smile back up at him. "You sure will!"

"Make sure you lock that door tight now; the night is still a little wild." He gives me another cheery wink and disappears off into the dark stormy night.

I do feel guilty not letting Noah wait out the storm after his kindness, checking that we were all safe. Was I intolerably rude making the statement that "Noah is going as well"? I wonder as I brush my teeth and slip into bed, letting the soft duvet embrace me. I can still feel the warm embrace of Noah's strong arms. But no, I have to keep my distance, I remind myself. Keep my walls up. Walls keep you safe. Safe. Safe…are my last thoughts as I drift off to sleep. Rumbles of thunder are white noise now filtering into my dreams as I sleep fitfully.

Chapter 42

Waking the next morning, I can see that the storm has passed over. I'm exhausted after a restless night. My mind plays back over the previous night. How silly I had been to think James had found us. It was Noah, kind Noah looking out for us on a stormy night. A normal thing for someone to do. To think of two people out in the woods alone in the middle of a storm. Normal maybe, but I am not used to normal. I slip my legs over the side of the bed, letting my toes curl into the soft rug beneath for a moment before padding through to the kitchen.

I never fail to feel a sense of calm wash over me when I see the neat and tidy order of this little cabin. Our little sanctuary in the woods. I busy myself making a cup of strong black coffee and head out to the front porch to drink it, wrapping a blanket about me as I curl up onto the swing seat watching the dolphins play.

As I sip the strong black liquid, I catch a glimpse of something in the corner of my eye to the left of the waterside in the trees. I look harder, is that a glint of glass? I feel the unnerving sense of someone watching me.

Stop being silly, after last night and faces at the window that was only Noah. You're just feeling jittery, I scold myself. I refuse to be at the beck and call of my overwrought mind. I sit firmly on the swing seat wrapped in the cosy rug to finish my coffee. I don't see any more glints and try to put my mind at ease. Finishing my coffee, I head back in to have a shower and change. I hear Sophie chatting away to Lola and Teddy.

Chapter 43

Did she actually think she could leave me? It hadn't taken him more than ten minutes to find her phone. Arriving back in the early hours of the morning from Edinburgh and finding the house in darkness. Empty. He had gone for a walk to see if they had gone out for a late-night walk with that damn dog. Walking along the verge and following the tracking from his phone, he spotted it straight away. He knew immediately that she had run away. The phone chucked carelessly to the side. Well, he knew just how that phone felt.

She thought she was being clever, chucking it away so he couldn't trace her. Well, not that clever, he thought victoriously. You didn't think the car had a tracking device as well. I knew I was right to do that. Just like the tracking device he had on her phone. You were cheating on me all along. I knew it. You will pay for this, he had thought as he logged onto his phone. The image in front of him blipped as it moved, he could see exactly where she was. A slow sneer spread over his face. But you can wait. You will pay for this, but it can wait.

He had been here almost a week now, camping out in the Range Rover, watching her. The rage had boiled up in James. He watched intensely through the binoculars as she sat on the front porch. Just look at her drinking her coffee as though she doesn't have a care in the world. The audacity of her to steal money from him. HIM! After everything he did for her, and this is how she repays him. He had been right all along. She was cheating on him. Remembering last night as he had almost been caught peering through the windows, until He had arrived. Who did he think he was? A knight in shining armour coming to rescue her. Well, he had stayed plenty long enough.

The rage bubbled up inside him as his mind went mad thinking about what they were doing in there. His hands touching her, the body that belonged to him…no he couldn't think that, he could very well kill her. What was he to do? Watching them sitting having breakfast together all romantic and family like out at that cafe. Well, it was his family, and he wasn't going to let anyone take her away from him. She belonged to him. She had married him. She was his and his alone.

Watching him come around that morning with all those cakes. Wrapping her up in that blanket. Making her drinks. The red mist had descended. He knew what he needed to do. It was his duty. His right to remind her. But first, he had to get her back home. He watched on as she sat on the porch swing, through the binoculars she looked as though he could reach out and touch her.

He raised his fist, unclenching his fingers; he could fit her in the palm, he closed his fingers, he could imagine her squealing out in pain, his fingers around her neck, her gasping her last breath. She stared at him and he dropped the binoculars and slid stealthily back behind the tree. No, she couldn't possibly have seen him. He glanced again through the binoculars; no, she was sat there. He watched until she got up and went back into the cabin.

Chapter 44

"Right McGinty, are you ready?" I call through from my room as I pull on my running tights and a sweatshirt. It's getting a lot cooler and my mind is in turmoil. A few miles' run would clear my head then we could head into Dotty's for breakfast.

"You're getting really good at running, Mummy," Sophie says loyally as we pull out her bike.

"Why, thank you, young lady, and you are getting really good on your bike!"

"Can we cycle straight to Dotty's? I think it would be good to let them know we are safe after the big storm."

"I think that sounds excellent." She is growing up so fast and wise beyond her years. I pull my hair up into a ponytail and we head off at a slow jog.

A few hours later, we head back to the cabin. I luxuriate in the feel of the breeze from the water, letting the fresh air caress my limbs. Dotty and Noah had been delighted to see us and had filled us full of sumptuous breakfast, they had both been in great form and it had been with reluctance that I had said we must head back home. I let my mind drift back to the evening before. The fright we had got in the storm. Then Noah showing up. How easy it had been in Noah's company, how welcome Dotty made us feel, how Sophie had taken to them both, unquestioning about the length of time we would stay here. How much the log cabin felt like home in such a short time.

I take in a deep breath, enjoying the warmth of the sun, the blue skies that had followed the storm, Sophie happily cycling in front of me, blonde tresses flying in the breeze. I can hear her calling out to Lola as she lolloped beside Sophie contentedly, black and white spotty body keeping pace alongside, full of Dotty's famous sausages. I was looking forward to a long hot shower and then a relaxing afternoon reading. I was excited to start work at Dotty's next week. I had offered to start sooner but Dotty had insisted we have 'a bit of a break, lass'.

It was a godsend, and I couldn't believe how lucky we had been to stumble upon this place.

"Come on, Mummy, nearly there!" Sophie calls out encouragingly from in front as I stride along. I love the feeling of running alongside the waterfront, knowing we are going back to safety. I've never seen Sophie more relaxed or happy, we are content in new surroundings, and I'm beginning to relax. The sunlight is peeking through the trees, reflecting off the water close by. I try to put the few odd things out of my mind as I let my feet fall rhythmically to the forest floor.

I get a flashback of pounding the roads back at the house. The hard tarmac. The escape that running there had given me before the prison of the treadmill. The escape. Yes, I had done it. I had got us out safely. We could start a new life here. It's perfect. We could be lost amongst the tourists, and in the quiet season, well, no one came out of season, we would just be locals. A local serving in a coffee shop. A no one. Yes. A no one is a good person to be. Safe. Being no one kept you safe.

As we turned the corner approaching the cabin, I let out a deep contented sigh. Home. A smile slides happily onto my face. I no longer need a mask. The smiles are genuine.

"Race you inside, Mummy!" Sophie shouts gleefully, hopping off her bike and propping it against the wall before bounding up the wooden steps onto the veranda. "I win!"

"Yes, you did! You are quite the little speedy now." I let out a contented sigh. It really is the simple things. "Okay sweetheart," I say as I unlock the door. "Right, I think I'm going to go for a lovely hot shower then I think a—"

"A hot chocolate and read by the water, Mummy," Sophie finishes for me.

"Absolutely, I think you read my mind!" I ruffle her hair as I kick off my shoes in the hallway. "Right, are you okay whilst I go for a shower?"

"Of course," Sophie replies. "Lola and I are going to choose a book to read, I love our princess palace and so does Lola!" and with that she ran up the hallway, blonde tresses flying out behind as she disappears into her bedroom.

I head into the bathroom contentedly, the thought of a delicious hot shower with bubbly suds in front of me. As I reach over to turn the shower on, a clatter catches my attention. I look up, the window clatters open and closed again, the little curtain swaying in the breeze.

That's odd, I was sure I had closed that? I am about to call through and ask Sophie, but I think again, I don't want to scare her, not after last night, I'd probably just forgotten to close it. I chastise myself for being so silly and jumpy. It was just after last night, I'd been so sure I'd seen his reflection, but no, it had been Noah. Noah had come to see if we were safe. That was all. No one is watching, no one has found us, we are safe. I pull the window shut and put the snib on before firmly closing the curtains.

Checking the water is hot, I slip off my clothes before sliding under the shower, enjoying the pressure of the hot water caressing my limbs. I let the water flow over me enjoying the fact that today we could just relax and enjoy reading. It had been such a lovely start to the day having breakfast at Dotty's then a lovely run. Soon it would be the start of another adventure. Working in Dotty's. I couldn't wait. As I shampoo my hair, rinsing off the bubbles, I lather thick conditioner into it, twisting it up into a unicorn spike I get a sudden flashback— a flashback to the old life, when I was excitedly getting ready to go out to the book club. The disastrous night…no! Don't let yourself go there. You are safe. I remind myself.

It's hard though. Hard to forget. It hasn't been very long since we escaped, but at some times it feels like a lifetime, at others it feels like I am in a dream and I'm still at home. It's worse during the night. I felt like I'm being watched. I wake up in the night and imagine I can see someone at the window. Other times I am sure I feel eyes on me, eyes on us as we walk, cycle, or run along the path. I'm being silly I realise, as I remember our escape in the depths of the night. Of my phone lying, likely now crushed under a hundred tyres. There was no way he could have found us. I rinse off the conditioner, switch off the shower and reach for the big fluffy towel. Rubbing myself vigorously dry, I slip on a robe and wrap a towel turban style around my wet hair. I think longingly of the hot chocolate, yes, just what I need to relax, it's been quite an eventful few days. I pad through to the kitchen and pull out 2 cups to make our hot drinks.

"Is that one for me as well?" a familiar voice appears from behind me.

I stop, every breath drained from my body, unable to move.

"Did you miss me, darling?"

Slowly, I steel myself to turn around, willing myself to be wrong.

I open my mouth and close it again, unable to utter a word because standing in front of me is James.

A slow smile spreads across his face. "You have been gone a long time. I thought you would have come home by now." His voice is eerily quiet. I know this voice. "You look different. You look good. I can't believe I found you. I missed you, but it's time to come home now."

"What are you doing here?" I utter hopelessly. "No, I can't, we can't, James, it's no life, please, please just let us go, I don't want anything from you, you can have everything, please just let us go."

"You want me to just walk away? Seriously? You actually think I would do that?"

"You kept hurting me, James."

"How many times do you want me to say I'm sorry? I give you everything, everything. What else do you want from me?"

"I can't live like that, please…"

"That's why you need to come home," he replies, deliberately misunderstanding. He lurches forward and I shrink back in fear. I can see the menace in his eyes, bloodshot and furious.

"Stop! Sophie is here. Stop!"

James stops hand mid-air, his steely eyes boring into me, dark beetling brows twitching below his wild, red curly hair, his sheer height looming over me. A look all too familiar to me passes over his face.

His voice is barely audible now. "My money. You took my money," the low tones of his voice are more terrifying than if he was shouting his mouth next to my ear, "you'll pay for this; oh yes, you'll wish you'd never been born, now come, you're coming home. You can do it the easy way, or you can do it the hard way, but one way or the other, you are coming back with me."

He grabs at my arm, twisting it painfully.

"James, stop," I gasp, "please stop, you need help, we need to get you help, explain what's going on, people will understand, they'll know how much pressure you are under."

"What! Who are you going to tell? Do you actually think anyone will believe you?" he gleefully spits at me.

I stutter and try to get words out, any words, pain is coursing through my body.

"Don't play with me, Isla, you won't win." James's jowls are shuddering, his eyes bulbous, teeth greener than ever. "You won't win, not anymore, I decide when this is over, not you."

"Please, let go of my arm," I plead hopelessly.

Ignoring me, he replies instead, "Don't test me, Isla."

"I will go to the police," I reply as a last effort.

"I wouldn't do that if I were you."

"Why not?" I reply defiantly, nothing to lose now.

"Because I will destroy everything, everything you love, and I don't make empty threats."

"You are crazy, out of your mind, you know that?"

Before he can answer, a small voice filters through the chaos. "Mummy?" I hear Sophie calling, hesitantly from the little hall. "Mummy?" she repeats appearing in the kitchen, the colour draining from her face as she takes in the scene. "Mummy?" she repeats again, her voice full of questions I can't answer. "Mummy?"

James turns to Sophie. "Go pack up your things, the holiday is over."

Sophie looks at me, her face now ashen white. I don't know what to do, I feel sick, physically sick. I wish the ground would open up and swallow me, anything was better than this.

James leans into me, his unwashed stench adding to my nausea, and says barely audibly, "I'll never let you go. Never."

I know I have lost.

The car journey has been inextricably long, the monstrosity of the house looms in front of my mind, and I know there and then the jail door is sealed, double-locked with no chance of parole. My heart falls. I had tasted freedom, how it could be, and this was my fate. I dare not think what the retaliation will be. Not a word had been spoken the entire journey. I didn't know what to say. I sat in the back. Sophie and Lola huddled together, frightened.

I feel sick. Sick that I had had this opportunity. Flashbacks replay over and over in my mind, Sophie's happy face, her delighted squeals as the water lapped at her little feet, as we sat reading at night by the log fire, blonde tresses flying in the wind as she cycled happily along the forest paths. Now back to this. This cold house. Back to the life everyone wanted…

Chapter 45

The weeks after arriving back in the village had been worse than even I could have imagined. I chose to cut those weeks out of my mind. If I didn't, I don't know what would have happened. I just know I have to survive. To survive, survive somehow for Sophie's sake. I had gotten used to closing myself off, I had long ago become a robot, focussing on survival—Sophie, my work, keeping the house clean, the bed and breakfast well organised. I put on the front that kept us safe, slipping my mask on daily whenever I left the house, whenever I met people. The face people expected. The happy, carefree face without any problems or cares. No one wanted anything different, they wanted what they wanted to believe. It's safer and simpler to do that. *Don't poke the bear,* I think. Our absence had been explained by a 'well deserved break' and was no longer spoken of.

That had been 457 days and 16 hours ago. I had never been more afraid or alone in my life. I often thought of Dotty and Noah. What had they made of our sudden unexplained absence? I had thought about sending them a message; however, I realised to do this would put them in danger, danger from James. They were lovely people and didn't deserve to be dragged into my mess. No, they were safer out of it. They would forget about us. After all, we had only been there a week. To me though, it was a week that would give me hope, hope in my darkest days. Hope that I would be able to escape again.

I am constantly in a house full of people but feel entirely alone. Every day with the guests is becoming harder. Only my plan keeps me going. The thought of a new life for Sophie and I, a future that was safe, a future with a life. We had had a taste of what life could be like. The plan that had to be executed properly this time. Nothing left to chance. I couldn't do that again. I wouldn't survive that. I knew I wouldn't.

I knew there would be a chance eventually, I had to keep hoping, keep praying, I needed the idea there would be an opportunity to keep me going.

Without hope, I had nothing. Today was particularly tough. I had worked late last night getting everything ready for the morning, ensuring everything was laid out ready for the guys needing coffee and toast at 5.30 am before they headed out. The noise they had made had awoken Sophie up and when we came downstairs, it was as though a bomb had gone off. It was now past 1pm the breakfasts had all been done and I was clearing away the last remnants of the debris when the phone rang.

"Isla?" an unfamiliar female voice queries at the other end of the line.

"Yes?" I answer hesitantly.

"Nothing to worry about, it's just Marjorie, the school liaison officer. I wondered if I could pop around to see you?"

"Umm, yes, okay, when?" I proffer, caught off-guard.

"Well, now actually if you can spare a few minutes, it won't take long, and I am passing your door anyway," she adds persuasively.

"Oh, umm, okay," I reply tentatively.

"Super, I'll see you in a few minutes then." Click. The phone goes dead.

What could this be about? I wonder. It's never good when someone says *nothing to worry about but…*

As I wait for Marjorie, I cast my eye about me looking for anything untidy or out of place. No, everything was as neat as a pin, finally. James wouldn't be back for a while yet, having gone out again hunting for quarry straight after the last group of guys had left, their holiday over. I hear a knock at the door.

Hesitantly and with a knot of concern building in the depths of my stomach, I answer the door.

"Isla, thank you so much for seeing me at such short notice," a bright-eyed, middle-aged woman articulates to me from the doorstep before I have time to say anything.

"Please, come in." I gesture as I take in Marjory's cheery face, blonde hair. She is medium height, slim build and wearing a pretty floral dress with a lightweight jacket, feet adorned with sensible pumps.

Marjory follows me into the kitchen, still fresh with the aroma of cooked breakfast, the bacon and coffee scents vying for top place.

"Oooh, what a lovely smell, doesn't that make you hungry?" Marjory smiles over to me.

"A bit," I lie knowing the answer she wanted. "Would you like a coffee?" I offer, automatically reaching for the kettle.

"Oh, yes please, that would be lovely."

Marjory makes small talk as I busy myself with the coffee.

"Black, no sugar," Marjory interjected my thoughts of working out why she was here.

"Oh, same as me then," I smile handing over the cup.

"I'm sure you are wondering why I'm here?"

I nod, saying nothing.

"We are a little concerned about Sophie. I've been seeing her a few times now about her reluctance to come into school, I just wanted to have a little chat about it with you, so…" she lists off a few questions. She has a gentle and no doubt experienced way of asking things and I feel my head start to spin, my heart quicken its pace. This is not going well and I have a sense of foreboding building deep within me.

"Isla? Did you hear what I just said?"

I click back to register Marjory's concerned face looking at me, her voice gentle as she repeats herself. *"That's domestic abuse."*

The words hit me like a bucket of ice water.

"No. No," I reply vehemently. "No, everything is fine."

"Isla," Marjory breaks in gently. "It is domestic abuse, and I'm going to have to feed this back."

My head whirls. No. If anyone finds out what really happens here, James will be so mad. It'll make matters so much worse. I try to convince this well-meaning lady everything is fine, but to no avail.

"I shall go now and let you get on with your day, but please remember we're here for you," she hands me a card with her number as well as a few different organisations on it. I don't really take in what she says. Something about phone calls and people getting in touch, but all I can think about is James's reaction. In the recesses of my mind, I know what he does is wrong. I have long disappeared from the person I once was. The happy, vivacious being, full of life and joy, to the quiet wreck I now am. It has been an almost imperceptible change, like the drip, drip that forms stalactites. You don't notice it happening but bit by bit, it forms a mighty presence, and just like a stalactite you hold on tightly for dear life or you fall, fall into a crumbly heap on the ground and you can't do that, not when you have a child to live for and protect.

I look at the half-empty coffee cup and the empty chair that only a few minutes ago had been occupied. How in that short space of time everything has changed. I could already feel it.

Left alone to my own thoughts, I become panicky. I set about my work on autopilot for what feels like seconds, or was it hours? Time has no meaning. I'm behind with my jobs after the meeting. I walk to school on autopilot, keeping my mask on. I pretend everything is normal. I am well accustomed to that. I am good at that.

Back home, Sophie is happy to go up and play in her room whilst I busy myself loading the last of the dishes through the dishwasher when my phone bursts into life again.

I take a deep steadying breath. *No Caller ID* flashes across the screen. Reluctantly, I hit the green answer button, fear fills me. This can't be good.

"Is that Isla Campbell?" The stranger at the other end of the phone queries.

"Yes," I murmur. I never like it when my full name is used. I sense trouble.

"And is this a safe place for you to talk?"

"Um, yes?" I reply, looking around me, slightly confused at her line of questions.

"I just need to go through a few questions before we can continue."

"Who is this, and what is it in relation too?" I ask the girl on the end of the phone who insists on answering a few basic questions, my DOB and a few other questions before saying, "I'm sorry about that, I just needed to ascertain it was you I was speaking too. It's DAAS." She goes on to briskly explain that they are a service for domestic abuse I've been referred to after my earlier meeting. *They work fast,* I think to myself.

"I need to ask a few questions. It is a set of 20 to assess if you are at risk." All very brisk and professional. I try to say that everything is okay, and I don't really need them, however she interjects brusquely that if I do not answer then social services will be in touch.

Knowing I have no choice, I whisper almost inaudibly. "Okay."

On and on the questions go. At the end, I feel physically and emotionally drained.

"Isla, I am going to have to refer this to the police. The firearms will need to come around, and the likelihood is the firearms will be removed from the property."

No, no, this can't be happening, this is going to make things worse.

The phone is silent, I stare at it still sitting traitorously in my open palm. It's just me. Alone. Again. But now things are worse. The lady hung up with words of advice to call 999 if any situation escalated. *Great suggestion that is,* I think to myself, *his friends are all in the police, how is that going to help? He will be so mad.* I begin to panic.

Sophie is upstairs playing in her room. It gives me time to think. I set about making her tea. I don't know what to do. All I know is this cannot turn out well.

The phone interrupts my thoughts yet again. It's Marjorie.

"Isla, is it safe to talk?"

I look around me. James is out with the boys at a late shoot.

"Yes," I reply in barely a whisper. This feels surreal.

"I just wanted to keep you in the loop, as you know I had to pass on my findings. I know you have already had a call, but just to say that the police will be calling in with you shortly to speak to James about his firearms. Now, he doesn't know yet, but it's just to give you a heads-up."

She continues with a few placatory comments, but all I can think of is that the fat is truly on the fire now and I am completely helpless. Not that I had any control before, but this is now spinning precariously and I am terrified of the fallout.

I hang up. Calm. That's what is needed. Calm. I feel anything but. I need to keep calm for Sophie. And in a routine. Teatime. Teatime is a good routine.

I walk across the marble to the bottom of the stairs and call up for Sophie.

"Teatime, sweetheart. Macaroni cheese, your favourite!" I sound more jovial than I feel.

I click on the TV. For a treat, we sit together watching CITV whilst Sophie has her tea. Lola is curled up next to her sound asleep on the sofa. I am too anxious to eat.

Just then I hear the back door burst open and ricochet off the wall, heavy footsteps clang along the hallway, getting closer and closer, my breath catches in my throat as the living room door slams open, getting the same treatment as the back door.

"Well, you have only gone and done it now, haven't you!" James rages from the doorway. "What have you been saying to the police? They are coming over now and they are going to take my guns off me. That's the end. I can't work.

244

There will be no money. We will lose the house. You stupid idiot," he rages on, face puce with anger, saliva spraying in all directions from his yellow teeth, red hair dancing wildly. "What did I say to you?" he demands. "Keep your stupid mouth shut. You have totally done it, now you are in trouble. *Big trouble.*"

Not waiting for an answer, James storms off up the hall door banging the door again off the wall in his wake. *When I'm through with her, she will rue the day she was born. And as for that meddling school, well, I'll soon sort them out.*

With great effort, he brought his rage under control, repressing the roar that was always threatening to erupt. He needed to think. To sort the situation. "Okay, you have influential friends in high places, thank god for that," he muttered into the silence that surrounded him, but he needed to act quickly. He needed to stop this one way and for all. He had just the answer.

A sneer appeared over James's ruddy face, separating his tight lips from each other, revealing a set of crooked, rapidly decaying teeth. He slipped along the hall and into his office, opening the locked filing cabinet and pulling out a set of keys. *Yes, he knew exactly how he could resolve this situation. Interfering bitch at the school, interfering friends, and his pathetic, idiot wife. Oh yes, he would make them rue the day they crossed him. They would pay. They would all pay. She won't get a penny, he would make sure of that!*

Sophie shrinks back into me and holds me so tightly I fear she will break. Lola, awake now, jumps up to cuddle into both of us. I am rooted to the sofa. The room is quiet. Gravely quiet. Sophie looks up at me, lips quivering.

"What did Daddy mean, Mummy? Why are you in trouble?" Tears slip from her pale blue eyes, wide open in her pale face, blonde curls bouncing as she struggles to get the words out.

Shaking deep within me from the verbal onslaught and the not knowing what was coming, I draw in a deep and calming breath, slowly letting it out.

"Daddy was just playing a silly game, that's all," I try as lightly as I can.

Sophie looks up at me, her face questioning but says nothing, slipping her hand into mine she hesitates before murmuring, "Lola is frightened, Mummy."

"Lola would maybe like a little treat, do you think? And maybe one for Sophie? I think we could make some hot chocolate and then go upstairs and read a book all together." Trying my best to calm Sophie through some normality, I

245

sweep as much of a smile onto my face as I can muster and bring her into a tight hug. "Come on, let's go see what we can find, McGinty."

Sophie nods but stays silent as I chat away, heading to the kitchen trying to distract her as much as possible. A subdued Lola follows, paws clattering on the floor as we reach the kitchen. I hear James on the phone. I can't make out what he is saying but he sounds very angry.

Hurriedly, I set about making the hot chocolate and trying to be light-hearted, feeling anything but as I plop some marshmallows on top of the steaming liquid.

"Ok, McGinty one and McGinty two, that's our hot chocolate ready." I try to sound jovial but even I can hear the tension in my voice. "Let's head upstairs with our scrummy hot chocolate and find a good book to read!" I'm desperate to be as far from James as I can. We slip upstairs and into Sophie's bedroom, from downstairs I can hear James rattling keys.

I go cold.

The gun cupboard.

What is he doing with his guns at this time of night? The police haven't arrived yet.

Fear sweeps through me as I look over at Sophie who was now talking to Lola asking her which book she would like to read.

"Ok, sweetheart, let's pretend we are camping! You hide under the bed and let's pretend it's a tent and it's all dark. Take Lola in with you and I'll pop the blanket over, you can read by this little torch. What fun," I add, trying to sound chirpier than I feel, desperate to get Sophie away to safety, I need to have her hidden. I don't know what James is capable of in this mood. Sophie slips under the bed without hesitation, Lola quickly joining her. Pulling the blanket down, I can see they are well hidden, no sight of the glow from the torch can be seen under the depths of this thick blanket. My heart pounds.

"Are you alright under there?" I whisper.

"Yes Mummy," I hear a muffled reply, "and so is Lola."

"Good girl, keep Lola in nice and close. I'll just be a minute then I'll come in too. I'm right here, sweetheart, and I'll join you very soon." I look around the bedroom. All is eerily quiet now as though time has stood still. The steady tick, tick betraying the reality of passing time from Sophie's Fifi Flower Tots clock on the wall. Stomach churning, I slip noiselessly over to the door. I try to hear what James is doing, any sound that will give me a clue. He's on his phone I can tell, but too far away for me to hear what he is saying, only muffled undertones. I hear footsteps thumping up the hallway, I press myself back against the wall, the footsteps pass, then the slamming of the car door, the screech of tyres angrily spewing gravel from beneath their rubber.

"He's gone," I whisper faintly to the empty hall in front of me and let out a repressed sigh of relief. A temporary respite.

Slipping back in Sophie's bedroom, I wriggle under the bed to join an awaiting Sophie and Lola.

"Lola and I are reading this book," Sophie whispers to me, showing me her new favourite sea adventures book.

"I think Lola would have enjoyed that adventure very much," I reply and spend a few minutes with her trying to maintain some sort of normality, continuing the pretence this is nothing but a game before saying, "Ok, I think our hot chocolate will be cool enough for us to drink now! What do you think?"

Sophie nods and gives a little smile of agreement before slipping her small hand into mine.

"Let's snuggle up here and drink them and read more of our book, shall we?"

Again, a little nod, I can see how shaken Sophie is with this experience despite my attempts at distraction.

Chapter 46

She deserved a good death, but a death was the only way out. He could not risk her taking everything, everything his family had stood for, all his life people had taken things from him, his mum, his dad, even the business that had been left to him had been taken from him. His insecurities come to the fourth, he took another long swig from the bottle and turned the car keys. Yes, death was the only solution, he thought as he pressed the foot down on the accelerator, the thrust giving him a thrill as the car sped forward.

A few hours later, there was still no sign of James; as I manage to get an exhausted Sophie off to sleep, I make my way downstairs to see if I have missed James's vehicle arriving back.

I slip in through the kitchen door. It is quiet. Like a tomb. Peering out of the window and into the steadily darkening evening I see no sign of any vehicle having returned. I am thankful the guests have left earlier in the day with the new arrivals not due until tomorrow.

I am wracking my brains what to do, when I remember I have Marjorie's number on the card she gave me. I punch in her number, not really expecting a reply at this time of the evening. I hear the ringing tone and barely a second beat before Marjorie answers. "Isla?" I hear the concern in her voice. "Is everything okay?"

"No, the police rang James to say they are coming to take his guns away." Briefly, I explain the situation as best as I can, heart hammering in my chest. Nothing feels real.

"Isla, are you safe? The police should never have contacted him. They were meant to just arrive. He must know someone in the police."

I say nothing, there is nothing I can say. Marjorie tells me to keep Sophie close by me and my phone in hand. If the situation escalates, I am to phone 999 if I feel in danger.

Great, I think, just great. We are now in a worse situation, but I realise with a heavy heart, I have no one. I have no friends anymore. I can't trust the doctors and now the police are on his side. I have no one and we are in danger.

I have no choice. For weeks now, a loose plan has been formulating in my mind. I had wanted to make sure everything was planned this time down to the smallest detail. We would have to leave, but how? I know we have no choice. I feel fear. Deep-seated fear that digs deep into the very core of me. I have no money, no friends. James has seen to that. He would find us wherever we go. The realisation bubbles up in me. I would need to get us new identities to keep us safe, but how? Surely those cost money.

I wouldn't be able to use the credit card, James would know where we were then and he would cancel them the second we were gone. I couldn't use my National Insurance number so how could I get a job to support us? Maybe I could get a wee cash-in-hand job? Cleaning perhaps? Anything to survive. We had done it before, but this time I would need to be smarter. We could change our hair, our names.

I desperately want to go back to Dotty's, but I couldn't risk them coming to harm; besides, it would be the first place James would look for us. I would take the car as far as the train station and would decide the details as best as I could after that; the main thing is we need to get out, and get out fast. The police would be here soon so James would also be back soon. I work quickly packing a bag. I would take just the essentials and Sophie could take her favourite toys. Heart thundering in my chest, anxiety gnawing wretchedly at my stomach, I grab a rucksack, pack a few of my clothes in it before slipping into Sophie's bedroom. Working quickly and quietly, I pull a few changes of clothing out and slip them into the rucksack. A couple of books and I am done. Sophie is still snuggled tightly with her bear so that could come when we leave. I slip down the long-split staircase into the kitchen to grab a few supplies when I hear the sound of tyres on gravel.

Nooo, he's back. I'm too late. Frantically, I look around for somewhere to hide the bag—he cannot not know of my plan. That would spell the end. I remember the last time and go cold. I barely survived that one. There is a loud knock at the door. That's strange.

Cautiously, I make my way to the door, forgetting the rucksack in my confusion. Opening the door, I see the police in front.

Of course, I think to myself, *realisation hitting.* In my haste to get away before James's return, I forgot that the police would be arriving.

I take a deep breath and slowly open the door.

Two police officers are standing there.

"Mrs Campbell?" The taller of the two officers ask.

"Yes, may we come in; we need to have a talk with you."

"With me?" I stutter, confused about this turn.

"Yes, if we could just come inside for a moment," the female officer says gently.

Confused, I open the door wider and let them in. As I walk into the kitchen, the two police officers following me, I feel a sense of foreboding wash over me. Why do the police officers want to see me? It is James they are here to see, right? I turn to see two faces looking at me, one gentle and sympathetic, the other blank, as though years on the force have removed all emotion. I open my mouth to ask how I can help them when the lady officer interrupts me.

"Isla, why don't you take a seat?" She gestures to the old, tattered sofa that is snuggled into the corner of the kitchen.

I look at her for what feels like a decade before I obediently sit down.

The male officer clears his throat.

"I'm afraid we have some bad news for you," his voice does not waver.

I look at him questioningly. I open my mouth to speak. No words come out. I close it again.

"It's about your husband," he continues, his tone unwavering.

Tick, tick, tick goes the clock, the sound of eternity passing.

"I'm afraid your husband has been in an accident," the officer continues to say. All I can hear is a buzzing noise in my ears as I look at him. I can see his mouth moving, his face expressionless. I can't make out what he is saying though.

This is surreal. Two uniformed police officers standing in my kitchen. I look past them to the neat cream units, the striking black granite polished so highly it gleams, the red aga offering a warm contrast.

The female police officer comes over to me and puts her hand gently on my shoulder. "She's in shock," I hear a voice float down to me as I sit staring at the battered old red-checked fleece covering the worn sofa.

"Make her a cup of tea and I'll see if we can find someone to sit with her," Deadpan Officer says matter-of-factly. I can't remember what their names are, they have floated straight out of my head. I have nicknamed them Deadpan Officer and Kindly Officer.

"Where is he? Is he hurt?" I ask Kindly Officer. I would need to go see him soon. If I didn't, he would be mad and he was in a foul enough temper already. "He'll need a change of clothes and maybe some magazines to read," I add, starting to get up.

Kindly Officer comes over to me and gently guides me back onto the sofa, pressing a cup of tea into my hands. "Drink this, it'll help with the shock," she says as I take the warm mug into my cold hands, the warmth a welcome sensation. "Isla, I am afraid the accident was serious. As I said before, James's vehicle left the road and went down a steep embankment. I am afraid James is dead."

I feel a humming in my ears. "Dead?" I repeat, looking quizzically at Officer Deadpan.

"Yes," Officer Deadpan confirms matter-of-factly.

"Can we get anyone to come and sit with you?" Kindly Officer asks.

This cannot be happening. James? Dead?

"There must be some mistake, he, he, he just went out. He'll be back at any minute," I whisper to the room, barely audible.

"The remains of the car are in the process of being removed, they will be examined and the identity of James and the other body will be officially confirmed."

"Can I go see him; will I need to identify him?" I asked hesitantly, still taking in the news.

"That won't be necessary," Deadpan replies briskly.

I look over at Kindly Officer for an explanation, and as gently as she can, she replies, "There wasn't much left of the vehicle, I'm afraid; forensics will be able to confirm everything we need."

My head is spinning, this is a dream, not real. How could it be? Any minute I'll wake up and find this is some sort of cruel, sick joke.

I sense the officers need to be going onto their next case. A few placatory words and a check again to see if there is anyone they can contact to sit with me and they are off. I sit in the tomb quiet of the kitchen at an utter loss. No. No there is no one I can ask to come sit with me. I am alone. James had sorted that. I know I need to break it to Sophie but that can wait until morning. She's had a dramatic enough night, the sleep will do her good; besides, I need time to think. My head feels thick, my limbs heavy. It hasn't sunk in. Dead? No, he can't be. It's only been a matter of hours since he was standing at the door of the living room shouting and threatening me. Things like that don't happen—not in real life—do they?

I get up and go to the sink, pouring my now cold cup of tea down the sink, watching it swirl down the drain, light brown followed by glistening sugar crystals that hadn't melted into the lukewarm tea. I don't like tea at the best of times, but milk and sugar make it worse. It was thoughtful of Kindly Officer to make it. *It will help with the shock*, she had said. I had accepted it with a slight nod of my head, without question.

I flick on the kettle and make myself a strong black coffee. I need time to think. I desperately want Zara by my side, I couldn't understand why she didn't get in contact.

I try to remember what the police officers had said. Car accident. Forensics. I try unsuccessfully to piece together the events of the night.

What a difference a few hours make. Only an hour ago, I was hurriedly packing a case for Sophie and I to flee, and now here I have a different set of problems. I have a house with a mortgage. I can't take out the shooters and they won't stay without the sport. How am I to support Sophie now? I put two large spoons of coffee into my mug and top it up with hot water. Taking it to the living room, I sit down. One set of problems have just been replaced with another, I think guiltily, as I realise that I will no longer live with the awful abuse.

The next weeks pass in a blur. I try to focus on what is happening, I feel like a robot just trying to make it through each day. Apparently, James had been carrying high volumes of petrol in the back of his truck, it had exploded on impact and burnt till it was just ash and cinder. The remains of James's body had been identified through his dental records and his wallet, which had been thrown from an open window before the explosion.

What was worse was the identity of the other passenger. My beloved Zara. I cannot think why she would be in the vehicle with James. I wracked my brains till I was exhausted, bereft at this loss. I was inconsolable. Only the thought of giving Sophie a new life kept me going.

I had phoned all the people I could to let them know the news, and there had been a small ceremony. Many were 'too busy, sorry love, but we send our condolences' to attend the service in person. Sophie had taken the news surprisingly well, tears at first, then questions—was he really gone?

It has now been four weeks since Officers Deadpan and Kindly had been around. It's early in the morning; I'm up and dressed, sitting at the kitchen table rubbing my forehead, subconsciously hoping this will give me some inspiration as to what to do now.

I have no income and no way to pay the mortgage. Without warning, tears spring to my eyes. I am overwhelmed, sobbing gently as I head along the marble hallway. It's the first time I've cried since the news. They're just gone. Erased. Nothing left of them. That's the hardest part. Understanding. I still can't comprehend they're gone. Zara, my best friend. James, when there's nothing. No fighting. No divorce. Nothing.

Softly, I make my way up the stairs, glancing at a photo of James and I on the wall, taken on our honeymoon. "I loved you," I whisper into the silence. The memories of us first building this house seem to flicker in front of me then die away like the last embers of a winter's fire. Where had it all gone so wrong? How could love turn to hate so easily, for he must have hated me to have treated me so.

I pad across the soft carpet and slip into my bedroom and into the ensuite. Moving across the warm floor, I open the shower door and flick on the shower, an action I have performed thousands of times before; however, this time I feel different. Slipping into the shower, I remember back to the girl of a long time ago. A different someone that had been giddily in love, a new baby in tow. Someone else who had felt the glorious jets from the power shower, someone else laughing as their husband slipped in beside them. A different someone before it had all changed. I only remember the sting from the jets, no longer caressing as the water flowed, stepping stiff-legged and sore; red-purple bruises covering previously pink-white skin. I am someone else now. Who, I am not sure, but I know I need to find out.

"I need to sell up," I murmur to the steamy air in front of me. A new start. Where? Somewhere no one knows us. A fresh start. I feel a tremble of excitement pass through me; I feel liberated. Yes, this house is a shackle around my ankles, not the home that it had promised to be, and would never be, too much water has passed under this particular bridge for that to ever happen. It's a beautiful house, a house that deserves someone else, someone who could make it a family home that it was always meant to be. I need to find myself, to be safe again, to get a life back for Sophie and myself.

Yes! That's it. Rejuvenated, I lather myself up quickly, wash my hair and spring out of the shower with renewed purpose. Real estate agents are what I need to find!

3 Months Later

A message comes through on my phone.

You alright? A brief message.

No, I message back, a faint smile passing my face as I recognise the number. *But I will be,* I add.

The End